King of

Steven A. McKay was born in Scotland in 1977. He is the author of two previous series of historical fiction, following Robin Hood and the warrior-druid Bellicus in post-Roman Britain. He plays the guitar, is the co-host of historical adventure podcast *Rock, Paper, Swords!* along with author Matthew Harffy, and lives just outside Glasgow with his wife and children.

Also by Steven A. McKay

Alfred the Great

The Heathen Horde
Sword of the Saxons
King of Wessex

STEVEN A. MCKAY

KING OF WESSEX

CANELO

First published in the United Kingdom in 2025 by

Canelo
Unit 9, 5th Floor
Cargo Works, 1-2 Hatfields
London SE1 9PG
United Kingdom

Copyright © Steven A. McKay 2025

The moral right of Steven A. McKay to be identified as the creator of this work has been asserted in accordance with the Copyright, Designs and Patents Act, 1988.

All rights reserved. No part of this publication may be reproduced or transmitted in any form or by any means, electronic or mechanical, including photocopy, recording, or any information storage and retrieval system, without permission in writing from the publisher.

A CIP catalogue record for this book is available from the British Library.

Print ISBN 978 1 80436 613 4
Ebook ISBN 978 1 80436 620 2

This book is a work of fiction. Names, characters, businesses, organizations, places and events are either the product of the author's imagination or are used fictitiously. Any resemblance to actual persons, living or dead, events or locales is entirely coincidental.

Cover design by Blacksheep

Cover images © Shutterstock

Look for more great books at www.canelo.co

Printed and bound in Great Britain by Clays Ltd, Elcograf S.p.A.

To Griff Hosker,

who inspired me to buckle down and write more.

PROLOGUE

AD 887, Athelney

It was almost as black as pitch outside the church that night. The moon had risen, but it was a mere crescent and gave off only a little light, which suited the two men who waited outside the building, furtively eyeing the door. Both wore dark clothes and would likely not have been noticed even if someone knew they were there, although the taller one's bald head did give them away a little, reflecting the moon's pale glow until his companion told him to put the hood up on his cassock.

'God's blood, where are the useless bastards?' The bald man, a Gaulish priest called Jehan, nervously fingered the handle of a long knife. The weapon was tucked into a length of rope tied around his waist as a belt. Had any of the other clergymen at Athelney Abbey spotted him, they'd have been shocked, for Jehan never wore a belt, and certainly never walked abroad carrying a blade. They would not, however, have been surprised by his blasphemous outburst, for the Gaul was not exactly a model priest.

His companion that night was smaller but heavier, with a belly that bulged from a lifetime of rich food and drink. Aimery was a deacon, and he too carried a knife or, more accurately, a seax. He was not as nervous as his companion, barely moving at all as they stood in the shadows despite the cold night air and the immensity of the task they'd given themselves.

As they waited – one shuffling and muttering anxiously, the other silent and brooding – there came at last the sound of

The abbot knelt before the altar and blessed himself, head bowed. The watchers did not make their move just yet, knowing the candle falling and being extinguished would leave them blundering around in the dark, and that would not be wise considering the blades they wielded. Jehan might injure Aimery by accident, or the other way around, which would be even worse, to Jehan anyway.

So, they waited, bile rising in Jehan's throat as he tried to remain as still and silent as Aimery.

The abbot rose and lit another candle which was on the altar, blowing out his own. Both were made from beeswax, and the extinguishing and lighting process filled the church with the distinctive, sweet smell. John the Old Saxon seemed to like the scent, for he breathed it in deeply, eyes closed, a small smile tugging at his lips.

Did the bastard know they were there? Jehan felt panic welling up within him again as he wondered if the abbot had come there prepared to confront them – it would be the arrogant man's style, after all. Was he, too, armed with a weapon? Jehan made ready to jump from his hiding place and begin swinging, but the abbot turned away, apparently oblivious to their presence, and returned to the place a few feet in front of the altar where he'd knelt before.

The abbot did not kneel this time, but instead remained standing, his hands clasped as he bowed his head, closed his eyes, and began to murmur a soft prayer.

Jehan stared at him, hatred filling his every fibre, or at least he tried to convince himself that it did, and then, when he was just about to look at Aimery, Aimery screamed, 'Kill him!' as he jumped out from behind the altar.

Jehan attempted to roar his own war cry but it came out as a choked whimper, and he too was moving, knife held high above his head, eyes wide, wishing he was anywhere but there in that cursed church. His rage and terror powered him forwards, and then he felt something smash into his mouth and realised he was lying on the ground.

He gaped. The metallic taste of blood filled his mouth as he watched the abbot grappling with Aimery, the muscles in the big man's arms cording as he called out for help. Somehow the horrible turd had managed to punch Jehan in the face while also fending off Aimery!

Jehan's blood was pounding in his veins now and his earlier whimper came out as a full-throated bellow as he lunged forward, grinning in bitter satisfaction as he felt his blade slicing into flesh and scraping against bone.

The abbot let out a cry of agony and fell onto one knee, crimson streaming from the gaping wound Jehan had carved in his calf. Aimery took the opportunity to free himself from the abbot's grasp and then he too was stabbing with his knife, in and out, two, three, four times.

The abbot's shouts for help had ceased, and he slumped down onto his back, unmoving, blood spilling onto the hard floor from his wounds.

'Come on, you damned lackwit,' Aimery gasped, dragging Jehan towards the door. 'We have to get out of here before we're found. His squeals will bring everyone running.'

It seemed the abbot's shouts had indeed brought people to his aid, as someone tried to open the main door then, only to find it locked. A fist hammered on the oak, but it was a sturdy door and would not give way easily.

'Oh God, what are we going to do?' Jehan said with a sob.

Outside, he recognised the voices of the two priests who'd let them into the church in the first place. They were shouting, 'Devils! The abbot was begging for aid as devils were attacking him!'

The mention of demonic beings clearly frightened the people gathered on the other side of the door, for the hammering stopped, and the voices grew more distant.

Aimery's lip was curled in a smile of disdain. 'The fools are too frightened to come in now,' he said. 'That will give us a few moments to escape. Come on.'

He led the way to a door behind the altar. It could only be opened from within, and he drew back the bolt quietly before pulling the door open and sticking his head through, checking the corridor was empty. 'Hurry!' he hissed, and then disappeared.

Jehan sprinted after him, not caring if anyone heard his sandaled feet slapping against the ground. Apparently everyone had gone to the main western door of the church for no one was around, and Aimery made it to the far end of the corridor where there was another door, this time opening out onto the south side of the building.

Stopping only to press his ear against the door, Aimery decided it was clear on the other side and pushed back the bolts before the small amount of light cast by the crescent moon illuminated the fugitives as they crept out into the night.

They could hear the shouts from the front of the church, but no witnesses were there to see Jehan and Aimery as they ran – crouched low and still grasping their bloodied blades – towards the nearby marshes.

—

Wulfric was frowning, not quite understanding what he was being told. He was not a stupid man – far from it. That was how he'd come to be King Alfred's most loyal advisor and right-hand man, after all. An ealdorman and a warrior of great renown, he was most at home on the battlefield or dealing with similar martial affairs. To be woken in the middle of the night by a priest carrying a guttering candle and be told that the Abbot of Athelney had been brutally attacked by knifemen was just… well, not what Wulfric expected to hear. At all!

He'd been sent there by the king to see how the newly built abbey was doing – Alfred had ordered it built after being forced to live in exile there in Athelney nine years before. But the place was not contributing taxes as the king had expected now that its construction was almost complete.

Being built in the middle of the marshes had always meant the abbey could not grow crops. But, even so, Alfred expected more from the place. More taxes, more goods, and, crucially, more scholars for his burgeoning kingdom. Yet all it seemed the abbot was truly gifted at producing was excuses, and Wulfric had been sent there to speak with the man. Remind him of his privileged position and lofty responsibilities to both God and Wessex.

When Wulfric had arrived in the abbey, however, he'd found the abbot – John the Old Saxon – to be an exceedingly pleasant, humorous man, and any thoughts of treating the fellow harshly faded from the ealdorman's mind like the sweetly scented smoke drifting from the censers in the church where they'd first met. The old man had given Wulfric a tour of the abbey grounds and then they'd spent a most enjoyable evening downing ale and trading war stories, of which the abbot had many.

The following day was spent in a similar fashion, although Wulfric had finally remembered why he was there and forced himself to speak candidly and even somewhat sternly with the abbot. Of course, John told Wulfric of the troubles he'd had with the lazy Gaulish clergymen employed in the abbey, and, by the end of their conversation Wulfric believed the abbot was not at fault at all for the estate's poor performance. Even the finest craftsman could only work with the tools he was given after all.

To be woken now, just a few hours after that meeting, with the news of John the Old Saxon's vicious stabbing… It was hard news for Wulfric to swallow.

'Do we know who did it?' Wulfric demanded as he put on his sword-belt, shoes, and cloak before leading the way out of the room he'd been allocated as his bedchamber. The priest who'd been sent to rouse him came along at his back, dwarfed by the ealdorman's great size and presence.

'No, lord,' the priest replied, doing his best to keep up.

Wulfric was in his late forties and bore many battle scars – including a prominent one down the left side of his face – but he remained hale and hearty, and even ruggedly handsome. His memory and sense of direction were also as sharp as they'd ever been, and he needed no guidance from the trailing clergyman as they hurried to the scene of the crime.

Murder was the most heinous of sins. And for it to have occurred within an abbey was doubly shocking. Wulfric knew they had to get to the bottom of what happened and make sure the perpetrator was brought to justice.

Someone had to know something, surely. Had it been a simple theft gone wrong? Or was there some other, deeper significance to the crime? Having met the abbot, Wulfric could see how his relaxed attitude to life could rub certain people the wrong way.

They came to the church and found a group of priests milling around outside, apparently too frightened to go in.

'Is there danger?' Wulfric asked, drawing his sword and heading for the door which had been forced open, its simple lock mechanism lying bent and broken from its fittings.

'No, the place is empty,' someone replied. 'But the abbot was attacked in there, and he was shouting about devils before the healers carried him away.'

'Devils?' Wulfric spat, then went into the building, eyes scanning the place and finding no signs of the attackers still within. He quickly examined the crime scene, noting the blood spatter. It looked to the ealdorman as if there had been more than one attacker, and he headed back outside, mind working as he tried to piece together what had happened.

His presence there was affecting the anxious priests in different ways. Some were too upset to care much about the big ealdorman's piercing gaze, while others were naturally fearful after such a violent attack. Two of the priests, however, were eyeing him with even more trepidation than their brothers, and they immediately caught Wulfric's attention.

'You two,' he barked, pointing at the priests and affecting the demeanour he used while training new soldiers in the fyrd.

Predictably, they almost soiled their breeches as they found everyone's attention suddenly upon them. 'Come here,' Wulfric commanded, and his tone was such that the two men walked towards him as if drawn on invisible strings. He decided to use their terror against them. If they knew something, now, when they were most vulnerable, was the time to get it out of them. He pointed his blade at the most obviously nervous of the two.

The priest blanched and swallowed.

'Who did this?' Wulfric demanded. 'And I want the truth. If you refuse to talk and God doesn't strike you down, I will.'

It was quite clear the man was desperate to unburden himself, and the threat of God, along with the glistening steel of Wulfric's sword, was enough.

The confession flowed out like a torrent, the terrified priest's heavy accent marking him as a Gaul. When his portly companion tried to walk away, Wulfric grabbed him by the hood and roughly dragged him back, sending him to the ground with an outraged whimper. 'Where are they?' the ealdorman demanded, looking from one to the other.

The one he'd thrown down must have thought it would do him good to also help now that their scheme had been discovered. He blurted out, again with a Gaulish accent, pointing towards the marshes, 'There. They said they would hide there once they were finished, until the fuss died down.'

Wulfric glared at him. 'Until the fuss died down'. He suspected any fuss might well have just faded away if he hadn't been there to take things in hand. Well, God be praised, the ealdorman *was* there, and he would make damn sure the abbot's would-be killers were found.

'Are there any warriors amongst you?' he called out, turning away from the two conspirators and addressing the rest of the priests who continued to stand around fretfully, still casting wary glances at the broken church door as if Satan himself might walk through it at any moment. Some of them, scared to be there in the dark, had lit candles, and those little flickering lights cast shadows on gaunt faces, lending the whole scene an eerie taint. Much to Wulfric's annoyance, only one of the priests answered his plea for warriors.

A short but muscular man with long hair beneath a type of shawl which was pushed back around his neck came forward. 'I was a soldier,' he said. 'What do you need, lord?'

'Take these two conspirators into custody,' Wulfric growled. 'Make sure they don't escape. If they try – kill them.'

The muscular priest nodded, eyes hard as he stared at his brothers. 'Yes, my lord. Where are you going?'

'To find the bastards who tried to kill your abbot,' Wulfric replied.

He walked around the church looking for clues, but it was so dark without even the light of the priests' candles that he despaired of finding anything. Then he came to the side door which lay open and, looking through it, he realised it led to a corridor which was attached to the church. It had to be where the murderers had escaped. He rose up to his full height of well over six feet, and cast his eyes about the lands before him.

Where would the fugitives go? Did they have a destination in mind, or had they simply planned to hide in the marshes until morning when, cleaned of blood and perhaps clad in fresh clothes, they would come back to the abbey and pretend they'd been there all along? That was what the priest who'd confessed to his part in the plot had claimed, so Wulfric decided he'd take a quick look around, purely to satisfy his own sense of curiosity and need to see justice done as soon as possible.

There was only one causeway leading off the island. Without evidence that the fugitives had taken a punt across the water, that was where Wulfric would start. He moved along the timber walkway quickly, hardly making a sound, sword still in his hand, the smell of the stagnant waters filling the air. At last, the causeway ended and he moved onto land, stepping carefully for he knew all too well how dangerous these marshes could be. The sliver of moon cast just enough light for him to see shadows in the darkness and, after walking for perhaps half a mile more, he spotted a square structure. With nowhere else to go, he headed in that direction, noting the small size and crude construction of the building as he grew nearer. A storehouse of some description, for tools or supplies used to keep the causeway in good condition. Nothing of real value would be stored there, just things that had to be protected from the elements until they were needed.

The perfect place to hide until dawn, if the attackers did not expect to be pursued.

The ground was wet, so that even when Wulfric stepped on a branch and froze – expecting it to crack loudly and give away his presence – it simply bent, making no sound. He waited, listening, and then he heard low voices coming from within the squat structure.

Two voices. One low and irritated, the other high and excited. Whoever was in the storehouse was not aware of the ealdorman's presence and he stepped right up to the door, pressing himself against the wall. What now?

He could wait. The men sounded drunk, so at least one would probably come outside to empty their bladder at some point. Wulfric could pick him off, and then deal with the other.

He shivered. It was cold, and he simply did not want to stand there, perhaps for hours.

Pressing his eye against the side of the ill-fitting door, he could see into the little building. The men inside had lit a candle and were sitting on the ground, skins of wine or ale in hand.

'You almost got us captured,' one of them was saying, the shorter of the two. 'Panicking like that.'

'The abbot moved faster than I expected,' the other protested, rubbing his jaw. 'Nearly knocked me out cold. He'd been a warrior remember, when he was younger. Anyway, what does it matter now? He's dead, and we escaped.' He tipped some of his drink into his mouth and sniggered nastily. 'Before the sun comes up, we'll sneak back and act like we slept through the whole thing. Too drunk to hear anything!'

His companion nodded agreement. 'We'll throw our old cloaks in the marshes, weighed down with a rock. That was a good idea, putting new ones here, along with the candle and the wineskins.'

Wulfric had heard enough. There was no lock on the door, just a latch, so he lifted it up and stooped as he moved into the tiny structure. The shorter of the priests had reacted quickly, lifting a long knife and struggling to get up, but he fell back as Wulfric thrust the point of his sword into his chest. It was a fatal strike, directly to the heart, and the light went out of the priest's eyes immediately.

The second fugitive was scrabbling towards him but Wulfric did not hesitate, kicking the man in the face. It was a heavy blow, and he followed it up with another, even harder kick. Then he sheathed his sword and bent down, dragging the dazed priest by the ankles right out of the storehouse. Quickly, he searched the man, finding a knife beneath the robe. He pointed it at his dazed captive and jumped back to his feet.

'Get up, before I kill you, too,' the ealdorman commanded. 'Come on, you piece of shit, back to the abbey. It's bloody freezing out here.'

What a night, he thought as he forced the protesting, bruised priest to stumble back towards the abbey to face justice.

CHAPTER ONE

'A visitor has arrived.' Ealhswith looked pleased as she delivered the news to Alfred upon his return from the morning's hunting. 'He's in the hall enjoying some meat and ale.'

'Who is it?' Alfred asked, removing his cloak and giving her a kiss.

'A monk,' his wife said, taking his cloak and shaking it out before wandering off with it under her arm. 'I think you'll like him. He's very pleasant.'

Alfred watched her go, frowning, for he sensed something hidden beneath her words. He went into the hall, half-expecting to see a young, handsome clergyman enjoying the hospitality of his hall. The man sitting at the bench closest to the firepit was at least as old as Alfred's thirty-eight winters though, and his tonsured head made him seem even older.

The king walked across to the monk. Two of the dogs who made the hall their home jumped up and came to sniff at him, licking his hand before realising there would be no treats, and disappearing. The monk had also stood up at Alfred's approach and bowed to him as he drew close.

'Asser! You've finally come!' They stood before one another and Alfred reached out to grip the monk's forearm. 'I'm so glad you made it here at last. Sit, please, finish your meal.'

They sat down opposite one another, and the monk proceeded to eat once more. He ate with gusto and Alfred was pleased to see the servants had piled his trencher high with roast meat, cheese, and thickly buttered bread. Despite his clearly prodigious appetite, Asser was slim, if not positively skinny, and the king remembered that he'd been suffering from some fever or illness for many months, which was why he'd not come to Alfred's hall before this.

'How are you keeping?' the king asked with genuine concern.

'Fine, now,' Asser replied, wincing slightly as he took a bite of the cheese and found it rather stronger than he was used to. It couldn't have been too unpleasant, however, as he quickly stuffed more into his mouth. 'I almost died you know, but God, in his infinite mercy, saw fit to heal me. As promised, I made the journey here as soon as I was fit enough.'

Alfred grinned. He had indeed summoned Asser to Wintanceaster over a year ago, around the same time he'd brought John the Saxon, Grimbald, and Werwulf there to act as tutors for his people. Asser, who hailed from Dyfed, had taken some persuading to join them at first, and then, when he relented at last, he'd fallen ill and been forced to remain in Caerwent to recover.

'I'm overjoyed to have you with us at last,' the king said, and he truly meant it. Alfred had met Asser once before and, despite their previous meeting being a brief one, the monk's presence and wit had made a great impression on him and he was genuinely pleased to have the man in Wintanceaster now. The scholars he'd summoned to his court recently were all very clever men, but none had filled the void left by the passing of his long-time priest and friend, Oswald, who'd died the previous year. Perhaps Asser would be the man to help Alfred get over his loss.

'What is it you want me to do here, my lord?' asked the monk, trencher now emptied, its contents being washed down with a refilled cup. 'I hear you already have a number of learned men busy at work, teaching your children and even your thanes to read.'

'Indeed,' the king said, nodding happily. 'But there can never be enough wise men in Wessex.' His smile faded, replaced by a deep frown. 'Have you heard what happened at Athelney Abbey?'

Asser nodded grimly. 'I have, lord. A terrible business.'

'Indeed. An absolute outrage, and a symptom of how far we've fallen. It was bad enough when the Danes were plaguing us, but now even our religious houses are tainted with evil! It's the inevitable result of moral degradation over generations, but I have vowed to reverse that trend. For too long there's been a decline in literacy and learning in general.' He leaned back and let out a sigh before swallowing a little ale and continuing in a more hopeful tone. 'Now I've bolstered our military defences, our ships, and our army. A kingdom cannot thrive on force of arms alone, though, can it, brother? With your help, I would have Wessex become the Rome of this island – a land filled with culture, poetry, song, libraries, and men and women of wisdom and learning!'

Asser placed his cup on the table, eyebrows raised, clearly impressed by Alfred's words and the force they were delivered with.

'I must admit,' the king went on, somewhat shamefacedly, 'that I didn't learn to read myself until I was twelve. I still can't read as well as I'd like – and I can't read Latin at all. I would like you to be my tutor, even my friend, if you would.'

The monk looked at him as if trying to gauge the king's character. At last, he must have decided Alfred was in earnest for he smiled broadly, bowing in assent. 'All right,' he said. 'Although, as we agreed before, I can only spend six months at a time in your court, the rest I will live at the abbey in St David's, yes, my lord?'

Alfred nodded grudgingly. That had been their agreement in the messages that passed back and forth between them over the past year. He hoped Asser would eventually agree to live in Wintanceaster with them, but, for now, six months stretched ahead of them, filled with possibilities.

For the first time really since Oswald had passed, Alfred felt a seed of joy growing within him.

'Are your people learning to read Latin?' the monk asked, wiping his mouth and stretching back on his stool like a dog before a roaring fire.

'No,' the king replied sadly. 'I'm afraid learning is at such a low rate these days that even our monks and bishops can't read it. Without anyone to teach it, I thought it best to simply use what we have, in terms of both teachers and reading materials. So everyone is learning to read Anglo-Saxon.'

'Well, it's also the language we all speak, so I suppose it makes sense to start with that,' Asser said. 'You, yourself would like to learn Latin, though, my lord?'

'Oh yes,' Alfred said enthusiastically. 'There's so many wonderful things written in Latin that are closed to me just now. My dream is to learn Latin, and then translate all those wonderful old texts like the *Historiae adversum Paganos* by Orosius into Anglo-Saxon so that everyone can enjoy them.'

Asser was smiling broadly. 'This is all very admirable, lord,' he said. 'Inspiring, even.'

'That's one of the jobs of a king, isn't it?' Alfred laughed. 'Inspiring his people. In truth, however, I've found it much easier to inspire my thanes and ealdormen into bloody battle with the heathen hordes than in getting them to read!'

'People become set in their ways,' Asser noted, nodding. 'Especially older people. Not everyone is as driven as you, my lord.'

'Well, they'd better learn to be driven, because I've threatened to strip them of their lands if they don't get studying.'

The pair laughed and Alfred refilled Asser's cup.

'That won't have gone down well I imagine.' The monk chuckled as he took a small sip, sighing in pleasure.

'Not at all well,' the king agreed. 'But they're doing as I asked. Thankfully I have the Witan on my side these days. I'm able to wield my power with more freedom than I could when I first took the throne, mainly because the Danes have been quiet for some time.'

They sat and chatted like this for a long while, drinking ale and enjoying the warmth from the firepit. They discussed the future and made plans together, with Asser promising he'd try to have the king reading, and even translating, Latin tomes before his six-month stay in Wintanceaster was over.

Men and women came and went while they chatted, but none disturbed them until Wulfric strode in through the main doors, his great bulk practically filling the entrance as he removed his heavy cloak and hung it on a peg on the wall. The captain had been spending much of his time lately training the Wintanceaster garrison. Many of the men were new, untested recruits, but even the veterans who'd seen action against the Danes had done so under the old system. Alfred's reforms, which created a full-time standing army, meant the commanders, like Wulfric, had much more time to spend drilling the troops, teaching them how to defend the newly fortified walls, and how to act if battle was met out in the open countryside.

Alfred saw the ealdorman come into the hall and, much to his surprise, felt a stab of annoyance. Jealousy, even – as if he wanted to keep Asser all to himself. It was an odd feeling, for Wulfric was not just his captain, he was his closest friend. The king felt terribly guilty as the ealdorman came across to greet them with his usual dour, but not unfriendly, smile.

'Another priest, eh? Just what we need to keep the Danes at bay.' He took a stool beside them and poured himself a cup of ale even before the king could offer.

'Take no notice of Wulfric,' Alfred said with a despairing look at his captain. 'He has little regard for religion and even less for culture or learning. He likes to kill Northmen, that's his favourite pastime.'

'Well, killing Northmen is what lets you spend time reading the bible and conversing with monks, my lord,' the captain replied with a shrug. 'We all have our part to play in Wessex, as you say yourself so often.'

'I don't remember ever saying that,' Alfred retorted, then a small smile touched his lips. 'It's good though, I'll need to start saying it.'

'Within a month I'll have you saying that, and a lot more, in Latin,' Asser said.

'Latin!' Wulfric theatrically 'spat' a mouthful of his ale towards the fire. 'That's all we need.' His look quickly turned to one of horror and he asked the king fretfully, 'You're not expecting everyone to learn Latin as well now, are you? I'm barely managing to read our own language!'

Alfred pretended to mull that over, allowing Wulfric to stew, before he snorted, shaking his head. 'Of course not. At least not until Asser has settled in.'

Wulfric glared at the monk then noticed the glint in Asser's eye and laughed himself. 'You had me going there for a moment,' he admitted. 'Pair of bastards.'

'Wulfric! You can't talk to a monk like that!'

They were all grinning now and Alfred's earlier jealousy had well and truly dissipated, replaced by a deep affection for his old comrade, and real hope that he'd strike up a similarly strong friendship with Asser. Men like these were the foundations a kingdom was built upon, and Alfred could hardly wait to get to work with the monk while Wulfric oversaw the growing military power of Wessex.

The other two were discussing Asser's earlier illness now, and more of the *hearthweru*, the king's hearth-warriors, were coming into the hall, ready to settle down to a hearty meal after a hard day's work. Part of the king wished he might have had Asser to himself for a while longer – the six-month period the monk had agreed to stay for already seemed to be slipping away – but his guts were grumbling and he knew Wulfric would need to be fed as well. He waved to one of the servants, holding up three fingers and pointing at Asser's empty trencher, fully expecting the man would manage another few mouthfuls in his quest to regain the weight stolen by fever.

A golden age beckoned to them, Alfred thought, not allowing himself to think of times in the past when he'd thought that only to be proven sadly mistaken. The Danes were pacified, his burhs were strong and growing even more so with every passing season, and his people had the time to learn from the finest scholars around. In fact, there was another important job Asser could do, now that Oswald was no longer around to do it...

'More ale, my lord?' Wulfric asked, breaking his reverie as he lifted the half-empty jug.

Alfred smiled. 'Aye. Why not?'

CHAPTER TWO

Aethelflaed was an impressive woman, Alfred thought, as he watched his eldest child with her new husband. Pride filled him as he watched her easily deal with the wedding guests, some of whom were already ridiculously drunk. Nothing seemed to faze her, and she'd taken the whole day in her stride, which made Alfred embarrassed, for he'd found it all incredibly stressful. Indeed, when the ceremony had started Ealhswith asked Alfred if he was feeling well, as his face had turned scarlet. That was a new symptom of his stress, one he'd never suffered from before as far as he knew, but it was preferable to the old, agonising gut pains, so he'd ignored it. Besides, he couldn't see his own face, so what did it matter to him?

The great and good of Wessex and Mercia had come to celebrate the joining of the two families – Ealdorman Aethelred and Princess Aethelflaed; a finer match none could remember. Not since Alfred and Ealhswith, at least.

Guthrum-Athelstan had also been invited, the Norse King of East Anglia, and godson of Alfred, arriving with a retinue of twenty warriors and carrying fine gifts.

Of course, everyone knew the wedding was not the only business that was to be attended to that week in Lundenwic. Alfred had charters he wanted witnessed and signed, including the setting out of borders and renewal of old alliances and trade agreements.

That could all wait until later, though. The wedding ceremony had been concluded and the feast was about to begin. Ealhswith, queen consort, had taken charge of the preparations, arranging the guests, food, drink, servants, sleeping arrangements, and so on with her usual aplomb. Alfred wondered if Aethelflaed would be as adept at running Aethelred's household in Mercia – somehow his daughter didn't seem the type. She might look like a stately young noblewoman, but in her heart there was a fire that burned like that of any mighty warrior's. If her new husband thought he was getting a little mouse he could order around, he'd be in for a rude awakening!

'You next, lad,' Alfred said to his eldest son, Edward, who was seated at a bench in front of the king's.

'That's enough,' Ealhswith said, laughing. 'He's only twelve. Stop trying to take all my children from me, Alfred.'

The boy grinned at his mother and Alfred felt another surge of pride as he looked from Edward to the rest of his children seated at the bench. They were all clever, mostly well behaved, and content with the tutors Alfred had found for them. A sudden pang of sorrow struck him then, for, although he was only jesting with Edward about marriage, it wouldn't be long before the boy was a man and, like Aethelflaed, moving on to live his own life away from his parents.

A king could control many things, but time was not one of them.

'Cheer up,' said Ealhswith, nudging his arm. 'It's supposed to be a happy day.'

He looked at her, noticing a few strands of grey hair around her temples, new lines beneath her eyes, and a slightly rounder face than when they'd first been wed. He smiled and leaned across to kiss her, still struck by her beauty, which had been little diminished by the passing of years. He hoped she felt the same about him, for he too had aged – constant war and the pressures of statecraft would do that to a person.

He lifted his cup and took a long swallow, enjoying the slightly burning sensation as the mead travelled down his throat and into his belly. He raised the cup aloft as he saw Guthrum-Athelstan doing the same and they shared a smile.

The Dane had been baptised – against his will – after Alfred's forces had defeated the heathen invaders and evicted them from Cippanhamme. Guthrum, fierce enemy king, had taken the name Athelstan when he became a Christian and, so far, he'd stayed true to his new faith and even wore a cross around his neck, joining in with the hymns and prayers throughout the wedding Mass. It was an inspiring sight for Alfred, who rejoiced in the power of God to tame a man who'd been as vicious and devoutly heathen as Guthrum. Hopefully the King of East Anglia would still be in a good mood once Alfred showed him the new treaty he'd drawn up between their two kingdoms…

That treaty would make it clear that the town they were sitting in, Lundenwic, was now formally Mercian, and belonged to Aethelred, now husband of Alfred's daughter.

Ealdorman Aethelred, who'd sworn fealty to Alfred…

Lundenwic, and the neighbouring site that had once been Londinium, would become one great trading town named Lundenburh, fortified and manned with enough warriors to make it forever safe from raiders. Guthrum-Athelstan would, Alfred hoped, not have an issue with any of that, or any of the other borders that would mark out East Anglia's territory going forward.

Aethelred himself sat in the centre of the table, the place of honour as it was his wedding feast. Aethelflaed sat at his left hand, while Alfred was on his right, his father-in-law as well as his liege lord.

The Mercian ealdorman was an impressive, likeable individual. He reminded Alfred of himself when he was first wed.

'More ale?' Ealhswith, as ever, took her duties as host seriously and, noticing Aethelred's cup was empty, stood up from her seat on Alfred's left and carried the ale jug around the guests at the high table, refilling everyone's drinks. When she was seated once more, toasts were made, oaths sworn, and the usual jokes made. Funny or not, everyone was drunk enough to find everything a great laugh, and it was a happy feast as the sun went down outside and a troupe of musicians came in to entertain the great and good.

'I have one last thing to say,' Alfred called, standing and lifting his arms for silence.

It took a while for the inebriated revellers to notice him, but, when Wulfric bellowed for everyone to shut up the people did as they were told.

'Today, I welcome Ealdorman Aethelred into my family,' the king said with a smile and a nod down to his son-in-law. 'In the years I've known him, I've been impressed by his piety and his organisational skills. He is the right man to lead Mercia going forward, with my beloved daughter Aethelflaed by his side.'

There were cheers at that, and the bride and groom looked into one another's eyes happily.

'The future holds much promise for us all,' Alfred went on, looking around at everyone gathered there. All were wealthy and powerful, and most had supported Alfred during his times of trouble. 'Our burhs continue to grow, as do our fyrds. Many of you have begun learning to read and write as I asked, and, as a result, a new golden age is upon us.'

There weren't so many cheers then, for the thanes and ealdormen of Wessex were finding their lessons hard, and would much rather have been spending their days hunting and whoring than trying to read the religious and philosophical texts their tutors forced upon them.

Alfred nodded to the servants, commanding them to refill everyone's drinks. Predictably, that lifted the mood again and beaming faces looked up at him as he went on.

'As you all know, my army took control of Londinium recently, killing the Danes who were camping here and causing so much trouble.'

Cheers and slamming of fists on tables, especially by those noblemen who'd been part of Alfred's army during that triumphant engagement. It had been a fairly straightforward battle, but had become the subject of many a scop's tale ever

23

since, thanks to Alfred facing the enemy jarl, Hjalmarr, in single combat. It had been a brutal fight which could have gone either way, but eventually ended with Alfred defeating Hjalmarr and savagely hacking off his head. The skull remained where it had been displayed, a warning to other sea-wolves who might think the Christians in those lands would be an easy target.

'Londinium, and Lundenwic have always belonged to Mercia,' he continued. 'And so it shall remain. Aethelred,' he placed a hand on his son-in-law's shoulder, 'Lundenburh, free from heathen raiders, is my wedding gift to you. Already, I've paid for work to begin on rebuilding the old fortifications and upgrading the docks. Welcome to my family, son.'

Everyone present might have been intoxicated, but they all understood exactly what the king was saying. There was no doubt that Alfred was now lord there in Lundenburh, as well as in Wessex. Aethelred might have been given command of the town, but he would rule it as a vassal of Alfred.

Wulfric, along with some of the noblemen, clapped and cheered — a prearranged response to Alfred's pronouncement — and everyone followed their lead. Only Guthrum-Athelstan and his men did not look pleased by what was happening, as the matter of who owned Lundenwic and Londinium had been rather ambiguous up until then. With the town now officially Mercian, and work underway on a wall around the place, the Dane saw his own territory shrink as he was pushed further east, away from Wessex.

Alfred nodded at Guthrum-Athelstan, silently letting him know there would be reparations for this unexpected turn of events. Again, the Dane's conversion to Christianity impressed Alfred — had this happened before, when Guthrum was still a heathen, there would have been cries of outrage, and most likely threats or actual acts of violence. Now, although the East Anglian king appeared far from happy, he caused no scene — in fact, he angrily told those of his men who would have caused trouble to sit on their stools and be silent. Those men, drunk and now belligerent, did not appear to be in the mood for silence, however.

'Take the children out,' Alfred murmured to Ealhswith. His wife, hearing the tension in her husband's voice, did not need to be told twice. Quickly, and without fuss, the queen consort shepherded Edward and their younger daughters into a side room. To their credit, the children went quietly although with obvious disappointmarr on their faces as they'd been looking forward to the musicians' performance.

'This town was not yours to give away!' A Dane, bigger than Guthrum-Athelstan – one of the thirty who'd been baptised at the same time – strode forward to stand in front of Alfred, eyes blazing with indignant fury. 'You're getting too big for your boots, Lord King!'

One of Alfred's thanes and closest friends, Diuma, jumped to his feet, as did many of the other warriors of Wessex, especially the younger ones. Or those more inebriated than the rest.

Wulfric did not stand, but merely looked at the irate Dane with an expression of boredom on his face.

'I defeated Hjalmarr and the rest of the raiders who were here,' Alfred replied coolly. 'So, by right of conquest, Lundenburh is mine to do with as I please. Do you have some claim to it, my lord? I can't see how, since you hail from across the whale road and have no claim to any lands in this island, other than those you stole from the rightful owners.'

'You,' the red-faced Northman pointed a meaty finger at Alfred, 'gifted lands to Guthrum, and he, in turn, gifted lands to me, and his other loyal jarls and hersirs. Londinium was never part of Wessex, and never yours to gift to Aethelred!'

Alfred looked at Guthrum-Athelstan and saw the king's mouth twitch in a smile. The former heathen warlord might not wish to publicly decry Alfred, but he seemed quite happy to let his jarl do it.

'You may be right,' Alfred retorted, growing angry himself now. 'Although how you can be so sure about what territories belonged to who without seeing the old charters, I don't know. But the fact is, Londinium, and Lundenwic, have traditionally belonged to Mercia. Until you sea-wolves arrived and started stealing land, this town, and the others nearby, were Mercian. So they shall stay!'

'Mercian!' The big Dane spat on the rushes carpeting the floor. 'You think us all fools here. We all know Aethelred is your lackey, and this marriage only cements that status. You would have this town for your own, Alfred. For Wessex.'

'You have a problem with that?' Alfred demanded. 'I never saw you coming to remove Hjalmarr and his raiders. In fact, we know there were certain noblemen – Danes – in East Anglia giving succour to Hjalmarr. Would that have been you?' His accusation was a grave one, especially here, surrounded by so many West Saxons and Mercians, and Guthrum-Athelstan's jarl paled. He did not back down, though.

'You accuse me of betraying my oath to Christ? Of aiding heathen raiders as they ravaged Christian lands?'

The words were indignant, but Alfred was sure he could detect a hint of mockery within them, and wondered if his barb had been closer to the truth than even he had believed.

'Sit down, fool, and let us get on with the wedding feast.' It was Diuma who spoke up, cheeks flushed from the mead he'd imbibed. His words brought a chorus of agreement, but the Dane rounded on him, shaking his fist.

'Fool, you call me, whelp? I'll show you who the fool is!'

Asser shook his head and stood up, calling for calm. His exhortation fell on deaf ears.

'Come on then, you big goat-humping fool,' Diuma demanded, spreading his feet wide and gesturing with his hands.

Wulfric looked up at Alfred and the two shared a knowing look. 'The entertainment is about to begin,' said the ealdorman.

The East Anglian jarl's fist flew through the air – there were no weapons allowed within the hall, hence Alfred's relative lack of fear for how things might pan out. When the thud of fist striking flesh came, though, it was shockingly loud, while Diuma's roar of outrage was even louder. He'd managed to dodge the worst of the blow, taking the full force on his shoulder rather than his face, but it spun him backwards, into his bench. Drinks spilled and men cried out in anger. Then Diuma parried a second punch and landed one of his own, right on the Dane's mouth.

More of Guthrum-Athelstan's sea-wolves charged towards Diuma, and the West Saxon thane's nearest supporters jumped up to defend him. Within moments punches and kicks were being thrown as the melee exploded. Wooden mead cups and bone drinking horns were lifted and used as bludgeons, long hair and even beards were pulled, and Alfred looked on as a number of men on both sides fell to the rushes, dazed or even completely out cold.

Asser returned to his seat, hands clasped as he murmured a prayer. The king could not hear the words, and he wondered if the monk was asking God to forgive the combatants, or to protect them from serious harm. Then again, from the look of amused interest on Asser's face, perhaps he was merely making wagers with himself on who'd come out of the fight in the best shape.

Alfred dodged a cup, thrown with venom at Diuma but mercifully missing the thane's head.

'Watch your aim, you fucking oaf!' roared the king, and the Dane who'd tossed the cup made a rude gesture. Alfred felt a surge of indignant rage at the show of disrespect and, before he knew what he was doing, he'd jumped over the table and punched the sea-wolf in the chin. The man rocked back on his heels, then, almost comedically, slumped down onto the bench Diuma had been sitting at.

The king's involvement heralded the end of the fighting, for Wulfric got into it too now, shoving men hither and thither, roaring at them to get back to their seats before he ordered the guards who had burst into the hall and were watching events with some confusion to come and deal with them. The threat of being skewered by a sword was enough to calm most of the combatants, although Alfred was forced to land another punch and hold his opponent down by the throat until his kinsmen came and dragged the throttled man back to Guthrum-Athelstan's table.

'Go on, move you big bastard,' Wulfric growled, shoving one of the Danes back towards his side of the room. The venom had gone out of the atmosphere already, as it so often did in these situations. No one, it seemed, had been killed or seriously injured, and the brawl had gone some way to defusing the tension that had been in the air. Punching people tended to have that effect, Alfred thought with a wry smile.

'My apologies, lord,' Guthrum-Athelstan called over the groans of pain and laughter as men recounted their exploits in the short fight. 'Brawling in the middle of a wedding feast is not acceptable. My men will be suitably chastised.'

Alfred laughed and waved his hand dismissively. 'Forget it, godson. You and I can talk later about our territories and the renewal of our treaty. You know I will deal fairly with you, as I always have.'

The Dane nodded. It seemed he'd grown wise over the years, or perhaps his earlier greed and desire for ever more plunder and land had faded with his advancing age.

Alfred turned to Aethelflaed, prepared to apologise for his role in the fighting. His knuckles were tender, and he rubbed them, then his eyes widened as he saw his daughter performing a similar action.

She met his gaze defiantly, her amusement making her eyes twinkle. 'What?' she asked innocently. 'They were ruining my wedding day. I think I'm entitled to knock some sense into them too.'

Alfred looked at Aethelred and he merely shrugged.

'A toast, then,' the king shouted, bringing some order to the hall again with his clear, commanding tone, as Ealhswith returned with the children. 'To Aethelred and Aethelflaed. And to the continuing growth and friendship between all our various peoples – Mercians, West Saxons, and Danes. *Wes hael!*'

Shouts of '*drink hael!*' and '*skål!*' went up, reminding Alfred once again of just how similar they all were, sharing a similar language, similar traditions, and coming from similar roots in generations past. It made sense for them all to be friends and allies.

The musicians struck up their tune then, with drums, a lyre, and a flute accompanying a pair of singers, whose powerful vocals filled the hall right to the rafters, encouraging all to join in. Alfred could see bruises on many faces, turning quickly purple and green in the flickering firelight, but there was no animosity now and the celebration moved on with the introduction of more ale and mead, brought forth by the barrel load by harried ceorls.

There would be days of this, with an incredible amount of drink consumed by the revellers, a similar mountain of fine foods, and all accompanied by songs and stories. As if on cue, the musicians ended their piece and Guthrum-Athelstan stood up, gesturing to Alfred.

'What about a tale, my lord?'

Alfred knew the Dane wanted to hear one of his Saxon scops regale them all with some story of adventure and mighty deeds, but Alfred had heard them all over the years.

'Go on then, godson,' he called back with a flourish of his hand. 'Let us hear one of your old heathen tales. I remember your predecessor, Ivar the Detestable, was well known for his storytelling. It'll be good to enjoy something new, eh, Aethelred?'

The Mercian ealdorman nodded enthusiastically, as did Aethelflaed and many of the others gathered in the hall. It wasn't every day one got to hear an exotic and exciting new story, and the Danes were renowned for their strange myths and legends, pagan as they were.

The Northmen grinned at one another and looked to their king. This was an opportunity for them to show the Saxons how rich their culture was, and they did not want to miss it.

'Ivar and his brother, Halfdan, were indeed great tale-tellers,' Guthrum-Athelstan agreed, getting to his feet somewhat reluctantly. 'I am not so well-versed in such stories. I employ... wise-women to entertain my people.'

'The völur,' Alfred said, giving the plural term for the heathen wise-women and apparent magic workers who, he believed, were analogous to the pre-Christian druids of the native Britons.

'Yes,' Guthrum-Athelstan admitted. 'My völva is not here this day because I feared her presence would not be welcome in your Christian court.'

Alfred did not mention the fact that East Anglia, and its king, was also supposed to be Christian nowadays. If Guthrum-Athelstan and his jarls still clung on to certain parts of their previous culture, it was to be expected. Change did not occur completely overnight, after all.

'Then you will have to take the place of your weaver of tales, godson,' said the West Saxon king with a reassuring smile.

'Tell us a story, lord!' agreed the Danes eagerly, some even thumping their fists on the benches now. Soon enough, Alfred's people were doing the same. The noise was deafening as Guthrum-Athelstan looked around, milking their encouragement. And then he raised his hands and nodded as if in defeat.

'All right, all right!' he cried, laughing and swallowing a long draught of ale as the thumping faded, replaced by an expectant hush. 'As this is a wedding, I will tell you a tale of love.' He looked from Aethelred to Aethelflaed, then nodded somewhat apologetically to the princess. 'You must forgive me, lady. Our stories are not very... romantic. At least none of the ones I know.'

'That's fine, my lord.' The bride nodded graciously. 'I'm sure I'll enjoy your story.'

'I hope so,' Guthrum-Athelstan murmured as if he wasn't sure about that at all and was perhaps even beginning to regret agreeing to provide the evening's entertainment. He shrugged and took another huge pull of ale then slammed the cup on the bench and drew himself up to his full height. 'A tale of love, then! This is the saga of Volund the smith.'

Alfred turned to Wulfric and shared a look of surprise. Volund? The name sounded much like Weyland, another smith that tales had been told about by the Saxons since time immemorial. The king hoped this story would be a new one, rather than one of the many he already knew.

'There was once a mighty king named Niddud,' began Guthrum-Athelstan, his voice ringing out into the silence, its only accompaniment the crackling and spitting of the firepit and the meat sizzling above it. 'He had two sons, and a daughter called Bodvild. When she came into her womanhood she was the most beautiful princess anyone had seen. Until the Lady Aethelflaed was born, that is.' He smiled at the bride who laughed along with everyone else.

'King Niddud asked his daughter if she had decided on a husband, and she said she had. "I would marry the famous blacksmith, Volund," she told the king. "For he is said to be the best of men, and the most handsome, and a fitting husband for me. He also makes the finest gold rings in all of Midgard."'

Guthrum-Athelstan stepped away from his bench, moving across to the one at which Diuma was seated, gingerly resting his backside on the wood to make sure none of the drinks spilled and started another fight. He crossed his arms and relaxed once he knew all was safe, and continued. 'King Niddud knew of Volund, and knew the smith was said to be the son of one of the Jötun – giants – and a mermaid. With this in mind, Niddud tried to persuade his daughter to choose a different husband. One with human parents. But Bodvild would not change her mind. Her heart was set on Volund and so the king, as all good fathers do, knew he must try his best to make his daughter happy.'

He glanced at Alfred who nodded in agreement, bestowing an affectionate look on Aethelflaed who returned it with a dazzling smile.

'So, envoys were sent by King Niddud to Volund's home in a place called Ulfsjar, on the shore of an ancient lake. They made the marriage proposal to the fabled smith, telling him of Bodvild's beauty, and of the great dowry that would be paid to Volund when the wedding took place. To their astonishment, the smith did not even stop working at his forge as he refused their offer. "Your princess's beauty, and her father's wealth, mean nothing to me, for I am already married," he said, dismissing them. The envoys peered into Volund's hall, noting the layer of dust covering everything, the mangy old furs that covered the bed, the filthy ale cups, and the cold firepit despite the frost and snow which blanketed the lands.'

There were murmurs from the audience, then.

'No woman would allow her household to be run so badly,' Diuma said, apparently unaware of the purple ring around his eye from the earlier brawl.

'Exactly.' Guthrum-Athelstan agreed, nodding at the bruised thane and continuing with his tale. 'The envoys said the same thing to Volund. "Your hall does not even have a fire in the hearth," they cried. "If you are married, where is your wife?" The smith sighed then and stopped his work at last. "It is a sad story," he told King Niddud's envoys. "One morning, many years ago, I went out hunting with my two brothers. We came to this lake and liked the place so much that we built our halls and settled here. One morning we went down to fetch water and found three strangers there – women. They were spinning flax and on the ground beside them were their cloaks, made with the finest white swans' feathers."'

Guthrum-Athelstan paused for a moment, to let that image sink into his audience's imaginations and also to take another cup of ale for himself from a servant. He sipped it, wetting his dry mouth and lips before going on.

'Volund told the envoys that the three women were Valkyries. One was named Hlaðguðr svanhvít, and she chose Volund to be her husband, while the other two married the smith's brothers and all lived in happiness in their halls by the lake. After seven years, though, Volund said to Niddud's envoys, "The Valkyries grew restless and decided to return to their work claiming the bravest warriors were killed in battle and escorting them to Valhöll. They took their cloaks of swan feathers and flew away, leaving us – their husbands – behind. My brothers decided to follow them, and search for their brides to this day, while I chose to remain by this lake, working my forge, and praying that the gods would one day bring Hlaðguðr svanhvít back to me. So," said the smith to the envoys, "I cannot marry your princess, or anyone else." With this answer, the messengers returned to King Niddud and gave him the bad news.'

The Dane looked at Alfred. 'What would you do, lord?' But before Alfred could answer, he held up a hand to forestall any reply, not wishing to put his fellow king at a disadvantage with such a difficult question. 'I do not know what I would do, but what King Niddud decided to do was send soldiers to bring Volund to his court. This they did, waiting by the lake until the smith passed out drunk after a hunting trip, and then binding him and carrying him on horseback to Niddud's far-off hall.'

Some of the wedding guests thought this quite right – when a king gave a command, a lowly smith must follow it after all. Others were outraged – kidnapping an innocent man purely to please a king's daughter was a flagrant abuse of power. Guthrum-Athelstan allowed the chattering to continue for a time, walking between the benches, helping himself to cuts of meat and crumbling cheese, and listening to what was said but never offering any opinion of his own.

At last, the storyteller continued.

'King Niddud commanded Volund be released from his bonds and welcomed the smith to his hall. "Now that you are here, you shall marry my daughter," said the king. "I am already married," replied the smith furiously. "And I shall never marry your daughter." "You will forget your old wife once Bodvild is beside you," the king promised, but Volund would not be swayed and continued to profess his love for his Valkyrie wife, Hlaðguðr svanhvít. Of course, this enraged King Niddud.' Guthrum-Athelstan whipped out his eating knife and leaned down, making a slashing motion in the air beside Diuma's legs. 'The king commanded Volund's hamstrings cut, and then had him carried to a nearby island where he would spend his remaining years, working a new forge and crafting fine golden items for Niddud and his folk.'

Now the cries of outrage from the people in Lundenburh's hall were universal, for such barbaric treatment of a skilled worker was outrageous.

'Volund worked on his own for years then, rarely having visitors other than supply boats, and forced to work for his captor, King Niddud. Then, one day, the king's two sons came to see Volund and demanded the smith show them all the fine jewellery he had stored in a chest at the side of the forge. He ignored them and continued working. "Volund," the princes shouted, "you are our father's prisoner, and you must do as we command, or you'll be sorry!"'

'King Niddud's family all sound as unpleasant as he was himself,' Alfred murmured. Wulfric grunted agreement, offering his own uncouth epithet for the arrogant princes.

'Volund listened to the young men, and then he cried, "Sorry? I'll be sorry? No, you two shall be the sorry ones," and, whipping out a fine longsword which he'd crafted in secret, he killed the princes, and, with two quick blows, cut off their heads.'

Cheers and laughter filled the hall, as the wedding guests cried out that the wronged smith had finally found some justice. Guthrum-Athelstan smiled around at his audience, holding up his ale cup in salute to the mythical Volund.

'Then, taking their skulls and cutting off the tops, he fashioned them with molten silver into fine drinking vessels. Then he boiled the eyes and polished them until they shone like fine gemstones. When the next supply boat arrived with Volund's meagre ration of food, the smith gave its crew the skulls and the eyes. "Give these to the king and his daughter, as gifts from me," he said, and the boatmen sailed away with the unusual treasures.'

Guthrum-Athelstan laughed at the crowd's reaction to this part of the story. 'I know,' he cried. 'What a gift, eh? The king had no idea what he was drinking out of, for he believed his sons away on a hunting trip in a neighbouring land. And as for the princess who had caused all this trouble? She thought the smith was finally growing weak, and would agree to finally marry her so, wearing her own brothers' eyes on a necklace, she went across to the island with her father, the king, and again demanded Volund wed her.'

'Had that family no shame?' Diuma demanded, his outraged words garnering whole-hearted agreement from most of the other wedding guests.

'Princess Bodvild was indeed a rare beauty,' Guthrum-Athelstan went on. 'And King Niddud promised to release Volund from his island prison if he would just take the beautiful girl as his bride. It would surely have been easy for the smith to simply accept, but he refused as he always had, crying out that he would only ever love his Hlaðguðr svanhvít.'

As he spoke, the Dane looked at Princess Aethelflaed who was enraptured by the story.

'I like this smith, Volund,' she said, nodding in approval. 'Did they kill him?'

Every ear strained to hear Guthrum-Athelstan's conclusion to the tale, knowing it would surely be brutal, for the stories of the Northmen usually were.

'They tried,' said the Dane with an enigmatic smile. 'But Volund had secretly crafted another treasure: a cloak of very fine gold, an exact replica of the swan cloak his Valkyrie wife had worn the first time they had met in Ulfsjar. This he threw around his shoulders and, despite his injured legs, was able to fly up, high over the island, away from the king and his hearth-warriors. Then Volund shouted down to Niddud the truth of his fine new drinking vessels and Bodvild's jewelled necklace and, with their horrified cries ringing throughout the kingdom, the smith beat the wings of his golden cloak and flew away, to the east.'

'Yes!' Alfred, Wulfric, Aethelred, and everyone else cheered in triumph, pleased at the hero's magical escape and the evil king's defeat.

Aethelflaed spoke up when the cheers died away, her voice high and melodious, easily cutting through the lower tones of the men gathered around her. 'Did Volund make it home?' she asked.

Guthrum-Athelstan nodded. He was in the centre of the hall now, cup still in hand although drained by now. Behind him was the firepit, making the edges of his beard seem to glow a fiery red, as if he himself was part of some mythical saga. 'He did,' the Dane said. 'To Ulfsjar the smith flew, but, when he got there he no longer thought of it as his home. Too much had happened since he had last dwelled there by the frozen lake. So, he flew on – eastwards, ever eastwards, until at last he came to Alfheim, and there he found his wife, Hlaðguðr svanhvít, and they were reunited. There, in the land of the elves, they remain to this day, man and wife.'

He watched as Aethelflaed's eyes sparkled as if suddenly filled with tears of joy, and he turned away, smiling, pleased to have touched the young princess with his tale. Of course, in the real tale Volund did not find his Valkyrie, and there was no happy end, but this was the story a wedding feast needed. Guthrum-Athelstan was very pleased with it, and it seemed the rest of the guests in the hall were too.

There was much discussion of the saga and the characters involved, and the rights and wrongs of each one's actions until, eventually, the musicians struck up another song – a bawdy, rhythmic piece which encouraged men and women to dance drunkenly around the firepit and Guthrum-Athelstan sat back down amongst his kinsmen, content.

He was handed another drink and he took it gladly, although the room was already beginning to spin. Alfred was looking in his direction and the kings' eyes met his from across the hall, both men smiling and lifting their cups in salute.

'He enjoyed your tale, Guthrum,' said the jarl who'd started the earlier fight and whose top lip was swollen, his left ear a fiery red from being punched. 'But will the terms of his new treaty with us be favourable? The new borders he's drawn up?'

Guthrum-Athelstan leaned back and took a deep breath, trying to steady himself as he took a sip of ale. He belched loudly and grinned at the jarl. 'I trust Alfred. He will look after us. Now relax and enjoy yourself, my friend, for you're going to feel it in the morning. Might as well make the most of it while you can!' And, with that, he forced the rest of his ale down his throat and stood up to join the merrymakers dancing clumsily about the hall.

CHAPTER THREE

AD 888, Spring

Wessex and its people enjoyed a time of peace during the next several years, thanks to their efforts in defeating the raiders and then building the infrastructure to keep those pagan hordes at bay. Alfred was able to spend more time doing the things he truly loved – not so much the carnal delights that had been such terrible vices in his younger days, but, now that he came into middle-age, he threw himself deeper into learning than ever before.

With the addition at his court of scholars like Plegmund, Werwulf, and Asser, it was always easy to find someone willing to show the king what a certain Latin phrase meant, or to read to him and Ealhswith in the evening. Their children also enjoyed the benefits of having so many learned men around, as a school was setup in Wintanceaster. Alfred's dream was to have many schools all over his kingdom, where even the poorest ceorl's sons and daughters could gain an education. That would not happen overnight, of course, but Alfred did make a start, founding schools in other places and exhorting his bishops to find suitable candidates to become students.

All this was possible thanks to the presence of strong allies on his borders. With Guthrum-Athelstan on the east of Britain, and his son-in-law, Aethelred, to the north, it meant Wessex had little reason to fear incursions by the Danes from those directions.

It was not impossible, of course – Guthrum might be a Christian nowadays, but many of his people remained proudly pagan and it wouldn't take much to entice them to join an army intent on attacking Wessex. It had happened in recent years, after all. And there was always the danger of an enemy fleet attacking from the sea to the south. Alfred had built bridges to nullify the threat of such a fleet coming deep into Wessex along the rivers, as they'd done in the past, but the kingdom would never truly be safe until the day when every Dane was a Christian, which Alfred prayed would happen soon. It might not happen in his lifetime, but he had faith it would come to pass eventually. God would see to it. The best way for the people of Wessex to hasten that glorious day was to praise God by learning, and by growing strong spiritually as well as militarily.

'Our Anglo-Saxon lands have been slowly devolving,' he opined to Asser as they sat in the sunshine enjoying cups of cool ale one fine, spring morning. 'Devolving,' he repeated firmly, 'into a pagan nation. That's why Mercia, Northumbria, and East Anglia were all so terribly ravaged by the Danes, and even ended up being subjugated by those heathen savages. Wessex would have ended up the same way, but God was merciful and saw our efforts to return to Him.'

'You see the Danes as a punishment from God?' Asser asked. It was an opinion held by many people, but it was the first time he'd spoken with Alfred about it.

'Of course I do.' The king nodded. 'Two hundred years ago Britain was full of scholars like Bede, writing his *De Arte Metrica*. The people were God-fearing and learned. We slowly grew away from that, forgetting how to read and write, and spending more time fighting and fornicating.' He paused, eyeing Asser almost suspiciously, as if wondering what the monk had heard about his own un-Godly exploits. 'I include myself in that criticism,' he admitted, as the monk peered back at him with a neutral expression. Either no one had gossiped yet, or Asser was good at hiding his thoughts. That would be a useful talent for a clergyman to have, the king had to admit, especially when hearing confession. 'Do you not think, Asser, that the pagan raiders are a punishment, or at least a test, from God?'

'Oh, I do, lord,' the monk replied enthusiastically. 'And I'm glad to hear you say so. If only other kings were as wise and as God-fearing as you, maybe Britain wouldn't have been overrun by those...' He shook his head, shuddering. 'Animals.'

'You must help me,' Alfred said, leaning forward and gazing earnestly into Asser's eyes. 'You, and your learned brothers. I can't do this alone, as I've been forced to discover over recent years, and my spiritual advisor, Oswald, is no longer with us.'

The monk nodded sympathetically, having heard many times about Alfred's departed priest. 'Lord, you've showered me with gifts since I took up your offer of service here in your court. But all of that pales in comparison to your infectious faith, and desire to see Wessex become a place worthy of God's blessings.' He raised his cup, the ale within glinting in the bright sunshine. 'I toast you, my lord, and pledge to do everything I can to help you succeed in your lofty goals.'

They sat, sipping their drinks and enjoying the day, birds singing and insects flitting from bright flower to bright flower in the royal garden. It was a far cry from the days when Alfred, his family, and his few hearth-warriors had been forced to scratch a meagre existence from the marshes of Athelney, hunted by Guthrum's bloodthirsty Danes. Yet, as he luxuriated in a truly blessed day, surrounded not by stagnant waters now, but by purple dog-roses, scarlet pimpernels, and fiery orange honeysuckle, Alfred knew those hard months in exile made him appreciate what he had even more. Asser was the very embodiment of everything that was good in Wessex at this point – a living representation of Alfred's hopes and dreams for the kingdom.

The monk only proved it further by taking a book written in Latin from beside him and, after clearing his throat and smiling at Alfred, began to translate it. It was Boethius's *Consolation of Philosophy*, one of the king's favourite books, and, as Asser read a certain passage, Alfred drew out a little tome of he carried on his person at all times.

Asser paused his reading as the king held ou to him.

'Lord?'

'Take it,' said Alfred. 'Please. And write down the passage you just read out, so I can recall it any time I like and think more deeply on it.' He rolled his eyes self-deprecatingly. 'One day I will be able to read Latin as you do!'

The scholar put down the book he was reading and took the one Alfred proffered. He opened it, eyes scanning as he moved through the pages searching for a blank one. Psalms, prayers, and all manner of Alfred's spiritual and moral thoughts had been noted down there over many years in the king's own neat handwriting.

Asser eventually spread his arms wide and looked up towards the sky, his eyes closed, and a look of great pleasure on his face.

Alfred gave a small chuckle of surprise. 'What are you doing?' he asked the monk. 'Surely my ramblings aren't enough to interest a man of your great learning?'

Asser opened his eyes, grinning. It was such a genuine, open expression without a hint of duplicity or pretence, that Alfred knew the monk was telling him the truth when he replied, 'Giving thanks to God, that I've come into the service of one so enthralled by the pursuit of divine wisdom. He has clearly sown the seed of learning deep within your heart, my lord, and it's inspiring. I can see now why Wessex, of all the kingdoms of Britain, remains outside the control of the Danes.'

'So far,' Alfred murmured. 'But go on, please – write down the passage.'

Asser nodded and looked through the king's handbook once more until, at last, he shook his head. 'There's no space left. You've had this a long time, my lord, eh? Why don't I get a new quire, and write it out there?' He stood and went to his chamber, returning a short time later with a little blank

...et – the quire he'd mentioned, which was simply four ...ets of parchment folded together in the middle to create eight pages one could write on. Taking his seat once more, he began to translate the passage which had interested Alfred so much, writing it down on the first sheet. Then, sharing a satisfied smile with the king, he set the quire aside and began to read from the Latin book of scripture again.

By the time they were finished and headed into the hall for the evening meal, Asser had written down another three passages for the king to browse and contemplate at his leisure.

When another month had passed, the quire was full of biblical passages and had been well-thumbed by Alfred. The book was seen by the king as analogous to how Wessex was blossoming – filling every day with new lessons, new teachings, new insights, and new ways of thinking, all of which must surely delight God, as it delighted Alfred himself. It was no coincidence, the king believed, that the Danes had been quiet in recent months.

A further blessing was bestowed upon Alfred, when news came from Mercia that his daughter, Aethelflaed, had borne a healthy baby girl named Aelfwynn, meaning 'Elf-joy'.

What heavenly future lay ahead for Wessex, and indeed all the Anglo-Saxon kingdoms of Britain that looked to Alfred for leadership? Only God could know for sure, but it was hard not to be optimistic when things were going so well, and peace reigned over all.

'Wessex will not always enjoy such peace,' Wulfric said, brows drawn together severely. 'You must work hard, lad, if you're to be ready for what will inevitably come.'

Alfred's son, the aetheling, Edward, looked up at the big ealdorman – his tutor that day – with a look of uncertainty that bordered on disbelief.

'What? You think the Danes will ignore us simply because we've built a few burhs and set up a standing army?' Wulfric shook his head in exaggerated amusement. 'Even if that turns out to be true, and the heathen warlords stay away from Wessex, d'you think your cousins, Aethelwold and Aethelhelm, will remain quiet on the eastern edges of the kingdom? They want Alfred's crown, you know.'

Edward frowned. He did not really know the two young men Wulfric spoke of. They were the sons of Alfred's dead brother, Aethelred, but neither had spent any real time with Edward and – in recent years – they'd been as good as banished.

The younger of them, Aethelwold, was incredibly headstrong and aggressive. He had caused quite a scene at the last Witan they'd attended, going so far as to punch the king in a dispute over what estates he'd chosen to leave them in his will. Alfred had retaliated in kind, and the whole thing remained a sore point within the royal court, especially as Aethelwold had sworn to gain support for their claim to Wessex's throne and return one day to take it by force.

'Your father's will should neuter your cousins' power,' Wulfric said. 'The estates that will go to them upon his passing are small and yield little wealth so...' He trailed off, shrugging. 'They should not be able to muster enough support to cause you too much trouble, but you never know. Aethelred was a clever, charismatic man, and his sons may turn out to be the same. Aethelwold at least – Aethelhelm is a sickly individual and likely won't be around for much longer.'

Edward absorbed all this although it was far from the first time he'd heard it all. It was sad to know his father had been very close with his brother. Alfred had never been supposed to end up as king – he'd been last in line for the throne, behind his four older brothers. When Aethelred died as the result of an infected arrow wound the kingdom had passed to Alfred and so had the problem of Aethelhelm and Aethelwold who believed, with some justification it had to be said, that they should be next in line, not Edward.

The line of succession was a tangled mess of family strife and politics, and Edward always hated when his tutors made him learn about it.

'Do we need to talk about this?' he asked Wulfric. 'Normally your lessons are about battle tactics and learning to fight. I get more than enough politics with my other tutors.'

'Well,' the ealdorman snapped, 'concentrate then! Get it into your head that Wessex's position will remain precarious as long as your cousins are around, and raiders cross the whale road seeking plunder. Which will never stop, so focus on what I'm trying to teach you, lad!'

Edward wanted to smile. Wulfric, for all his dourness, was strangely enjoyable to be around. Even when he was irritated and scolding the aetheling.

So they continued with the morning's lesson, as Wulfric explained in great detail how battles against the Danes at Ascesdune and Ethandun were won. They studied troop positions and movements, the importance of supply chains, morale, missile attacks, and how best to use terrain. Edward, like his older sister Aethelflaed, enjoyed such lessons and, when he concentrated, was able to absorb the information easily.

Wulfric did not teach from books, that was not his way, although he could read passably well thanks to Alfred forcing him to learn just like all the other noblemen in Wessex. Instead, Wulfric spoke from years of experience while Edward took notes, sometimes mental, sometimes written down. His father had learned much from the bluff ealdorman, but mistakes had been made along the way – harsh lessons that were taught to them by the bloodthirsty Danes. Edward hoped to avoid making the same errors when he was king.

The lesson came to an end just before midday, the sun high overhead. They were outdoors in the gardens of Wintanceaster's royal court, spring flowers blooming as insects buzzed around them and birds sang from the branches of blossom trees. It was a pleasant place to learn but, as Wulfric stood, stretching out his neck which made audible pops as he did so, Edward was looking forward to a meal in the hall.

It was not to be. Not yet at least.

'Up,' Wulfric commanded. Edward stood – he was not yet fully grown, but was already taller than his father even if he still only reached Wulfric's nose. The aetheling's other tutors were very respectful now that he was almost a man, addressing him as 'young master' or some similar variant. Not Wulfric, though – he generally spoke to Edward the way a superior officer spoke to a subordinate.

They faced one another, and Edward felt pride at his own burgeoning physical stature. He would never be as big as Wulfric, few men were, but the aetheling was tall, although he had some filling out to do, and retained his boyish, lanky frame.

'Come on,' said the ealdorman. 'It's not time for a rest just yet.' He walked towards the back of the hall, rather than the doors, and Edward felt a slight thrill of trepidation as he realised where they were going.

'Take one,' Wulfric ordered, lifting a wooden practice sword from a rack and stepping out into the centre of the training area.

'You want to spar with me?' Edward asked, choosing a sword and testing its balance before returning it for one that suited him better then following Wulfric onto the worn grass.

'Aye,' the ealdorman said. 'You have a good understanding of battle tactics and the logistics of war. I'd like to see how you actually fight, though.'

Wulfric did not normally spar with Edward; it would have been an obvious mismatch when the lad was younger, and not do much for his learning for the ealdorman was not the type to go easy. So this was something new, and an indication of how Wulfric thought the aetheling was progressing, physically.

It was also a little frightening, as Edward walked across and began to circle his opponent. Wulfric was older, but still in excellent condition, and the scar on his face only made him appear even fiercer.

Without warning, Wulfric aimed a blow at Edward's side and the young man skipped back, parrying the wooden blade easily enough. The shock that ran up his arm was unexpected though, and warned him he'd need to be better prepared as the bout progressed, for Wulfric was not holding back.

They traded jabs back and forth for a time, trying to feel one another out while giving little away themselves. Edward felt his muscles loosen up nicely and settled into a steady rhythm while reminding himself continually not to get complacent. He lunged and feinted and very quickly found himself sweating in the midday heat while Wulfric appeared cool and barely out of breath.

'Was Aethelflaed as good as me?' the lad asked, batting aside another attack and narrowly missing with a shot of his own.

Wulfric laughed and replied, 'As good? She was better!' which made Edward's face flush even hotter, and he came on, launching blow after blow before somehow finding himself flat on his back, gazing up at the sky in astonishment.

'Got angry there, didn't you?' the ealdorman asked, peering down from directly over the fallen aetheling. 'Never allow yourself to get angry.'

Edward had indeed allowed his irritation to master him, but it had drained out of him now. Still, he felt there was an opening, a chance to even the score. Holding Wulfric's stare, he swung his right leg at the ealdorman's calves, ready to roll out of the way when the bigger older man fell.

Wulfric knew all these tricks, however, and easily jumped out of the way, slapping Edward's backside with the practice sword as he did so. The sound of it reverberated around the sparring area and the youngster let out an indignant squeal for the blow had been extremely painful.

'Come on,' Wulfric said, stepping away to allow his charge to regain his footing. 'You've improved a lot since the last time we sparred—'

'I should bloody hope so,' Edward replied petulantly. 'That was about two years ago, when I was a child.'

Wulfric nodded slowly, thoughtfully. 'You're not quite a man yet, lad,' he said. 'But it won't be long, and by then you might even be able to beat me.' He grinned then, instantly removing any anger Edward was still feeling from being put on his arse. 'I doubt it though. Perhaps when I'm three score and ten and in my dotage, although even then I fancy I could still take you.'

'We'll see!' Edward laughed, rubbing his backside and then letting out a relieved breath as Wulfric headed towards the rack of wooden swords, depositing his weapon back where it had come from.

'Indeed,' the ealdorman agreed. 'Come on – time for some meat and drink, eh? I think we deserve it – we've covered a lot this morning.'

They made their way towards the hall, mouths beginning to water at the wonderful scents of cooking meat that emanated from the smoke hole in the roof. As they walked, Edward discreetly examined his tutor, noting how well the big man moved, how he carried himself with an air of easy authority, and how everyone who looked in their direction clearly respected the ealdorman.

Wulfric had been Alfred's captain for many years now, and offered the king a powerful presence to fall back on when he most needed support.

They came to the hall, its doors open to let in the crisp, warm air, and they went inside, squinting as their eyes adjusted to the relative gloom.

Who will be my right-hand man when I'm king? Edward wondered, praying it would be someone as competent as Wulfric. Then he pushed those thoughts aside, unwilling to contemplate a time when his father would not be there to look after him. Hopefully it would be many, many years before Alfred's throne passed to him.

He grinned, accepting the mug of cool ale that Wulfric handed to him and sat down with a comfortable sigh as a serving girl hurried to fetch them bowls of beef broth.

CHAPTER FOUR

Things were not quite as idyllic in Mercia that summer as they were in Wessex. Although Aethelflaed was now mother to a happy baby, it had been a difficult birth for the eighteen-year-old princess. Aethelflaed would never bear another child, she'd been told, although, to be fair, she did not want any more after her experience the first time. Little Aelfwynn had been worth it, of course, and brought her parents much joy in the weeks after she was born. Their joy was tempered, though, when Aethelflaed's husband, Ealdorman Aethelred, fell gravely ill with a fever.

She had quickly come to believe that she'd left the court of one powerful but sickly man to come to that of another. Aethelred was a fine warrior and a wily leader, but – much like Alfred – he seemed to take ill regularly. Usually, it was something minor which he would work through without much trouble. But this fever had come on quickly and lasted a long time. He could barely eat, so he lost weight and grew weaker, which was always a bad thing when one's body was attempting to fight off some malady. Eventually, perhaps as a result of the herbal concoctions the priests and so-called healers foisted upon him, Aethelred began to see things that weren't there and to cry out in his sleep even more forcefully than baby Aelfwynn when she needed her nursemaid.

There were men in Mercia's Witan who offered, or perhaps demanded would be more accurate, to take control while Aethelred was unwell, but Aethelflaed was not having that.

'You?' The thane who asked the question gaped at her incredulously. 'But you're a woman!'

Aethelflaed's lip curled, and she rolled her eyes at him. He was a tall man, very broad of shoulder with a thick, dark beard and hard eyes. She knew she had to deal with him in the right way, or the rest of the gathered Witan would never take her seriously. So much was riding on these next few moments. 'I am indeed a woman, Morcar. Well spotted. Not much gets past you I see.'

Some of the other council members sniggered and Aethelflaed took note of them. She'd been taught that such information, the dynamics of the Witan such as who liked who and who would like to murder whom, was always useful to know. Similarly, Morcar's reaction to her gentle but very public insult would also be worth noting.

'No need to be glib, my lady,' the big man replied dryly, rather surprising Aethelflaed for she'd half expected him to grow angry at her. That he didn't was definitely a point in his favour and belied his fierce looks. 'You know what I mean,' he went on. 'Women don't usually rule in Mercia.'

'It would only be temporary,' Aethelflaed replied, standing up and walking around the hall, eyeing the mostly middle-aged men who formed the Witan. 'Until my husband is over his illness.'

'And what if he does not get over it?' a red-faced, bulbous-nosed man asked bluntly.

'Then we'd need to look at the matter again, Edgar,' Aethelflaed barked, annoyed at the question for she'd grown close to Aethelred in the relatively short time they'd been married. 'But, for now,' she stopped walking right behind Edgar who was forced to turn in his chair and crane his neck upwards to see her, 'my husband is alive, and I shall take his place as head of the Witan.'

'But you're not even Mercian,' Edgar argued.

'I am Mercian now,' Aethelflaed retorted, her patience growing thin with the dense thane who had actually got to his feet, forcing her to look up at him now. 'I married your ealdorman, Aethelred, didn't I? Or does marriage not count for anything these days?'

Edgar shook his head, clearly annoyed. He was only a little taller than her, with thinning white hair, and he ground his teeth as he glared at her, almost as if he wanted to take her over his knee and smack her backside like a naughty child. 'You might have married Aethelred,' he growled, 'but you are your father's daughter first and foremost. Your loyalty lies with Wessex, not Mercia.'

'Surely it's the same thing?' Aethelflaed asked in a low voice, her steely eyes boring into his.

'What? Because Alfred has declared himself king of all the Angles and Saxons?' Edgar asked. His breath was sour and Aethelflaed realised he was drunk.

'Yes,' she replied, as if it was obvious. 'My father is the only king that Mercia has, since Aethelred is but an ealdorman. I would remind you, Edgar, that King Alfred, and his fyrd, are the only things standing in the way of the Danes overrunning Mercia completely.'

'Are you calling us cowards now?' the inebriated thane demanded, his flushed features contrasting deeply with his white hair. 'You're lucky you're not a man, or I'd show you the men of Mercia are not afraid of anything.'

He was so angry at her that flecks of spittle struck her face as he ranted. And, as he went on, he actually reached out and grasped her sleeve, digging his fingers into her bicep.

Instinctively, Aethelflaed grabbed his hand, twisting his wrist and forcing him to spin around so he was facing the table again. Despite knowing she'd done enough, she could not keep her temper in check and thrust her knee into the back of his, making him stumble and, as he went down, she pushed his face, hard, into the trencher of meat and cheese that he'd been eating from.

The food went everywhere, and she let go of the stunned thane, stepping back as he fell onto the rush-covered floor and lay there, shaking his head.

Some of the men roared in delight, impressed by her skill and how easily she'd managed to put the man on his arse. Others were not so happy, and decried her for using violence against a member of the Witan although, in truth, fights at these gatherings were not uncommon for mead, ale, and wine were always flowing. Women beating up men was not a common occurrence, however, and those who didn't find it hilarious were grossly offended by it.

Aethelflaed did not care. Edgar had invaded her personal space, which was bad enough, but grasping her arm as he'd done could not go without reply. She stood glaring at him, waiting for him to regain his senses, practically willing him to come at her again so she could put him on his backside again. The thane was bigger than her, but she had no doubts she could best him. A small smile tickled the edges of her mouth as she silently thanked her father for making sure her childhood lessons were not those most women of noble birth received. Aethelflaed had learned how to fight, and how to use her weight to best effect, as Edgar had just discovered.

When the humiliated and enraged thane struggled back to his feet – no one bothered to help him which gave Aethelflaed an indication of how his peers viewed him – he rounded on her, fists clenched.

'You fucking little—'

He came for her, but before he was embarrassed even further Morcar was there, pinning his arms and forcing him back into his seat. Edgar might have been stronger, physically, than Aethelflaed, but he was like a child compared to Morcar and, eventually, the struggling thane's threats and attempts to break free subsided. His expression of fury was replaced by one of fear, as the ale-fog lifted from his mind, and he slowly understood just what he'd done, who he'd got into an altercation with… and who her father was.

Morcar eyed him with some amusement and then, as the danger was clearly past, he turned to Aethelflaed and gave a shallow bow. 'Mercia has always needed a strong leader,' he said not only to her, but for the benefit of the entire Witan. 'We've not always had one, especially in recent years when we've been forced to suffer puppets of the Danes. Your husband is doing a fine job, however, and now it seems you're ready to step into his place and continue to lead us forward with an iron fist.'

'It's just as well for Edgar that she doesn't really have an iron fist,' one of the other thanes piped up, drawing a ripple of laughter from the noblemen. Even Edgar himself, perhaps trying to ingratiate himself with Aethelflaed, smiled at her.

'I can only agree,' he said, self-deprecatingly. 'Having my forehead bounced off the table was bad enough. I apologise, lady, for my behaviour.' He lifted his cup and held it out ruefully, looking from Aethelflaed to the contents within before setting it back down. 'It's not the first time the drink's got me into trouble.'

The fire crackling merrily was the only sound in the hall, then, as everyone watched Aethelflaed for her reaction to the drunk thane's excuse. Her earlier battle-lust had faded, and even the disgust she'd felt as he tried to save himself from further, even worse punishment, was replaced by pity. The man was a fool who should not be in the lofty position he was in, that much was obvious. She thought of her father's reforms and his demands that his nobles learn to read. It was doubtful if Edgar had ever so much as smelled a book, never mind learned to read one. He was symptomatic of the problems the Anglo-Saxon people faced these days. Still, he was not hated by his peers – some even seemed to like him – and Aethelflaed needed the support of everyone in that hall if she was to be accepted by the people of Mercia.

'I understand,' she said, smiling graciously at Edgar and walking back to her seat. She did not sit but lifted her cup and raised it in Edgar's direction. 'Even the best of us are nothing but slaves to the ale at times. My own father is famous for his love of the drink, after all!'

Edgar grasped with open arms the opportunity she was offering him, laughing much louder than was necessary and nodding vigorously, his face scarlet in the firelight. 'That's true,' he cackled in obvious relief. 'Alfred loves his ale! But he's also revered for his leadership, and I should have remembered you were his daughter before I opened my sot's mouth to berate you. Again, lady, I am sorry. You can be sure of my complete support.' He hoisted his cup into the air, matching Aethelflaed's, and looked around at the rest of the Mercian Witan. 'Who's with us?'

It would be a brave, or foolish, thane who spoke out against their new female leader at that moment. None did. In fact, every single man there bowed their heads towards her before raising their own cups and pledging their support.

Aethelflaed felt like she could do anything at that moment as she took in their admiring glances. Morcar was smiling, won over just like the rest of the council members. She was glad it hadn't been him who'd started a fight with her, for she knew her limits very well – she could match, even best, a man like Edgar, but a warrior of Morcar's size and skill was another matter. Still, even Alfred, as vicious and skilled a fighter as many in Britain, could not defeat everyone. He relied on the likes of Wulfric to be his strong right arm.

Aethelflaed looked at Morcar and gave a small nod of thanks for his part in stopping the fight from getting seriously out of hand. Could he be her Wulfric? He was certainly big enough, but the fact that she was even asking herself that made her feel guilty. Her husband, Ealdorman Aethelred, would stand by her side, and vice versa, once he was over his illness, would he not? She realised at that moment that she really was not sure if Aethelred would ever get over his ailments and, if he didn't, the support a man of Morcar's standing would be invaluable.

She'd only been in Mercia for a short part of her eighteen summers, but already she felt at home there; even if God saw fit to take her husband into his arms, Aethelflaed would remain a lady of Mercia.

'Drink up, men,' she said to the Witan, supping deeply of her own cup and pushing aside the strange melancholy that had come over her as she thought of her sickly husband. 'Now that we're all agreed I'll lead Mercia while Ealdorman Aethelred is poorly, it's time we got down to business. Now...' She took another sip and then placed the ale cup on the table with a thump. 'How do our fyrds stand, in terms of weapons and armour, and training? Lord Morcar, you can go first.'

The burly thane's eyes glittered as he nodded and began to deliver the information Aethelflaed had requested.

They've accepted me, she thought, looking around at the contented noblemen, no longer put out by the fact a woman was in charge. Now I just need to prove that I'm up to the task they've granted me. Not just a lady of Mercia, but the Lady of Mercia!

She prayed she would prove equal to the task.

CHAPTER FIVE

The task of rebuilding Wessex to fit Alfred's vision continued well into the next year. Word had come of Mercia's strong new leader, which surprised Alfred and Ealhswith not at all, for they knew better than anyone how Aethelflaed was perfectly suited for command. A resolute Mercia was key to the region's stability, and allowed the people of Wessex to spend more time on their literacy lessons. Alfred was proud that his daughter was playing her part so well.

Still, the West Saxon warriors could not be allowed to grow flabby and soft. It was important that the fyrds continued to train hard with spear and shield, spending time on duty even if that was merely patrolling their lands. Still just fifteen, Alfred's oldest son, Edward, was too young to go off to war, but he spent as much time being drilled by Wulfric as he did studying bible verses and philosophical treatises. The months of peace allowed the king to enjoy more time with his son than he was able to during the raids of the heathen armies, and Alfred took advantage of that, for, the older he grew, the more important his family became.

'Children are a gift from God,' Asser said to him as they shared a meal with Ealhswith that summer. 'You should make the most of them now, lord, before they're too old and moving on with their own lives.'

Edward had just come in from sparring with one of the hearth-warriors – tired, bruised and grubby from being knocked down repeatedly. The boy's eyes were shining, though, as he came to sit beside his mother at the high table and told them of his successes that day. He was almost as precocious as Aethelflaed had been, and viewed his sparring defeats as opportunities to learn, rather than growing upset over them. Alfred watched him regaling Ealhswith with a tale of being sneakily tripped by his older sparring-partner, only to remember the move and use it in their next bout, defeating his opponent and earning the praise of their tutor.

'You're right,' he said to Asser, grinning. 'Children truly are God's greatest gifts. It's pleasing to see mine grow into good people. Even their time in Athelney seems to have been a blessing, showing them how hard life is, and how blessed they are to be in the positions they are.' He nodded thoughtfully, gazing at his son who continued to speak excitedly to Ealhswith. 'Edward will be king one day. He must be prepared for everything that will come with that title.'

'No father ever gave their son a better education, lord,' said Asser and it was an honest statement, without any undertones of sycophantic flattery. The monk spoke his mind, as his predecessor, Oswald, had done. If he said Alfred was a good father, he meant it, and Alfred valued that judgement for it was important to him to do the best he could in every endeavour God gave him, be that as a king, politician, diplomat, warrior, husband, or father. No man could be perfect at everything, and Alfred knew he had limitations and flaws, but it was important to try one's best.

If he could impart that sense of duty to Edward it would give the lad a head start when it was time to take up the red and gold banner and rule Wessex as Alfred's successor. The thought inspired pride but also a sense of deep melancholy, for Alfred knew better than any how lonely, and how terrifying, it was to be a king.

He felt that old, feared twinge in his guts then. Just a tightening, a little pain which so often led to much worse agony and saw him confined to his bed, sobbing and being cradled by Ealhswith until it passed. A similar malady had killed Oswald too... He put down his ale cup and pushed away the trencher of greasy roast pork which he'd been enjoying so much, knowing too much rich food and drink were often what triggered his abdominal pains.

Along with fear and stress, of course, which he was most certainly feeling now as he looked into Edward's possible future. All his children's possible futures, for each would face different and difficult challenges, even if only Edward would be king.

'Are you well, lord?' Asser was asking.

Alfred realised his eyes had glazed over and he was probably staring at Edward with the expression of a deer startled by a hunter. He gritted his teeth and blinked, refusing to give in to the ache that had settled into this belly. He stood up, forcing a smile, and gestured to his son.

'Show me this move you described,' he said, setting his feet in a defensive stance and raising his hands as if he held an invisible sword.

'Not in here,' Ealhswith protested. 'I don't want anyone getting hurt!'

'We won't get hurt,' Alfred laughed as Edward eagerly came away from the table and faced off against him.

'It was like this,' said the boy, also holding up an invisible blade and stepping in close to 'strike' Alfred. They went back and forth like that for a short time, Ealhswith and Asser watching in amusement, until Edward moved forward with the grace of a dancer and used his foot to hook Alfred's heel. The boy was tall but not heavy and Alfred – who knew the move well – could have easily turned the motion back on Edward and upended him. Now was not the time for such a lesson, however, especially when the aetheling was so excited at his earlier success.

So, Alfred allowed his foot to be caught, and – with a short cry – fell backwards, hoping the rushes covering the floor would be fresh enough to offer some sort of cushion against his fall. He was a warrior of no mean skill though, and had learned how to take a tumble himself just as much as he'd been trained to make an enemy fall, so he managed to hit the ground without too much damage.

'You see?' Edward said, turning to his mother and Asser who were both nodding in appreciation. 'It even allows one to trip a bigger, heavier opponent.' He reached out to help his father up.

'It's a good move,' the king admitted, putting his arm around the boy's shoulders and giving him a proud hug before they returned to their places at the table, with Alfred giving him more advice on when to use such a move and when to avoid it. Edward listened intently, even when a servant placed some food in front of him and he began to eat.

When the lad's trencher was empty and he excused himself to go and change into clean clothes before evening Mass, Alfred realised the pain in his side had gone, and he felt wonderfully happy.

Asser was right, he mused as he sat and watched the monk chat with Ealhswith, children truly were a blessing. That was why Alfred knew they had to make sure even the poor ones would one day enjoy the same education as the offspring of the wealthy thanes and ealdormen. That would be Alfred's legacy to Edward, and to all the future generations of Anglo-Saxons in Wessex and beyond.

Filled with hope, and the faith in God that had carried him through so many trials and difficulties in his forty years, Alfred took his wife's hand in his and nodded happily at Asser. 'The hall is filling up with my hearth-warriors. How about you read that passage we were discussing earlier to Ealhswith? The Latin one that we noted down in my handbook.'

The monk beamed, taking out his own copy of St Augustine's *Soliloquies* and quickly finding the page. He began to read. Not loudly, but still his powerful baritone could be easily heard over the mounting hubbub within Wintanceaster's great hall. Food and drink were being served to his most loyal men and his closest friends, and the most learned man in the kingdom was reciting scripture to Alfred and his wife.

This was the life peace brought, and, to Alfred, it was about as close as it was possible to get to Heaven on earth. He'd been making plans for a life like this for years but never had the chance to put them into action until the Danes were properly pacified. Now, expanding his own learning as he was, even more plans and dreams came into his mind every day and he could hardly wait to put them all into motion.

Tonight, however, they would feast and make merry. He knew he should not drink any more ale, for it was still early and he'd already enjoyed a few cups, but he'd passed the tipping point where he felt so comfortable that another drink would not hurt, and besides, tomorrow was a long way away. He would awaken fine and refreshed and perhaps Ealhswith would even want to make love, if he did not grow belligerent or obnoxious.

'More ale, lord?' asked a blue-eyed serving girl with a narrow waist, wide hips, and strawberry blonde curls.

He looked at her and grinned, holding out his cup. 'Aye, fill it up, lass,' he said. 'Tonight we're celebrating another day free from Danes, and I mean to make the most of it.'

He noticed Ealhswith's critical stare and felt irritated. He knew what that black look meant, and any hopes of bedding her faded. Still, he mused as he sipped his overflowing cup and watched the serving girl walk away to another bench, hips swaying as if to proclaim the miracle of God's creation, Ealhswith wasn't the only attractive woman in Wintanceaster.

It was as black as the grave and, despite the obvious chill in the air, his body felt sweaty and… unpleasant. Alfred had no idea where he was at first, but then the memories came back. Sometimes, when he got really drunk, the memories did not come and he remained oblivious to what he'd done and what had happened forever. It was often a blessing, so with a sudden desire to vomit, he wished his mind would grant him that black, merciful oblivion, for, as he pictured the events in the hall from just a few hours ago, he felt utterly ashamed.

He rolled onto his side and fell out of the bed, not realising how close he'd been to the edge in the blackness. As he landed on his hands, he threw up, a stream of bitter liquid and half-digested food, the smell of which made him vomit again, and again, until there was nothing left to come up and he lay, panting, on the cold floor of the bedchamber.

The physical discomfort, as horrendous as it was, paled in comparison to the knowledge of his pitiful weakness. Again, even now in middle-age, he had been unable to resist Satan's temptations. He, the king who thought of himself as God's warrior, as the pious Christian who stood so righteously against the heathen hordes, was as weak as any child when offered a shiny bauble.

Alfred's shiny baubles had always been the same: ale, rich food, and, worst of all, women. God must have been disgusted with him at that moment, after what he'd spent the night getting up to with the serving girl.

He suddenly vomited again, as another wave of terrible guilt wracked his body and left him sobbing for breath with bits of wet sick on his chin, in his long hair, and all down the front of him.

Ealhswith. He had a vague recollection of going to bed as usual with her, but, when she rejected his advances, he'd threatened to go and find the servant with the deep blue eyes and the swaying hips. Ealhswith had told him to do as he pleased – he was the king, wasn't he? And so, he had.

He knew his wife would not mention what he'd been doing with the servant, and neither would he. It would be forgotten about, for Ealhswith accepted her husband's faults and rarely berated him for them. She knew very well that there was no need – he would punish himself far more for his actions than Ealhswith could do. Besides, Alfred was not the only nobleman who took lovers – most of them did, unless they were too old to get it up. Many of them even forced themselves on their unwilling wives and barely gave it a thought, unlike the pious Alfred who set himself high standards, if not always reaching them.

Ealhswith was not naïve. She knew how the world worked. But the thought that she did not complain about him rutting with some young serving girl because she feared Alfred might rape her made the gorge rise in his throat again. He would never do that to Ealhswith – he loved and respected her far too much. And yet, here he was covered in vomit while the girl he'd slept with remained in the bed in silence, too aware of her lowly station even to ask if he was all right.

Or perhaps she didn't give a damn.

That thought brought another wave of shame, but it faded quickly – he had not raped the servant. She'd come willingly with him to this chamber and, given his reputation, she must have known what exactly he wanted her for. No, the girl had been a willing partner, and he would reward her for it when he regained his senses. He was not an ugly man, he knew that well enough, and he retained the lean, muscular figure he'd had since he was an aetheling, but the women and girls who came to his bed in times of his drunkenness appreciated something more than just his ale-scented kisses and clumsy fumbling.

The desire to vomit had passed now that his guts were truly emptied, but the crushing sense of failure and shame had only grown more intense as he lay on the floor, going over everything in his mind.

He stood up, shaking and still unsure of his bearings. Stumbling, hand pressed against the wall, he moved away from the bed, his foot stepping in the warm contents of his voided belly and he swore in humiliation. What kind of sight would he be when he finally left this room, and who would be there to see him? His grasping hand finally found the iron latch on the door and he lifted it up, wincing at the clatter it made, and then the door was creaking open and he was stepping out into the main body of the hall, rubbing the filth off his feet on the rushes as he went.

'My lord?'

From the bed behind him came the small, questioning voice and he sucked in a deep, steadying breath before turning back. 'Thank you,' he said. 'I will make sure you are well rewarded for—'

'Thank you, my lord,' came the voice, cool and neutral so Alfred had no idea what emotions must be going through her mind. Excitement, he hoped. Happiness at the bounty that would soon come her way.

He moved on, eyes darting about the gloomy hall, which was populated with sleeping warriors, just visible in the soft orange glow from the fire which had been allowed to burn low once the night's revelries had come to a conclusion. Alfred knew no one would dare question him, much less upbraid him for what he'd done. It was his right as king, after all, and only God could punish him for his vices. Still, the thought of seeing Ealhswith or Asser made him move quicker until he reached the main doors and, with a nod to the sleepy spearman on guard duty, unbarred them himself and went outside.

He ignored the murmured greetings of the two guards out there, and walked towards the stream that ran through the town not far from the royal residence. The chill air, and the stars twinkling overhead, calmed his racing mind and somewhat lessened his awful feelings of having done something truly heinous. His actions had been bad, of course, but he would make his peace with God, and with Ealhswith, and he would never behave in such a way again. Or at least, he would try not to behave like that again. He was not foolish enough to believe he had the mental resilience to resist temptation forever – that kind of faith in himself had long since died.

He came to the stream and, gritting his teeth for the water was like ice, he washed the puke from his feet and then knelt to clean his face and rinse out his mouth. When he was done, gasping and shivering, and starting the return journey to the hall, he felt more normal again. By the time he was standing next to the low, yet still warming, fire with a cup of ale in his hand, the very worst of his anxiety had faded.

He refilled the cup and took a seat closer to the fire, gazing into the dancing flames and enjoying the warmth of both hearth and drink. It must have been later in the day than he'd realised, or perhaps he'd simply been sitting there in a comfortable stupor without noticing the time pass. The household began to come alive, with servants clearing the previous night's used cups and trenchers from the hall, going in and out fetching water, replacing the rushes, and all the other tasks they carried out each day. Alfred even noticed the blue-eyed girl he'd spent the night with busily working away, hair freshly combed, ruddy cheeks washed clean of Alfred's sweat. Their eyes met and he smiled sheepishly; she returned the look respectfully before her eyes were averted and she hurried into the back section of the hall.

He suddenly realised someone was sitting at the table behind him and he turned, surprised to see Ealhswith, a cup of water and a piece of buttered bread in her hands. She was eyeing him sardonically, and that was enough to bring back his earlier crushing feelings of guilt and failure.

'I'm—'

'I'm sure you are,' she interjected, eyes still boring into him, like a dagger being slowly plunged through his chest. She took a bite of her meal and chewed slowly, never looking away from him for even a moment. 'You make sure you reward that girl well for whatever she did.'

He nodded. 'Of course. I always—'

'You always do,' she broke in again, finishing his sentence for him.

'I truly am sorry,' he muttered. 'The ale…'

She lifted her eyebrows archly and sipped her water, still, somehow, never seeming to avert her gaze for even a heartbeat, or even blink. It was quite a skill she had, and it always made him wish he could disappear into the earth to escape her accusatory stare. It had been a long time since they had got into a heated argument over Alfred's wandering cock, however, and his wife was apparently in no mood for one now either. In truth, she didn't seem too bothered as she sat munching contentedly on her buttered bread.

At last, she was done breaking her fast and finally tore her eyes away from him, licking butter from her fingers and then washing it all down with the last of the water in her cup. 'Go to the church, Alfred,' she said. 'And make your peace with God.'

He bowed his head, hoping that her words meant there would be peace between him and Ealhswith at least. 'I'll go now,' he said, but she was already striding off towards the royal bedchamber and never so much as glanced back at him.

Suddenly the firepit, and his hall, and the glances of his now fully wakened hearth-warriors did not seem so comforting any more.

CHAPTER SIX

AD890, Wintanceaster

'Bad news, my lord.'

Alfred looked up from his sword, which he was sharpening with a whetstone. He'd spent the morning trying his best to understand a passage Asser was showing him, but the Latin had proved beyond him, and he'd eventually given up. Sometimes the mind needed a break, Asser reassured him, telling him to find something less mentally draining to do for a time.

That was when he'd remembered he hadn't been maintaining his war gear as fastidiously as he had when the Danes were constantly raiding. Alfred had the sharpest, shiniest sword blade in all Christendom, and his byrnie and helmet were as polished and free from dents as the day they'd been given to him. Recently, though, he'd neglected that maintenance, for there had been no real fighting in Wessex for some time and there were books demanding to be read.

Bringing his arms and armour back up to perfect condition was proving therapeutic that afternoon, however, offering a rewarding but simple task that he was able to lose himself in as he sat in the sunshine and watched the folk of Wintanceaster go about their daily business.

Of course, Wulfric had to come along and ruin his pleasant reverie, didn't he?

'Bad news?' Alfred said with a sigh, looking up at his captain and searching the man's face for clues as to just how bad the tidings might actually be. It was hard to tell with Wulfric, for he tended to look grim pretty much all the time, unless he was drunkenly singing a song, in which case everyone else's face was grim. The big ealdorman might excel in most things he pursued, but he was an atrocious singer.

'Aye.' Wulfric nodded. 'It's not good, lord. It's Guthrum.'

Alfred frowned as his mind began to work. Guthrum-Athelstan had been a strong ally, and caused Wessex no trouble at all since he'd been baptised as Alfred's godson over a decade before. Yet the man was a Dane after all, and Alfred knew the life of a sea-wolf would forever be a temptation to him as he existed mostly peacefully in East Anglia. If Guthrum decided after all this time to return to his days as a *vikingr*, raiding and plundering the Saxon lands beside him, would it really be such a shock?

Alfred thought about it and came to the conclusion that, yes, it would actually be extremely odd for Guthrum-Athelstan to take up his axe again and return to a life as the brutal warlord he'd once been. So it was almost a relief when Wulfric said, 'He's dead, my lord.'

Alfred's first thought was *I knew he wouldn't renounce God and return to his heathen ways!* His second thought was *Dead? What will that mean for East Anglia?* And then, perhaps with a little surprise, he thought, *Another friend gone*, and realised he would actually miss the man who'd once been the scourge of the Saxons, raping, killing, and enslaving so many of them.

'How?' he asked softly, his voice a hoarse whisper.

Wulfric shrugged and gave a little shake of his head. 'Nothing violent, as far as I know. He just seems to have died.' He shrugged again and spread out his palms. 'He was pretty old, lord.'

'Old!' Alfred pictured Guthrum-Athelstan in his mind. The first image that came to him was of the man he'd first met, when the enemy king was young, arrayed in war gear, and a rather frightening, powerful presence. But then Alfred realised that had been what, fifteen, sixteen years ago, and, sure enough, Guthrum-Athelstan must be quite elderly by now.

'Aye, I suppose he is – was – rather old,' Alfred murmured, staring down at his gleaming sword blade – a sword he'd wielded in battles against Guthrum-Athelstan's army. 'Now I feel old, too.' He sighed heavily and silently prayed that God would take the dead man into his care. Would his final years as a Christian be enough to see him into Heaven, or would there be some other final destination for the departed King of East Anglia?

Younger Guthrum would certainly have preferred an eternity in Valhöll, where he could fight, and drink, and fornicate all day, surrounded once more by his fallen friends. Alfred smiled sadly. When he thought of it like that, Valhöll really didn't sound like such a terrible place. Guthrum would be right at home there.

Whether it was Heaven, Valhöll, or some other resting place for him, Alfred prayed it would be pleasant.

'Are you all right, lord?'

Alfred came back to himself with a start, suddenly realising he'd been silent, lost in contemplation for quite some time. Strangely, he also had tears in his eyes and he turned away from Wulfric, embarrassed. Why should he be upset over the death of a man who'd been directly responsible for the slaughter of hundreds, even thousands of West Saxons? A man who'd caused so much trouble for Alfred, and for Wessex, during his life.

'The memory is a strange thing,' he said, surreptitiously wiping his eyes although he knew fine well Wulfric would have noticed they were damp. 'Don't you think?'

His captain pursed his lips thoughtfully and nodded. 'I suppose so. You're remembering the years we fought Guthrum with fondness now, aren't you, lord?'

Alfred smiled, turning back to Wulfric and nodding. 'Yes. At the time, it was hell. Especially those first months on Athelney when we were forced to live like the lowliest of ceorls, fearing for our lives as Guthrum's Danes sought to find us and make an end to us. And yet…' He trailed off and his face fell as those days flooded his memory. Long days spent in close proximity to his wife, and his hearth-warriors, and his children. Aethelflaed had moved away now, and a sudden longing to return to that time in Athelney when he'd enjoyed laughter and stories and games with his little daughter filled the king. Tears filled his eyes again and he forced a laugh.

'I miss those days, too, lord,' Wulfric said softly, surprising Alfred. 'We were afraid, and there was little hope of ever beating the sea-wolves, but, oddly, we were all happy.'

'We were, my friend,' the king agreed. 'Those were some of the best days of my life and Guthrum played a large part in that. He's the one who drove us there after all.' Alfred placed his sword down on the ground and stood up, arching his back and rolling his head to work out the tension in his neck. The sun was still shining, and he looked out at the town, breathing deeply of the summer air, giving thanks to God that he, at least, had been afforded another day on this middle-earth.

'He was a good man, eventually,' Wulfric admitted. 'I never believed he'd truly renounce his heathen gods and live as a Christian, but he did. It was a masterstroke on your part, lord, to force him to be baptised.'

'He wanted to settle down,' Alfred said. 'All he needed was the opportunity, and that's what I gave him.' He sighed heavily. 'I will miss him.'

'Aye,' the ealdorman agreed. 'And his passing isn't just sad – it raises a problem for us.'

'Who will take his place as king in East Anglia?' Alfred murmured, watching a pair of jackdaws fighting noisily with one another, falling from the sky to the ground, pecking one another furiously while a dozen more shrieked and flew about in consternation or, perhaps, amusement. 'And will he be a friend to Wessex?'

'I'd suggest sending messengers to our burhs,' Wulfric said as the squabbling corvids flew off, neither of the combatants apparently worse for their battle. 'Warn them to be prepared for trouble.'

Alfred nodded slowly. 'Do it,' he said, turning back into the armoury and lifting his sword which he eyed critically before wiping it with a rag and pushing it into its recently renewed sheath. 'Hopefully this won't be needed, but we'd better be prepared, Wulfric. The death of a king rarely leads to a time of peace.'

'No. But at least we have a proper standing army in place now, thanks to your reforms.'

The reforms Wulfric referred to had long been in Alfred's mind, but with all the upheaval in his kingdom since the day he'd taken the throne it had been impossible to enact them. Now, though, they had become a reality. First, a system of fortified towns – burhs – were set up at regular points along the length of Wessex. With stronger walls and gates than previous settlements, they would be much harder for raiders to take without a siege. And, should such a siege begin, the soldiers in nearby burhs could quickly march along the herepaths – the army roads – to aid their neighbours. And there would always be warriors ready to march, for half the men of the kingdom would serve in the army at any one time, while the other half worked the fields and did the other industrial and commercial tasks required to keep Wessex productive. The men would change positions at regular intervals, soldiers swapping with workers, avoiding any battle fatigue. It was a simple system, which Alfred thought should have been put in place generations before. But it had taken his foresight and leadership to make it a reality.

'Any raiders looking to attack Wessex would do well to take note of how easily we defeated them at Hrofescester,' the ealdorman continued, referring to a battle five years before when the army and system of burhs had combined to see off a major attack led by the jarl named Hjalmarr. 'We're prepared for raids now, and the age of Ivar the Detestable and the Sons of Ragnar are gone.'

'Indeed,' the king agreed with a grim smile. 'Our lands are secure. It would take a hundred longships filled with enemy warriors to cause any real trouble for us these days!'

They laughed, knowing, or at least hoping, such an invasion was highly unlikely.

'Our lands are secure,' Alfred said, humour fading, 'from outside raiders. It's within our borders that has me worried at times.'

Wulfric frowned. 'You're thinking of your nephew, Aethelwold.'

The king nodded, gazing off into the middle distance. 'He's plotting, I just know it. Plotting to take the throne from Edward when I die. He hates us.'

They stood together, thinking of the aetheling Aethelwold and the threat he posed to the future safety of Wessex.

'I've done what I can to prepare the way for Edward,' the king said heavily, forcing himself to forget his nephew and cheer up. 'Come on, I'm done sharpening and oiling my sword. I suppose we better see what's to be done regarding Guthrum-Athelstan's funeral. It'll be a Christian service, after all, and we should be there for it. With any luck, Guthrum-Athelstan's son, Eohric, will take East Anglia's throne and honour the agreement we made with his father.'

Wulfric nodded as he closed and bolted the armoury door behind them. 'And then?'

'And then, my loyal captain,' Alfred said with an expansive smile, 'with things set to right in our world, we can look at finally uniting all the Anglo-Saxon lands under one king, whether that be myself or, more likely, my son, Edward. That – that! – is what we must strive for in the coming months and years, Wulfric. A kingdom of all the Anglo-Saxons: Ængleland!'

CHAPTER SEVEN

'Danes!'

There were few cries that inspired anxiety in the hearts of those who heard them. 'Help!' was one, 'Fire!' another. But the most terrifying shout to be raised within the Mercian capital, Glowecestre, was that which the mounted warrior was calling out now as he rode hell for leather along the main street towards Ealdorman Aethelred's hall.

It was the ealdorman's wife, Aethelflaed, who appeared in the doorway, flanked by two burly bodyguards. Her hair was tied back, and she was pale, for although her husband was recovering after his long illness, he remained poorly and, when he could not sleep, it disturbed her rest too. That made her irritable, and she glared at the rider cantering along the street, sending workers and pedestrians scattering hither and thither. For a moment she wished she'd travelled to East Anglia for Guthrum's funeral, and to see his son Eohric be crowned in his stead, but she'd ignored her father's missive requesting her presence there. With Aethelred ill, Mercia needed Aethelflaed's leadership, and, with that in mind, she steeled herself to do her duty.

'Danes?' she demanded when the wide-eyed man reined in his mount before her. 'Where?'

By now everyone in Mercia knew the Lady Aethelflaed had taken control of the Witan until her husband was fully recovered from his illness. Even so, many of the warriors found it difficult to take a woman seriously. How could this princess, little more than a girl, command the men of Mercia? Ridiculous.

71

Aethelflaed could see all this and more flash across the rider's face as he jumped down from the horse and stood before her, panting as if he'd been the one running across heath and field. She gazed past him, out at the countryside surrounding the town. Everything seemed peaceful – a shepherd boy was busy on a nearby hill, tending his flock; smoke from the blacksmith's to the east rose languidly into the blue sky; and a large merchant vessel plied its way lazily towards the docks, bringing trade from some exotic foreign land. Still, just because there wasn't a marauding band of sea-wolves screaming towards the town did not mean all was well. This messenger had clearly come with a warning from somewhere.

'Witenhert,' the rider said, before adding as an afterthought, 'My lady.'

Aethelflaed fought the urge to look to her bodyguards for confirmation of where Witenhert was, knowing it would only make her seem like she had no idea about the geography of Mercia. That was not true. She'd familiarised herself with as many of the towns and villages as possible, and, quickly bringing up a mental map she realised that Witenhert, 'white wooded hill', was a small settlement just six miles south of Glowecestre itself.

'Don't you think you should muster the fyrd?' the rider demanded, suddenly grown irritable at the sight of the girl standing, apparently unable to decide how to proceed.

There came the sound of horses' shod hooves clumping towards them, and a dozen men appeared from around the side of the hall, each leading an animal, saddled and ready to ride.

'She commanded us to get ready as soon as she heard you shouting,' the tall, broad ealdorman, Morcar, growled. He was leading two horses, and he headed for Aethelflaed, handing her the reins to one of them with a respectful bow of his head. He turned back to the rider. 'Next time you address the lady, have more respect, man, or it'll go badly for you.'

The messenger blanched, mouth working as he tried to offer some apology for his rudeness. Aethelflaed ignored him, knowing it would do no good to embarrass him even further, but unwilling to excuse him either. She took the reins from Morcar with a word of thanks and expertly jumped onto the horse's back, sitting with her legs on either side of the beast's flanks, like a man would ride. The expression on the messenger's face was priceless as he took in the sight of her, only noticing now the sword slung across her shoulder on a baldric, the coat of mail that glinted beneath her grey cloak, and the helmet that was buckled to her horse's saddle.

'Come, Morcar,' she said, turning away from the messenger without another word and nudging her mount into a walk towards the town gates. 'We'll gather more men and ride for Witenhert with all haste.'

Glowecestre was not a burh in the sense of those Alfred had constructed in Wessex, but Aethelflaed had taken note of her father's reforms and brought the idea to Mercia. So, although it was not as advanced as those in Alfred's kingdom, the town was slowly progressing towards that status, with strengthened walls and gates, and a burgeoning standing army. It would take time, of course, but there were enough warriors manning the defences that day to quickly form them into a fyrd and head towards Witenhert.

Aethelflaed had donned her helmet now that they'd left the safety of the town's walls, and collected a spear when they stopped at the gatehouse. She was smaller than Morcar who rode at her right hand, and smaller than the rest of those she commanded, but she sat atop the palfrey with such poise and confidence that none there thought her out of place. Of course, much would depend on how this day went, and how she performed, and that thought did make her guts churn. If she could hold her nerve and manage to avoid being skewered by a sea-wolf's sword, or cleft in two by a war-axe, it would be a good way to prove she really was worthy to be in charge of Mercia's Witan.

If the Danes managed to kill her though, well, she thought with a wry smile, she wouldn't be around to worry about it...

She took in the scenery as they travelled, noting how similar, yet also different, this part of Mercia was to Wessex. They shared the same green fields, glittering streams and rivers, and meadows strewn with summer flowers, and the hills were mostly gentle slopes without the towering crags or misty mountains found in neighbouring Northumbria or the lands of the Wealas. Even so, there was something – the colours, the smells, the sounds, or something completely undefinable – that was different here in Mercia. It was neither good nor bad, just… different.

She smiled. Whatever it was, she enjoyed travelling in these lands, even when so led to a possible gory death.

'Are we just riding straight into the settlement?' Morcar asked, interrupting her thoughts and bringing her back to the task at hand.

Aethelflaed looked at the warriors with her – there were not enough of them to make it worthwhile splitting into two groups. That would simply weaken them. Besides, if she was remembering Witenhert right, the place only had one gate.

'I think so,' she said, nodding thoughtfully. 'That messenger was in a real hurry. I don't think we've got time to send a scout on ahead – we're probably too late to help the townsfolk as it is, but, if we can save even one of them from death or rape, we need to do our best.' She looked again at her riders, noting the grim set of their mouths and the fierce determination in their eyes to deal with this outrage perpetrated against their people. 'Are we ready to bring death to the Danes?' she demanded.

Every man there roared an emphatic reply. As Witenhert drew into view, the wooded hill it was named for rising up in the distance before them, Aethelflaed kicked her heels into her mount, urging it into a gallop. They thundered across the ground, the lady in front and her fyrd close behind, no war-cries or shouted boasts preceding them, just quiet determination. Somehow that was more impressive to Aethelflaed, and she felt the blood beginning to course faster through her veins, the nauseous sensation that had grown tighter in her guts the closer they got to their goal slowly beginning to ease.

'Have you ever led men in battle, my lady?' Morcar asked, bringing his mount close to hers so the answer would remain between the two of them.

Aethelflaed snorted with dark humour. Led men in battle? She'd never even fought in a battle, but she could hardly admit that now, could she? Her father had allowed her to train with his warriors and to learn the strategies of war with Edward's tutors. She knew how to wield a sword and a spear, how to protect herself with a shield, and, in her mind, she'd been preparing for this day since she'd learned to walk. Not for her the life of a maiden – Aethelflaed had always wanted to be a warrior. Would she be able to go toe-to-toe with the screaming, blood-crazed Danes, or would the spear and shield prove too heavy for her?

'No,' she admitted to Morcar. 'So you make sure I don't make any mistakes, all right?'

The big ealdorman gazed at her, his expression unreadable, and then he simply nodded and looked ahead again.

She knew he'd guessed the truth of it, but decided it was too late to change their course now. If she froze and ended up being gutted, it was not his fault. Still, she was sure the ealdorman would not have let her carry on towards Witenhert if he did not have some confidence in her abilities.

She had no more time to worry about it, for their destination was growing ever nearer and the sounds of wailing rose above the town, mingling with the black smoke of fires set by raiders rather than cooks.

'At least some of the people are still alive!' Aethelflaed shouted, taking one white-knuckled hand off the reins to make sure her helmet was still firmly buckled in place. 'Let's keep them that way!'

The gates had been smashed open, and were hanging from their hinges, while the remnants of the bar that had held them shut were strewn about the ground. Aethelflaed took in the sights, sounds, and smells as she reined in her mount just outside the town and dismounted. Her men followed suit, forming up in a line four deep with her at the centre. She was glad Morcar was beside her, his great brooding presence offering reassurance that, even if she failed in her role as leader of the fyrd, he would be there to take over.

'Shields up!' the ealdorman roared, practically deafening Aethelflaed in her right ear. 'Spears ready!'

'Remind me when this is over,' the princess murmured to the ealdorman. 'I must learn how to shout like that.'

'I'm not sure it's something that can be taught,' Morcar replied, and she could tell without looking that he was smiling.

'Maybe not, but I still intend to learn,' she returned, and then her eyes were wide and her nostrils were flaring, for the Danes had noticed them and came to meet them now, shieldwall to shieldwall. 'Those on the wings, watch out for enemies flanking us,' she cried. 'There's cover for them in the buildings there. Ready?'

'Ready!'

She took a long, steadying breath, fearful that the sweat on her palms would make the spear slip from her grasp. 'Give the command, Morcar,' she said hoarsely.

'Forward!'

His great voice boomed out, reverberating against the houses and workshops nearest the wrecked gates and the Mercian fyrd began to move forward, step by step, in tight formation. There was no room for missiles, indeed the opposing groups of warriors were almost upon one another, mostly silent apart from one or two Danes who'd realised Aethelflaed was a woman and were making crude insults and threats towards her. She bit her tongue, knowing it would do no good to rise to them. There was only one way to make the bastards eat their words.

'Brace!' she shrieked, hating the lack of power in her voice as she turned away from the spear point that tore through the air towards her face.

Somehow it missed, and Aethelflaed thrust her own weapon forward, feeling it clatter against the boards of a shield. It did not become stuck in the wood, however, scraping past it and finding purchase in something soft and yielding. There was a terrific scream of shock which mingled with a dozen similar cries and, desperately, she pulled back on the spear, praying to God that it would come free, for this was no place for the shorter reach of her sword. The shaft shuddered in her hand, as if whomever it had lodged inside had torn themselves away from it and a second cry confirmed her thoughts. It was free and, teeth bared like an enraged wolf, she ducked behind her shield, narrowly avoiding another attack before shoving her spear forward again. She could not see the Danes from behind the linden boards that kept her alive, but it did not matter, the leaf-shaped iron blade drew blood once more.

The horrified shouts of mutilated and dying men seemed to swirl around Aethelflaed, and it felt almost as if the sounds came from inside her own skull. It was terrifying, and disorienting, and all she could do was continue to thrust out her spear and hide behind the shield, all the while fearing some fallen enemy would stab her in the legs, below the shield's protection. Or perhaps one of those glinting enemy spear-tips would plunge right into her eye and through her brain, or maybe her mouth, smashing her teeth and pinning her tongue against...

Roaring 'Godemite! For Mercia!' she pushed her fearful thoughts aside and fought with renewed vigour, replacing terror with rage, at least for now.

Soon enough though, her arms began to ache. Her shield felt as if a dead Northman was hanging upon it, and her right hand could barely keep a grip of the spear never mind continue to push it forward and back.

Drawing in one massive last breath, she shouted, 'Front row – fall back!' Hearing her command repeated along the line she tried one last ineffectual thrust and then took a step backwards. The warrior behind her slipped past and took her place in the first row of the shieldwall and the princess moved to the very rear of the formation.

'Did I give the command too early?' She gasped, sucking in breaths as if she'd just been dragged from the sea on the verge of drowning. 'To move back I mean?'

Morcar shook his head. 'We've earned a rest. Take it while you can, we may be needed again.' He was breathing heavily too, and his arm was soaked with blood from a deep gash but he hardly seemed to notice as he said, 'Well done,' and then turned back to watch as well he could the battle that continued before them.

Aethelflaed felt buoyed by the ealdorman's praise. It was like being praised by her father and she might have grinned had the sounds of dying not continued around her, reminding her of the peril they were in. 'You,' she called to the man in the line next to Morcar. 'Bandage his arm before he collapses from loss of blood. And make sure you're patched up too, I need you ready to go again if these bastards don't break soon.' She did grin then, hoping it looked reassuring, as she imagined Alfred would do in the midst of a battle, inspiring the men serving under him.

It seemed to work, as the warrior she'd addressed returned her grin and immediately set to work, pulling a clean cloth rag from within his tunic and binding it tightly around Morcar's forearm. Aethelflaed stepped back, trying to see over the helmeted heads of those in front of her. She did not have Morcar's height though, and ended up climbing up on one of the damaged gates, using it as a ladder to see what was happening.

With a surge of elation, she saw her Mercian fyrd now outnumbered the group of raiders by a good margin, perhaps even as much as two to one. She might have called for the enemy leader to surrender but she knew her voice would not carry over the clatter and clangour. Hopefully the Danes would realise they were losing and throw down their weapons before too many more had to die.

'Lady! Look out!'

The cry came just as Aethelflaed felt someone grab her leg and haul her down from the gate. She fell like a sack of grain, thumping against the wood to land on her back, breath blasted from her. She tried to get up, but the face of a Dane swam into view, blackened by smoke and twisted with hatred. He fell on her, punching her in the side of the face with one hand and grabbing her between the legs with the other.

'Mercian bitch!'

He was screaming as he tried to tear her leggings down, and she was too dazed to try and stop him. Her ears were ringing and the stench of sour ale from the sea-wolf was so strong it made the princess gag.

'I'll enjoy this!' he shouted right in her face, and she realised that he'd ripped her breeches open. At last, Aethelflaed managed to fight through the shock and the fog in her brain. As he pressed his face close to hers, she lifted her head and bit the end of his nose. Blood spurted instantly, and she spat it into his face along with the lump of flesh she'd torn off. He reeled back in horror, and she punched him in the temple. It was not a heavy blow, but it was enough to dislodge him so that she could get out from under him and roll to the side.

He knelt beside the gate, cross-eyed as he tried to see the damage done to his ruined nose, and then the side of his head crumpled as Aethelflaed smashed her sword against it. Silently, the Dane fell sideways, but the princess chopped down again, and again, before thrusting the tip of the blade right through his mouth.

She was sobbing, shocked by what had just happened. She'd known battle would be dangerous, terrifying, and horrific, and she'd known what would happen to her if she was ever on the losing side. But this...

'Are you all right, lady?'

Morcar's calm voice brought her back to the present and she turned to him, trying her best to appear strong and coolly detached from her ordeal. She knew he could see through her front, but it had to be maintained or this could be the last time any of the Mercian fyrds would follow her. 'I'm fine,' she said. 'Have we won yet?'

He smiled but there was more of relief than triumph in it. 'Just about.' He took off his tunic and held it out to her. 'Tie that around yourself, lady. That whoreson…'

Aethelflaed took the garment, not understanding what he meant until her eyes travelled down and saw her torn leggings. She shuddered and quickly tied Morcar's tunic around herself. It was not perfect, but it was better than nothing and she nodded her thanks to the ealdorman.

Behind them the battle was over. Only a handful of Danes were left, and those had thrown down their spears, begging the Christians to show them mercy.

'What would you have us do?' one of the warriors from the shieldwall's front row asked as he ran up and delivered the news to Aethelflaed and Morcar. 'Should we let them live, lady?'

Briefly, she wondered what her father would do, but then she pushed such thoughts aside. She was not Alfred, and they were not in Wessex. She was Aethelflaed, Lady of Mercia, and the Danes must learn to fear her as much as any man. More!

'Kill them,' she said, lip curling as she glanced back at her would-be rapist, realising what he'd intended for her had undoubtedly been done to many of the inhabitants of Witenhert that day. 'Kill them all.'

CHAPTER EIGHT

'You can't kill them all!' Her voice was high and plaintive, but she didn't care. She was in charge, and she would not sanction such violence.

The nun rolled her eyes, sighing heavily, as if dealing with petulant young noblewomen was even more irksome than slaughtering lambs. 'But, my lady—'

'Don't 'my lady' me, I don't care how many important men are coming to dinner! They can eat mutton. Those lambs are not long born into this world, and they should have a chance to live for a time before you feed their flesh to a bunch of fat old thanes.'

Despite her obvious irritation the older nun smiled ever so slightly at the description of the nunnery's guests. She was tall and very thin, with iron-grey hair and more wrinkles than an old prune, but Alfred had chosen her specifically to help his daughter run the nunnery there at Sceaftesburi.

'Are the older sheep's lives less important than the young ones?' Lady Ealhswith asked, and Aethelgifu snorted.

'Of course,' the girl argued, ignoring her mother's raised eyebrows. 'The older ones have had their time. Now we must afford the same courtesy to the babes. Does the bible not say: 'He will tend his flock like a shepherd; he will gather the lambs in his arms; he will carry them in his bosom'?'

'It's fine.' The king laughed, nodding to the nun. 'As Aethelgifu commands, we will eat mutton.'

His daughter nodded imperiously. 'Mutton, and beef. We have plenty of that, I'm sure. There's cows all over the place in Sceaftesburi!'

Alfred shared an understanding, sympathetic look with the grey-haired nun as she swept out of the chamber to see to the new dinner arrangements. He knew better than anyone what Aethelgifu was like.

At just fourteen summers his daughter was rather young to be made Abbess of Sceaftesburi Abbey, but this was what the girl had wanted for her life, and, as hard as Alfred could be with his thanes and ealdormen, he was notoriously soft with his children, especially the two girls. Aethelflaed had always wanted to be a warrior and was performing admirably in that role as recent reports from Mercia proved – not only had she taken charge of the Witan, but she'd led a warband to victory over raiding Danes. Alfred would have liked to send his own hearth-warriors to guard her, but he knew his children had to make their own way in the world now and, by all accounts, Aethelflaed had performed as well as any man in battle and immediately set about rebuilding the sacked Mercian town. She did not need his help, it seemed.

In contrast to her older sister, Aethelgifu had never been interested in fighting or learning the ways of war. She was a sickly child, very small and frail and, for most of her youth, Alfred and Ealhswith had feared she would not make her next birthday. The girl had an inner strength, however, and defied all expectations to reach this stage in her life where she'd told her parents she wished to dedicate herself to God's service, celibate, and consecrated to the rules of monastic life.

Sceaftesburi Abbey, like the one on Athelney, had only recently been founded and it seemed the ideal place for the princess to take up the role of abbess, despite her lack of years or knowledge of the role. Alfred had made sure there were enough experienced nuns in residence there to make the transition as simple as possible, and to help Aethelgifu learn the skills she would need for the abbey to be successful. Although she was not as precocious or confrontational as Aethelflaed, Aethelgifu was clever and driven.

She also loved animals, particularly young ones, hence her refusal to sanction the slaughter of lambs for her feast... Alfred couldn't help grinning at the haughty expression she wore as she gazed at him. There were worse traits to have than a love for baby animals, he thought with a sudden surge of affection.

'Are you absolutely certain this life is what you want?' Ealhswith asked seriously. 'It's not too late to change your mind. We can find you a good husband.'

Aethelgifu sighed in exasperation. She had never thought herself an attractive girl and Alfred suspected it was that skewed opinion of herself that had driven her desire to leave courtly life and become a nun. It hardly mattered what she looked like – any ealdorman in Anglo-Saxon lands would gladly take her as wife, since marrying one of the king's daughters brought obvious political power and prestige.

'I don't want a husband,' the girl said firmly. 'I've never wanted that.' She paused and eyed her parents suspiciously. 'My cousin, Aethelwold – he isn't here for the feast, is he?'

Alfred looked at Ealhswith in surprise, and both shook their heads emphatically.

'Of course not,' the king said. 'We don't talk to him, unless we need to. He certainly wouldn't be invited here for this happy occasion. He'd only cause trouble. Him and his brother, and bloody Sicgred.'

'Why do you ask after Aethelwold?' Ealhswith wanted to know.

Aethelgifu gave a small sigh and pulled the head from a flower, plucking the petals absent-mindedly. 'He sent a message,' she said. 'Asking for my hand in marriage.'

'What?' Alfred exploded. 'That little—'

'Are you sure it came from Aethelwold?' Ealhswith asked in a calmer tone than her husband's.

Aethelgifu shrugged. 'Maybe not, I don't know. The messenger *said* he came from Aethelwold, and he said my cousin wished to know if I would be interested in marrying him. The message was very complimentary about my beauty and my intelligence.'

Alfred was chuckling in disbelief at the audacity of his nephew. 'So, he thinks that marrying my daughter will strengthen his claim to the throne? Well, he can think again.'

Ealhswith looked worried, as if she feared her daughter might be swayed by the attention of the aetheling, but Aethelgifu set her parents' minds at ease quite firmly.

'Don't worry,' she said. 'I already told you – I don't want to ever be wed. Ever! And I told the messenger that. I enjoy reading, and learning, and praising God. That's what makes me happy, and living here with others like me will give me all I need.' She stood up and looked out the un-shuttered window at the abbey grounds which were bursting with colourful flowers at that time of year. The sunshine shone on her, making her almost seem to glow, as if God was framing her in his light and, of course, Alfred could not help but be moved by the sight. It did not take much for him to think something was divinely inspired.

'If this is what Aethelgifu truly wants,' he said to his wife, 'let's support her as much as we can. She's obviously settled in well since arriving here a month ago, and at least she's not far from Wintanceaster or the other royal residences; we can visit her often.'

He smiled at Aethelgifu, and she returned it, beaming in gratitude. 'Of course,' she said. 'You'll always be welcome here – just don't expect to be fed lamb when you visit!'

They all laughed, and the conversation moved on, everyone trying to forget Aethelwold's proposal as Alfred and Ealhswith offered advice on how to deal with the older nuns and how they imagined a nunnery should best be run. As they spoke, they went outside, glorying in the warm day and the peace of the abbey grounds. Nuns worked amongst the gardens, tending to the flowers and vegetables, while insects buzzed to and fro and birds sang from the branches of the fruit trees that were dotted around.

No wonder Aethelgifu wanted to spend her days here, Alfred thought. It was like Heaven! He prayed the novelty did not wear off in time, leaving her wishing she'd done something else with her life. He looked at her chattering gaily to Ealhswith as they walked, and the old fears over her health returned. At least she should be in no danger from marauding Danes here for Sceaftesburi was part of Wessex's new system of burhs and boasted strong, high walls and enough trained warriors to guard them.

No, violence would not be the end for Aethelgifu. Not here. Aethelflaed on the other hand, riding around Mercia like a warlord… She was a different matter. He sighed and forced himself to put aside such melancholic thoughts – it was a parent's lot to fear for his children, even when they became adults and went out into the world to make their own way.

God would take care of them.

'How goes your learning, father?' his daughter asked, turning and beckoning impatiently for him to keep up with them. 'Has Asser taught you to read Latin yet?'

Alfred laughed. 'We're getting there,' he admitted. 'Although I can't read it as well as I'd like, if I work hard, I can get there eventually. I've managed to translate Gregory the Great's *Pastoral Care* into English, and I'm working on more with Asser. Soon we'll have a whole library that any literate person in the kingdom can read and enjoy!'

Aethelgifu's joy was as apparent as her father's. 'And the other grand project you've been talking about for years? How is that going?'

They came to a bench and sat down. Ealhswith noticed a servant watching them surreptitiously from a shaded archway near what – from the delicious smells and clatter of pots and utensils emanating from the windows – must be the kitchen. 'Bring us refreshments,' she called, and the servant bowed before hurrying away.

'My Anglo-Saxon Chronicle?' Alfred asked in the familiar, enthusiastic tone that always accompanied his talks on favoured subjects. 'Finally, work has started on it! Bishop Plegmund and John the Old Saxon are busy with it in Wintanceaster as we speak – he, and others, will record every important event that happens in our lands over the coming months and years. At the same time, more scholars will compile previous historical documents and, once completed, we'll have one great collection of writings that future generations can refer to.'

'It's a wonderful idea,' Ealhswith said, drawing her feet back as the servant appeared carrying a jug brimming with freshly brewed, aromatic ale, three cups, and a trencher of cool fruits including cherries, apples and plums. When the royal party were furnished with their food and drink the servant, bowing obsequiously, hurried back to her place in the shadows in case she was required again.

'It is a wonderful idea,' Alfred agreed, biting into a plum and wincing slightly at the delicious sourness that filled his mouth. 'I don't know why no one thought of doing it before. Just imagine, if the Romans had kept such a chronicle of all the events that happened here during their time? And then the people who took their place when the legions sailed away?' He shook his head, gazing out at the gardens, mind filled with the wonder of what those unwritten annals might have recorded.

'Well, at least those who come after us will have your Chronicle,' Ealhswith said, chewing a slice of apple. 'Eat up,' she ordered Aethelgifu. 'Fruit is good for you. I don't care if you are abbess here, you still need to eat well, or you'll get sick.'

The girl muttered something under her breath but did as her mother bade and took a couple of cherries, biting one in half and daintily picking out the stone to throw into the earth behind them. Alfred smiled, appreciating Aethelgifu's manners, and knowing Aethelflaed would have revelled in spitting the stone as far across the garden as she could manage.

'Let us pray,' said the young abbess, 'that your chroniclers in Wintanceaster have nothing more exciting to record than marriages and births. Britain has seen enough of Danes over the past hundred years.'

Ealhswith nodded, finishing her apple and, like her daughter, neatly discarding the core in the earth. 'Indeed. It might make for a boring read, but, by God, that's the book I'd prefer over one filled with the likes of Ivar, Ubba, and Ragnar Lodbrok.'

"'*Therefore, since we have been justified through faith, we have peace with God through our Lord Jesus Christ...*'" Alfred intoned, quoting Romans 5:1. 'Let that be my legacy. Let my children, and their children, flourish and prosper without the threat of violence hanging over them.' He grinned then, unwilling to dampen the joyful mood that had filled their day together so far. 'Let's not think of war, though. The Danes are pacified and know their place – we should have no more trouble from them. Now, my lady, Abbess Aethelgifu, I think it's time we went indoors and showed ourselves to your guests. The "fat old thanes" as you so eloquently described them earlier.'

'You know I didn't include you in that description, father,' protested his daughter with just enough of a glint in her eye to make him wonder whether she was teasing him or not, but she stood and led the way towards the abbey door before he or the smirking Ealhswith could say another word.

Alfred's nephew returned to his thoughts as they walked. Aethelwold's proposal of marriage to Aethelgifu was astonishing. Of course, there was no way to prove it had really come from the aetheling, who would likely deny it if challenged, but it showed Aethelwold was still trying to manoeuvre his way closer to Wessex's throne. There wasn't much Alfred could do about it, short of having someone kill his nephew which he couldn't bring himself to do.

Edward would simply need to be wary of Aethelwold when the day came that Alfred was no longer king, and the throne was vacant.

Hopefully that day was a long way off.

CHAPTER NINE

AD 892, October

The regrowth of Wessex continued as one of the holy scholars Alfred had brought to his court, Plegmund, was elected Archbishop of Canterbury. The previous incumbent, Ethelred, had died two years earlier, and had never been a great supporter of the king. With Plegmund's elevation Alfred's position grew even stronger, and the task of producing what he thought of as 'the books most necessary for all men to know' continued apace.

All was well within the kingdom until, in 891, there appeared in the sky what the scholars called a '*cometa*', and the lay people termed a 'hairy star'. Few in Wessex, including Alfred, believed it presaged good tidings and so it proved.

'I knew we were in for trouble,' the king said, shaking his head and trying to ignore the knot in his stomach that the messenger's news had triggered. 'The moment that bright star arrived last year, with its fiery tail, it was never going to be a good omen.'

Wulfric grunted. 'I don't place as much stock in omens as you, my lord. I think it was obvious that recent events in Francia, although celebrated by all in Christendom, were only ever going to prove troublesome for us.'

Alfred nodded grimly, fiddling with his ale mug without drinking from it. Ealhswith, sitting beside him in Wintanceaster's hall, did not offer to refill it and, in truth, he knew he needed a clear head to deal with what was happening. What

Wulfric had alluded to was the crushing defeat an army of Danes had suffered on the banks of the River Dijle in Francia the previous November, followed by further beatings at the hands of the Franks. On top of that the Danes had faced famine and blight until, at last, they'd decided to give up raiding those lands and packed their families, animals, and stolen booty into their longships.

Now, with the tidings brought by the messenger from Alfred's new burh in Eorpeburnan, it was clear where those desperate sea-wolves had decided to sail to.

'I can't believe there's so many of them,' the king said, staring into the dancing flames in the firepit. 'Are you certain you counted correctly?'

The messenger was cradling a mug of warm ale, his eyes still wide from what he'd seen in the burh he'd been helping to build. He shivered, from the memory of it as much as the gust of icy autumn wind that rattled the door to the hall and sent embers scattering about the chimney-hole overhead, 'Aye, lord,' the man said. 'I counted them twice. I could hardly believe it myself.'

'Two hundred and fifty longships,' Ealhswith murmured, exhaling softly as she refilled her own drink from the jug on the bench before them. 'That's an incredible number of warriors, even taking into account the fact they have their women, children, and horses with them.'

Wulfric grunted agreement. 'We could be looking at an army of anything from two to six or seven thousand Northmen. More than we've ever faced before, even in the days of Ivar and Halfdan.'

Alfred swallowed, forcing his gaze from the fire and placing his mug on the bench. 'It is,' he agreed, voice hard and as confident as he could make it. 'But now we have a standing army ready to face any threats, and our burhs. Who leads these newcomers? Do you have any idea? Did their sails bear any symbol? Did they have a banner?'

'They did, lord,' the messenger confirmed. 'Red, with a black eagle.'

There was an ominous silence at that news and Alfred shared a worried look with his captain.

'Haesten.' Wulfric suggested.

'God help us,' Alfred intoned in a low voice. 'He must be an old man by now though! He's been raiding for decades.'

'True,' Wulfric said, lip curling in disgust. 'But, unlike Guthrum, it seems Haesten has never grown out of the desire to pillage.'

'Then it's up to us to put an end to his wickedness once and for all,' growled the king.

'Pray it's so, but I wouldn't hold out much hope for Eorpeburnan,' Wulfric said, and his expression was dark.

'Why not?' Ealhswith asked.

'The defences are only half finished,' Alfred replied. 'I told them to get those damn walls built! I asked them nicely, I threatened to strip the thanes of their titles and lands, but they had excuse after excuse and now...' He looked at the messenger who nodded sadly.

'I left before any fighting started,' he admitted. 'And others did the same – riding to the nearest burhs for aid but...' He shook his head and swallowed a long draught of ale. 'As you say, my lord, the fortress was not complete. Those walls could not hold back so many Northmen for long.'

'God help those poor people,' Asser said, clutching the cross that hung around his neck and murmuring a soft prayer which Alfred and Ealhswith joined in with.

When the monk finished, the five of them sat in silence, digesting the terrible news, their imaginations describing for them the slaughter that must have taken place within Eorpeburnan. Thousands of enemy warriors, against a half-finished burh manned by more workmen than soldiers.

Alfred saw Wulfric eyeing him with obvious impatience and he let out a heavy breath, getting to his feet and kissing his wife on the head. 'Wulfric is desperate to muster the fyrd and I suppose I'd better don my helmet and shield for another war with these bastards from across the whale road.'

'God protect you, my love,' Ealhswith said, gripping his hand as if she did not want to let him go.

'He has so far,' Alfred replied with a wry smile.

'We'll pray for you,' she said, glancing at Asser. 'Won't we?'

'Oh, yes,' the monk agreed. 'Daily.'

'That's good,' said the king, looking from his wife to Asser. 'But I want you with me, my friend. With Oswald no longer here to offer spiritual guidance before and after a battle I'll need you riding with the army.'

Asser blanched at that. There had been no discussion about something like this, for the idea of hundreds of longships sailing along the Tamyse estuary had seemed so improbable in the years that the monk had been part of Alfred's court. Asser had never celebrated Mass in the middle of a field before men began the brutal work of slaughtering one another. His role with Alfred had been to teach him to read Latin, to translate books into English, and to discuss theology and philosophy.

Alfred watched the emotions play across the monk's face – naked fear giving way to determination and then pleasure at being invited along on this holy war against the heathen invaders.

'I'd be honoured, my lord,' the monk said at last.

Wulfric, predictably enough, was not too interested in enjoying this happy moment. 'I'll go and muster the fyrd,' he said dourly, stalking from the room as if desperate to meet the sea-wolves as soon as possible, which was only right. The longer they tarried there the more time their enemies had to strengthen their own position, stealing, enslaving, raping, and killing unchecked as they went.

'Gather some clothes and your prayer books then, Asser,' said the king. 'We ride as soon as possible. If Haesten thinks the warriors of Wessex will be easier to deal with than those in Francia he's got a horrible surprise coming his way.'

'This?' The Dane sneered, gesturing at the silent streets of the settlement they'd subjugated practically without breaking sweat. 'This is one of Alfred's fabled burhs, Rune? The burhs we've heard so much about?'

'*Ja*, Haesten,' a younger man, a jarl named Rune Eriksson, said, bowing and laughing along with the warlord who'd led them across the Southern Sea from Francia. 'It makes you wonder why Hjalmarr was unable to take Hrofescester, eh?'

Haesten waved a hand dismissively. 'Pah, Hjalmarr was a fool. He thought he was a warlord to match Ragnar himself. He should have joined us, and maybe Alfred wouldn't have stuck his ugly head on a spear beside the Tamyse. Come, let us take a look around this burh and see what's supposed to be so special about it.'

The two men walked further into the town, stepping over the bodies of West Saxon defenders who'd been stripped of any valuables then left to rot where they'd fallen. Haesten was no fool – he knew there should have been more soldiers resisting them, and he could see that the walls and gates were in the midst of construction. He doubted every settlement they attacked there in Wessex would be so easy to take, but it had lifted his people's morale to gain such a devastating early victory while suffering hardly any casualties themselves. Haesten had been a *vikingr* for most of his sixty-seven years, but he'd never had such a run of bad luck as he'd suffered in the past year or two. The Franks had finally stood against them with such ferocity and, well, luck, that Haesten's army had been forced to retreat or face being wiped out completely.

Eorpeburnan had given them all hope that here they might have found a place to rest and rebuild in relative safety.

Despite his age, he remained firm enough in body and mind, and his flowing grey beard was a source of pride for him. He was of average height, neither tall nor small, and he had many broken or missing teeth and a dozen or more scars on his heavily seamed face, but he wore them all without shame. Only the most skilled and beloved of Óðinn's warriors lived through as many battles as Haesten had seen. And, although there were those like Rune Eriksson who followed him and coveted his position as king, none had enough support to usurp him, despite being decades younger as Rune was.

He looked at the jarl as they walked, noting the weak chin which Rune tried to hide beneath a small, narrow strip of beard that, in truth, merely accented how fat and round it was. He also had a moustache and large, if flabby, arms. He did not look like much of a warrior, but he was cruel, and utterly vicious in battle and had proven to be a good second-in-command to Haesten so far.

A dog whined at them as they walked past, stupidly hoping for a morsel of food. It would be more likely to get a kick, or even an axe in the head from either of the Danes, but they were in too good a mood to care about the sad mongrel. Eorpeburnan was theirs, and all the treasures they'd found within, gods be praised! The sounds of victorious warriors celebrating with plundered mead and ale had lasted all through the previous night, punctuated with songs of war and the screams of Saxons being raped. Glorious sounds that Haesten had not heard for far too long.

'Should we throw the gates back into position?' Rune asked, turning and waving towards the entrance that had offered such pitiful resistance to their ingress. 'We can shore them up with rubble. Alfred's warbands will be heading here by now.'

Haesten looked about. Eorpeburnan might have been an impressive settlement if it had one day been completed – there were straight roads from one end to the other, well-constructed dwellings and workshops, and the walls would have been tall and sturdy. It was an ill-omened place now, though, Haesten thought, eyes scanning the burnt-out shells of buildings and scattered corpses staring up towards the sky and the White

Christ that had so badly failed to protect them when the Danes turned up.

'No, leave the gates,' said the king. 'We will move on from here, and find a place more suited to our needs. Have it stripped of all the food and valuables you can find, Rune.'

'Of course, lord. What will you do?'

Haesten's grin was lupine as he patted the jarl on the back and nodded towards the centre of town. 'I might be an older man,' he said, 'but I still like to empty my balls at every opportunity. I will go and take my pick from the women we've captured before our horny men use them up!'

Rune laughed nastily. 'Leave some for the rest of us then,' he begged.

'Oh, don't worry,' the king replied, stretching up to his full height and working the kinks from his neck and back. 'There'll be plenty more women to come over the next few months. I mean to settle here amongst the Saxons for a time, bleed the bastards completely dry before we move on again. That's why I brought my wife and little boys with me. We'll be here for a while yet, Rune, so make yourself at home amongst their women and their treasures.' Haesten laughed and strode off towards the middle of Eorpeburnan. 'Trust me, my friend,' he called over his shoulder. 'Alfred, and his Wessex, have no idea what's about to hit them.'

CHAPTER TEN

Despite the dire circumstances, Alfred was feeling surprisingly positive about things as they rode towards Eorpeburnan. The weather was not too pleasant considering it was October, but the golden and red leaves on the elm, ash, and birch trees they passed seemed to the king to be a good omen, mirroring the colours of his dragon banner as they did.

The Wintanceaster fyrd was ready to move very quickly, thanks to the recent military reforms and Wulfric's efficient leadership, so it wasn't long before the massed ranks of riders and spearmen were moving along the herepaths towards their destination. They gathered reinforcements as they passed towns and villages, with most of their numbers coming from the burhs at Eashing, Burpham, and Lewes.

Alfred examined his burgeoning force with a great deal of satisfaction and pride – not only were there plenty of them, but they were well drilled and properly armed and armoured. Gone were the days of his early reign, when the fyrds were made up mostly by untrained levies carrying spears with nothing more than a fire-hardened point and a cloth cap to turn aside the crushing blows of the Northmen's terrible axes.

'Haesten's going to get a shock when he sees us coming,' Alfred said to Wulfric as they mounted up once again after a stop at a village for supplies, refreshments, and to take on more troops.

His captain nodded sourly. 'The bastard's sailed here thinking we'll be easy pickings. He'll have heard all about Ragnar's whelps lording it over the folk of Mercia and East

Anglia and thought he'd come here in his old age and do the same. Unfortunately for him, those days are gone. Still, though...' He trailed off, removing his helmet so the sweat beneath its leather lining could dry out.

'Two hundred and fifty longships *is* a terrific number,' Alfred finished for him. 'I know. But Haesten is an old man, and he doesn't know these lands the way the likes of Guthrum did. We'll not give him time to get to know them. Our army will grow as we travel, and more will join us once we reach Eorpeburnan, like Ealdormen Diuma and Aethelnoth, who'll bring their fyrds as soon as our messengers reach them.' He gripped the hilt of his sword and gazed out fiercely at Wessex. His Wessex, with its bountiful fields, glittering, well-stocked rivers, and hardy, God-fearing people. 'Aye, two hundred and fifty ships full of sea-wolves is a daunting prospect, but our months and years of preparation have made us ready for this kind of invasion force, Wulfric. We'll be too much for Haesten and his heathen rats.'

He truly believed it, unlike earlier years when raiders had beset his kingdom and when the end had seemed so close on more than one occasion. He'd remained faithful to God throughout those troublesome years and been rewarded many times over for that faith. Haesten would be dealt with just as previous warlords of the Danes had been.

'What say you, Brother Asser?' he asked the monk who was riding beside them, keeping pace without much trouble for he was quite an accomplished horseman and Alfred had gifted him a fine animal, one of many extravagant rewards for his service.

'I've never seen two hundred and fifty longships,' Asser replied thoughtfully, gazing into the middle distance as he tried to picture such a huge force. 'It seems an impossible number. The logistics of keeping so many people and animals fed and watered must be a nightmare.' He pursed his lips, frowning. 'I simply can't imagine how it can be done, but I do know that God is with us. He provided a miracle before, when he caused a great storm to whip up at Polle, smashing a similar number of Guthrum's ships and drowning their crews before they could land in Wessex. We must have faith that He will provide for us once again.'

'Well said,' Alfred said with a laugh.

He wasn't the only one listening to the monk's words. Those of the fyrd – thanes and ealdorman mostly – riding nearest to them had also heard what was being said and a low chorus of agreement rumbled even over the thump of hooves and clatter of harnesses.

The king, recognising he had a rapt audience of noblemen, if only of those closest to him, raised his voice and turned his head so as many as possible could hear. 'We are better trained than we were even five years ago. Better equipped. Better provisioned. More experienced. Less afraid of the reputation of tired old Northmen like Haesten!'

Grim laughs and jeers greeted his cries, fully agreeing with him and promising to meet these new Danes with more belief and aggression than ever before.

Asser seemed a little taken aback by the vehemence in the soldiers' words, raising his eyebrows, a forced smile on his face. 'For Christians, they don't seem to be in a forgiving mood,' he noted.

'Forgiveness is for after the war,' Alfred replied, still pitching his voice to carry as far as possible, knowing his words would spread throughout the army once they stopped to rest. 'Until the moment of victory, we must show absolutely no mercy to the sea-wolves, for they'll simply take advantage of us, as shown in the past. Well, my friends, not this time. This time we'll teach the bastards a lesson that will ring down throughout the centuries, and make sure no more Danes ever seek to pillage the lands of the Saxons!'

It was a dreary day with a fine mist in the air which seeped insidiously into cloaks and breeches, making the journey quite unpleasant. As Alfred called out though, the sun broke through an opening in the grey clouds and bathed the fyrd in golden light. The king was not the only one who took that as a sign, as if God was lighting their way towards Haesten and his heathen host.

'That's it!' Alfred laughed as a carrion crow that was almost as big as a raven saw them coming and, shrieking irritably, soared into the air and headed northwards. 'Fly, Óðinn, fly from these lands with the rest of your false gods. Christ is coming, and there is no love in his heart for the likes of you!'

Wulfric, although nowhere near as pious as his king, could see the effect Alfred's words were having on the men, and began chanting 'Godemite! Godemite!'

The simple call to God Almighty was taken up by the thanes nearest to them and soon rippled outwards to the furthest ranks until the entire fyrd was moving through the Wessex countryside with that cry on their lips.

Alfred's eyes shone, for he could not remember ever being part of an army so ready to face their enemies. Asser was clearly moved too, silently mouthing prayers as he gripped his pectoral cross and gazed at the king in wonder.

None could stand against them in this mood, Alfred knew. Not even two hundred and fifty longships led by one of the most infamous Danes in history!

The clouds inexorably swept across the sun once more, but the mood remained light as the fyrd continued towards Eorpeburnan.

'How much farther?' Asser asked. He did not seem tired, just curious for he did not know Wessex as well as he did the lands of the Wealas.

'We're about halfway there,' Wulfric said. 'We should arrive tomorrow.'

'And, God willing, be on the way home again, victorious, the day after that!' Alfred said with a vicious smile.

'Lord!' One of the thanes in the vanguard called out, looking from Alfred to the northwest. 'Someone approaches, my lord.'

All eyes turned to the fields on their left where two dark shapes could be seen moving towards them. Riders, moving fast.

'God, they're riding as if the devil himself were behind them,' the thane who'd spotted them muttered. He grasped his spear and stared at the horsemen, his actions mirrored by all around him.

Were the newcomers friend or foe? Were they merely the scouts for a much larger group, perhaps from one of the burhs in that direction?

The fyrd had slowed now, awaiting the answers to those questions and it didn't take long before the galloping horses brought the riders within shouting distance.

'Lord King!' one of them called, his accent marking him as a man of Wessex and allowing Alfred's soldiers to relax somewhat. Their ease was quickly destroyed, however, when the rider drew closer, delivering the message he'd come there to deliver. 'Danes, my lord!'

Some of Alfred's men chuckled sarcastically at that. 'We know,' they shouted back. 'Where d'you think we're going?'

'Silence!' Wulfric commanded, giving them such a dark look that they instantly shut their mouths, like scolded hounds.

'Where?' Alfred asked as the two riders reined in their sweating mounts before the fyrd. Clearly, they'd come from the northwest, while Eorpeburnan was to the southeast. An icy fist had gripped his intestines and the confidence that had suffused his being just moments before was gone.

'Middletun,' one of the messengers replied. 'Beside Saedingburga, my lord.'

Alfred turned to Wulfric, trying to place the settlements in his mental map. It took only a moment for him to realise that this new force had arrived directly north from Eorpeburnan. Wulfric knew it too.

'This is no coincidence,' the ealdorman growled, teeth clenched bitterly. 'It's a coordinated attack. A classic pincer movement.'

Alfred swallowed, knowing his captain was correct. 'How many?' he asked the riders, and, even before they answered, the king knew it was bad news, for they glanced at one another as if too frightened to deliver their message. 'How many?' Alfred demanded again, angrily.

'Eighty longships, lord,' came the reply and it brought forth low moans and mutterings from those of Alfred's army who were close enough to hear.

'Eighty...' The king calculated quickly. 'Over two thousand warriors.'

'On top of the thousands at Eorpeburnan,' Wulfric added, and even his voice held a note of despair.

How could the West Saxons fight a war against such numbers, and on two fronts?

There was silence then, as the news filtered to the rear of the army and the magnitude of the task facing them struck home.

'What should we do?'

Alfred did not bother turning to see who'd asked the question. It hardly mattered. The only thing that mattered was his reply, but he could not bring himself to say the words that were churning within his mind.

I don't know! he thought, fighting back the desire to kick his heels into his horse and flee back to the safety of Wintanceaster. God help me, I don't know what to do!

CHAPTER ELEVEN

'What the hell are we going to do, Wulfric?'

Alfred had managed to calm himself after the messengers' terrible tidings, not riding back to Wintanceaster but instead calling a halt and ordering the fyrd to take the chance to rest while their next move could be discussed. While the thanes and ealdormen marshalled their men, the king took his captain aside and sought his advice in a hushed tone that, he knew, betrayed his terrible anxiety.

Eight thousand Danes? More? They'd need a miracle to defeat so many! How could Alfred have let his people down like this again?

As ever, Wulfric remained steadfast and grim. No trace of fear touched the grizzled warrior's face, and neither did any judgement on Alfred's barely concealed panic. That was enough to shame the king and bring him back to reality.

Asser could offer as many prayers as he liked, but in his heart, Alfred knew it was going to take everything he, Wulfric, and Wessex could muster in terms of troops, supplies, and sheer courage, if they were to defeat what was probably the biggest invasion force these lands had seen in generations.

And with Haesten at its head, too! Alfred had played down the Dane's influence and vitality, making much of Haesten's advanced age, but such a man could not be taken lightly. The sea-wolves did not follow weaklings and, despite their defeats in Francia, Haesten's name struck a fearful chord within Alfred. He had heard much about the man's cruelty and single-mindedness, and the thought of the infamous *vikingr* leading attacks on the people of Wessex was a horrifying one.

'What are we going to do?' the king asked again, gazing out at the autumn landscape he loved so much.

'We don't have many choices,' Wulfric replied. 'Either we divide our forces and meet the Danes on two fronts, or we choose to take our whole army to face one of the enemy forces. We defeat them, and then travel to face the second horde.' He shook his head. 'Neither option is a good one.'

Alfred felt the bile rise in his throat, hawked and spat it out sourly. 'What would be your counsel, old friend?'

Wulfric thought about it for a long time, the two men lost in their thoughts, oblivious to the sounds of their men going about their business behind them. At last, the ealdorman said, 'Muster all our fyrds, and split them in two. One army bigger than the other, led by you, should go to meet Haesten. The second, smaller force, should try to contain – not engage, if possible – the other group of Danes.'

Alfred was nodding for those were his own initial thoughts. 'Agreed,' he murmured. 'And Edward shall lead that second army.'

Wulfric's brows drew down at that, and no wonder. Alfred's son had never led in battle – to throw him into this, untested, could be devastating for both Wessex and the boy.

'What?' the king asked somewhat testily. 'Edward is eighteen. I wasn't much older myself when I first faced the sons of Ragnar. It's time Edward learned to lead.'

Wulfric shrugged. 'It's up to you, lord. It could prove costly but, in truth, Edward has been trained for this all his life. He's a smart young man, with your intelligence.' A smile lit up his face which he tried, unsuccessfully, to hide. 'I don't think he'll be as merciful to the Danes as you've often been, however.'

Alfred snorted but appreciated the joke, even if it was close to the bone. 'Good,' he said. 'It's time the heathen rabble were destroyed once and for all. If my boy's the one to do it, all the better. All right then, Wulfric. Let's discuss it with the nobles, see if they agree with our plan.'

The nobles were divided, with around half thinking Alfred and Wulfric's choice of splitting their forces in two would be the best way to contain the raiders, while the rest argued in favour of continuing on to Eorpeburnan as a single, unified army. The latter group changed their mind when the messengers from Middletun told them who led the group attacking their town.

'Haesten?' Alfred asked in confusion. 'But he was with the Danes who laid waste to Eorpeburnan.'

'It was him, my lord,' one of the messengers confirmed. 'No doubt about it. He was recognised.'

'Bastard must have wanted to lead from the front when the longships made it to our shores from Francia,' Wulfric said, scowling. 'Then taken some of his vessels along the Tamyse estuary, north, to Middletun.'

'So are there even any sea-wolves left to the south?' one of the thanes asked. 'Or did they all move on after sacking Eorpeburnan?'

Alfred sighed bleakly. 'We won't know until more messengers reach us and we can piece together a full picture of how things stand. For now, though, I think we have no choice but to split our army. I will lead the main force to Middletun and deal with Haesten.'

The other commanders looked at one another, muttering amongst themselves, coming up with possible scenarios – good and bad – until, at last, they bowed to Alfred's wishes and agreed to follow whatever path he chose.

'Good,' said the king, chewing the inside of his cheek and staring towards the northern horizon as if he could see the sails of Haesten's fleet massing there. 'Send riders back to Wintanceaster. Have Edward bring his personal guard and meet up with the rest of the fyrd.'

'Where?' Asser wondered.

'Halfway between Middletun and Eorpeburnan,' Wulfric suggested. 'Goudhurst? That'll make it harder for the two forces to join up, if there even still are two groups. It'll also mean Edward can quickly engage whichever army proves most troublesome, or come north to aid us against Haesten if need be.'

'See to it,' Alfred agreed, smiling without humour at his captain's use of the word 'troublesome'. His earlier feelings of panic had been replaced, initially with sadness that so many of his people would, yet again, suffer at the hands of enemy invaders, but now a firm resolve filled his heart. 'We'll continue on to Goudhurst for now. Have the messengers gather the fyrds there, my lords. Once we have enough numbers to defend the area I'll lead an army north.'

'To Haesten,' Asser murmured nervously.

'Aye,' Alfred agreed. 'To Haesten.'

—

'By Þórr, wench, will you leave me alone? I'm nearly seventy winters old; once or twice a day is enough for me to spill my seed! Go and make yourself useful before I blacken your other eye.'

The young woman winced, gazing up at the Dane in fear. She left his breeches alone, however, and got up from her knees, hurrying away and promising to do whatever he asked if he would not hurt her.

Haesten watched her go, angry at himself. Ten years ago, he'd have been happy to empty his balls inside the scared slave girl, but those drives had completely faded recently. He hid it from his men of course, but it had only made him wish to prove his virility in other ways – mainly violence and conquest.

Besides, he had a wife who knew best how to please him, and he'd brought her, and their two young sons, here to Wessex for that very reason. A man of his age needed companionship more than he needed sexual gratification.

'Are you well, husband?'

Haesten looked up. Peering through the curtain was an attractive, tall woman in her mid-thirties, with dirty-blonde hair and green eyes. His wife, Ulfhild, was the very epitome of a woman of the Danes, with her striking looks and powerful physical presence. She had even fought alongside the men in her younger years, before marrying Haesten and bearing him his children. He nodded at her, irritated by her knowing look – his men might not know about his inability to hump the slaves, but Ulfhild certainly did. She did not mock him for it, she knew better, but he could tell by her eyes, and the little smirk that sometimes curled her full lips, that she did not find him as impressive as she once had.

'I'm fine,' he replied curtly. 'Bring me mead, and bread. No, not bread, this Saxon stuff is too tough for me to chew. Cheese, I'll have some of that. What are the boys doing?'

'Playing,' she replied.

He nodded and waved her away to fetch his meal. His sons were ten and eleven, and still had a long way to go before they would be warriors or men. They would be playing with toy boats or racing the other children that had come across with them from Francia. Haesten was not an attentive or caring father, but the boundless energy of Knud and Erik brightened the days for him, reminding him pleasantly of what it was like to be so young and carefree.

That was another rather depressing sign of his old age, he thought, staring through the un-shuttered window at the trees behind the hall he'd taken control of when his forces sacked Middletun. He'd fathered dozens of bastards during his long life, but it had never crossed his mind to take anything to do with them. His life was that of a proud *vikingr*, traversing the whale road, killing those who stood in his way, humping their women, stealing their wealth, and sailing onwards to do it all again in some other place.

Nowadays he still enjoyed leading men in battle as much as ever, but at the end of the day he was content to watch his children playing amongst themselves while Ulfhild brought him meat and drink and massaged his tired muscles.

He snorted with grim humour. There were worse fates, he supposed. At least he was still here, and still able to hold spear and shield. A thrill of fear ran through him at the sudden thought of losing his ability to fight. He shook his head — that day would come eventually. Until then he would do his best to leave a legacy the skalds would sing of for generations to come.

Ulfhild pushed through the curtain separating the chamber from the main body of the hall. She carried a jug of mead and a trencher of food which she placed on the storage chest that was set against one wall.

'Anything else?' she asked.

Haesten shook his head. 'No. Join me, though. Share the meal with me, wife.'

She smiled, her pretty face seeming to light up the room as she sat down on the bed beside him. Haesten took some of the cheese and bit into it, enjoying the bitter taste as it crumbled in his mouth. He wondered what kind of wife he'd have if he wasn't a king? If he was a simple farmer back in his homeland. A wry smile came to his seamed face as he imagined some withered old crone, berating him endlessly for his laziness. Thank the gods that had not been his life!

'What will we do next?' Ulfhild asked, washing down her cheese with some of the mead.

'We will march southwards, attacking every Saxon settlement between us and the other army that landed at Eorpeburnan,' Haesten replied happily. 'When our forces are combined no one will be able to stand against us, not even Alfred. Wessex will be ours.' He shrugged expansively, getting slowly up and leaning on the window frame to gaze out at the autumn countryside.

His wife came to stand beside him, bringing the heavy woollen blanket from the bed. She placed it across his shoulders and pulled it in at the front so the chill air did not make him uncomfortable. He allowed her to tuck him in as if he were a child, glad of the extra layer even though he already had two knee-length tunics and a winter cloak on. Wessex was colder than Francia, if not quite as bitter as the frostbitten homelands of the Northmen.

'And once Wessex is ours?' Ulfhild asked, looking at him with the same fierce pride that had been in her eyes since the day they were wed. 'What then?'

'Then?' he murmured, gazing at her and almost feeling the once-familiar twinge in his loins. 'Then we will continue on to Mercia, and the lands of the Wealas, and Northumbria, and even further north, until all of this island belongs to me...!'

CHAPTER TWELVE

AD 893, January, Middletun

'Loose!' Alfred stood in the front rank of his army and, with a terrific grunt, released the short spear. He watched it rise into the air beside dozens of others, seeming to hang, unmoving for just a moment before gathering speed as they fell back to earth. There were the usual sounds then as the iron tips thumped home in grass or wooden shields or, more pleasingly, in human flesh. The West Saxon king could not rest and enjoy the agonised shrieks of his enemies though, for they were retaliating in kind and he was forced to cower behind his own shield, savagely praying to God that the linden boards would protect him. When he judged it safe he stood fully erect once more and threw the second of his throwing spears and then the third and last.

His force outnumbered the Danes who were dug in to the south of Middletun, and the deadly hail of missiles stripped the invaders of even more warriors.

'Ready, men?' Alfred bellowed, battle fever fully upon him now as he envisioned how this engagement would go. 'Forwards, then!'

Unencumbered by the throwing spears, the king's army marched towards the sea-wolves. Wulfric was on his right, as always, and behind them Asser's voice was raised in a hymn. The monk was not the only clergyman with them and a heavenly choir could be heard praising God and begging his aid against the heathen host that had left these shores in flames. Alfred had experienced such an atmosphere before, many times, yet it still stirred his blood and drove him forwards even though he knew he might be cut to ribbons before the day was done.

Eighty ships the sea-wolves had brought there to Middletun, with Haesten at their head. Many of those vessels carried women and children as their cargo, however, rather than fighting men. Still, the enemy army had numbered almost two thousand and caused much trouble for the Saxon settlements in the area. The nearby burhs at Southwark, and at Sashes, deployed their fyrds as soon as possible and these did enough to contain the worst excesses of the Danes, eventually pushing them back to Middletun and penning them there until Alfred and his army could arrive.

Alfred remembered his first sight of Haesten then, the memory of it filling his mind as he rapidly closed on the enemy shieldwall. The Dane was not that impressive at first sight — not like previous warlords Alfred had faced in the past. Ivar the Detestable, Ubba, Halfdan, Guthrum, even mighty Bagsecg — these had been imposing physical specimens that had struck fear in the hearts of the West Saxons.

Haesten was bent with age, however, and although Alfred had not got too close to him, he could see the old man squinting from rheumy eyes as they traded insults and threats before battle began. Still, one should never underestimate an opponent, and Alfred had afforded Haesten the same respect as those earlier, more fearful, enemy jarls and kings. He tried to see the old warrior within the ranks of the Danes' shieldwall but before he could locate him the two sides came together and everything was forgotten except spear and shield and the mechanical movements that would keep Alfred alive.

The battle did not last long. Outnumbered as they were, the Danes traded blows for a time but soon decided they'd had enough. Perhaps Haesten was surprised by the ferocity the warriors of Wessex displayed, or maybe he just wanted to hide behind the defences his army had built around Middletun until reinforcements could arrive. Alfred had no way of knowing what was in the enemy king's mind but, with a further two hundred and fifty longships not that far south of their position, it was possible Haesten expected them to join him sometime soon.

Alfred could not allow that to happen, for it would be disastrous for his kingdom.

'Die, you goat-humping squirrel turd!' Wulfric was kicking one of the Danes who'd fallen as the enemy troops tried to retreat. The downed warrior must have done something to particularly annoy the big ealdorman for Wulfric was incandescent with rage, stamping on the bawling sea-wolf and then smashing the tip of his spear down until the unfortunate fellow was a bloody, silent mess.

'What was that all about?' Alfred asked, chuckling as they jogged after the routed enemy soldiers.

'Bastard tried to kill me,' Wulfric growled, and that simply made the king laugh even harder.

The Danes were mostly behind their fortifications now, so Alfred commanded his men to halt and regroup where they were, out of range of any possible missile attacks. He spoke with his commanders, getting an idea of how many casualties they'd suffered and what their opinions were on the battle. It seemed everyone agreed the Danes had never really been looking for a fight, merely testing the water and seeing what Alfred's army could throw at them.

'Well, I think we showed them plenty,' Wulfric said sourly, drawing shouts of agreement from the other noblemen. 'They know they're not in for an easy time of it.'

Alfred was nodding as he scanned the enemy earthworks, trying to figure out if his men could storm the fortifications or if it would prove too costly. He was loath to lose more of his warriors than necessary but the threat of more longships coming along the swan's path to reinforce Haesten was always at the back of his mind.

The sooner these Danes in Middletun were dealt with the better, for then Alfred could take his whole army and march south to meet Edward and attack the second, even bigger, enemy force at Eorpeburnan.

'Surround their fortifications,' he commanded his thanes. 'Make sure they can't make it through to forage. There won't be much by the way of food and drink in Middletun, so Haesten won't last long if we keep him penned in.'

'What about their longships?' Wulfric asked. 'A few of them have been moved but there's still some around the Swale.'

'Send men to capture them,' the king said. 'Or destroy them if that's easier. If the Danes know there's no way for their women and children to escape they might be more likely to try and break our siege. We'll be more than ready for the whoresons when they do.'

Wulfric hurried off, roaring orders and marshalling the warriors he'd chosen for the task of sweeping the river clean of enemy vessels. Alfred watched him go, a deep feeling of satisfaction filling him. He removed his helmet and shook out his shoulder-length brown hair, a slight breeze blowing through it and quickly drying the perspiration.

'Lord.' A young ceorl bustled up to him carrying an overflowing jug of ale and a sack full of wooden mugs. The king helped the lad empty them onto the ground for his commanders to take and then the ceorl filled them, his skinny arms shaking until most of the contents of the jug had been poured out.

'Good man,' the king said, patting the boy gratefully on the back. 'You're a lifesaver.' He took a long swallow of the ale, which was surprisingly fresh and tasty, or perhaps he was simply so thirsty that any old slop would taste like it had been brewed by angels. The ceorl hurried off, grinning proudly at performing such an important task.

'Well fought, my lord,' one man said, and Alfred's heart swelled with joy as he saw a broad, middle-aged ealdorman with straight dark hair, grizzled beard and an old scar that ran almost the full length of his face.

'Diuma! You turned up at last, eh?'

'Aye, just in time to join in the fun.'

They embraced like brothers, and Alfred couldn't stop smiling. Diuma had been a friend and supporter of his for over twenty years now and they'd shared much as they grew into manhood. It had not always been easy, for Alfred had believed Diuma betrayed him the night the Danes chased him into hiding in the marshes around Athelney. That had all been settled a long time ago now though, and Alfred valued Diuma almost as much as Wulfric at this point. He was glad to have the ealdorman with them now, the journey from his lands in Brycgstow taking longer than expected.

'Did you see Edward on your way here?'

Diuma nodded. 'I did. We passed that way before turning north to travel here. A fine boy you've got there.' He smiled ruefully. 'A fine man I should say. Edward's not a boy any more – he's bigger than you.'

'And you!' Alfred laughed, swelling with fatherly pride. 'How did he seem? How are things there?'

'He's in control of things,' Diuma said. 'There's been no trouble so far. The Danes in the south seem content to remain where they are.'

'And where is that now?' the king asked. 'They were still at Eorpeburnan when I brought my army here. Have they remained there?'

'No, they left there after stripping it of food and valuables.' Diuma's lip curled as he pictured in his mind what a shell of a settlement Eorpeburnan would be now that the sea-wolves had sacked it. 'They moved onto Apuldre,' he growled. 'Built their usual earthworks and made themselves at home. God help the people thereabouts!'

'Indeed,' Alfred said, his earlier happiness fading somewhat. 'God help them, until we can get there at least. Come, old friend, join us in a drink.' He looked around for the ceorl with the ale jug, but the lad had already noticed he was wanted and came rushing across, his jug freshly filled.

Soon Diuma was resting on the grass beside the king and the other noblemen as their spearmen combed the battlefield, stripping enemy corpses of booty and making sure their own fallen comrades were dealt with properly.

'Asser!' the ealdorman said, noticing the monk who looked absolutely exhausted despite taking no part in the fighting. 'Your prayers worked, brother! We won a solid victory here this day.'

Asser managed a smile and wiped beads of sweat from his tonsured brow. 'Praise God!' he agreed. 'But I feel like I could sleep for a week. Being part of an army is tiring work.'

'How d'you think we feel?' a young thane asked, a smile taking any hint of criticism from his words.

'Asser and his brothers played their part,' Alfred said, his words similarly light although the fact that he'd said them at all made sure there were no other comments on the monk's exhaustion. Not that there would have been, he thought, for everyone was revelling in their rather easy victory and all knew that, without God on their side, things might well have turned out differently.

'Where the hell is Wulfric?' Diuma asked, leaning up on his knees and shading his eyes from the pale sunlight as he searched for Alfred's captain.

'That'll be him over there.' The king chuckled, pointing at a plume of black smoke that had slowly drifted into the air as they rested.

'Burning the bastard's ships, eh?' Diuma nodded approvingly. 'Good. Haesten will see the flames and realise there's nowhere to run. With any luck his own people will turn on him and save us the hassle.'

As unlikely as that seemed his comments received some support from his peers and they settled in once more to enjoy their ale and the sight and smell of the blackened wisps that curled into the air on the other side of Middletun.

The war was far from over, Alfred knew that better than anyone, but defeating the infamous Haesten and cutting off his escape routes was the perfect start. Now they just had to sharpen their blades, mend damaged shields, and wait to see what the notoriously vicious warlord would do next.

CHAPTER THIRTEEN

'Alfred, King! We surrender.'

Diuma grinned fiercely, while Wulfric simply curled his lip in disdain, clearly mistrusting Haesten. Alfred's feelings were somewhere in the middle of his two advisors', happy to have brought the Danes to the point where they were forced to parley, but also fearing the wily old enemy warlord might have some trick up his sleeve.

'Come, you three,' the king said, striding towards the earthen rampart that Haesten stood upon. Ealdorman Aethelred of Mercia had arrived with his fyrd by now, and he, Diuma and Wulfric followed Alfred, hands resting on the hilts of the swords they wore in belts, or baldrics over their shoulders. A dozen of Alfred's *hearthweru* came behind them, ready to defend their king with their lives if need be although it was highly unlikely it would come to that.

Haesten, if he had any sense, must know there was only one way out of Middletun.

The siege had not lasted long – just three days since the Danes had been defeated in battle and retreated to the safety of the newly fortified town. The effect the loss of their ships had on them was marked and Alfred was not surprised. Everyone knew the Northmen all loved their longships. The sight of them being eaten by flames or simply sailed away by the Saxons had struck at the heart of every warrior trapped in the town with their grizzled king. Alfred could imagine their dismay and their outraged discussions with Haesten, demanding he somehow get them out of this predicament.

Truly, the Danes were finally coming to realise Wessex was not the easy target it had been in the days before Alfred took the throne.

'We surrender, Alfred!' Haesten called again although his stance remained proud, as if he did not want his people to see him humiliated.

'Remember how the Danes fooled us before,' Wulfric muttered to Alfred, and his hesitation before he said 'us' made it clear he did not blame himself for any of the past troubles. Alfred had been the one who, through a desire for Christian charity and forgiveness, had been merciful with the likes of Guthrum and Jarl Hjalmarr. Usually, the king's mercy was rewarded by the Danes simply marching off, immediately renouncing the oaths of peace they'd sworn, and slaughtering and enslaving more West Saxons.

Wulfric quickly learned not to trust the Northmen, but Alfred had taken much longer. Guthrum eventually proved himself worthy of Alfred's patronage, becoming a Christian and living peacefully in East Anglia but only after he'd broken his oaths more than once before that.

'I'm no longer a young idealist,' Alfred said quite tartly to his captain. 'I won't let Haesten pull the wool over my eyes, you can stop worrying.'

'Good,' Diuma said. 'This old bastard might not look much, but his reputation goes before him. He could have proved to be the worst of all the enemy warlords we've faced so far if we hadn't managed to contain him so quickly.'

Alfred didn't reply. There were still two hundred and fifty longships on the southern coast of Wessex, the warriors that had crewed them dug in at Apuldre. As far as they knew, those warriors, like the ones here at Middletun, followed Haesten.

The threat he carried was not dealt with just yet, even if he was calling on Alfred to parley with him.

'We surrender,' the veteran warlord shouted yet again. 'Come Alfred, let us talk of peace.'

The Saxon noblemen were close enough now that they wouldn't need to bellow to be heard, although still out of range of enemy throwing spears, hopefully.

'Why should I talk peace with you, old man?' Alfred called out as if he was amused by Haesten's request. 'We have you hemmed in, surrounded on all sides, your longships destroyed or taken away to be part of my own fleet. It's only a matter of time before you and your kinfolk starve.'

Haesten nodded. 'This may all be true—'

'It is true!' Diuma shouted. 'You have nothing to bargain with, you heathen sack of dog shit!'

'Like I say, it may all be true,' the Dane continued irritably. 'Or it may be that the other part of my army – the bigger part – are making their way here right now. Thousands of brave warriors, veterans of raids in Francia and beyond, coming to kill every one of you.'

'He's bluffing,' Diuma snarled.

'Of course he is,' Alfred agreed softly before raising his voice to address the pagan king again. 'Why are you surrendering to me then, if you have a vast army on the way to save your worthless skin?'

'Because there's no reason for us to fight, Alfred,' Haesten called. 'You are a Christian. I am one too.'

'Oh no,' Wulfric groaned, drawing in a deep sigh and side-eyeing Diuma. 'Here we go again.'

'Be quiet,' Alfred hissed, frowning at the big ealdorman. 'He's not finished.'

'It's true,' Haesten continued. 'I was baptised in Francia, and so was my wife. We are good Christians like you, Alfred.'

'We've heard this before,' Diuma said, shaking his head dismissively.

'You can't trust him,' Aethelred added. 'If he's such a devout Christian, why did he attack our lands at all?'

On the earthen rampart Haesten was loudly reciting the Lord's Prayer, a broad smile on his face, hands clasped devoutly.

At this distance it was impossible to tell whether he was mocking them or not, although Wulfric certainly made his opinion known to Alfred.

'Look,' said the king softly. 'I believe he's bluffing about the other part of his army. They're far to the south and pose no immediate danger to us here. But they do need to be dealt with as soon as possible.'

'So we accept that old bastard's surrender,' Aethelred said, jerking his head towards Haesten who was clasping his hands as if in prayer, gazing up at the sky in a pose Alfred had made himself countless times during his life.

'We accept his surrender,' Wulfric said firmly. 'But we make sure he can't then cause us more trouble.'

'How?'

Alfred smiled at Diuma's question. 'We do what we did with Guthrum.'

All three ealdormen frowned at that.

'But he's already been baptised,' said Diuma, stroking his unkempt beard. 'And so has his wife.'

'He didn't mention his children.'

Wulfric was not pleased at all by this solution of Alfred's. 'It won't work,' the ealdorman said in consternation. 'You can't trust their kind. They've proven it time and again.'

'What do you suggest then?' Alfred demanded. 'Wait them out, while the southern part of Wessex burns? We must deal with this situation here as quickly as possible, Wulfric. The only way to do that is to offer Haesten a way out.'

'But baptising his sons won't make them, or that crazy old fool, beholden to us,' said Aethelred.

'Why not?' Alfred asked. 'It worked with Guthrum, and his men. We enjoyed many years of peace after that ceremony, once they understood that being a friend to Wessex brought greater rewards than being an enemy. It can work. Besides,' he held up his palms impatiently, 'even if it's only a short-term solution it will allow us time to secure the south so… Unless one of you has a better idea, I don't see any other way out of this.'

None of them did, so, nodding in satisfaction, Alfred turned to look up at Haesten who was staring down from the wall at them with a smile on his weather-beaten face.

'We accept your surrender, Haesten,' Alfred shouted. 'But we will take prisoners from your jarls and hersirs, we will expect reparations for the damage you've caused in these lands, and your sons will be baptised. Ealdorman Aethelred of Mercia will be godfather to one, and I will sponsor the other. These are our terms, there will be no discussion. Come out from behind your rampart when the sun begins to set, and we will seal the agreement. Bring thirty of your noblemen to act as hostages.' He pointed at the Dane, wagging his finger as a parent would do to a naughty child. 'And make sure they are noblemen, Haesten! I want none of your ceorls or lowborn lackwits. Jarls and hersirs, Haesten!'

Alfred stood for just a moment, allowing the enemy king time to refuse the terms if that was to be his decision. When no reply was forthcoming, Alfred waved a hand dismissively and turned away, striding back towards the army, telling his three companions to follow.

'Time will tell if this treaty will hold,' he murmured, more to himself than the men with him. 'But for now the problem of Haesten is sorted, and we have one less issue to deal with.'

The ceremony was nothing like as grand as the one that had seen Guthrum baptised alongside forty of his warriors. That had been an occasion that spread out over multiple days, with many gifts given to the Danes who'd renounced their heathen gods and pledged themselves to Christ. Of course, the war had been over with Guthrum at that point and Wessex was in no danger, which was totally different to the situation now. Haesten might be neutered, but the southeastern lands were still held by thousands of enemy warriors.

So, while the ceremony that had seen Guthrum take the Christian name of 'Athelstan' and become Alfred's godson was a grand, ostentatious, and time-consuming affair, the one that followed the battle at Middletun was almost obscenely fast — much to Asser's annoyance. Even Alfred found himself disappointed for he had fond memories of the earlier ritual and the feasting and celebrations that followed it. There was nothing else for it, though, and Wulfric complained constantly that even this hasty baptism was taking too long.

Haesten's sons were surprisingly gentle boys, given their warlike parents. Perhaps in time Knud and Erik would become bloodthirsty *vikingar*, but on the day that Asser welcomed them into the church they were wide-eyed and quiet.

Alfred watched the boys as they recited their ceremonial lines and then the monk submerged them in the water of the baptismal font. Alfred and Aethelred helped them out, and they were dressed in white robes as Asser anointed the boys on the crown of their heads, intoning, 'You came into this House of God as heathens. Now, you have become Christians, filled with the glory of the one, true God. Go in peace, and be guided in your new faith by your godfathers, King Alfred of Wessex and Ealdorman Aethelred of Mercia.'

It was a touching experience for the Saxon king, as any such event invariably was for him — although this deeply spiritual occasion seemed to mean nothing at all to Haesten who fidgeted and chattered to his wife all through the ceremony. Much more to the wizened warlord's liking was the feast afterwards in the hall at Middletun.

There, Alfred bestowed gifts on Haesten, his sons, and those of his jarls who hadn't been taken as hostages by the Saxons.

Mead, ale, and wine were consumed in ridiculous amounts, and as fine a feast as Alfred's subjects could manage at short notice was laid on. Beef, pork, and poultry were all enjoyed by the revellers. And then, when everyone was sated and happy, the entertainment began.

Feats of strength were performed by muscular warriors – Danes as well as Saxons raced, arm-wrestled, threw missiles at targets, and boxed, before musicians performed and Asser read from the bible.

'It has been a fine feast,' Haesten said to Alfred as they sat side by side at the high table picking at a trencher of sweetmeats laid out before them. 'Your hospitality is impressive, my lord.'

Alfred looked at him. In the flickering light of the fire Haesten's every wrinkle was accentuated, making it seem almost as if the man had been carved out of stone, or perhaps fashioned from the bark of an old oak tree. It was astonishing to think such an aged man still commanded an enormous army of sea-wolves. 'It has been a pleasant day,' Alfred agreed, trying not to stare at his counterpart's craggy features. 'But no feast is complete without a tale of adventure and heroism.'

'You have a skald here?' little Knud asked, eyes lighting up. 'We love stories, don't we, Erik?'

His brother nodded vigorously, and they reminded Alfred so much of his own children that he couldn't help smiling.

'We do have storytellers within the rank of the army,' he told the boys before turning to Haesten. 'But I was rather hoping you might tell us the tale of how you attacked Rome, my lord.'

Haesten's seamed face flushed red and, for a moment it seemed like he would react angrily to Alfred's request. He held his temper in check, however, and then, after a great mouthful of mead, nodded. 'All right then,' he agreed, raising his voice to be heard over the din of the celebrations. He gestured at a very thin man seated close to him. The man nodded, smiling happily, and got to his feet.

'This is my skald,' Haesten slurred. 'He will tell the tale. It's a fine one, so enjoy!'

CHAPTER FOURTEEN

'Haesten the Bold was always a warrior,' the skald began, 'and always travelling, seeking to make his fortune and to find fame and glory in the songs and poems of the storytellers. Broad, muscular, and charismatic, men flocked to fight beside him as he sailed from coast to coast in his fleet of longships.

'So quickly did his reputation grow that even Bjorn Ironside, fabled son of Ragnar Lodbrok, came to Haesten, asking if he could join him in his travels. Together, they mustered dozens of ships and thousands of eager *vikingar*, and set out to win renown along the Iberian peninsula.

'With Óðinn on their side, Haesten and Bjorn could not fail, and they moved from one settlement to another, battling vicious warriors but never once losing.'

Alfred did his best to keep a straight face. He knew very well that the Danes had not had it all their own way. They'd suffered more than one defeat on that expedition, notably in both Asturia and the Emirate of Córdoba. Alfred understood the benefits of propaganda, however, so he held his peace as the skald continued with his tale of Haesten and Bjorn Ironside's godlike military prowess.

'Their longships were so filled with slaves and plunder that they almost capsized,' said the man with exaggerated wonder. 'So Haesten was forced to send much of the booty home. Continuing along the coast, they ended up in Išbīliya, where the cowardly people had invented a way to fight from a distance using fire.'

'Greek Fire!' said Alfred excitedly. 'I've heard of it. Sounds terrifying!'

'It truly is,' the skald agreed, eyes wide. 'The thunderous noise and smoke it created was bad enough, but the flames that spewed out and could not be put out by water… Terrifying indeed! Now, Bjorn Ironside was no fool, and he saw that their brave warriors could not win such an unfair fight so, although Haesten would have gladly taken on the craven Spaniards, the Danes reluctantly sailed on to find foes willing to fight like real men.'

Alfred shared an amused look with Wulfric at the skald's obvious attempt to portray his lord as fearless even when faced by Greek Fire. Some in the hall even sniggered, drawing black looks from Haesten, but the skald hurried on before more could be made of his words.

'Our mighty heroes knew they would find more worthy opponents in Italia, a place neither of them had raided throughout their illustrious careers. "We should sack Romaborg," Haesten suggested, and Bjorn agreed that doing so would bring them great fame and glory, as well as untold wealth.'

'Where?' Aethelred murmured. 'Romaborg?'

'Rome,' Alfred replied, and the Mercian ealdorman nodded, mouth shaping an 'ah' of understanding.

'Romaborg was well known throughout the whole world,' the skald said, spreading his arms expansively. 'Seat of the ancient emperors, home of the greatest and most decadent civilisation in history… and, to this very day, a place filled with priceless treasures!' His eyes were wide again as he hammed it up, moving between the benches, smiling at the warriors listening to his story. 'Gold everywhere! Valuable works of art that cannot be replicated even today, so skilled were their creators! Jewels piled high in the homes of rich noblemen! And the women? By Þórr, those beautiful dark-skinned women, with their long black hair, white teeth, and tits out to here!' He held up his hands, grinning lasciviously at a group of inebriated warriors who roared lecherously, rubbing their crotches and proclaiming their appreciation for such exotic slave-girls. 'How could any red-blooded *vikingr* resist such a wondrous place?'

'It does sound tempting.' Aethelred smiled tipsily.

'You already have a beautiful wife,' Alfred reminded him.

'Of course.' The ealdorman laughed. 'No Roman woman could compare to Aethelflaed! Still, I might have a trencher laden with beef, but that doesn't stop my mouth watering at the sight of a succulent side of ham.'

'A side of ham wouldn't cut your balls off,' Wulfric growled.

Alfred laughed at the dismayed expression on his son-in-law's face, and they returned their attention to the skald who was describing Haesten's first sight of Rome.

'A place filled with wondrous ancient ruins, towering far higher than anything we see here in Wessex, or in any place other than Romaborg,' the storyteller said, lifting his hands as if gesturing towards the mighty columns, temples, and ruined buildings that Alfred had seen with his own eyes during two childhood visits to the holy city. 'A place fashioned by the gods themselves,' the skald cried. 'And the sight of the incredible seaport drove Haesten and Bjorn's warriors into a frenzy.'

'Seaport?'

Alfred turned to Wulfric with a sardonic laugh. 'Indeed. That should have been the point at which Haesten began to question his navigator...'

'Such an important settlement was, naturally, very well defended however,' said the skald, shaking his head, brow furrowed as if he himself were searching for a way to make it into the city. 'So Haesten, with all the guile of Odysseus himself, came up with a ruse!'

This sounded interesting, reminding those who knew the story of Odysseus and the great wooden horse that had allowed him to make it inside Troy and capture the city. The folk gathered in the hall listened eagerly, still eating and drinking but doing so quietly enough that the skald's words could be heard easily as he resumed his tale.

'Messengers were sent by Haesten and Bjorn, telling the people of Romaborg that they were merely travellers seeking supplies and sustenance. Also, to convince the Romans further, the messengers claimed Haesten was sickly and needed medical assistance. Unfortunately, the messengers were sent away and the gates to the town remained firmly locked shut. Haesten would not be put off, however, so the messengers were sent back once more, this time to tell the Romans that he had now died of his illness and, since he was a good Christian, the Romans should provide him with a burial suitable for his faith.'

Wulfric was frowning as he turned to Alfred and whispered harshly, 'What the hell is this, my lord? Why did you ask for this story to be told? Tricking and mocking Christians won't go down well with our people!'

Alfred's eyes were shining with mirth as he watched the skald moving about the hall. 'It's a great tale, just listen to the end,' he advised. 'You'll see.'

Wulfric snorted but lifted another piece of roast beef and tore off a chunk, shaking his head as he chewed, clearly astonished that Alfred – the most pious king in all Christendom! – should allow a tale like this to be recounted within his own lands.

'The people of Romaborg, lamenting the death of one who followed the White Christ, relented at last and allowed Bjorn Ironside to lead a funeral procession into the city, carrying Haesten – who pretended to be dead – to a Christian burial ground.' The skald was chuckling away merrily at his heathen king's duplicity although the Saxon warriors within the hall were scowling, just as Wulfric had predicted. Their humour did not improve with the next section of the story.

'When the funeral rites were in full flow,' said the skald, 'mighty Haesten sprung up from his place of resting, drew his sword, and cut down the fat bishop, who was in the middle of one of his prayers!' This truly tickled the skald, who laughed long and hard, joined by Haesten himself, and those of his jarls who'd been permitted to attend the feast. To their credit, it seemed Haesten's young sons, Knud and Erik, did not appreciate the dark humour the way their older kinsmen did, as both shuffled on their stools uneasily, casting anxious glances at Alfred's hearth-warriors.

'Now that Haesten and Bjorn's army was within the city the Romans were completely at their mercy and it was not long before the triumphant Danes had completely crushed all resistance,' the skald crowed, miming the actions of a swordsman, hacking and cutting at the air with an invisible sword, his teeth bared like the mongrels beneath the benches in Middletun's hall as they faced off over fallen scraps.

Haesten was grinning at the performance, no doubt pleased to recall such a glorious victory over Christians considering Alfred's fyrd had so recently defeated him there in Wessex.

'And that, my lords,' the skald finished, breathing heavily after his mock battle, 'is how Haesten the Bold, and Bjorn Ironside sacked Rome!'

The Danes thumped their mugs on the table in appreciation although Alfred could see many of them casting suspicious or even sceptical looks in their venerable king's direction. Haesten for his part was preening and basking in the skald's praise.

Wulfric, Aethelred, Diuma, and the rest of the West Saxon noblemen were muttering darkly and throwing their own king dark looks. Alfred allowed the scene to play out for a while longer and then, when the noise had calmed somewhat, he called out, 'And yet, skald, I have visited Rome myself, twice.'

The sea-wolf storyteller was making his way back to his seat near Haesten, but he hesitated now, slowly turning back to Alfred with a worried frown.

'I made friends when I was in that great, holy city,' the Saxon king went on, voice as loud as the skald's had been during his tale. 'None of them have ever sent any message telling me that an army of Danes had successfully sacked the place.'

That was true — such a momentous event would certainly have engendered songs and tales that inevitably would have found their way to Wessex and, indeed, all Christendom. Yet none there, apart from Alfred it seemed, had ever heard this story before.

Haesten was glaring at Alfred, and he called something across the hall in harsh, heavily accented tones.

'What was that, my lord?' Alfred shouted back. 'I couldn't hear you. Would you repeat it please, slower, so we Saxons can understand your words a little better?'

'I said,' Haesten replied in no less harsh a tone but placing more emphasis on his words so they could be heard more clearly, 'it was not Rome we sacked. It was Luna.'

Alfred waited, allowing his men to hear and understand, and then he said, 'Luna! Yes, I do remember hearing about that small port town being ravaged by Northmen. A sad day.'

There was silence for a moment and then Diuma said with an amused frown, 'You sacked the wrong place? You thought you were in Rome, but you were, in fact, hundreds of miles away?' His voice, and his mirth, had risen as he spoke, and he was laughing heartily by the time he finished. He was not the only one. Every Saxon in the hall joined in, openly mocking Haesten's terrible navigation skills.

Alfred shared in the laughter and even Wulfric had tears running down his face as the feast descended into uproar. It went on for a long time and all Haesten and his unarmed, humiliated warriors could do was sit and take it.

CHAPTER FIFTEEN

'I'm not so sure it was a good idea to humiliate Haesten like that.'

Alfred rubbed his head and winced, the hangover from the baptismal feast striking hard and without mercy. He shrugged and reached out to lift a cup of ale from the table. 'Why not? What can he do about it?'

'Nothing, today,' the ealdorman replied. He was, as always, apparently untouched by yesterday's celebrations although Alfred had seen the big bastard downing quite a few drinks.

'So he gets angry and resentful? Who cares?' the king muttered, forcing a long swallow of ale down his throat and willing it to do its magic as quickly as possible. 'Don't you understand what I was doing, allowing them to spin that fanciful tale? They told of overcoming Christians, but, in the end, they were made to look like the fools they are. I wanted to show Haesten and his men who's in charge here in Wessex, and it's not them.'

Wulfric accepted that but still didn't seem too happy. 'Maybe,' he said, biting into a piece of bread and chewing slowly. 'But, unless you were planning on killing Haesten, I just don't think it was wise to mock him when he still has thousands of men ostensibly under his command at Apuldre. And, by the way, I think you should kill him, Alfred. Do it now, and save any trouble from him in future. You must know—'

'Enough, Wulfric,' the king murmured, shaking his head as a wave of nausea swept through him and he belched, praying he would not vomit. Just a little while more and the ale he was downing would make him all better and ready to deal with Haesten and the Danes' annoyance. 'Let me break my fast in peace, would you?'

Alas, it was not to be, as much as Alfred hoped for it.

'Where is he?' A voice came to them through the sturdy walls of the hall and the king recognised it as Diuma's. The guards at the door had not seen Alfred that day but they guessed he must still be inside sleeping, so they told the Ealdorman of Brycgstow as much and he came bursting into the hall, squinting as his eyes adjusted to the shadowy interior.

'Wulfric!' he called, seeing the older man at the table, and then, 'Alfred, my lord, there you are!'

'God's blood, man, can I not get a moment to wake up? What's all the shouting about?'

'Dire news, lord!' Diuma said as loudly as before, practically running to stand beside their bench, consternation on his face as he gazed at the king as if waiting for permission to speak.

Alfred took another pull of ale and then shook his head, shrugging and lifting his palms as he demanded, 'Well? What is it?'

'The Danes have attacked.'

'Haesten?' Wulfric asked, rising with his hand on his sword's pommel.

'No, at Apuldre,' Diuma said. 'They've sacked settlements in Hamtunscir and Berrocscir then headed back to Apuldre laden with plunder.'

'Bastards!' Wulfric spat, thumping his fist on the table and making Alfred wince.

'Edward has cut them off though,' Diuma went on. 'The aetheling managed to intercept them and the two sides are at a stand-off.'

Alfred's hangover had been slowly fading as the ale worked its way from his belly throughout his body and now, as he thought of his son facing such a massive horde of heathen warriors, the king came fully alert, pushing back his stool and getting to his feet.

'Muster the army, Diuma, if you haven't already. We must ride south as quickly as possible.'

'What about Haesten?' Wulfric asked.

'Forget him, for now,' Alfred said, heading towards the door. 'We have dozens of his jarls held hostage, he and his family have all been baptised, and he swore an oath of peace.' He was glad Wulfric did not argue with him for he was in no mood for it. They had done what they set out to do there in Middletun by securing peace with the enemy king, and now all that mattered was reinforcing Edward's army.

'This could be the chance we need to smash the whoresons for good,' Diuma said as they came out into the cool morning air. 'If we can get there in time, and Edward still has them contained, we might be able to destroy their whole army.'

Alfred made his way towards the stables, glad to see his men rushing here and there as they made ready to march. He had faith in his son, but this was going to be a massive test for the lad who'd never faced such a huge force of Danes before. The sooner Alfred reached him the better.

'Best send a messenger to Haesten, Wulfric,' said the king as he took the reins of his horse from a stablehand. 'Apologise for my bad manners in leaving without farewells. Hopefully the rich gifts we bestowed upon him and his boys will go some way to making it up to him.'

'Where should the messenger say we're going?'

'I don't know Wulfric, think of something, but don't tell him the truth! The last thing we need is to have Haesten's sea-wolves coming up behind us as we're just about to attack his kinfolk…'

'Haesten wouldn't do that,' Wulfric muttered sarcastically. 'Not Haesten the Christian, whose wife and sons have also been baptised.'

Had it been anyone else showing such insubordination Alfred would have been angered by the comment, but the ale had kicked in and besides, Wulfric had kept his voice low so only Alfred could hear what he said. And, the king had to admit, his captain's opinion was not that outlandish.

'Well, I'll tell you what, Wulfric,' he said, nimbly jumping onto his horse's back and settling himself comfortably. 'I don't believe that'll happen, but if he does break his oath and follows to attack us on the road to Apuldre, I'll serve you your meals for a week afterwards. How's that?' He waited until the ealdorman was also mounted and they were riding towards the town gates and the gathered army. 'If he holds true to his oath and does not attack us, you must serve me. What say you?'

Wulfric seemed unsure. The idea of acting as a servant was hardly a pleasant one, but he shrugged and agreed.

'Good,' said Alfred. 'Then pray that you lose, for if you win, neither of us might be alive to enjoy the results of the wager!'

'God's bollocks, that was close!' Edward ducked as the spear whistled over his head, heaving a sigh of relief that it had missed him. He'd already seen a dozen men skewered by such a missile that day and the results were not pretty. Even those who survived an attack would carry their injuries for the rest of their lives. Just eighteen, the aetheling would like the opportunity to see a few more summers before some sea-wolf cut him down. 'Hold the line!' he roared, glad to hear his command echoed along the shieldwall.

Edward's army had been camped where Alfred told them to remain unless the Danes at Apuldre moved on. That had eventually happened, with reports coming in from Hamtunscir and Berrocscir that the sea-wolves had sailed their longships along the Tamyse and were attacking and, since most of the men in those areas had gone off to join either Alfred's or Edward's fyrds, the Danes faced less resistance than they should have. Edward had never been in a position like this before, commanding such a large army yet knowing the enemy he faced boasted even greater numbers. He could not simply sit and let Wessex be ravaged, of course, so they'd made their way west and managed to cut off the Danes who were returning by land to Apuldre.

By God's grace Edward had been able to choose terrain that suited him best, allowing him to position his men on a low hill. With that advantage the volleys of throwing spears his warriors unleashed on the Northmen had caused horrific and numerous casualties while facing relatively little retaliation. The slope had then given them much needed momentum for their charge as the opposing shieldwalls had met and then that added height, as little as it was, propelled them on while the Danes slipped and slid backwards.

It had been a learning experience for the aetheling. He'd fought beside his father before, even led warbands himself, but never had he been responsible for the lives of so many soldiers of Wessex. It was a heavy burden to bear, and one he'd been terrified he'd bend beneath, but, once the fighting began, the anxiety faded and was soon replaced by a terrible bloodlust. Alfred, Wulfric, and his other tutors had tried their best to prepare him for this, and Edward believed they had. The reality of battle – the sounds, smells, sights, and sensations, magnified a hundredfold from normal life – had quickly shown him that experiencing it for oneself was truly the best way to learn for a warrior and a commander.

Similarly, Edward's men had followed him willingly enough before then, simply because he was the aetheling and the son of their beloved King Alfred. After this day, though, those men would know Edward was as brave and fierce as any in the shieldwall and follow him willingly as a result.

Assuming he survived.

Like most battles between two sizeable armies of Saxons and Danes there was little, if any, opportunity for clever tactics. Edward did not deploy cavalry for he knew horses did not perform well when faced with the massed spears of a shieldwall, and there had not been much time to prepare flanking forces of any great number, so it came down – as usual – to the opposing sides to simply line up and hack and thrust for all they were worth.

Edward's priests said Mass for the army before the Danes reached their position, and he was glad of that for it could not hurt to have God on their side. Although the aetheling was not as pious as his father — who was, after all! — he had great respect for the Christian faith and the men who preached its good word. In a fair fight he had no doubt the one true God would prevail over the disparate pantheon of crazed, bloodthirsty deities the Danes followed. And so it was proving now.

'They're getting desperate, my lord,' shouted Edward's captain, Dunstan. The thane had been a loyal supporter of Alfred during his exile on Athelney and later oversaw the building of the burh at Wilton. When Edward came of age and required someone experienced to watch his back and advise him Dunstan seemed the ideal choice. He was small in height, but sturdily built and ferocious in battle, and Edward had been glad of his presence for he took no nonsense from anyone and made sure the young aetheling avoided making obvious mistakes.

'Aye, they are getting desperate,' Edward agreed. 'And their desperation is a good sign for us. Look! They've abandoned their wagons of stolen treasure, the craven bastards. No wonder they had to travel back to Apuldre on foot — so much booty would never have fitted in their cursed longboats.'

He and Dunstan continued to advance with the rest of the army as the Danes left their plunder and continued to retreat in the face of the Saxons' disciplined approach.

Some of the wagons had become stuck in the soft grass, but others were on firm ground and could have easily been pulled along by the oxen that were tethered to them had the Danes not realised they were in for more of a fight than they wanted. And it wasn't just silver, jewellery, weapons, and other valuable inanimate objects that had been stolen during the raids — living people were tied up and either in the wagons or tethered to them. Mostly women and girls, these unfortunates had been destined to see out their days as thralls to the Northmen. Edward shuddered at the horrors planned for them had his fyrd not turned up and rescued them.

It was one thing recovering coin or goods, quite another to save dozens of terrified, weeping humans from the clutches of their brutal captors.

When they were freed from their bonds many of the captives asked for weapons and joined Edward's army – men as well as women, desperate for a chance to avenge the wrongs that had been done to them and their kinfolk. Considering that day was Edward's first real taste of war it was quite a sight to see a fyrd full of hard-eyed women – clad in whatever outsized tunics and armour they could be furnished with from the bodies of the slain – raising shield and spear and joining his army. Their shrieks of rage were enough to turn his blood to ice so he could only imagine what the Danes must have felt as the shieldwalls came together once more.

The enemy jarls clearly did not want any part of the battle. The Northmen famously hated a fair fight, seeking instead to strike hard and make a fast getaway before any sizeable resistance could be mustered. Those had been their tactics for generations and they'd served them well, so Edward could understand why they tried to stick to them. What the Danes wanted was to get the hell away from the infuriated Saxons and make their way back to their fortifications at Apuldre. With Edward's army blocking their way, the enemy commanders must have decided to make their way to East Anglia instead, since there were many Danes living there who would, presumably, offer them succour.

'Should we let them go?' Dunstan asked as it became increasingly clear the Danes were not prepared to stand and fight and their path wound ever northwards.

Edward had been wondering about that for some time and his mind was already made up when his captain asked the question.

'No,' said the aetheling firmly. 'If we give up the chase the bastards will just start raiding again. We can't allow that.'

Dunstan nodded in satisfaction. 'My thoughts exactly, lord.'

That gave Edward confidence that his decision had been the correct one and so they marched on, harrying the retreating Danes for miles, refusing to let them rest, picking off stragglers when possible and attacking any foragers the enemy sent out to look for food.

At last, after six days of this, the Danes must have been running so low on supplies that their jarls were forced to call a halt at Thorney. There, they dug themselves in, surrounding themselves with the now familiar earthwork ditches and ramparts that were hastily built and crude but ever so effective at repelling attacks.

'What now, Dunstan?' Edward asked the stocky thane as they stood watching their enemies raise the great mounds of dirt that separated them from their quarry. 'We can't storm those fortifications, as inelegant as they are. We don't have enough warriors, do we?'

The question betrayed his inexperience but that was exactly why Alfred had placed Dunstan within Edward's court. The thane shook his head now. 'No, you're right,' he agreed. 'We would need double the men we have to storm those walls. I'd suggest we do our best to surround them and stop them from gathering food from nearby settlements. They'll have sent messengers on ahead to East Anglia though, begging for reinforcements from the Danes there.'

Edward chewed his lip, continuing to watch the enemy warriors erect their fortifications with impressive speed and efficiency.

'Our relations with King Eohric in East Anglia are good,' he noted. 'So those reinforcements might never turn up for them.'

Dunstan nodded although his face betrayed his uncertainty. Who could tell what the Danes of East Anglia would do now that Guthrum was no longer there to keep them firmly in check?

Edward read his captain's expression and sighed deeply. 'We've sent messengers of our own,' he said. 'To my father at Middletun, informing him of what's been happening. My plan is to remain here, holding the Danes under siege, while we wait for the king to arrive with his army. We'll have more than enough men to storm that dirt fortress then.' He waved disgustedly at the Danes' position and then, seeing Dunstan's firm nod of agreement, said, 'Come on, then, my friend and advisor. We've not stopped marching and fighting for what seems like forever. We might as well make the most of this time to rest and recuperate.'

'Ale, lord?' the thane asked with a broad grin.

'Aye, Dunstan,' Edward agreed with a laugh. 'Ale! Come on, we've definitely earned a few cups.'

CHAPTER SIXTEEN

It was raining. Not hard, but the type of persistent drizzle that, even when it eased off, left a damp smirr in the air so one's cloak, breeches, or hair couldn't dry out.

'I wouldn't want to fight in this,' Aethelred said, lifting the edge of his cloak to show how wet it was. 'I don't envy Edward marching after the Danes, probably being forced into skirmishes every few miles.'

Alfred swallowed, trying not to think too much about his son fighting the savage Northmen. Edward would be in the front rank too, showing he was a leader to be followed – courageous and inspirational. At times like this the king almost wished Edward had sworn to serve the church, like Aethelgifu, rather than become a warrior.

It was a warrior Wessex would need though, once Alfred was either too old or too dead to stand against the pagan raiders from across the whale road. Edward would just have to take care of himself, and pray God would protect him.

'You think Edward will be fighting those bastards just now?' Wulfric asked with a sardonic smile. 'I doubt it. The Danes will have stopped running at some point and dug themselves in somewhere they can't be got at. They'll be hoping Edward's men will have to return home soon. That's what's always happened in the past, so why would they expect anything different now?'

'Fair point,' Ealdorman Aethelred admitted, his lips pursed as he thought about Wulfric's suggestion. 'And they attacked Eorpeburnan, too – a burh only half finished. If the Danes expect all the burhs to be like that, undermanned and incomplete... well, they'll hopefully get a nasty shock.'

Alfred was following the conversation, but his mind returned to what Wulfric had said, trying to grasp a crumb of comfort from his captain's words. 'You think the Danes will have dug in?'

'Of course,' Wulfric said. 'In fact, Edward's probably sitting right now with a cup of ale in his hand, bored out of his mind. He's got enough troops to chase the enemy but not enough to storm one of those bloody forts they throw up once they think they might need to stand and fight.' His tone became reassuring, as if he knew what Alfred feared. 'There won't be a proper battle for a while, I'd think. Not until we get there at least, and the Danes will realise they've no way out other than to attack.'

Alfred threw him a tight smile, praying he was right. In truth, the king had already thought of the scenario Wulfric had described, for it was exactly how the sea-wolves would act, going on past experience. Just look at how Haesten had hidden away in Middletun after all, rather than facing the Saxons in a fair battle. Hit and run, that was how they behaved, unless they had superior numbers.

Wulfric was right. Edward would be sitting enjoying an ale with his warriors right now. Safe.

'He'll be a sight warmer than us too,' Aethelred said, smiling ruefully and rolling his eyes upwards at the continuing drizzle. 'In his cosy tent, dry, half-drunk, listening to his *hearthweru* tell tales of old.'

'I wish I were there with him, the way you describe it!' Diuma laughed.

'Aye, shut up,' Wulfric grumbled. 'You're making us all feel bad.'

Alfred joined in with their mirth, his heart lighter now that he saw the truth of things. 'We'll be able to join him in his tent in just a few days,' he said, filling with pleasure as he imagined that happy reunion. 'So, let's hurry up and see an end to this war. Hopefully the last we'll see for many years!'

The mood amongst the commanders was light then, despite the gloomy weather, and Alfred joined in as one of the fyrds behind them struck up a ribald marching song in time with their footsteps. Soon, the whole army was singing and laughing, the cleverer or more imaginative amongst the warriors changing lines here and there, cruder each time. Even Asser was laughing as he shook his head at the filth that was being sung, although he did bow his head at the worst of it, making the sign of the cross at times.

It was a happy, confident group of men that travelled onwards when the song faded away at last, fresh from their crushing victory over Haesten and more than ready for another fight.

'Clear the way! Clear the fucking way you oafs!'

Alfred became aware of the commotion on the road behind them and he slowed his horse that he might turn in the saddle and see what was going on.

'Clear the way, I say! I've got a message for the king!'

The rider had been shouting the same phrases for a while before he'd come into Alfred's earshot, but now that the distant, unintelligible cries had resolved into actual words the king glanced at Wulfric. 'What now?' he wondered, feeling suddenly terrified that the messenger carried terrible tidings about Edward.

'He's coming from the southwest,' Wulfric noted, as if reading the king's thoughts.

'So he is,' Alfred replied with great relief.

Diuma did not share his feelings – his lands were to the southwest after all. 'Clear the way you men,' he commanded, turning his horse and riding towards the messenger who was slowly but surely coming closer to the front of the great, snaking column of soldiers. 'Let him through!'

At last, with much cursing and growling at the massed ranks who blocked his way, the messenger sat atop his horse before Alfred and the other noblemen in the army's vanguard.

'Well?' Diuma demanded without preamble or pleasantries. 'What's happened?'

Alfred could guess what the man was going to say even before that first, terrible word was spoken.

'Danes.'

'Oh, fuck off!' Aethelred cried, raising his hands heavenwards and letting out a heavy sigh that perfectly encapsulated the feelings of Alfred and the rest of them.

'Where?' Wulfric asked levelly.

'Exanceaster,' the messenger replied, drawing another loud curse from Aethelred and even Wulfric joined in this time.

'How many?' said Alfred, emotions roiling within him as he contemplated this wholly unexpected turn of events. How many armies of Danes were there in his kingdom, by Christ? They dealt with one and then another seemed to appear as if by magic!

'Hundreds, my lord,' the rider replied. He'd clearly ridden hard as he looked exhausted, and his poor horse was lathered in sweat. He went on, however, delivering his news as was required of him. 'They turned up in dozens of longships – more than a hundred! – and attacked the town. Some pirate named Sigeferth commands them.'

'God in Heaven,' Aethelred muttered. 'Where did this lot come from?'

'Doesn't matter,' said Diuma. 'We need to stop them.'

Alfred forced his mind to calm, his thoughts to cease their churning. There seemed little doubt now that this invasion had been planned in advance by Haesten and the jarls who followed him. As Diuma noted, it mattered little where the enemy armies had come from, all that mattered was defeating them. He had an idea where Sigeferth hailed from, though – there was a Dane in Northumbria with that name. A man who'd once been a raider but settled down in the fertile northern lands and grown to become powerful in that area. If it was the same Sigeferth who commanded the fleet at Exanceaster it meant the Danes in Northumbria had attacked Wessex.

Alfred truly was beset on all sides. By God, he was getting too old to deal with these constant raids.

'There's a jarl from Northumbria named Sigeferth,' Aethelred said thoughtfully. 'I wonder if it's the same man. Vicious bastard, so he was, before he gave up the life of a *vikingr*. Ugly bastard with a face that would make a maggot gag.'

Alfred couldn't help but laugh at that vivid description of the sea-wolf, but his mirth quickly faded. That Sigeferth was said to have been every bit as brutal as Haesten during his raiding days – if the people of Exanceaster were fighting him at that moment... God help them.

All eyes were on the king now, waiting for him to make a decision. He wanted nothing more than to continue northwest to join Edward. To protect his son, as a father should do.

Alfred was not merely a father though, he was a king, and he had a responsibility to his people in Exanceaster.

'What do you think, Asser?' He turned to the priest, hoping for some sage advice of the kind Oswald once would have provided.

Asser looked back at him for a moment, then said, 'Follow your heart, my lord. God will guide you.'

Alfred was disappointed by that answer, but Asser was not Oswald and, ultimately, the king must do what was best for Wessex. 'Damn Haesten,' he murmured, looking around at his commanders and hearth-warriors. 'There's only one thing we can do.'

'Are you sure, lord?' Wulfric asked. 'We could split the army, send half to join Edward?'

Alfred thought about that. He could gather more men as he headed for Exanceaster far to the west, but Edward would not have the same luxury. 'All right,' he agreed. 'Aethelred, you take your fyrd to Lundenburh and join my son. Do what you can to destroy the Northmen hiding in Thorney.'

The Mercian ealdorman nodded, smiling grimly. 'Your son and your son-in-law side by side against the Danes,' he said. 'You can count on us, my lord.'

'I know,' Alfred told him. 'May God go with you, and see you safely back by my daughter's side in Mercia once this is all over.' Then he looked back to Wulfric and Diuma and the rest of his commanders. 'As for us? We march for Exanceaster!'

'Ha, the stupid Saxon bastards must think the sky is falling upon them!' Haesten roared with laughter as he took in the words of his scouts, informing him of Alfred's frantic marches hither and thither.

The hall there in Middletun was filled with happy Danes enjoying yet another day of feasting and flyting and games like hnefatafl. A skald had recited poetry of great beauty, bringing tears to even the toughest warrior's eyes, and musicians performed tunes either accompanying the storyteller or on their own. Animal skin drums and rattles beat out the rhythm, setting feet all around the hall to tapping, while melodies were woven on pipes, flutes of bone and even a lyre. Haesten loved music and poetry, as did his people, and it always astonished him when he heard the Saxons call Danes 'savages'. Of course, Haesten's folk fought with unmatched ferocity, but culturally they were at least on the level of Alfred's subjects, and a sight better groomed too!

His wife stood, resting her arm on top of the high-backed chair Haesten was using as a throne, and shared his mirth at the scouts' reports. 'Even a man as righteously pious as Alfred will find his faith in the White Christ shaken by the various attacks of our kinsmen,' she averred.

Haesten looked up at her and they laughed together again. Ulfhild really was a stunning woman, he thought, wishing with deep regret that he was a little younger and could take her right there and then. He wondered, for the thousandth time, if she took her pleasure with his jarls and hersirs. Surely she did, for everyone had needs. But she'd never admitted it to him, and he'd never caught her with another man. Just as well – for Haesten would kill them both.

That was probably why he'd never caught her rutting with anyone else, he thought with a grim smile that she shared, oblivious to his dark thoughts. He would prefer Ulfhild to be content, but no king of the Northmen could be so weak as to allow another man to bed his wife – any respect Haesten had amongst his warriors would soon be lost and, at his age, that would prove fatal. So, if Ulfhild used some hersir to satisfy her lust, as long as she did it without anyone ever knowing, Haesten would not try to catch her out.

Besides, she would put up quite a fight if he tried to kill her, he thought wryly. The woman was like a cornered wolf if you got on the wrong side of her. It was Ulfhild's warrior-like nature that was keeping Haesten raiding, truth be told. If he'd had a wife his own age, he'd probably be content to find some farm in a pleasant, warm land, and settle down to a quiet life. But Ulfhild continually pushed him on to one more adventure, one more battle, one more conquest, and one more chance to write his name into the songs of the skalds. He did not protest, much, having seen what happened to many warriors when they grew old and gave up the life of a *vikingr*. Death often came soon to them, and it was a pitiful death, of apathy and decrepitude, rather than the glorious one that every true warrior deserved.

Óðinn would not reserve a place at his table for a farmer, Haesten believed, so if he should find his death here amongst the Anglo-Saxons, sword in hand and a battle cry on his lips, he would not fear it.

He would appreciate a rest every now and again, but it seemed even that was not to be afforded him for Ulfhild was already badgering him about their next move.

'This is exactly what we planned,' she was saying. 'Our messengers to our kinfolk in East Anglia have done their job and now Alfred's forces are stretched.' She came out from beside his seat and used her hands to show just how effective the Danes' attacks had been.

The musicians saw what she was doing and softened the tune they were playing so that her words could be heard.

'He marches now, west, to Exanceaster with his fyrd to deal with our allies there,' she said, pointing to her left as she faced Haesten. 'His inexperienced son, Edward, is here, in the middle, besieging another of our armies. And we, my king, are here.' She pointed a little to the right. 'We have the Saxons stretched thin. Beset on three fronts already, with the possibility of more of our people coming to join us every day from Mercia and Northumbria.' She turned to face the rest of the Danes gathered in the hall, spreading her arms wide, grinning, her hair swirling as she turned. 'Our attacks have reminded those of our kin who settled here that they were once *vikingar*. They march to join us! Now is the time of those the Saxons call "sea-wolves"! Now is the time for us to smash the Christians and make all these lands one – united under one king: Haesten Troll-Burster!'

Haesten had found himself growing more excited as his wife spoke, but he blinked in surprise at the nickname she bestowed upon him. He'd had various such monikers over the years, some less than complimentary, but this was the first time anyone had called him 'Troll-Burster'. Where had Ulfhild come up with that? Haesten had never met any trolls, never mind burst one!

It hardly seemed to matter, as the men in Middletun's hall, aroused by Ulfhild's speech, began slamming cups and fists on the benches, following her lead as she chanted, 'Haesten! Haesten! Haesten!'

He sat in his high-backed chair, and it seemed like the aches in his joints faded as the chant grew louder, the musicians accenting every thump with a blast on a horn or a bang of the drum. The drowsiness that usually settled over him around this mid-point in the afternoon was absent and, instead of needing a nap, he wanted to face Alfred of Wessex in single combat at that very instant. Face Alfred, dispatch him in bloody, brutal fashion, and then fuck Ulfhild in front of his cheering jarls!

Haesten had only had a völva in his entourage once, and it had been decades before. The so-called wise-woman had proved to be anything but and he'd soon tired of her presence. He watched Ulfhild now though, imagining how powerful she might have been had she been trained in the ways of the völur. If she could rouse a crowd — and Haesten — like this with no formal training, what might she have done as a völva?

The men in the hall were not thinking of her as a wise-woman, he could tell. Their hungry stares betrayed naked, animal lust and desire. Well, let them covet her — she was his, and would remain so until the day he could no longer lift a spear to enforce his claim. At that moment, his jarls and hersirs were loyal to him, and, with Ulfhild at his side, they would do whatever he asked, go wherever he led.

'Onwards!' Haesten bellowed, jumping from his seat and holding his clenched fist aloft as the horn players blew triumphant, ascending notes. 'We march onwards, my friends. With Þórr and Óðinn and Týr on our side, deeper into Wessex, until every Saxon bends their knee to us, or lies slaughtered at our feet. Who's with me?'

The roar that answered him shook the hall to its very foundations and Haesten grinned, fiercely returning the kiss that Ulfhild stepped across to bestow upon him.

Halfdan, Ivar, Ubba... they had been young, famous warriors with armies of thousands at their backs, but they'd been unable to defeat Alfred. Now, it was time for the old dog to show the youngsters how it was done.

CHAPTER SEVENTEEN

Edward's scouts told him of the arrival of Ealdorman Aethelred's fyrd when it was still miles away from Thorney. At first, the aetheling had been overjoyed, expecting enough reinforcements to attack the besieged Danes. But the scouts had quickly spoiled his pleasure, informing him that it was only a fraction of the king's army that was coming. Edward had no idea what had stopped his father from bringing all his men to Thorney, as he'd expected, but it left the aetheling in a dire position.

Although Alfred had enacted major reforms, reorganising the army so that half would be available to fight at all times, while the other half performed the work that upheld the kingdom, it was by no means a perfect system.

'Why the long face, brother?' Aethelred asked as they met in Edward's tent, rain thundering off the leather and making them both happy that their rank allowed them the shelter, unlike the majority of the soldiers, who were forced to sit beneath their shields, hoods up, praying that God would blow the clouds to some other land.

'Long face?' Edward asked, pouring a cup of ale for his guest and refilling his own. 'My men are at the end of their period of service. Any day now, they'll head home, ending the siege and allowing the Danes – who I've managed to keep penned in all this time – to wander away without so much as a skirmish. It's galling!'

Aethelred gulped down his ale and shrugged. 'I'm an experienced warrior, my lord. Nearly twenty-five years your senior. I've commanded armies of my own over the years that were forced to give up sieges in order to bring in the harvest or plant crops. It's a fact of war, Edward. Aye, it's irritating as hell when you're so close to victory, but there's no point in getting too upset over it.'

Edward was astonished by his words. How could Aethelred be so calm, when the Danes who were at their mercy would soon be marching on to attack another West Saxon town? 'Upset?' he spat, reaching for the jug of ale. 'You're damn right I'm upset! I want those bastards dead, so they can never attack us again. Eh, Dunstan, what say you? You're about the same age as my brother-in-law. Is he talking out his arse, or does he have a point?'

Dunstan's face was sour as he also contemplated the thought of letting their enemies go free, but he shrugged his wide shoulders, and his mouth at least hinted at a smile. 'He does have a point, lord. But I don't think the situation is quite as black and white as you suggested. We now have Aethelred's Mercian fyrd with us, and only about half of our levies are nearing the end of their term of service. We'll still have a decent-sized force, so the Danes won't just bugger off without any resistance.'

'See?' Aethelred laughed. 'And then you'll have a fresh set of soldiers coming to reinforce you when the other half head home. All is not lost yet, Edward.'

The aetheling sighed, long and heavy, much like he'd seen his father do so many times. 'If only the king had brought his whole army here, we'd smash those bastards in Thorney and have one less pack of sea-wolves to worry about.'

'True,' Aethelred agreed. 'But you're young. You don't remember what it was like before your father built the burhs.'

'He's right,' Dunstan put in, standing and stretching his neck up, rolling the muscles and grimacing as there were audible cracks and pops. 'If this invasion had happened a decade ago Wessex would already be a memory. Haesten would be king and there would be no miraculous return from Athelney for Alfred. The situation is far from ideal, my lord, but we've faced worse and come through it.'

Edward chuckled, a sheepish look on his youthful face. 'Fair enough,' he said. 'But what about Mercia? How's my sister treating you?'

Aethelred's face lit up at the mention of Aethelflaed, and Edward was glad for it was a genuine expression that spoke volumes of the ealdorman's affection for his sister. Of all his siblings, Edward was closest to Aethelflacd, and he hoped she would be happy in life.

'She's in charge of Mercia while I'm away,' Aethelred said proudly. 'The thanes love her! Well, most of them anyway. Some find it hard being told what to do by a woman, but she takes no shit from any of them, and they'll soon learn, as I have, that life is easier if one lets her do as she wants.'

'Aye, we all learned that,' Edward admitted with a sympathetic laugh. 'Woe betide any Danes who look to raid Mercia while she's in charge of the fyrd.'

He stroked the wispy beard he'd been cultivating for over a month and part of him wished his sister was there with them in Wessex. He'd always looked to her for leadership and advice as a child and her strength would be welcome right then. He eyed the ale jug, wondering if it would be prudent to drink more. *Damn it, I might as well*, he thought. *We're going to be stuck here for a while longer anyway.*

As he was placing the jug back on the table, footsteps approached the tent and the bearded head of a gaunt young soldier poked through the entrance flaps. 'Forgive me for disturbing you, my lords,' said the guard. 'The Danes have sent a messenger.'

Edward glanced at Dunstan, who shrugged. 'They'll be looking for silver to leave Thorney,' he guessed. 'That's what they do.'

The aetheling grunted. He knew the tactics of the Northmen very well – from the lessons of his tutors, if not yet from personal experience. This war was proving to be a fine learning experience, he thought, trying desperately to take something positive from the fact so many of his countrymen had already been killed or enslaved by the barbarous sea-wolves.

'We have silver here in Lundenburh,' Aethelred noted. 'Let's see what the emissary has to say before we begin counting it into wagons for the whoresons though, eh?'

Edward stood up, not wishing to meet any Dane while he was seated. 'Don't let slip the fact half our army will be pissing off to their homes any day now,' he said as footsteps approached the tent. 'All right?'

Dunstan and Aethelred shared an amused look. They did not need him warning them to be reticent, Edward realised a little self-consciously. Oh well, he was learning as he went, they wouldn't hold it against him.

The same soldier who'd shoved his face through the entrance a short time earlier did so again now, and again apologised for the intrusion. 'The sea-wolf is here. A hersir. We've disarmed him, as much as that pissed him off, and he's been warned that we'll not hesitate to cut him to pieces if he tries anything.'

Edward's lip curled. He wouldn't mind if the Dane did try something. The guard disappeared though, and, when the enemy messenger was ushered into the tent, the aetheling had second thoughts for the man was enormous. At least as tall as Wulfric and much heavier too. Edward didn't fancy his chances in a one-on-one fight, even if the aetheling had been trained by some of the best warriors in Britain and had youth on his side.

The Dane stood before them, head almost touching the roof of the tent, yet despite towering over them all he did not appear threatening or overly imposing. His demeanour was respectful, and he nodded to all three of the Saxon noblemen, finally resting his gaze on Edward.

'My lord,' he said, his words accented but easily understandable. 'My name is Olaf. My jarls have sent me to seek peace with you.'

Edward gestured to one of the empty folding camp chairs, praying it would take the huge emissary's weight. If the man ended up flat on his back, flopping about like a landed fish, it would hardly be the best way to start negotiations! The Dane must have had similar thoughts for he took the proffered seat and lowered his great frame gingerly onto it. The wooden legs creaked, protesting loudly at the unusual force they were being asked to bear but, at last, the hersir was seated and accepted a cup of ale from Aethelred's hand.

'What are your terms?' Edward asked without preamble. The messenger might be respectful, even pleasant, but the aetheling had no interest in spending any longer than was necessary with him. He examined the big man, noting the perfectly trimmed hair, freshly scrubbed face, and the full set of almost-white teeth that flashed when the Dane smiled.

'You don't waste time, eh, young lord?'

'Your kinsmen are besieging Exanceaster while I sit here pretending to enjoy your company,' the aetheling replied levelly. 'I do not have time to waste so, I ask again, what are the terms your jarls propose for their surrender?'

The man looked up at Aethelred and Dunstan, although even seated he was almost at eye level with the latter. His face was that of a grizzled veteran amused by the behaviour of an overly enthusiastic new recruit. If he expected the Saxons to share his humour, he soon realised his error, as both men simply stared coldly at him. He shrugged, chuckling softly as he upended his cup and drained it in a long swallow. When his eyes once more met Edward's the Dane's face was as stern as the others'.

'We will leave our defences and march northwards—'

'Out of Wessex,' Edward stated, framing it as a statement, not a question.

The Dane smirked. 'Of course. We want no more battles with you, my lord.' His words might have been seen as sarcastic, especially given the sardonic look on his face, but it was no joke. The Danes had met much fiercer resistance than they'd expected in Wessex – it would make sense for them to seek easier pastures to plunder once they left the protection of Thorney. 'We'll leave your lands in peace, and we will even leave you with forty hostages as security against us breaking our oaths.'

Dunstan snorted mirthlessly. 'We've heard that before,' he growled. 'Your kind do not honour oaths.'

'It depends who we swear the oaths to,' the Dane replied, leaving Dunstan to make up his own mind about what exactly that meant.

'That's it?' Edward demanded.

The Dane shrugged. 'We came here seeking plunder. If you wish us to leave without any more bloodshed, it's only fair you share some of your silver, don't you think?'

Again, Dunstan snorted, and his hand gripped the handle of his sword as if he'd draw the blade and use it to put an end to the nonsense spilling from their guest's mouth.

'Calm down,' Aethelred commanded the thane. 'He's only delivering the message. Save your anger for the next time we meet the sea-wolves in battle. On past experience,' he barked a sardonic laugh, 'that won't be long in coming.'

'How much of our silver do you think would be fair?' Edward asked sweetly.

The Dane grinned at the overt sarcasm in the aetheling's tone. 'Your father has paid Danes off before,' he said. 'Everyone knows of it amongst my people. Seven thousand pounds of silver Alfred paid Halfdan to leave Wessex. And four thousand he paid to Guthrum.'

'Halfdan and Guthrum had much bigger armies than the one you're with, Olaf,' Dunstan said. 'I know. I fought them.'

'We don't have anything like as much as that here anyway,' Edward added. 'One thousand pounds is what you'll get, in silver and whatever other treasures we can load onto wagons.'

The wry amusement that had been part of the Dane's demeanour since the moment he'd stepped into the tent evaporated now, like the steam from a piss on a cold day. 'One thousand pounds? That—'

'Is all you're getting,' Edward shouted, slamming the flat of his palm onto the table where the ale jug rattled and almost fell over. 'Be thankful you're getting anything at all, you great, ugly bastard!'

Olaf got to his feet, towering over the aetheling, but Edward's temper was up, and he did not back down.

'Take my terms to your jarls,' the aetheling snarled. 'Tell them I will not negotiate with them further. One thousand pounds is what you will get, and we will take forty of your "noble" men as hostage. And if you do not leave Wessex as promised, I will personally slit the throats of every fucking one of them, do you understand me?'

Olaf's anger faded and he smiled down at Edward now. 'I understand,' he said. 'I like your fire, boy. If more of you Saxons had the same fire in their bellies, maybe we Danes wouldn't raid your lands so often.'

'This will be the last time your kind raids Wessex, Olaf,' Edward said through gritted teeth. 'My father and I will see to that. Now get out. Run along and deliver my message to your betters.'

Olaf chuckled again and waved his hand in salute to Aethelred and Dunstan before bowing theatrically to Edward and turning to push his way through the tent's opening. Half a dozen Saxon guards shadowed his every step as he was escorted back towards Thorney.

When he was gone, Edward looked at his two companions and let out a long breath, finally dropping back into his seat and laughing softly. 'Let my temper get the better of me there,' he said, hoping for some reassurance or advice from the others.

Dunstan shrugged. 'That's all right,' he muttered. 'You let the big hairy twat know where we stand.'

Aethelred was smiling. 'You have the same short temper as your sister.' He walked to the tent's opening and put his head through, breathing deeply of the clean air. After a couple of breaths, he came back inside and poured some ale although the jug was now practically empty. 'I wouldn't allow yourself to get so irate every time a messenger delivers their message, Edward,' he advised, swallowing the ale in a quick gulp. 'I always think it's better not to let your enemies see what you're thinking. Besides, Olaf seemed quite an affable fellow.'

'As Danes go, aye,' Dunstan admitted.

'Affable or not, if they don't hold up their side of the deal,' Edward said darkly, 'I'll happily give the order to kill him, and all his kinsmen.' He stood up, lifting the empty jug and peering into it dolefully. 'Come on, Dunstan, we'd better start collecting the silver we've to pay them.'

'What about me?' Aethelred called as they ducked between the tent flaps.

'We'll be back soon,' Edward shouted. 'Find us some more ale!'

CHAPTER EIGHTEEN

AD894, Beamfleote

'How do I look?'

Ulfhild tilted her head and examined Haesten for a few moments before nodding in satisfaction. 'Like a king,' she proclaimed. 'I like those greaves. Not many warriors have those.'

The warlord beamed. He could tell his wife was not just being kind to him; she meant what she said, and it pleased him. Over the past few years, he'd lost much of his muscle definition – once bulging biceps and thighs slowly atrophied until what had once been impressive bulk was now little more than hanging flaps of skin. To mask the inexorable result of time's ravages, Haesten's wife had advised him to dress in clothing that would make the most of what he still had.

Today he wore baggy green trousers, a tunic of similar colour with a long mail coat over it, and on top of all that a wolfskin which served to bulk out Haesten's upper body. A sword hung at his waist on a baldric, while he carried a bearded axe decorated with silver inlay on the head – an eye-catching weapon that only the truly elite warriors could ever hope to carry. On his own head he wore a simple iron helmet with a nose guard. It afforded no protection for the eyes or cheeks, but Haesten had always liked to see what he was doing and so eschewed helmets of grander, bulkier design. The greaves, thin metal plates which reached from his knee to his instep, were worn over his trousers and, again, added bulk to his skinny legs.

Overall, as Ulfhild attested, Haesten looked like warrior twenty years younger, as long as no one looked too closely, or noticed his shield was smaller and lighter than those he'd once carried, as was the exquisite axe.

'You'll do,' his wife said at last, coming across to kiss him on the mouth. 'The Saxons will shit in their breeches when they see you coming to kill them, my lord.'

'Are the men ready to march?' he asked, breathing on the silver inlay on his axe-head and polishing it to a gleaming shine with the edge of the wolfskin. While he'd been dressing with the help of a captured Saxon slave-boy, Ulfhild had been out amongst the jarls and hersirs, making sure those Haesten had chosen to go raiding with him that day were ready.

When Alfred had taken his army west, away from Middletun, Haesten travelled northwards, coming at last to Beamfleote where they were camped now. Those of his longships that had escaped Alfred's fires were with him and, to the Saxons in Beamfleote, it had been a terrifying sight when Haesten's hordes arrived. A few minor skirmishes had not been enough to drive the Danes away and they'd quickly done as they always did, throwing up earthen defences and making themselves at home while plundering the nearest settlements.

With Alfred and Edward's forces far away, Haesten knew he could do as he pleased without fear of being attacked. His confidence only grew when the Danes who'd been besieged at Thorney came to add their numbers to his after the aetheling, Edward, had let them go.

What really pleased Haesten today was the prospect of raiding yet another Saxon town, hence his full array of war gear and a skinful of mead for the journey. He could hardly wait to get into the saddle and be on the road.

'They're ready,' Ulfhild said. 'As am I.'

He looked at her, wondering why he hadn't noticed she was wearing her fighting garb and carrying her sword at her waist. All she needed was helmet and spear and she'd be able to step right into a shieldwall, yet, somehow, that had not registered with him. Flushing, he mentally berated himself for his dotage, for what else could explain his lack of perception?

'So I see,' was all he said, nodding at her as if unsurprised by her decision to come with him on that day's raid. He was raging inwardly at himself though and, when the cowering Saxon slave handed him his skin of mead, Haesten took it and, by way of thanks, slapped the child across the face, sending him sprawling.

To his credit, the boy did not make too much of the blow, merely crying softly to himself and keeping his eyes on the ground as Haesten and Ulfhild went out into the morning.

'You're in a violent mood today,' his wife said, cleaning her upper teeth with her tongue as she grinned lasciviously at him.

'I always feel violent towards the Saxon, Christian scum,' he replied, feeling his mood lighten as he watched her stride confidently through the town they'd subjugated together.

'Watch your tongue,' Ulfhild scolded. 'Our sons are Christian.'

'So are we,' he reminded her. 'We've been baptised, too!'

They laughed long and hard at that and were still laughing when they reached their jarls in the centre of town.

'Are we ready to slaughter cowardly Saxons this day?' Haesten called out to them once they were quiet enough to hear him.

'We are!' came the reply. 'By Óðinn, we are!'

'Good,' Haesten bellowed back and soon they were heading out through the shattered, pitiful little gates that the people of Beamfleote had laughably placed their trust in.

'The Gods favour us this day,' Haesten told those of his nobles who were near enough to hear as they joined up with the main body of their army and started the journey westwards.

'Of course,' one of the hersirs agreed, nodding fiercely. 'But why do you say so, lord? What makes this day different to any other in these lands?'

Haesten turned to him, eyes twinkling with merriment for he was greatly looking forward to proving his virility yet again.

'What makes this day different,' he said with a wink to his hersir, 'is the fact that, for once in Wessex, it's not bloody raining!'

Haesten shook his head, water flying from his helmet as he chuckled at his earlier pronouncement. The rain had started not long after they'd begun the march to the next sizeable settlement and had not let up since. Despite his wolfskin, he was soaked through, and it was hard to keep his footing on the slippery ground. At least he wasn't feeling the cold. That would come later.

A spear thudded into his shield, and he grunted in pain as the shock ran right through his arm and into his shoulder. One day that kind of pain would reach his heart, he thought ruefully, and that would be the end of him. Not today though. He brought his axe down on his attacker's arm, roaring with joy as the Saxon screamed at the sight of the horrifically shattered bones. When the crying man fell to his knees in shock, Haesten, still laughing, used the blunt side of the axe, thundering it down and shattering the skull.

'I might have seen too many winters,' he cried, turning momentarily to glance at his wife who was fighting alongside him. 'But I can still hold my own!'

Ulfhild did not answer for she was desperately trying to stop a fat Saxon from spitting her on his spear. Luckily, his initial thrust was slow, and she batted it aside easily enough with her shield, and then he slipped in the mud before he could do anything else and Haesten laughed again as the warrior-woman smashed her axe into the downed Saxon's legs. Neither her or her husband's axes were very big, but their blades were honed to a lethal sharpness and Ulfhild's weapon easily clove through flesh and bone, actually severing the man's leg in two.

As her axe came down, one of their other foes roared a war cry and lashed out with his shield, striking Ulfhild in the side of the head. The iron boss caught her, and she collapsed like a dropped sack of carrots.

The gleeful attacker raised his spear aloft, calling out thanks to Christ and revelling in his glorious victory. It was only half a spear he held, for something had snapped it in half during the melee, but it was more than enough to kill the prone shieldmaiden.

Before the killing blow could be struck, however, two of Haesten's men, much younger and quicker than their king, laid into the Saxon with sword and axe and savagely cut short his triumph, and his life.

Haesten bent and looked at his wife, praying to Freyja for her safety. His supplication worked, as Ulfhild blinked, vomited, and then, with the king's help, got back to her feet; alive, though bearing something of a grey pallor.

Man and wife moved on, carefully stepping across the blood- and mud-soaked grass, eagerly hunting for more enemies to murder. Haesten cast about, blood thundering in his veins and making him completely forget the usual aches and pains that accompanied his movements these days.

'It seems we've killed them all,' Ulfhild grated, wiping a smear of blood across her face. 'Shame. I was just getting started.'

Haesten nodded slowly. She was right – the town looked devoid of life. The inhabitants had either run off or been killed by the Danes in the short and one-sided brutality that could barely be called a battle. There would be some survivors hiding in the squalid little hovels though, Haesten knew that. There always were. He did not need to tell his warriors what to do – they were already going about their business efficiently. Soon enough the screams of women and children would be heard drifting from the open doors of the houses, and Ulfhild would grit her teeth in displeasure, but would say nothing. Haesten's wife knew her place, and she knew it was a warrior's right to violate those unfortunate enough to be captured in the aftermath of battle.

Haesten wondered idly what Ulfhild would do if some Saxon fyrd managed to capture her. It didn't bear thinking about. For her, or them!

Then he reflected on how close she'd just come to death. He looked at her and she vomited again, holding her head as if in terrible pain.

'Are you well?' he asked her.

'Not really,' she admitted.

They were at the first, and nearest, settlement to the west of Beamfleote Haesten knew. He did not want Ulfhild following them to the next one if she was still suffering the effects of that shield blow to her head.

'You will return to Beamfleote,' he said decidedly, steeling himself for an argument. It did not come, which proved his decision was correct. 'Some of the injured will be returning in wagons with some of the booty we've plundered, and you will accompany them.'

She was breathing heavily and looked much paler than normal, but he had no real fears for her. She would rest back at Beamfleote with their sons and be ready for battle another day.

It didn't matter how skilled or strong a warrior was, Haesten reflected – there would always be someone stronger, or better, or more devious, or simply luckier.

The people of this settlement were not lucky. Not this day.

This day belonged to Óðinn and Haesten and, once this place was picked clean of its supplies, valuables, and people worth enslaving, the Danes would move on to the next settlement, while Ulfhild and the rest of the wounded returned to Beamfleote.

CHAPTER NINETEEN

Beamfleote was a small town on the Tamyse estuary, which meant it was always susceptible to raids. There was little to stop Danes from sailing across the whale road and striking at will before disappearing with slaves and stolen booty packed into their longships. When Haesten had turned up there had been nothing the people could do, and it wasn't long before they realised this particular group of Northmen would not be leaving any time soon. The town wall, a pitiful affair, had been bolstered with earthworks by Haesten's men and with astonishing speed the settlement became a heavily fortified Danish camp.

For all the rumours and tales of their barbarism, the sea-wolves were surprisingly organised.

Ealdorman Aethelred stared at the newly strengthened walls of the town, hawked, and spat into the rain in disgust.

'I know how you feel,' Edward murmured, scanning the length of the defences and seeing no obvious weak points. 'It looks like we're in for yet another long siege — one that ends with us paying the bastards to piss off again!'

When news reached the aetheling in Lundenburh that the Danes he'd allowed to leave Thorney had headed north to Beamfleote and joined Haesten he'd felt physically sick. Despite Dunstan reassuring him, quite forcefully in the end, that there'd been no other viable option open to him at Thorney, Edward hated the fact that those sea-wolves he'd had penned up so neatly had taken his silver and simply gone to raid elsewhere in Wessex with the old whoreson Haesten.

And raiding they were, for reports came in from various settlements around Beamfleote, recounting the savagery the Saxons had been faced with as the Danes tore through their towns and villages like a dose of dysentery. Using their feared longships, the invaders moved up and down the coast and along the estuary, striking terror into Christian hearts as they went.

'We can't even burn their damn ships,' Aethelred groused, gesturing and standing on his tiptoes to try and get a better view over the town wall. 'They're gone.'

'Bastards learned their lesson after Middletun,' Edward said with a grim smile. 'When my father either seized their boats or simply burned them to ash. They'll have sailed them out to sea, or further along the coast in case anyone – like us – came hunting them.'

'So what do we do then?' Dunstan asked. He had the most experience of the three of them in fighting the Danes, and as a result he was the most pragmatic and least enraged by the situation there at Beamfleote.

'Well, we're here now,' Aethelred said resignedly. 'Might as well surround the place and at least contain Haesten so he can't raid any more of our settlements.'

'See to it,' Edward said with a nod, and Dunstan strode off to give the orders to their troops.

'There must be a lot of them in there,' Aethelred said, still trying to get a look inside the town. 'Olaf and his lot from Thorney, added to Haesten's army.' He shook his head sadly. 'Must be thousands of them camped inside, if we could just bring them to battle.'

Edward felt a lump in his throat, growing anxious as the image the ealdorman painted filled his mind. That was what they were there for though, and he forced down his fears, grasping his sword's handle for reassurance.

'Then again,' Aethelred went on, almost in a daydream as he began to pace, eyes fixed on Beamfleote's wall, 'if there's thousands of Danes in there, wouldn't you expect there to be more of them standing guard on the walls?'

Edward took a moment to think about that, eyes moving from one end of the town to the other, taking in the spears and heads of soldiers he could see staring out at them from the wall's walkway. 'Maybe,' he said, shrugging. 'Would you?'

'Indeed!' Aethelred replied excitedly. 'Haesten is no fool. He's not survived into his hundred and twelfth year by being stupid!'

Edward was too intrigued to laugh dutifully at the exaggeration of their enemy's age. 'Where are all the guards, then? Couldn't they just be "celebrating" their recent raids? You know? Getting blind drunk and raping our kinswomen? That's what they're best at.'

Aethelred was shaking his head vigorously, still gazing up at the men on Beamfleote's wall. 'There should be a lot more of them up there. Double their number. Especially now that they know we're here.'

Edward felt his own excitement building as he allowed the older warrior's words to take root within him. 'Haesten would have come to see us,' he agreed.

'Unless he can't,' Aethelred said, eyes shining as he turned to look at the aetheling.

'Haesten and many of his men are away.' Edward grinned. 'They've gone on another raid, and Beamfleote is there for the taking!'

'Certainly looks like it.' Aethelred nodded.

'Come!' Edward called, turning and hurrying after Dunstan. 'This is our chance to really strike at the very heart of Haesten's invasion! We must attack Beamfleote right now!'

When they caught up with Dunstan he was talking with the thanes and ealdormen in charge of the various fyrds that formed Edward's army.

'Change of plans,' Aethelred called out as they approached the noblemen.

'What's going on?' Dunstan asked Edward in surprise.

'We attack the town,' replied the aetheling. 'Now.'

'Now?' More than one of the thanes reacted with disbelief, having seen the freshly strengthened town walls and firmly locked gates.

'But we've only just got here,' Dunstan said. 'The men are tired, lord. Is there any reason for this haste?' He looked from Edward to Aethelred, clearly amazed at the sudden change of plans.

'Listen to me,' Edward said, grinning fiercely. 'Haesten is not in there.' He flung his arm back, towards the strangely quiet town.

'Then what's the point in attacking the place?' someone asked.

Edward frowned and threw Aethelred a look that suggested he thought the man who'd asked the question was a fool. 'The point?' he demanded. 'The point is, the Danes still hold the town and it's our duty to free our people. Not to mention the fact that, although Haesten isn't there, hundreds of his people, and a hoard of looted treasures, will be on the other side of those walls!'

At last the others were coming around to the idea of storming the town, and Edward pushed on. 'We have to strike immediately, though. Haesten might return at any time. If we can retake Beamfleote before he gets here, we'll be in a much better position to deal with him. This is our chance, lads! If we can wipe out Haesten's army here the war will be as good as over, do you understand?'

The men were all grinning now, realising their young commander was right. They would win glory and renown and their names would ring down through the ages in the tales and songs of the scops.

'Are you with me?' Edward demanded, eager gaze roving across each and every one of the older warriors.

There was no hesitation – to a man they shouted their support for the aetheling.

'Then let's move,' Edward roared. 'It's time to take back our kingdom!'

It amazed Edward how fast his army – tired and ready to make camp as they were – adapted to the new orders the thanes began dishing out. It was all thanks to his father's military reforms, he guessed. Having a proper standing army that had been trained well, rather than the unskilled levies from past decades, made all the difference. Now the soldiers knew what they were about, and performed their duties quickly and efficiently. In a surprisingly short time, they were lined up around Beamfleote. Aethelred had commanded the formations be kept loose for now, in case the enemy had a good supply of missiles at hand. No point making an easy target for them.

Dunstan had overseen the felling of a number of sturdy trees, and those within the army who had engineering or carpentry experience quickly turned the trunks into battering rams. There was no time to craft ladders but Edward did not think they'd be needed anyway – Beamfleote's gates, and even the walls, would not withstand many blows from the rams.

'Is everyone in position?' the aetheling asked, striding to Aethelred. The men smiled, fully ready for battle, and their obvious support reassured Edward that he was doing things right so far. If they could win this fight today it would go even further to cementing his position as a commander to inspire loyalty despite his youth. If he was to be king one day, he would need to perform well in this battle.

A lump came to his throat and he had to cough to clear it, spitting out a small amount of phlegm but feeling better for it as Aethelred turned to him with a cool smile.

'We're all ready, lord.'

Edward nodded, eyes running across the walls and gates for the hundredth time, wondering if this truly was the correct path he'd chosen. It had to be.

'No fancy tactics, or clever ruses,' Aethelred said. 'Just strike them hard and fast, then overrun them with – hopefully – our greater numbers.'

'Hopefully,' Edward agreed in a cracked voice.

'You'll be fine,' Aethelred told him quietly. 'We all feel nervous, and it's even worse when you know you bear the responsibility for the survival of so many men.'

'I wasn't even thinking about that,' Edward admitted. 'Not yet. I was just thinking about getting a spear through my own guts.'

'You'd have to be a bloody fool not to fear that,' the ealdorman said reassuringly. 'Or crazy. Don't let the fear master you though, Edward. That's the most dangerous thing that can happen. Aye, you might die here today, but you might die tomorrow just by falling down some stairs, or from eating something that's gone off, or simply because God thinks it's your time.'

Edward nodded, swallowed nervously, and then pushed his shoulders back and blew out a long breath. He felt better already and said in a clear, strong voice to Aethelred, 'Let's do this.'

Dunstan appeared then, slapping warriors on the back and offering words of encouragement as they waited. 'Your father would have had his priests say Mass for us before attacking,' he said. There was no trace of criticism in his tone. It sounded more as if he wanted to remind Edward of his family's protocols. 'Your uncle, Aethelred, was even more pious... if that's possible.'

Edward snorted. 'I've heard all about the Battle of Ascesdune. My uncle refused to leave his tent until he'd heard Mass, while my father and the rest of the army fought with Halfdan and very nearly lost before King Aethelred finally joined the battle. Are you saying we should make the men wait, Dunstan? When they're all lined up and ready to slaughter heathen scum?'

'I'm not the commander, lord,' Dunstan said.

Laughing, Edward hefted his spear and stared again at Beamfleote's gates. 'We need to take the town now, before Haesten returns. We go now, and have the priests say the best Mass Wessex has ever witnessed once Beamfleote is once again in Saxon hands. All right, Dunstan?'

'Sounds good to me, lord.'

'That's settled, then. God protect us.'

On the walls of the town there were more defenders now, but they were quiet and none hurled the usual insults or threats. As the West Saxon army began to move in Edward had a momentary sensation of panic, as he wondered if perhaps this was a ruse – a trick by the Danes to make him think the town was poorly defended when, in fact, the opposite was the case. He forced himself to calm down, breathing slowly and steadily, putting one foot in front of the other as those charged with manning the battering rams ran ahead and started thundering the great logs against Beamfleote's gates.

Similar booming noises could be heard from other parts of the town. Now, the Danes began to make sounds, screaming and roaring their hatred as they launched missiles at the men with the battering rams. Stones, spears, and arrows clattered off the shields that were held aloft by men beside the rams, offering protection to themselves and their comrades who continued to step backwards and run forwards, putting everything they could into shattering the gates.

Edward did now feel that terrible weight of responsibility that Aethelred had mentioned, as he saw enemy spears slipping through gaps in the 'roof' of shields over the battering ram at the gates. Already a handful of his men were on the ground, some dead and silent, while others, horribly injured, were screaming in pain and fear.

'God,' Edward prayed, watching as one of those screaming men was silenced by a boulder thrown directly at his face. 'Break open the gates. Please, God!'

There was a sudden, massive splintering and the gates did swing open as the battering ram tore through the timbers and shattered the bar that held them closed.

Edward felt his heart lift and he opened his mouth to command the rest of his fyrd to charge through the opening, but the gates jammed before they were wide enough even for a single man to slip through.

'The Danes have piled debris or something there to hold them shut,' Dunstan shouted. 'Push! Fucking push! Wait, lord, while we clear the way!' He sprinted forward pointing at men in the line beside Edward to add their weight to the gates.

'Defend them!' Edward bellowed, throwing one of his spears at a man on the wall who was carrying a great rock along the walkway, ready to drop on the Saxons. Edward's weapon must have been guided by God's own hand as it sailed up and slammed into the Dane's shoulder, throwing him and his rock sideways. He could be heard screaming as he flew off the side of the walkway, and then Edward's men were cheering and throwing their own spears.

It wasn't long before the gates were shoved inwards – one even tearing from its hinges in the process – and the army filtered inside, helping their fallen comrades as they went.

The Danes had formed a shieldwall inside but it was quickly overrun. The enemy soldiers had no stomach for the fight, as the other battering rams did their jobs and more Saxons poured into Beamfleote eager for blood, hacking apart all who stood in their way.

'No prisoners!' Edward ordered, dodging a piece of debris that had come from God knew where. 'Kill them all!'

'The place is filled with women and children,' Aethelred shouted, appearing from a street on the right.

'Danes?'

'Aye, lord!'

'Kill the men!' he amended, hoping his command would be heard and heeded. 'Do not harm the women or children!'

The battle did not last long. Edward's hopes that Haesten had taken most of his warriors off on a raid proved true although there were still a few hundred men left to defend the town. It was not nearly enough to hold off the West Saxons who showed no mercy, all the rage that had built up in them over the weeks of traipsing around Wessex coming to the fore.

Within Beamfleote, as well as the families of Haesten's warriors, Edward's triumphant troops discovered much looted treasure and silver, and even many longships. It seemed they'd been dragged into the town on rollers to keep them safe.

'What should we do with them?' Dunstan asked when the fighting was over and quiet had settled over the town again.

'Burn them,' Edward said. 'Or sink them, as my father did at Middletun.'

'We could use them,' Aethelred argued. 'For our own fleets. The Northmen build superb vessels, Edward. Burning them would be a waste of resources.'

Edward quickly realised the older man was exactly right. He nodded. 'Commandeer as many as we can then, Dunstan. Have them absorbed by our own fleet, and that of Mercia.'

Aethelred grinned, but then his face fell and his expression became thoughtful. Perhaps even anxious. 'If we remove their ships,' he said, 'we are removing their only way to leave our lands. Haesten will no longer be able to sail away and leave us in peace.'

Edward thought about that. Did they really want to trap so many enemy warriors in Wessex? It would mean a fight to the death, with one side or the other winning a decisive victory. Now, this truly was a momentous responsibility to fall on the young aetheling's shoulders, and he wished Alfred was there to make the decision.

What would his father do if he were there? Edward was not entirely sure, but it didn't matter. He was his own man, he must make his own choices or no one would ever think him worth following.

'Do it,' he said with a boldness he did not really feel. 'Take their ships. Destroy any not worth keeping. And have a fyrd scout along the coast for the rest of Haesten's fleet, take those into our possession as well. Let's see if the old sea-wolf still has the stomach for a war when he finds out his escape route has been stolen away from him.'

Dunstan's smile was as wide as the battered town gates as he bowed and hurried off to carry out the aetheling's orders.

Edward was amused, too. He'd noticed how much Saxon warriors enjoyed sinking or burning the Northmen's ships. It seemed to slake their thirst for revenge on the vicious whoresons who'd wrecked so much of their countryside.

'What about the women and children?' Aethelred asked with a sour expression.

'What about them?'

'What are we going to do with them?' the ealdorman asked. 'We can't just kill them, but they'll need to be fed and guarded. Another drain on our resources, by God, these sea-wolves really are a pestilence!'

Edward wasn't particularly interested in the people they'd captured – the town was theirs and that was the important thing. His opinion changed moments later when two soldiers came running along the street from the direction of Beamfleote's hall.

'My lords!' the foremost soldier called, waving to Edward and Aethelred. 'You must come and see this!'

Edward felt a twinge of anxiety at the excited tone of the man's voice. Had Haesten's army been spotted on the road back to town? Was the aetheling's great victory about to become a massacre? His momentary panic was quickly dispelled as he saw the two runners were smiling, their eyes shining with merriment.

'What is it?' Aethelred demanded.

'You need to come to the hall,' the second running warrior gasped as the pair skidded to a halt, still smiling despite being out of breath.

'You won't believe who we've captured,' said the other man.

'Spit it out, for God's sake!' Edward shouted, but he was laughing too, infected by the men's excitement. 'Who have we captured?'

'Haesten's wife, Ulfhild! She was supposed to be away raiding with him, but she got injured and returned here last night.'

'She put up quite a fight, lord,' the second man added, and his face darkened as he went on. 'Killed one of our lads before she was knocked out and tied up.'

Edward glanced at Aethelred and they shared a look. The good news was not done, however.

'That's not all, my lords,' said the first soldier, standing fully upright now that he'd caught his breath again. 'Ulfhild wasn't just fighting for her own sake. Her sons were with her.'

'Her sons!' Aethelred hooted in happy disbelief. 'Knud and Erik? Oh, this is wonderful.' He turned to Edward and grasped him by the forearms. 'We've routed Haesten's defenders, captured his baggage train and treasure, retaken Beamfleote…'

'And, on top of all that,' the aetheling said with a laugh, 'we've captured the ugly old bastard's whole family! Break out the ale lads, I think a celebration is in order!'

The two soldiers moved off to spread the good news and Aethelred waved at some other troops who were gleefully unloading a captured wagon filled with barrels of drink.

This would prove decisive, thought Edward as a ceorl began rolling one of the barrels towards him. It might even lead to Haesten's surrender, and the end of the war! Praise be to God, this day's triumph would fuel the songs and stories of the scops for years to come and truly show the people of Wessex that Edward was a man to follow.

And then he remembered his earlier moment of panic as he feared Haesten's army's premature return and all thoughts of celebration were temporarily placed on hold. The barrel Aethelred was broaching could wait – the smashed gates and walls of Beamfleote needed repairing as quickly as possible.

CHAPTER TWENTY

'They're simply not like us. They're savages!'

Aethelred was so angry that he kicked his stool, sending it flying across the hall to clatter against one of the benches, thankfully unoccupied as it was mid-morning and their hearth-warriors were out training or working to refortify Beamfleote.

While the Mercian was furious at the news their scouts had brought them that morning, Edward, in contrast, was stunned. 'How can any man just abandon his family like that?' he wondered. 'His wife? His children?'

'I'll tell you why,' Aethelred replied viciously. 'Because Haesten knows fine well we won't kill women and children, unlike his own barbarous followers! We Christians are too civilised, perhaps even too soft, to do what should be done.'

Edward swallowed, eyeing his brother-in-law uncertainly. Should they kill Ulfhild and the two boys? It is what warlords throughout history had done. Certainly the likes of the Romans would have executed them without a second thought. But such slaughter went against everything Christ taught – it would be evil! Would it show the Danes what they were up against though, and perhaps even send Haesten's hordes back to Jutland or Francia or, well, anywhere other than the lands of the Saxons?

'Besides,' Aethelred ranted on, 'Haesten probably has dozens of families dotted around the world. He's seen about seventy winters, most of them spent raiding. How many women has he raped do you think, Aethelred? Most likely hundreds, with a similar number of bastard offspring the result! How many wives did he take before Ulfhild?' The ealdorman shook his head in disgust. 'We really should have known he'd not give a shit about Ulfhild and his sons when we captured them. It's the nature of the sea-wolf – use what, and who, they want until it becomes too much trouble and then move on and start afresh leaving all behind. God's bollocks, will we ever be done with the Danes?'

Edward accepted some bread and butter from a young ceorl and bit into it, barely tasting the food as he contemplated Aethelred's words and the report from their scouts.

Haesten had not returned to Beamfleote. Clearly some of his men had escaped the town before the Saxon army attacked it and carried the news of what was happening to their king. Rather than attempting to break through the newly repaired walls, Haesten had simply abandoned his people and possessions, marched past the town and continued on to the coast, where he made a new camp at Scobrih, ten miles from Beamfleote.

Edward sending emissaries to try and get Haesten to bargain with them for the return of his family did not end well. None came back. Meanwhile, the Danes continued to raid the nearby towns while the Saxon army did their best to try and catch them in the open without much success.

To make matters worse, Haesten's army was growing again. Apparently the Danes who'd settled, and now ruled, in East Anglia and Northumbria felt Alfred's position was about to collapse and so more and more warriors came to join Haesten. Edward had sent word to his father of course, to apprise him of the situation there in the east, and to ask him for reinforcements.

'Have those extra levies you asked your father for turned up yet?' Aethelred asked, changing the subject slightly, his rage finally dissipating.

'They've been spotted on the road,' Edward replied. 'They should arrive here today. Enough to bring Haesten to battle from what I've been told.'

'Who commands them?'

Edward shrugged. He'd not heard back from his father who was still doing his best to catch the Danes attacking Exanceaster and the other lands in the west of the kingdom. 'No idea. Hopefully someone with experience. I feel like I don't know how to think like the sea-wolves.'

Aethelred snorted humourlessly. 'Don't worry. No matter how experienced you become, Edward, you'll never be able to understand the likes of Haesten. He's inhuman. They all are.'

Edward chuckled bleakly, fearing his brother-in-law was right. Still, it would be better if the fyrd marching to join them was led by someone who'd faced the Danes in battle before and could help Edward come up with strategies to defeat them.

They did not have long to wait. Just two hours later, their reinforcements arrived. The leaders were brought into the town and escorted to the hall to meet Edward, Aethelred, Dunstan and the rest of the aetheling's commanders.

When the door opened to admit the newcomers, Edward was surprised. It was gloomy within the hall but he could tell the first of the thanes to be ushered inside was young, perhaps only a few summers older than Edward himself. The next man was much older though, with a bald head, pale-red moustache, and broad shoulders. Strangely, that one reminded Edward of Wulfric – he was not quite as tall but carried himself in a similar manner, his confident, even arrogant, presence filling the room despite his advancing years.

Then Edward noticed that Dunstan and the rest of the men already in the hall were staring at him and he frowned. What was happening? What were they all looking at him for? Was he supposed to be doing something more to welcome them? He flushed, fearing some terrible lack of etiquette on his part, and then the guard who'd brought the newcomers inside announced their names in a parade-ground bark and the aetheling's embarrassment turned to fear.

'Lord Aethelwold, and Ealdorman Sicgred.'

It was the royal cousin who despised him, and Edward was no longer the only aetheling in Beamfleote.

'God in Heaven,' he heard Dunstan murmuring. 'Why did Alfred send us those two? I'd rather share a hall with Haesten!'

There was nothing for it but to welcome the two noblemen and, in truth, Edward had no memory of either of them. He was not even sure if he'd ever met them before. He had heard the stories about what had happened at the Witan six years before, when Aethelwold and his older brother Aethelhelm had turned up with Sicgred – the man who'd been their captain and protector when they were children – and caused all sorts of bother. That meeting between them and Alfred had ended in a fight outside in the torrential rain – even Edward's mother, Ealhswith, had somehow ended up in the mud. After it was over, Alfred had banished the three men from Wintanceaster, threatening them with death if they ever returned.

Still, Aethelhelm and Aethelwold were noblemen in their own right, aethelings, being the sons of Alfred's dead brother, Aethelred. Alfred was their uncle and, once his anger faded, he'd done his best just to ignore them, allowing them to live in peace in their estates in the southeast. As long as they did as they were supposed to, protecting the coasts from raids, and sending taxes to the king's coffers, all was well.

Edward had been warned by many in Alfred's court, and Alfred himself, on many occasions, that his cousins wanted the throne, believing they should be next in line rather than Edward. It was all very messy, and complicated, and Edward had never bothered about it too much, especially recently when Wessex had a full-blown invasion to deal with.

The sight of Aethelwold and Sicgred being shown to his own table had shocked him so much that he could barely think what to do. Wessex was in dire peril and his father would not have sent these men to join him if there'd been an alternative. There was nothing for it but to welcome them and do his best to get along with them.

Edward had never had any personal issues or falling out with Aethelwold so perhaps they might even become friends. They were kinsmen, after all.

He stood and bowed to the pair as they strode up to the table and they returned the gesture coolly before all took their seats and the low hum of excited chatter slowly filled the hall. Ceorls and servants brought ale and food for those who had none yet, and then, when everyone had been served, Edward took a long pull of his drink. Steeling himself, he forced a smile and said to Aethelwold, 'Welcome, Ealdorman Sicgred, and cousin! I'm happy to see you. Your fyrd should hopefully allow us to deal with Haesten properly – your numbers will prove a Godsend.'

Neither man replied and Dunstan snorted, but Edward refused to let this meeting get off on a sour note. He would be the bigger man. 'Where is your brother? Aethelhelm? I trust he's well? I had hoped to meet him too.' That was a complete lie, of course, but politics was full of lies – they were a necessity, and even Aethelwold would understand that, surely.

'My brother is dead,' Aethelwold replied harshly.

Edward gaped at him, wondering if this was some strange joke or trick, but Aethelwold simply chewed on the roast pork he'd been given and stared balefully back.

'I'm… I'm sorry,' said Edward, doing his best to keep his voice level. 'Was it sudden?'

'He'd been ill for a long time.' Sicgred grunted. 'He died just as we were preparing to march here and join you.'

'The stress was too much for him,' Aethelwold added, and Edward felt his heart sinking.

Alfred, and his faction – including Edward – were to be blamed for Aethelhelm's death as well as everything else Aethelwold held against them? It seemed absurd but the sullen expressions of the two men facing him could not be mistaken. Such hate they must feel for Alfred and his line… Or did they? Aethelwold's next words suggested he might not despise at least one of Edward's siblings.

'How is your sister, Aethelgifu?' the broad-shouldered young man asked with an unpleasant smile.

'Aethelgifu?' Edward repeated in confusion. He hadn't seen her for months. 'Quite well, as far as I'm aware. Why?' He did not like the look on his cousin's face, or the tone of his voice.

'I've always greatly admired your little sister,' said Aethelwold. 'We met once. I think it would be good if we were to get to know one another better.'

'Marriage,' Sicgred put in.

Edward turned to Dunstan, eyebrows raised in amazement and, again, he parroted the words he was hearing. 'Marriage? Aethelgifu and Aethelwold? That's preposterous! She's a nun. Sworn to God.'

Aethelwold shrugged. 'Maybe one day she'll grow tired of such a boring life, and then we can be wed. For now, I will fight beside you, cousin, as my uncle commands.'

Edward made no reply to that. His head was spinning as he tried to make sense of the strange conversation. He put aside thoughts of Aethelgifu – she had no interest in marrying anyone, never mind the scheming Aethelwold, but the fact that Sicgred and the aetheling had come to join Edward proved that they were at least willing to do as the king ordered them to do.

Or did it? What choice did Aethelwold have but to follow Alfred's command to come to Beamfleote? If he ignored the king, any chance he ever had of convincing the people of Wessex he was the rightful heir to the throne would be gone forever. How could a man who refused to fight the Danes be crowned king?

So, Aethelwold had come, but he was not happy about it, and it was clear he would be making no efforts to befriend Edward, or even be civil.

So be it, thought Edward. If Aethelwold wished to be his enemy, that was fine. For now, all that mattered was using their combined forces to defeat Haesten and bring peace back to the kingdom. Edward had been proving himself a loyal servant of Wessex in this war.

Let Aethelwold do the same, if he could.

Edward was not the only child of Alfred's doing their best for the Anglo-Saxon people that year. To the north, in Mercia, Aethelflaed had been left to take care of far more things than she'd expected. Her stewardship was supposed to be a short-term thing, just to look after things until Aethelred got over his bout of illness which had ended up lasting for almost two years. When the ealdorman recovered, he'd taken charge again and Aethelflaed had been able to spend more time with their daughter, Aelfwynn. It had been a happy period for them all, but then Aethelred had marched off with his fyrd to join Edward in the fight against the Danes who'd attacked Wessex, and Aethelflaed had been forced to grasp the reins and guide the Mercians again.

Morcar was called to her side once more, offering a powerful physical and political presence to her court although, at twenty-four summers, she was even more confident in her role as Lady of Mercia than when she'd first taken charge of the Witan.

The people had grown to appreciate her after she'd led her warband to victory over the raiders at Witenhert, and their love had only grown in the intervening years as their lands remained mostly safe from Danes, Irish and other threats. None in the Witan questioned her authority now, especially with Morcar supporting her. He too had risen in prominence since the battle at Witenhert, as he was rewarded for his service to Aethelflaed with lands and wealth to add to his already considerable fortune.

Perhaps the Danes had heard of her ruthless streak after she'd commanded the deaths of the enemy prisoners at Witenhert, or perhaps they were simply too busy attacking Wessex to pose much of a threat to Mercia but, whatever the reason, Aethelflaed had not been forced to face any raiders since her husband had gone south to join Alfred and Edward.

So, it was an unexpected and not very pleasant surprise when a group of visitors arrived at Glowecestre.

'Who are they?' she asked Morcar as they hurried towards the town's great hall. She'd been at the nearby church and the ealdorman had come to fetch her when the travellers turned up.

'Danes,' Morcar told her. 'Warriors. Be very careful dealing with them, my lady,' he advised.

'How many of them are there?'

'A dozen,' he replied sourly. 'I was hoping they'd refuse to give up their weapons when they sought entry to the hall, but they handed them over readily enough.'

Aethelflaed's mind was working hard, trying to make sense of this unexpected visit. Danes! What in God's name could a dozen sea-wolves want in Glowecestre? Morcar didn't know because the hersir in charge of the newcomers refused to tell him, saying he'd only speak with whoever was the head of the Witan at that time.

'Are you expecting a fight?' Aethelflaed asked Morcar as they came to the hall and nodded a greeting to the anxious door guards.

The big ealdorman shrugged. 'Who knows with these bastards?' he said. 'They're outnumbered, and we took their weapons from them but perhaps they're just the outriders of a much bigger warband.' He shook his head in exasperation, just as puzzled by the visit as Aethelflaed.

What could the Danes possibly want there in Mercia? All their kind ever wanted was war and plunder and the glory of battle – why would this visit prove any different? Had it been a dozen farmers or scholars who'd turned up at the hall that would be one thing, but, from Morcar's description the visitors were experienced, grizzled warriors. Aethelflaed paused before going into the great hall, taking a deep breath and gathering her composure as the guard threw open the door and announced her and Morcar's arrival.

She was armed of course with her seax, and she was as competent with that as with a sword, so she felt no great fear of attack as she went into the hall's gloomy, smoky interior. Still, there was a tight knot of trepidation in her guts as she strode to her chair on the raised dais. She eyed the visitors as she walked, noting their armour and fine clothing. These were men of high rank, that much was obvious even from her cursory glance, and her curiosity was piqued even further. She took her seat and Morcar stood just behind her, a reassuring presence.

'You are in charge here?' one of the Danes said, marking himself as their leader.

'I am,' Aethelflaed replied with just a touch of disdain in her tone. She did not want to be rude, it was her duty to offer hospitality to travellers after all, but she would not allow the conversation to be dictated by this man. 'I am Aethelflaed, Lady of Mercia.'

The Dane smiled at this, and it was not a pleasant expression. He turned back to his companions, sharing an amused look with them. It seemed they thought this – whatever 'this' was – would be easy for them. She could understand their good humour – she was still just a young woman after all. If they underestimated her, that would be to Aethelflaed's advantage.

'Who are you?' she asked coolly. 'And what do you want here in Glowecestre?'

'I am Sweyn,' the man replied. 'I am a hersir.'

'That's nice,' Aethelflaed said, unimpressed. 'Why are you here?'

Sweyn laughed, eyeing her appreciatively, his gaze moving unashamedly along her slim legs and up her body to her face. 'We request passage through your lands, my lady,' he said with a rakish smile.

Aethelflaed wondered if he thought himself handsome. Did he think he could charm her into doing whatever he asked? Her laughter quickly disabused him of the notion, and his face fell further when Morcar joined in, the ealdorman's low rumbling chuckle seeming to fill the hall with its disdainful sound.

'You find me amusing?' Sweyn demanded, balling his fists in anger. 'We have come here as a courtesy to you, girl. We could have simply marched through your lands.'

'You could have,' Aethelflaed agreed. 'But we would kill you if you did. If you do.'

Sweyn's smile had been replaced by a scowl and he looked from Aethelflaed to Morcar and back again. Behind him, his warriors shuffled uneasily, eyeing the Mercian guards who were dotted about the hall and armed with spears. Aethelflaed's lip curled in a bleak smile, hoping the Danes would attack. Their presence in her hall offended her greatly, especially since they were seeking passage to what could only be Wessex.

'You want to march through these lands,' she demanded, eyes glittering as she stared at Sweyn, 'to attack my father in Wessex?' She laughed in disbelief. 'And you think I would agree to that? Are you insane, or merely stupid, Sweyn?'

The Dane's face turned scarlet and it was obvious he was not used to being insulted by a woman. He took two steps towards Aethelflaed, teeth bared in anger, but, instead of shrinking into her chair, she stood up and stepped down from the dais towards him. It was a foolish thing to do and, on later reflection, she knew her temper had got the better of her but, at that moment, she wanted nothing more than to put Sweyn on his arse in front of his men.

The hersir was so taken aback by her reaction that he halted, and his thoughts were easily readable to everyone within the hall as he gazed at her, fists clenching and unclenching. If he threw a punch at the Lady of Mercia, Morcar and the guards would not waste time in using their weapons against the Danes. He was so enraged – snubbed so openly by a mere girl, and a Saxon to boot – that it took a huge effort for him to calm down and step back to his original position.

'Why did you come here?' Aethelflaed asked again. 'Really?'

'As a courtesy,' Sweyn returned through gritted teeth. 'We have an army ready to march from Northumbria—'

'To Wessex?' Aethelflaed demanded.

'*Ja*, to Wessex!' the hersir cried, rage making his eyes bulge. 'Haesten seeks men to join him, and we have answered his call.' He forced himself to be calm again. His smile even returned, although it was not so pleasant any more. 'Alfred cannot stand against the army that Haesten is assembling, and we will march to Wessex whether you agree to let us pass freely through your lands or not, girl.'

'Alfred has stood against everything you sea-rats have thrown at him so far,' Aethelflaed growled, grasping the handle of her seax hopefully. 'And so have we here in Mercia.' She walked forward, standing directly in front of Sweyn who was a little taller than her but she did not let that put her off as she went on. 'If you bring an army into these lands we will attack you, do you understand me? You may win the battle, I have no idea how many warriors you will bring, but we will kill many of you. What kind of army will you take to Haesten then, Sweyn?'

The hersir's rage had cooled by now, and as he looked down into the face of the young woman who called herself the Lady of Mercia, he seemed to shrink. His arrogance faded, his confidence diminished visibly, and, in their place, fear came into his eyes.

'Aye.' Aethelflaed nodded, smiling grimly at him. 'You are at my mercy, Sweyn. You and your men. Unarmed, and outnumbered. What will you do now that you have my answer to your demand? Will you attack me?'

Morcar had come up behind her now and the Dane swallowed, licking his lips.

'We will leave,' he said at last, trying unsuccessfully to sound confident again. 'We will leave, *my lady*. But this is not the end of it. You cannot hold back the tide with a single seax.'

'You are no tide,' Aethelflaed spat, drawing her seax, its oiled blade glistening in the light from the firepit. 'You are nothing but scum. Surround them!'

Her command brought an instant response. The Mercian guards moved forward from their positions against the walls, spears held out, pointing at the Danes who had no response, unarmed as they were.

'I would ask you to send a message to your army, Sweyn,' Aethelflaed said. 'To tell them that Mercia and Wessex will no longer be terrorised by your sea-wolves. But,' she shrugged and looked at Morcar who was standing beside her, sword in hand, 'I can think of an even clearer message to send to your kinsmen.'

The hersir's mouth opened as he took in her words and understood their meaning, then his face twisted and he lunged towards her, hands grasping for her neck, seeking to squeeze the life from the girl that had humiliated him and his proud warriors.

Aethelflaed never even had to move, as Morcar's sword tore into Sweyn's chest, hurling the man backwards, away from the lady, blood spurting from his open mouth.

It took only moments for the dust to settle and, when it did, the Danes were all dead.

Morcar pulled his sword from Sweyn's body and wiped the blood off it on the hersir's cloak before sheathing it. He lifted an eyebrow and looked at Aethelflaed with just a hint of a smile. 'That wasn't very hospitable of us,' he said.

'Damn them,' Aethelflaed said harshly. 'They would have taken their army to kill my father and my kinfolk in Wessex, and then they'd have come back here to kill us and take Mercia for themselves as well.'

'True,' Morcar said, nodding. 'But what now? What of the army of Danes that's massed in Northumbria that the hersir spoke of?'

'Let them come,' Aethelflaed spat, looking at the mangled corpses scattered about the floor of her hall. 'Let the bastards come. Our shieldwall will be ready for them.'

CHAPTER TWENTY-ONE

'Shields up! Get your fucking shields up!'

Edward felt the pull of his training as the command was bellowed out and he instinctively threw up his own shield just moments before a hail of spears blackened the sky and crashed down, tearing through Saxon flesh and bone. The sound was horrific, first the thumps of iron meeting linden wood, and then the agonised cries of the injured.

'Now!' Dunstan roared. 'Loose!'

Edward and the rest of his fyrd followed the order and the aetheling gritted his teeth, hoping with vicious relish that their missiles would do ten times the damage the Danes' attack had done.

'Forward!' he shouted, and the cry was echoed along the Saxon line. The shieldwall moved ahead in tight formation, their throwing spears spent, ready now for the thrust and parry that would settle this battle one way or the other.

Aethelwold's fyrd had started forward before Edward's line and he could see them meeting the enemy now, more cries of rage and pain filling the air as crows sailed in languid circles overhead, awaiting their chance to land and feast on the eyes and flesh of the slain. Sicgred was right there at the front beside his master, his height making him easy to spot, and his voice was so powerful that it somehow carried across even the screams and thumps and shouts of dying men begging for their mothers.

Something struck Edward's shield then and he forced his attention to the front again. The Danes had come for them at a run and now there was nothing to do but fight desperately for their lives.

Beside him, Dunstan's spear had either slipped from his grasp or broken, and he'd drawn his sword in its stead. One of the sea-wolves stepped in too close, swinging wildly and ineffectually with a bearded axe, and Dunstan slashed downwards, tearing completely through the man's unprotected forearm.

Edward blanched as the blood gouted from the Dane's terrible wound, splattering up and across the aetheling's face before the gasping, horrified man collapsed and was stamped mercilessly into the ground by the booted feet of the advancing Saxon line.

The blood on Edward's face dried quickly – first becoming sticky and then hardening uncomfortably. But he thanked Christ that it had not been his blood, or him that had died in such a manner. No man believed he would die in battle like that, did they? Or there would never be any battles like this, for the fear would be insurmountable, surely!

Bizarrely, despite such thoughts, Edward did not feel frightened as he batted aside enemy blows and did his best to rip them open with his spear. He felt more alive than ever and, each time a Dane was sent to Valhöll by his hungry weapon, he laughed and called out praises to God.

Before the battle begun that day Edward had recalled Dunstan's talk of his father's and his uncle's piety, and made a point of having his priests celebrate Mass. Their sermon reverberated around his mind now as he killed bearded, leering Northmen with a savagery Christ would surely have shrunk from.

Haesten's army had continued to be a nuisance, raiding from their new camp in Scobrih, killing and carrying off the unfortunate inhabitants of nearby settlements. With Aethelwold's fyrd added to theirs, Edward and Aethelred decided they had enough men to take the fight to the enemy king.

Haesten must have been heading out on yet another day of pillaging for he was caught out in the open, too far from his defences at Scobrih to retreat there. He'd been forced to meet the Saxons in the field and, although his numbers had been replenished with the new recruits from East Anglia and Northumbria, Edward's army was still bigger, and had the advantage of choosing the terrain for the skirmish.

It was exactly the kind of battle the Danes famously hated to be caught up in, and this fact was borne out by the fact that some of those in the enemy's rear ranks seemed to be disappearing into the countryside to the north.

'They're breaking!' Dunstan cried, noting the same as Edward. 'The bastards have lost their heart, lads. Give 'em hell!'

Edward's heart soared and he redoubled his efforts to maim and kill as many foes as possible. Soon, the shieldwall facing his fyrd had utterly fragmented and the Danes began to drift backwards, defending themselves but no longer attacking.

Edward looked around, trying to see how the rest of his army fared. The other commanders seemed to be having similar success to him, routing their opponents and continuing to move forward steadily without losing their discipline.

Only Aethelwold's fyrd were still beset with numbers similar to their own and Edward wondered if that was where Haesten was. Certainly, someone of high rank was managing to hold the Northmen in fighting formation at that part of the field.

'We should send men to aid Aethelwold,' Dunstan said as they watched the fighting progress to their left.

For a moment, Edward imagined ignoring his captain's suggestion. This could be the perfect chance to get rid of his cousin and remove forever any threat to his throne. With Aethelhelm already dead and gone, only Aethelwold remained to dispute Edward's claim to the crown.

But Aethelwold was not the only Saxon facing annihilation – Edward could not bring himself to allow good men to die just to make his own life easier. Dunstan was right, they must reinforce Aethelwold's fyrd, and end the battle. Besides, if Haesten was amongst those still fighting, this was a chance to remove the twisted old warlord from Wessex for good.

'Do it,' the aetheling said to Dunstan and his captain saluted before running towards Aethelwold and calling for Edward's fyrd to go with him. Edward did not run with them. It was one thing sending aid to his cousin, but he had no desire to help the sour-faced twat personally.

Instead, Edward found a small hillock which would afford him a better view of what was happening and he scrambled up it, only now realising that his arm had a long gash in it that was bleeding quite heavily, and something had struck his left knee, making him limp. When he stood on top of the raised section of ground he ripped off a strip of his tunic – an easy task for it was already torn through by some enemy's weapon – and bound his arm tightly, stanching the bleeding until he could have the wound properly treated.

He could see Aethelred's fyrd, along with some of the others, had pursued the Danes quite far into the countryside until the routed enemy army disappeared in some woods. The Mercian ealdorman must have decided they'd done enough for the day and was leading the men back to join Edward and the others. His attention returned to Aethelwold, and he chuckled darkly to himself as he saw the fighting still raged on there.

Hopefully, God willing, Haesten really was there for there was no escape for him now. That section of Northmen was all but surrounded, an island of sea-wolves amongst the victorious Saxons.

Given the fact the battle was still, technically, not won yet, Edward felt a glorious sense of calm – joy, even – as he stood towering over the field, Aethelred's men like ants in the middle distance, and Dunstan savagely laying about the last bastion of Danes. Aethelwold was there and, Edward had to admit grudgingly, his cousin was fighting like a demon, even now, when most were thoroughly tired out.

To Aethelwold's right was his captain, Sicgred, and the old ealdorman appeared almost as fresh as his young lord. There was no shieldwall at this stage, it was more a collection of small groups hacking at one another with swords and axes, and Sicgred was obviously a master at this, with decades of experience to call upon. He made a formidable team with Aethelwold which, on one hand, was enjoyable to see as they hacked down enemy warriors with brutal ease, but, on the other, did not bode well for the future of Wessex. Edward did not relish the idea of facing these two, either politically or, God forbid, on the battlefield one day.

As these thoughts filled his head, Sicgred seemed to stumble over something Edward could not see on the ground. Perhaps an old tree root, or a divot, or a fallen foe – whatever it was, the bald ealdorman cried out, red moustache bristling almost comically as he lost his footing. It was only for an instant that he was bent double but, in that heartbeat, a Dane raised his axe and Edward watched in fascination as the blade came down, smashing straight into Sicgred's hairless pate.

The ealdorman's head seemed to explode – bits of blood and bone and brain matter coating those around him.

Aethelwold saw it happening too, and came to his captain's rescue, plunging his blade into the Dane's chest so hard that the point erupted out the back, through the man's brynja.

Edward's head spun as he watched, fatigue and emotion making him weak, and he was forced to crouch on his haunches for fear of falling over. When the wave of nausea passed and he stood back up, the only warriors still standing were Mercians or men of Wessex.

The battle was over. Edward had led his army to another great victory over Haesten. Happiness filled him as he scanned the field, seeing his triumphant troops celebrating wildly and setting about the grim but welcome task of stripping the enemy bodies of their treasures.

And then Edward's eyes travelled back to see Dunstan laughing and slapping his comrades on the back, and Aethelwold...

The aethelings gazed at one another over the corpse-strewn grass and, even at that distance, Edward could feel the anguish

Aethelwold was experiencing over the loss of the man who'd been his protector, advisor, and confidant for his entire life. Anguish, aye, but also hate – hate for the Danes that had killed Sicgred, but hate too for Edward, standing smiling in victory on that hillock. If his cousin still retained one of his throwing spears he would surely have thrown it at his despised rival at that moment.

Fuck him, Edward thought, smile not leaving his face as he jogged down the slope to go and join Dunstan. *Sicgred's death means one less threat I'll have to worry about in years to come.*

'My lord!' Dunstan bellowed like a great bull, laughing and putting his arms around Edward to lift him off his feet, overcome with the release of tension now that the battle was won. 'You did it again!'

'We did it again, my friend,' Edward said, laughing as he was put back on the ground, not caring at all about the fact his subordinate would behave in such a familiar manner towards him. 'We all did it, lads! Praise be to God, you fought like demons!'

The men nearest to him, his own as well as Aethelwold's, cheered lustily at his words and, before he knew it, he'd been hoisted in the air again by Dunstan, but this time more of the warriors joined in and Edward was soon being carried aloft by them as the combined fyrds chanted a bawdy victory song and marched towards Aethelred.

'Stop, you fools.' Edward laughed, Aethelwold completely forgotten. 'Stop! You're going in the wrong direction! The barrels of ale are back that way!'

CHAPTER TWENTY-TWO

Alfred, Wulfric, Diuma and Ealdorman Aethelnoth of Sumorsaete were enjoying cups of ale, content although not happy – for although they'd managed to contain the invasion force that had come to Exanceaster, they had not yet been able to decisively defeat them, or remove them. There were too few of the enemy to take the kingdom while Alfred's army was there, but plentiful enough to still be a thorn in the Saxon king's side.

'It's as I said from the start,' Wulfric grumbled, staring balefully into his cup. 'This "invasion" of Exanceaster was mostly a ruse to bring us here so that the rest of Haesten's sea-rats could plunder our eastern lands.'

'Undoubtedly,' Alfred agreed. 'But if we hadn't come, the west would have been overrun.' He shrugged. 'From the reports that have come in from my son I'd say things are going as well as they could have. Edward and Aethelred are more than holding their own against Haesten, while the Northmen in these parts have had their arses kicked any time we've managed to catch them for long enough to bring them to battle. We've also heard from Aethelflaed – an army of Danes was apparently massing in Northumbria, and they wanted to pass through Mercia. Aethelflaed killed the hersir who sought that permission and no army ever arrived in Mercia!'

'Good on her,' Wulfric said with a grim smile. 'I doubt the army just dispersed because your daughter killed some hersir, though. They might not pass through Aethelflaed's lands, but they'll come, most likely along the whale road in their longships, avoiding Mercia altogether.'

Diuma took a sip of his ale and smiled at Wulfric. 'You're never happy, are you? Come on, man, it's a nice day! We are well provisioned with meat and ale which is more than can be said for the Danes, and Wessex is still ours. Cheer up, by God!'

Wulfric merely grunted and swallowed back the last of his ale before standing up and informing the others that he was going to check the troops were maintaining their equipment properly. He stalked off and soon enough his great booming voice could be heard upbraiding some unfortunate soldier for the poor condition of his shield.

'Is it just me?' Diuma asked. 'Or has Wulfric become even more grumpy these past few months?'

'He's bored,' Alfred said, making a space as Asser came to sit with them. 'Fed up chasing shadows. We all are.'

'Well, here's something that looks like it might lift the boredom for a time,' Ealdorman Aethelnoth said, lifting his portly body from the camp stool he was seated upon and gazing northwards where a group of heavily armed travellers were coming their way, escorted by some of the perimeter guards.

'Messengers?'

Alfred nodded at Diuma's question. 'Looks like it. There's a lot of 'em though.' He felt a surge of interest; Aethelnoth was right, this was a welcome change from what had been their usual routine recently. Then he remembered messengers brought bad news just as often as they did good and he felt the old, feared pain beginning in his guts. What would require so many soldiers to deliver a simple message? A sudden, terrible image came to him then and he was terrified that these men were bringing him Edward's dead body. Had the aetheling fallen in battle? Had the reinforcements he'd sent to him proved too few, and Haesten had managed to defeat them?

'Is that a woman?'

Alfred turned, feeling an incredible surge of relief as he realised Wulfric – faithful old Wulfric – was by his side again.

'Looks like it,' said Diuma. 'God's blood, she's quite a looker too!'

'It's Haesten's wife!' Alfred recognised the tall, well-built warrior-woman as the group drew closer. She was in the middle, escorted by hard-looking Saxon troops in front and behind, and she stood out like a sore thumb, her poise, cat-like grace, and well-groomed straw-coloured hair marking her as a woman of high status.

'What the hell is she doing here?' Diuma murmured.

'She's not here by choice.' Aethelnoth chuckled. 'Look at the expression on her face! I would not want to get on the wrong side of her if she was armed.'

The newcomers had almost reached them now so Alfred could get a better view of them, and he gasped as he noticed the other Danes in the centre of the group. 'God's bones, they have Haesten's sons with them as well.' He was filled with relief, and joy, then for he knew these prisoners must have been sent by Edward, and that surely meant Haesten had been defeated.

'You wait here.' The warrior in charge of the prisoners said firmly to Ulfhild as he held up a hand for the group to halt. She sneered and spat in his direction as he walked ahead and bowed to Alfred and the other noblemen. 'My lord, my name is Merwin, thane. I come from Scobrih.'

'Is Edward all right?' the king demanded.

'Yes, lord, he's in good health and good spirits.'

'And Ealdorman Aethelred?'

'He is also well, lord. Your nephew Aethelwold survived the recent battle with King Haesten's Danes too, although his comrade, Sicgred, was killed by an axe blow to the head.'

Aethelnoth, Diuma, and even Wulfric made the sign of the cross at this news and Alfred absent-mindedly followed suit. He had once been on good terms with Sicgred, a warrior who'd served the royal family, especially his brother, well over the years. Yet now Alfred felt only relief that the man would no longer be there to drip poison into Aethelwold's ear. Perhaps now, without Sicgred's influence, the troublesome aetheling would forget his claim to the throne and Edward's life would be simpler.

Perhaps. For now, however, one of the highest-ranking ealdormen in Wessex had died and etiquette had to be followed.

'That's terrible news,' Alfred said levelly. 'I'll have my priest celebrate Mass in Sicgred's honour later. He was a true warrior to the end. How did you come to be in the company of Haesten's wife and children though, Merwin?'

'When we stormed Beamfleote those three were in the hall. The woman killed one of our men – she's bloody crazy. Our journey here would have been much more pleasant if I hadn't been given explicit orders not to gag her.'

Alfred looked at Ulfhild and received a scowl and an obscene gesture in return and he laughed softly. He could well imagine what a nightmare it would be travelling with her. 'Did she give you much trouble?' he asked.

'Only earache,' the thane replied. 'She was securely bound to save her attacking any of us, but that tongue of hers is sharper than any bearded axe, lord.'

Alfred gazed at her. God, she truly was a stunning woman, he thought. Haesten was a lucky man, having her in his bed of an evening! He realised he'd been staring at her for rather longer than was polite and forced his eyes away. She must have guessed what he was thinking though as she laughed lasciviously at him, earning another rebuke from Merwin.

'Are the boys in good shape?' the king asked, changing the subject and desperately hoping he wasn't flushing in embarrassment.

'Yes, lord,' Merwin said. 'Quiet lads. They've been no trouble at all.'

Alfred looked at them now. They appeared calm but clearly anxious, their eyes darting from Alfred to his thanes and ealdormen and taking in the army camped around them.

'You need not be frightened,' the king called to them, drawing another disdainful snort from Ulfhild which he pointedly ignored. 'You will not be harmed. Aethelnoth – take the boys to my tent. Make sure they're given refreshments and made comfortable. They'll be tired from the long journey, eh?'

His godson Knud nodded in relief, his youthful face drawn and pale. The older boy, Erik, was looking at Ulfhild.

'Don't worry, I can promise you no harm will come to your mother. Go with Ealdorman Aethelnoth and rest, boys. You are all safe here with me. You are part of my family, after all.' He smiled and ruffled Knud's hair as the boys walked past to join Aethelnoth, and the plump nobleman led them towards the large tent that had been Alfred's home for weeks now.

'How has Haesten taken the capture of his family?' Alfred asked Merwin once the boys were gone.

'Badly, I hope,' Diuma said with a nasty smile.

Merwin's eyebrows lifted and he shook his head vigorously. 'Not at all, it seems! He's made no attempt to parley with Edward to get them back. In fact, he's taken his army and begun marching west.'

'West?' Alfred demanded.

'Aye, lord, towards Mercia, or perhaps the Wealas. Edward and Ealdorman Aethelred are pursuing Haesten while your nephew Aethelwold is journeying back to his own lands in case more Danes strike there.'

'God's bollocks,' Wulfric swore. 'Will nothing stop Haesten?'

'What will you do with me?' Ulfhild interrupted. 'I know what you'd like to do to me, Alfred. You've always liked the ladies, haven't you?' She sneered at him. 'Noble Alfred, pious Christian king of Wessex. Pah. Your vices are legendary, even amongst my people. You'd like nothing better than to drink yourself into oblivion tonight and then entice me into your bed, wouldn't you?'

Everyone stood in shocked silence. No one had ever heard a woman speak to the king in such a manner before! It started to rain then, great, fat drops that would not take long to soak through clothing, yet not a soul moved as they waited for Alfred's fury. Asser even grasped the cross that hung around his neck and began to murmur the *Pater Noster*.

Instead of anger, however, Alfred just laughed. 'I can think of worse ways to spend an evening,' he said, and his glib reply brought immediate laughter, the tense atmosphere lightened with just those few words.

Ulfhild did not laugh. If anything she looked even more murderous, and Alfred's plan to have her untied was put to the side for now.

'You can rest easy tonight, my lady,' he said. She was a guest, and a king's wife after all, so deserved to be treated with respect. He would not be going anywhere near her bed though – he would not even be turning his back on her, never mind giving her the power a bed-mate could often wield!

'What will you do with them?' Diuma asked quietly. His tone was grim and Alfred knew exactly what his friend wanted him to do with the warrior-woman. She'd killed at least one Saxon after all and, if the tales were true, was as bloodthirsty and vicious as Haesten himself. Alfred would be well within his rights to have her executed.

He turned to ask Asser his opinion on that, but he could see from the expression on the bishop's face that he would merely advise Alfred to be guided by God. He thought of his old priest, Oswald, imagining the churchman's outrage over such an un-Christian course had he still been alive. Alfred ignored the rising melancholy that always accompanied memories of his departed friend, but heeded the counsel Oswald would certainly have given him.

'As a Christian, and a man of honour, I will not harm you, Ulfhild. And I will certainly not harm your children.' He glared at Diuma and the other men who were muttering at his leniency. 'You will rest here for the night,' he told the Dane. 'You will enjoy whatever meat and drink you wish, and you will sleep in as comfortable a bed as can be found for you, in a warm, dry tent.'

Ulfhild's expression did not change. She still looked as if she'd been forced to eat manure. Her brows did rise in disbelief as he went on, though, outlining his plans for her.

'On the morrow you will go with Merwin and his companions once more, but this time you will ride to Haesten's camp, if it can be found, where you will be reunited with him.'

'What?' Diuma burst out. 'But, my lord—'

Alfred gave his friend, his subordinate, a warning glance and Diuma fell silent but remained openly furious.

'Merwin, take the lady to her children, if you would.'

The warrior nodded, and he too had a look of utter disbelief on his face as if to say *We captured her, and brought her all this way, only to let her go free?* He did as he was ordered though, taking Ulfhild in the direction Aethelnoth had gone, along with three of the other soldiers who'd come from Edward. The rest were sent off to find refreshments.

'This is madness,' Diuma said quietly to Alfred once they were mostly alone again.

'I have to agree,' Wulfric added. 'That crazy bitch could cause all sorts of trouble. Indeed, she already has, if the rumours of her hold over Haesten are true. The old man would likely not be here destroying your kingdom if it wasn't for her baleful influence.' He shook his head darkly. 'It might not be "Christian", Alfred, but you should have her done away with, and save us all future trouble.'

'Come, my friends,' said Alfred, not at all angered by their advice which, he had to admit, was sensible, if not quite palatable to a man of his convictions and morals. 'Would you have me kill the children, too? One of them is my own godson, remember, while the other is Aethelred's godson.'

There was an awkward silence then, as the others chewed their lips and cast bleak looks at one another. Killing the boys would be a step too far.

'Well then,' said Alfred. 'I can't just murder their mother – you've all seen the results of that kind of killing. Vengeance is something that is passed on through generations. Those boys would never forgive me, or any of us, for such a heinous act. Remember the sons of Ragnar, who came here to exact revenge on those who killed their father?'

Again there was silence, although Diuma and Wulfric still did not look too happy about things.

'On top of all that,' the king continued, smiling to try and alleviate the gloomy atmosphere somewhat, 'by returning his family to him, I show Haesten, and all the world, that I do not need them as a bargaining tool. We have the upper hand in this war, and we do not need to resort to blackmailing our enemies.' He waved a hand dismissively. 'Let Haesten have his wife and children back. We'll defeat him regardless.'

Wulfric at least was coming around to his way of thinking and he shrugged, jerking his head in the vague direction of where they believed Haesten's army to be. 'Your argument makes much sense, lord. And, let's be honest, when has any Dane cared much about the death of a hostage?'

'Exactly!' Alfred muttered. 'The bastards always hand over hostages with oaths to keep the peace, and then they march off and go straight back to their murderous ways, full in the knowledge those helpless hostages – their own kinsmen! – will be killed by us. It's happened many times while I've been king and Haesten has shown a clear lack of concern for those two boys or his wife since Edward took them prisoner.' He idly kicked a stone at his feet, sending it rattling against a nearby rock. 'No, we can't kill them, and I have no desire to babysit the three of them – that would be a waste of resources, and Ulfhild would constantly be a danger to those around her. Sending them back to Haesten is the only option.'

Diuma let out a long sigh and shook his head in resignation. 'I suppose you're right, my lord.' Then a thought struck him and his expression became severe. 'We must send men to join Edward and Ealdorman Aethelred though. Their fyrds alone may not be enough to defeat Haesten should the Dane decide to turn and face them.'

Aethelnoth reappeared then, murmuring to Alfred that Haesten's sons were having something to eat with their mother. He caught the end of what Diuma was saying and immediately offered to take his fyrd to reinforce Aethelred's.

'Good idea,' said Alfred. 'This lot here at Exanceaster seem to have no appetite for a fight anyway. We can afford to lose some of our numbers, especially if it means the end for Haesten.'

'I'll go too, lord,' said Diuma. 'My fyrd, along with Aethelnoth's, Edward's, and Aethelred's should be enough to secure a victory.'

Alfred hesitated, looking at Wulfric and then back at Diuma. The thought of both Diuma and Aethelnoth – two of his most loyal supporters, as well as two of his closest friends – leaving his side to face Haesten was not a pleasant one. Still, in war hard choices had to be made and this plan made sense. Besides, Wulfric would remain by his side, and Asser.

'All right,' he said at last. 'Depart in the morning then, and be careful around Ulfhild! I wouldn't take my eyes off her for a heartbeat.'

'I don't blame you,' Diuma smiled impishly. 'She's a good-looking woman.'

'That's not what I meant!' Alfred retorted before he realised he was being made fun of and burst out laughing. 'Just be wary Diuma, and you, Aethelnoth. I'd hate to lose either of you, but it would be even worse if it was at that Valkyrie's hands.'

'Don't worry about us,' Aethelnoth replied. 'She'll be well guarded by Merwin's lads. Just be sure and deal with the bastards here in Exanceaster harshly, lord.'

'I will,' promised the king. 'No payments for them to depart, not this time. We will slaughter every last one of them, won't we Wulfric? So they can't sail off and help Haesten, or strike again at one of our other coastal towns.'

'That's the best strategy,' Wulfric agreed. 'If they're all dead, they can't be a threat to us any more.'

With that settled, Alfred felt a strange lightness in his heart. The news of his son's victories in the east had given him a real feeling of satisfaction – of pride – and his overall well-being had been given a lift by all that had happened over the past hour.

This war could be won by his forces, he was sure of that now, when before he had never really known what to think, given the number of attacks on different fronts and the size of the armies facing them. God was with them though.

Haesten had no ships to escape in, thanks to Alfred and Edward. He would be comprehensively defeated, and the Danes would finally – *finally!* – learn never to invade these lands again.

CHAPTER TWENTY-THREE

Haesten did not waste any time leaving behind his base in the east. After the defeat by Edward's army, he regrouped and followed the Tamyse and the Severn rivers into the lands of the Wealas, where the Danes attempted to enlist the aid of the folk there. In the past, the Wealas had been friendly towards the Northmen, but not now, and it was in large part thanks to Asser.

Asser had been impressed by Alfred from the first day they'd met. The king was more intelligent than any of the other warriors the monk had met over the years, and his genuine love of learning, his thirst for knowledge, combined with his piety, greatly endeared him to Asser.

So, he'd been more than happy when Alfred asked him to be his personal biographer. As far as Asser could tell, Alfred was the greatest military leader of the time, and his life and works proved that a king could be warlike, protecting his people with valour and ferocity, while also improving the lot of his people, spiritually, socially, and economically. Even despite the near constant raids of the Northmen! Asser had written the biography that year, using Alfred's own testimony as well as the *Anglo-Saxon Chronicle* to flesh it out, and then distributed it amongst the noble Wealas – his own people – who'd been greatly impressed by the glowing picture it portrayed of Alfred. Many of the Wealas were already supporters of the West Saxon king, or even allied to him, so Haesten was dismayed not only to find no succour in those lands, but to actually be chased out of them!

Eventually, Haesten's desperate army came at last to Botingtvne. Edward and Aethelred followed but, when at last the Danes stopped moving they did as they always did and dug themselves in, surrounding themselves with earthworks and essentially creating a fortress. It might not be on a par with one of the completed burhs of Wessex, but it was to all intents and purposes impregnable unless some attacking force was prepared to throw away the lives of hundreds of men.

Edward, of course, did not have such numbers to waste even if he thought it necessary. But it was not long before the Wealas, and more of Alfred's ealdormen, came to join him. Again, Haesten found himself utterly surrounded with no way to break out of his crude defences.

'Diuma!' Edward knew the Ealdorman of Brycgstow well enough, and liked him a great deal, appreciating his forthrightness and easy smile. 'My father sent you, did he? I must admit that surprises me, since you're one of his closest friends.'

Diuma dismounted and gripped Edward's wrist as his horse was taken away to be tended by one of the camp ceorls. 'Alfred is in no danger,' he said. 'In fact, as we were on the road, messengers came to let us know the Danes at Exanceaster have sailed away.'

'What?' Edward cried happily, before his face fell and he became pensive once more. 'Have they truly gone though? You know what the sea-wolves are like. Those damned longships!'

'True,' Dunstan spat. 'They sail off and you think they're gone for good, only to reappear a few miles along the coast and attack another settlement.'

Diuma made a sour face. 'You're right, but Alfred was convinced they had only landed at Exanceaster to draw him away from Haesten's army in the east. They were never really there for a fight so, when Alfred turned up with such a big army...' He shrugged. 'They had hoped to spread the forces of Wessex thin and overrun us, that's how Haesten managed to get the support of the Danes in East Anglia, Mercia, and

Northumbria. That's why veterans from those lands took up arms once more to join him. But things haven't gone to plan for them.'

Aethelred was nodding with grim satisfaction. 'Alfred's burhs, and his standing army, have done their job. The Danes didn't know what they were sailing into when they attacked Wessex.'

'Indeed,' Diuma agreed, teeth flashing from beneath his grizzled beard. 'And the help of your Mercians has been crucial, my lord.'

'It has,' Edward said, smiling at his brother-in-law. 'We're all grateful for your help.'

Aethelred waved away the thanks. 'I'm your ally,' he said. 'I swore allegiance to Alfred when I married Aethelflaed. Besides, if Wessex falls, Mercia will be next, and all the lands of the Anglo-Saxons will be crushed beneath Haesten's boot.'

Edward noticed then the other thanes and ealdormen who'd been sent by Alfred as they arrived in the camp and dismounted, groaning as they tried to ease the stiffness from the long ride. He recognised them all, with Aethelnoth and Ethelhelm being the highest ranked. He began to lift his hand to gesture them all over, to offer them hearty greetings and refreshments, and then he noticed more familiar faces and his arm froze in mid-air.

'What the hell are they doing here?' he demanded, turning back to Diuma who noted the direction of his gaze and gave a wry laugh.

'Ulfhild, you mean? And her personal guard, Merwin? I'll explain it all to you over a meal, my friend. Trust me, your father's reasoning makes sense, as much as we all wanted to kill the woman at first.'

'But why is she here?' Edward asked again, more insistent now. 'What the hell am I supposed to do with her? By God's hairy arse!' He suddenly threw his hands up in the air in disbelief and again turned to gape at Diuma and Aethelred who were openly laughing at his reaction. 'Has my father lost his mind?' he cried. 'Is that Haesten's sons as well?'

'It is,' Diuma said. 'And I told you I'd explain it all shortly. Come, I'm starving, and thirsty.'

'As am I,' Aethelnoth said, grasping Edward's arm as he strode up to join them.

'And me,' boomed Ealdorman Ethelhelm of Wiltshire, a tall man with long red moustaches and hair tied back in a ponytail. 'Where's the drink?'

Edward's initial dismay at seeing Ulfhild dissipated as he remembered his duties as host and began calling on his servants to bring out the food and drink for their guests. He nodded to Merwin and received a respectful but exhausted salute in return. It was quite clear the poor soldier was even more tired than the other men in the army, undoubtedly thanks to Haesten's wife and her sharp tongue.

When everyone was happily devouring roast meat and downing refreshing mugs of ale Edward finally turned to Diuma and demanded to hear the story of Ulfhild and what was to be done with Haesten's family.

When he was told, he did not know how to react at first. 'My father is just letting them go back to that miserable old prick?' he asked. 'And you will deliver them to him?'

Diuma set out Alfred's reasoning and, by the end of it, Edward grudgingly accepted the plan.

'You'll need to be careful though, my friend,' Aethelred warned Diuma. 'Haesten is your typical sea-wolf. He places little weight on the conventions of war, such as seeing to the safety of hostages... or emissaries.'

'You think he'll harm him?' Ethelhelm demanded, flicking his ponytail as if it was irritating him. 'Surely not!'

Aethelred shook his head and heaved a bleak sigh. 'Haesten is a bitter, vicious old man,' he replied. 'We sent messengers to let him know we'd captured his wife and sons when he was at Scobrih. Not only did he not give a shit about getting them back, but we never saw our messengers again. God only knows what happened to the poor bastards. Put it this way,' he looked directly at Diuma, his gaze stern and unsettling, 'I wouldn't have thought Alfred would entrust a task like this to one of his most loyal and beloved commanders.'

His pronouncement was met with silence, broken eventually by Diuma himself.

'Well, if he kills me, so be it,' the ealdorman said lightly, lifting his cup and raising it as if in a toast. 'I've had a good long life. I even have grey in my beard now! But we're here to kill Haesten and his Northmen – first and foremost, that's our mission, regardless of my other job of returning the hoary old warlord's family to him. Many of us will die in the coming days and weeks, it can't be avoided.'

He shrugged and returned to his meal and Edward couldn't help but admire his courage. No wonder Alfred valued this man so highly that he even forgave him for his betrayal the night the king was forced to flee to Athelney for his life.

'You'll be all right,' Aethelnoth remarked, piling another load of beef onto his trencher. 'Haesten knows he has nowhere to run to now that he's surrounded, and without his beloved longships to save his skin. He won't harm our messengers here.'

No wonder the man was so round, thought Edward. He ate enough for two men. And yet, Aethelnoth was another who'd fought with great courage and distinction over the years and, when others failed Alfred, Aethelnoth had been right there, loyally helping him survive the trials of Athelney.

Aye, these were all good men thought Edward. It was a shame Diuma's gloomy prediction about their impending deaths was likely to prove accurate. He decided to follow Diuma's lead and push such dire musings to one side. God would deal with them as he saw fit.

'When will you deliver Haesten's family to him?' he asked, downing his ale and immediately refilling it.

Diuma looked up at the roof of Edward's tent, then glanced towards the entrance flaps which were half open despite the chilly autumn air. It was still light, and they were camped close to the Dane's earthwork fortress.

'I should probably get it over with right now,' said Diuma, eyeing the contents of his mug. 'But your warning has given me pause, Aethelred. If Haesten is as morally corrupt, and bloodthirsty, as you say, I think I'll leave it until tomorrow. I'd like to enjoy one last night of good drink and good company.'

The thanes and ealdormen cheered his words and Edward laughed along with them. The thought of a forthcoming battle was always enough to focus one's mind and make them enjoy each moment as if it were their last. They would make this a good night, and tomorrow would bring what it would.

CHAPTER TWENTY-FOUR

The next day was overcast. Edward knew the previous night had been an enjoyable one from the amount of groaning and puking he could hear coming from the tents near his. He shivered and filled a cup with water from a jug on the table beside his bedroll, sipping it gingerly. He was not as big a drinker as the older men, yet he was sure he had as much of a headache as anyone else that morning. Vague memories of bawdy songs, riotous tales, arm-wrestling and flyting contests, and a game of hnefatafl that ended in board and pieces being strewn about by a sore loser.

Who was it that had done that? Edward couldn't remember, and it gave him a sharp pain in his skull to try. He thought it was Aethelnoth – he could sort of remember the portly ealdorman's belly pressing against the table just before the game board was upended. Edward chuckled, and groaned as a wave of nausea washed over him. Water was not the cure for what he was feeling, and he soon swallowed a mug of stale ale which tasted unpleasant but at least took away the sickly feelings.

Anxiety was not so easy to shift, however, and he felt a moment of panic as the hangover struck one final time, reminding him of the massive responsibility that had been placed upon his shoulders. He was so young, yet he held the lives of an entire army in his hands... How did his father cope with this pressure every day? How would Edward cope with it when he became king?

He heard a woman shouting some obscenity and, thankful for the diversion, struggled to make out her words, finally realising it was not merely the effects of last night's drinking session that was confusing him. It was Ulfhild shouting, and she was cursing some unfortunate soul in her own tongue – Edward could follow it well enough now that his brain had aligned itself to what was happening. He wondered if the woman was so abrasive with Haesten. If so, maybe that explained why the old man had not made any attempt to get her back when she was captured!

He dressed and threw his thick cloak over the mail coat, shrugging into it and revelling in its weight and warmth. A chill wind was rippling his tent and he expected it would rain, if not even snow, at some point in the day.

Would Haesten finally try to parley with them once he had his family back? Would Alfred's magnanimous gesture sway the grizzled old warlord?

Edward suspected the fact Haesten was completely surrounded with no way to forage for food would probably play a bigger part in any bargain the Dane sought to strike with the Saxons.

And what would such a bargain consist of? Edward's army outnumbered the Danes by quite some margin and, with winter closing in, Haesten's men were likely to starve within their encampment. Edward pictured the place, using his knowledge of previous sites the Northmen had vacated as a guide. It would be a shithole, he knew that. The Danes were famously proud of their personal hygiene, carrying valuable combs for hair and beards, bathing more than Edward believed necessary, and even making tiny scoops for extracting ear wax part of their travelling kit. Yet, for all that, they liked to make a mess of anywhere they wintered. It was as if they knew they'd be moving on in a few weeks or months so made no attempt to keep the area tidy.

No wonder the fabled *vikingr* Ragnar Lodbrok had famously almost died from a dose of the shits after illness ravaged his army in Francia! Bloody savages...

Edward was looking forward to seeing the inside of the seawolves' lumpen ramparts, no matter what state the place was in, for he knew the only way he'd get inside was when his army managed to overcome the defenders.

Not so for Diuma, however, who was thumping on Edward's tent at that very moment.

'You awake in there, my lord? Come and have an ale with us, man, I'm dying out here. Don't ever let me drink too much again. Well, at least not until after I've spoken with Haesten today!'

Edward winced as he opened the flaps and daylight flooded in. 'God, that hurts,' he groaned. 'Come on, I'll join you for a drink. Only one though – that'll do me. When are you leaving?'

'As soon as I've downed enough ale to feel normal again,' Diuma replied, leading the way towards a wagon loaded with barrels. Some of the other ealdormen and thanes were already congregating about the thing, nursing mugs handed out by smug-looking ceorls who were clearly enjoying their superiors' hangovers.

The ale on this particular wagon was good, strong stuff, and it wasn't long before Diuma was laughing with Edward and Aethelred and the others, discussing the previous night's events. When Aethelnoth mentioned Ulfhild and her impending return to Haesten, Diuma's exuberance faded, and Edward wished Aethelred had never warned the ealdorman about the messengers they'd sent to Haesten at Scobrih who'd not returned. All it did was make Diuma pensive and helped no one.

'Are you sure you have to go with Ulfhild and the others to meet with Haesten?' Edward asked. 'Merwin is more than capable of performing the mission.'

Diuma shook his head. 'Haesten will take things more seriously if we send someone of higher rank,' he said, swallowing another mouthful of ale. 'He won't discuss a bargain with someone who doesn't have the authority to make promises that will be held to.' He smiled, face flushing with the drink. 'I'll persuade the old prick to bugger off into Northumbria or to join his kinfolk in East Anglia, you wait and see. What else can he do? He's not breaking through this army.'

'Might not stop him trying,' Ethelhelm noted. 'It's that or starve.'

'Or make a bargain,' Diuma said. 'And I'll make damn sure the terms favour us.'

Merwin appeared then with his stern, hard-looking warriors in tow and, in the middle of their small formation, Ulfhild and her sons. The children looked excited, and eager to be amongst their own people again although they'd not been treated unkindly by the Saxons. Even Ulfhild seemed happy, her eyes blazing fiercely as she glared at the noblemen around her.

'Are we going, then?' she demanded as Merwin opened his mouth to ask the same thing – if in a more respectful manner.

Diuma gave her a mocking bow. 'Yes, my lady, we're going. Shame – I'm sure we all wish you could remain here a while longer.'

'You'll be wishing you were dead soon enough,' she said, then spat some hideous sea-wolf oath at him which he ignored, instead asking Merwin if all was ready.

'Aye, lord. Ready to go when you are.'

'Right.' Diuma's eyes turned to the ceorl who was filling the cups but then changed his mind about a refill, perhaps realising he'd need a clear head if he was to negotiate a decent deal with the experienced Haesten. 'Let's go then.'

Without further chatter Diuma joined Merwin's little troop and they marched off, heading north, to the camp of the Danes.

'You think Haesten will parley?' Dunstan wondered as the figures receded into the middle distance.

'Who knows? He's as unpredictable as the Mercian weather,' Aethelred muttered. 'There's as much chance of him agreeing to Diuma's terms as there is him attacking us in an attempt to break through and move on to some new settlement where he can plunder enough food to last through the winter.'

Ealdorman Aethelnoth murmured a blasphemous oath at that and, with a wave of farewell, walked away towards his own fyrd.

'Where are you going?' Edward called after him.

'To make sure my men are alert and ready for anything,' Aethelnoth shouted over his shoulder. 'I suggest you all do the same.'

It did start to rain later that day, an icy drizzle that seeped right into Edward's bones despite the fact his cloak kept the worst of it off. He was loath to retire to his tent until he knew what was happening. Would Diuma return with Haesten's pledge to leave Botingtvne without a battle needing to be fought? As much as the aetheling wanted desperately to smash the sea-wolves right back into the frothing sea that had washed them up on these shores, he did not relish the thought of another fight with them.

'God's toenails, what's taking so long?' Aethelnoth demanded, shaking the hood on his cloak so a deluge of rain drops went spattering onto the sodden grass.

'Negotiations are delicate matters,' Aethelred said. 'They take time. Have patience, my lord.'

Aethelnoth snorted. 'Delicate! Diuma's probably in there downing horns of mead and listening to Haesten's skald recounting tales of Óðinn and Þórr.'

'Or humping Haesten's völva,' Ealdorman Ethelhelm suggested gloomily.

'Haesten doesn't have a heathen wise-woman,' Edward replied, staring at the Danes' earthen walls. 'He's a Christian, remember?'

That at least brought a round of sardonic laughter and jokes about just how much of a Christian Haesten was. The humour soon faded as the miserable weather continued, eventually sending the men back to whatever shelter they could find. Edward looked out from the canopy of the large tent, glad that he and his fellow commanders could at least stay dry in a place that allowed them to stand up. Most of the army – those not on guard or performing other tasks – were forced to sit within their low shelters, entertaining themselves as best they could or even catching up on sleep.

Aethelnoth eventually returned to see if there had been any word from the Danes, cursing when Edward shook his head dourly. It was late afternoon by that point and, although the sun had not been seen all day, its warmth had at least been felt a little. Now, as evening slowly engulfed the camp it grew even colder and a bitter wind picked up too, blowing the sheeting rain into the command tent and drawing curses from the men within.

'Where in God's name is he?' Edward murmured, finally giving in and accepting a cup of ale from Ethelhelm. There would be no battle now, not in that weather and at that time of day. Haesten would not come out of his fortress this late in the day, so Edward thought he might as well have a few drinks. Perhaps they would raise his spirits and warm him up a little!

The nagging anxiety that settled in his guts that morning had never dissipated, however, and the drink did little to help. Was Diuma enjoying himself in Haesten's camp? Working out a deal that both parties could agree to? Sharing meat with the enemy king while a fire kept them warm, and beautiful serving women brought them drinks?

The aetheling snorted. Why was he picturing the heathen encampment as if it was some well-appointed Saxon town, with a sturdy hall bedecked in finery? He gazed into the gloom at the lumpen earth walls that had been thrown up to protect the enemy army. There were no buildings within those walls – just stinking sea-wolves, their horses, and their tents.

Something – Edward did not know what – made him feel suddenly on edge and he laid a hand on his sword's pommel. He wondered what had caused that uncanny shiver, but he wasn't the only one to feel it for some of the others in the command tent also touched their weapons or were muttering prayers as if some darkness had touched them. What was happening? Had an evil smell drifted on the air to them from the Danes' fortress? Some unclean stench that offended the nostrils or even one's tastebuds?

'Christ and all the saints!' Dunstan, who was near the front of the tent, suddenly cried out, turning to look at Edward with a horrified expression. 'Did you hear that?'

The aetheling shook his head and then paused, listening, noticing then what the thane had heard. What they all must have just barely sensed, touching the very limit of their hearing, but now could not fail to be fully aware of: a man's scream.

The sound rose over the Dane's camp and was carried south to the Saxons, rising in pitch and volume and seeming to go on forever, the man's vibrato ringing out in a wholly unnatural way.

'Someone is being killed,' Aethelnoth growled, face red from drink and the cold. 'Damned savages are torturing some poor bastard.'

Edward had already come to the same conclusion, and he listened intently as the screaming stopped, only to begin again, this time morphing into an agonised, shuddering roar. The aetheling could picture the victim's sweat-streaked face, teeth gritted as Haesten and his sea-wolves did... whatever it was they were doing.

'The blood eagle,' someone muttered, conjuring up horrendous images of that near-mythical execution method the Northmen were infamous for perpetrating upon unfortunate prisoners. First, the victim would be forced face down, then some sharp tool such as a seax, saw, or even an axe, was used to cut open the back, severing the ribs from the spine. Then the lungs would be pulled out and laid on the dying person's shoulders, like the wings of some hideous eagle. In one final act of insane savagery, salt would then be added to the gaping wounds.

It would be an excruciating way to die, and all to praise the twisted, bloodthirsty gods of the Danes. Edward would not wish it upon even the worst of the sea-wolves. It was said the sons of Ragnar had murdered King Aelle of Northumbria in such a barbarous fashion, and now...

'That's not Diuma,' he heard himself saying, relief, and then guilt flooding through his body. 'It's not him.' As if it was all right for some other unfortunate soul to suffer Haesten's brutal savagery. But it was not Diuma crying out, Edward believed – this victim's voice was lower in pitch.

Ethelhelm forced a laugh. He, along with most of the others beneath the tent, had stood up on hearing the dying man's cries, but he sat back down again now, chuckling softly. 'The scum must have had a falling out,' he said. 'Let them kill one another, it'll save us having to do it.'

His explanation for the horrific noises was eagerly accepted by the other thanes and ealdormen in the army. Some laughed, some raised their cups to toast the supposed Dane-on-Dane violence, and others crossed themselves, thankful it wasn't any of them suffering within the earthwork fortress.

Edward could not bring himself to laugh. The pitiful screaming had stopped at last, ending suddenly, as if whoever was being tortured had finally been put out of his misery. The ealdorman thanked God for ending the man's pain, and for silencing the sounds that were so disturbing, even to warriors who'd seen and heard many horrific things over the years.

'I'm glad it's over,' Aethelred said, eyeing his fellow commanders grimly. 'I feared it might go on all night. We all know how brutal the Northmen can be – there's nothing they enjoy more than torturing a man for hours; a sick sacrifice to their twisted gods.'

'Aye,' Aethelnoth agreed. 'Thankfully it's done. I'd like to know what the dead man did to deserve such a fate though.'

'Probably looked the wrong way at that crazy Ulfhild,' Dunstan suggested lightly. It was supposed to be a jest, but no one took it as such. It seemed too likely to be true.

'It's done now,' Edward said. 'Hopefully they all kill one another during the night but, if so, they do it quietly so we can get some sleep!' He laughed and cast about for one of the scops who travelled with the army. A poem would entertain them all and help them forget that terrible screaming…

'By the body and blood of Christ!' Ethelhelm jumped up from his seat again, spilling ale all over the ground. The whole Saxon camp seemed to hold its breath, listening once more as another agonised cry rent the night air.

This time it wasn't simply an unintelligible wail that carried on the icy breeze. Words could be made out, and that was even worse than a mere noise.

'Please!' the distant voice was calling. 'Please, God, no!' The final syllable became a screech of purest agony and terror and, when it finally faded, it was only for a moment's respite before it rose again. 'Help me! Help me! God, save me!'

Edward felt a wave of cold run through him, making him shiver. He looked at Dunstan and both men had tears in their eyes for they recognised the voice that was begging for help.

It was Diuma's.

Edward stood rooted to the spot, shivering, tears of impotent rage rolling down his cheeks until he felt like he could not stand there any more. His hand reached out, flailing wildly as it sought a chair. When he finally found one he fell onto it and put his head in his hands, covering his ears to try and shut out Diuma's horrific final moments.

Please, God, kill him! the aetheling prayed silently, frantically, unable to stop imagining what might be happening to Diuma to make him scream like that. End this now, please, God, fucking end this now!

CHAPTER TWENTY-FIVE

When Diuma's cries finally stopped, and Edward's shock had passed, the aetheling wanted to attack Haesten's camp immediately. He'd known Diuma for his whole life, and he had liked the ealdorman's company and come to think of him as almost an uncle. To hear him being tortured to death was soul destroying, and Edward swore to see Haesten suffer a similar fate.

It was fully night by this time, however, and the other, more experienced, commanders had to talk him out of his grief-driven plan to assault the Danes' fortress right away.

'Rest,' Aethelred had said to him, pale and stricken himself in the flickering light from a nearby torch. 'Sleep off the ale. Pray that God will take Diuma into Heaven and grant us vengeance when we do meet Haesten in battle. But that cannot be now, Edward. We'd lose hundreds of men trying to scramble up those earthen walls. Diuma wouldn't want that.'

Ealdorman Ethelhelm was in full agreement. 'We'll see what can be done in the morning, when it's light again and, God willing, the rain might have stopped.'

'We will avenge our comrade,' Aethelnoth promised. 'But we'll not throw away the lives of our men needlessly. You'll agree when your shock and fury have passed, my friend.'

Edward listened to their words, raging within, wanting nothing more than to charge at the enemy encampment and kill every living thing within. He was not quite drunk enough to act on the wild impulse though, and soon he'd been led back to his own tent by Dunstan and was numbly listening to a priest read from some prayer book. Edward heard the words, but could not take them in. His mind swirled endlessly with images and imagined sounds as he saw Diuma and Merwin and the rest of their party being butchered by the fearful axes and sharp-toothed saws of Haesten's gleeful warriors. The anxiety he'd felt earlier that day returned and he wanted to cry, to run to his mother and...

'Are you well, lord?' the priest asked him, and Edward sighed, shamed by his panic.

'No, not at all,' he admitted, drawing a breath and trying to hold himself together. 'Leave me, brother. I'll rest now, if I can.'

The priest rose and nodded pityingly at him but did not offer any words of advice. 'Sleep well, my lord,' was all he said, for which Edward was grateful, and then he went out into the night, leaving the aetheling alone.

He did sleep, almost immediately in fact for the emotional turmoil of the evening had left him shattered and as spent as if he'd fought in some great battle. When he awoke it was as grey and bleak as the day before, but Edward knew he could not wallow in his anger and grief.

Who was he to mourn Diuma's loss so deeply? He was not related by blood to the man. There were many hundreds of men in the Saxon army who'd seen close friends, brothers, fathers, even mothers and sisters and children, torn from life by the sea-wolves. Edward must put aside his emotions and behave like an aetheling.

He splashed some lightly scented water on his face, thankful that one of the ceorls had left it there fresh for him to awaken to. He imagined the water washing away not just the grime and sleep from his eyes, but the sadness from the day before. He did not down any ale that morning, just took a long draught from a water jug, rubbed his teeth clean with a birch twig, and once more threw on his thick cloak. He didn't have to dress for he'd fallen asleep wearing his clothes and he stepped out into the morning, sucking in a deep, cool breath and steeling himself for what was to come.

'Edward!' Ealdorman Ethelhelm was in the mess tent, standing erect, and dressed in full war gear. 'I hope you're well, lord,' he said, eyeing the young warrior with some concern.

'I'm fine,' Edward replied. 'A few hours' sleep has helped me see things clearly again.'

Ethelhelm cocked an eyebrow and grunted. 'Oh? You no longer wish to attack the Danes' encampment then?'

Aethelred appeared, along with more of the thanes and ealdormen.

'Then we continue the siege?' Dunstan asked.

'We must,' Edward agreed, looking to Aethelred, Ethelhelm, and Aethelnoth for confirmation. All three nodded with obvious relief, as if they'd spent the night dreading arguing with him over assaulting the enemy fortress.

So that was that. The siege would be maintained, but Edward did go out with Aethelred and a detachment of his hearth-warriors and demand to speak with Haesten.

The Dane took his time, the sky lightening as they waited although the clouds did not part, making the day as gloomy as Edward felt. He tried once more to spy weak spots in the piles of dirt that formed the enemy walls but, as crude as they were, they would do a very effective job of keeping Saxon attackers at bay. Aethelred had commanded the army to cut down trees from the nearby woods which they'd fashioned into simple ladders – little more than long trunks with hacked off branches for rungs – and, if it came to it, they would need to be used. For now though, the Saxons could not get in. But neither could the Danes get out, and Edward knew which position he'd rather be in.

Haesten might gloat within his stinking fortress, but he wouldn't be so smug when the food was running out and his men thought of mutiny.

'What is it, boy?' a reedy voice called down from atop the earthen wall and Edward stared up. It was the enemy king, clad in an enormous wolf pelt. Edward smiled, guessing the huge fur was supposed to disguise Haesten's skinny frame. Still, he was not there to judge the man's appearance.

'Where is the group of men we sent to escort your wife and children back to you?' the aetheling shouted up, making his voice as powerful and strong as possible, hoping it would contrast with the thin tones of his elderly counterpart.

'Dead,' Haesten called back bluntly. 'You might have heard them calling for their mothers.' He was smiling and the warriors who'd accompanied him laughed nastily at his words.

'Why?'

Haesten's smile disappeared at that. He seemed genuinely surprised by the question. 'This is war, Saxon,' he shouted down, gesturing outwards to encompass the army camped not far behind Edward and Aethelred. 'Men die. It is the way of things. You're new to this, boy, but you'll learn one day, if we don't kill you first.' Again his men laughed at their lord's wit.

'They were emissaries, Haesten.' Edward raged, spittle flecking his lips as he fought to remain calm. Showing his anger would merely amuse the filthy sea-wolves even further he knew. 'They were returning your family to you, by God! We could have raped and killed your wife and children, but my father chose to return them to you. And you show your gratitude by murdering Ealdorman Diuma and his men?'

Haesten's face grew dark then and his eyes bored into Edward, although he was forced to squint, making his expression less terrible than he probably would have liked. His words, when they came, were harsh enough, though.

'Your Diuma, fine Christian that he was,' Haesten spat a thick globule of phlegm onto the ground before continuing, 'treated Ulfhild like a thrall! He assaulted her, and the other whoreson with him, Merwin was it? He raped her more than once!'

Edward gazed at him in surprise. Merwin did not seem the type to behave so – he was an honourable man, a good Christian soldier. That was why he'd been chosen to escort Ulfhild and the two boys across Wessex in the first place. And Diuma? Assaulting the woman? Again, that seemed extremely unlikely.

'Lies,' Aethelred growled. 'Heathen lies.'

Edward remembered Ulfhild's last remark to Diuma then, before they'd left the Saxon camp and made their way to Haesten: *You'll be wishing you were dead soon enough.*

The clouds parted behind the enemy warlord at that moment and, as a thin shaft of sunlight shone down on them, understanding filled Edward's mind. Ulfhild had persuaded Haesten that she'd been mistreated – it likely didn't take much to make the old fool believe her, either. It was said the woman had persuaded him to wage this war in the first place, and to continue it. So many had died already, what would a handful more dead Saxons mean to Haesten? Especially when Ulfhild claimed they'd abused her.

Edward gritted his teeth and tried again to keep his temper in check. It was all too easy to imagine what had gone on within that encampment the day before. Haesten, probably drunk and bored, was suddenly confronted by the wife and children he'd essentially abandoned. She'd then told him the Saxons had done bad things to her and Haesten, well, what else could he do but punish Diuma and Merwin and the others?

'Your wife has deceived you, Haesten,' the aetheling shouted. 'But what's done is done. God will judge you for your sins.'

'My gods will reward me for the sacrifices I gave them yesterday!' the Dane cackled, and he had never sounded more like an old man to the Saxon nobles. A capering, twisted old buffoon who should be resting easy on a little farm in Jutland or some other icy northern waste, not there in Wessex causing death and misery on a scale rarely imagined in those lands.

'May we have the bodies of the men you brutalised, Haesten? They deserve a proper Christian burial at least.'

The enemy king squinted down at him, working at one of his remaining teeth with his tongue. Then, at last, he shrugged and spat again. 'If you like. I don't want their carcasses rotting in here. It's all right for a day or two but then...' He wafted a hand in front of his nose and his men laughed as if he'd made some hilarious joke. 'Are you going to come in and get them?'

He didn't even let Edward reply, which was just as well for only now did the aetheling realise he hadn't really thought this through – there was no way in hell he would walk into that camp, or ask Aethelred or any of their warriors to do it. Not after what had happened to Diuma.

'No, never mind, I don't want to clear the rubble from the opening,' Haesten shouted. 'Wait there, boy. I'll have your men brought to you.' He turned and muttered to the man standing nearest to him and Edward waited, wondering where the Danes would bring out the bodies. It wasn't long before he understood Haesten's plan.

'Are you ready for them, Saxon?' shouted the king after some time had passed, and then he gestured to someone behind him. Two burly Danes appeared atop the wall, dragging Diuma's corpse by the arms. When they reached the edge they grunted and lifted the body, and then threw it. Edward watched in outraged horror, but he had no time to react for Merwin was tossed out next, and the rest of Ulfhild's Saxon escort party followed in quick succession, their lifeless limbs flailing horribly in the air before each body thumped down on the grass beneath the earthen rampart.

'There you go,' Haesten shouted cheerfully. 'Don't say I'm not good to you, Saxon. I had planned on burning them, so you should be grateful.'

Edward did not trust himself to reply, so he simply stood there in silence, eyes moving from Haesten to the pile of twisted, battered flesh, and back again until, at last, the Danes waved a sarcastic farewell and disappeared.

Still, Edward remained rooted to the spot, sickened, wondering what he should do next. Would Haesten's men rain missiles down on them if they tried to collect the bodies? He stared at Diuma, whose lifeless eyes seemed to stare across at him accusingly. Every one of the dead Saxons had bruising to their pale flesh, some seemed to be missing eyes and even lips, as if they'd been cut away or perhaps more likely taken by crows.

Diuma… Edward stared at the body of his friend, somehow unable to tear his gaze away. The flesh of the dead man's back had been cut open and the ribs hacked apart so they stuck out like white, stunted eagle's wings, leaving a terrible gaping opening that Diuma's lungs would have been dragged out of. They were not visible now and Aethelred wondered what had happened to them. It was probably for the best that he would never know.

'My lord?' One of his hearth-warriors spoke, finally breaking the spell that had settled over the aetheling. 'What would you have us do?'

'Bring more men,' Edward replied, fighting to keep his tone level. He felt lost and out of his depth, too young and inexperienced to deal with this horror, but it was his place to command, so he did. 'Bring men with shields. Have them protect you while you gather the bodies and bring them back to our camp. All right?' He looked at the soldier who nodded firmly, face betraying no emotion, and then hurried away to do as he was commanded.

The Danes did not trouble the Saxons as they collected the corpses, dragging them away out of missile range and then placing them onto a wagon drawn by a pair of oxen. Edward watched the gruesome cargo being hauled away and the rest of the morning passed in a daze for him.

The bodies were prepared for burial with all the respect due to fallen Saxon soldiers. Ethelhelm examined them before they were covered, telling Edward and Aethelred that only Diuma had been forced to endure the blood eagle.

'The others had bruises and things like that,' he told them. 'They'd taken a bit of a beating but then they were killed quite swiftly from what I can tell, even Merwin, who had a broken jaw and some fingers missing. Diuma…'

'I don't need to know,' Edward growled, glaring at him.

'Well, if it makes you feel better, I don't think he suffered for long,' Aethelnoth told him. 'I think he died almost as soon as the whoresons began cutting him.'

Edward sucked in a breath through his nose and tried to hold himself together. He tried to focus on Aethelnoth's words, telling himself they made sense. The blood eagle had long been spoken of in hushed tones by the Saxons for decades, but many of those who spoke of it did not think any man could withstand such shocking agonies without dying almost instantly. Or at least passing out, and then being too insensible to feel themselves being hacked apart.

It was, the aetheling told himself, some small comfort to know Diuma died quickly. He remembered again the tortured screams ringing out over the land the previous night and shuddered, thanking God it hadn't been him at Haesten's mercy.

And then he thought of his father. If Edward felt this emotional over Diuma's loss, how bereft would the king feel when he heard the news? What would Alfred expect from the army at Botingtvne now?

Edward wished desperately that his father would ride up to join him at that moment, to take the weight of command upon his own shoulders and relieve the pressure that the aetheling felt might break him. Would he ever become used to this horrific stress? He did not think he would, and a bitter smile twisted his mouth as he thought of all the grasping noblemen who coveted the throne of Wessex. Was the crown really worth a lifetime of such unrelenting fear and anxiety?

There was only one course of action open to them Edward thought, forcing himself to focus on the present: they must maintain the siege throughout the winter, slaughtering without mercy any foraging parties that tried to sneak out of the fortress, and starve the Danes into submission. There would be no more emissaries sent into that hellish camp, and no parleys or payments bribing the enemy army to leave. If Haesten wanted to escape the prison he'd made for himself, or even just to eat, he would need to break through the Saxon lines.

It would be hell inside that camp after a few weeks, Edward knew, and a moment of pity touched him as he remembered the two young boys that were now penned up inside with their witch mother and sadist father. Well, Edward had not made the rules of this war, that was all down to the Danes. They had made their beds, they could die in them.

CHAPTER TWENTY-SIX

Diuma's body was sent south to Brycgstow, there to be buried with full honours in his own homelands. Alfred was, of course, informed of everything that had happened, and the king sent messengers himself to command Edward and Aethelred to maintain the siege and make sure Haesten did not escape.

Winter was fully upon the land now, meaning Alfred could not easily travel to join his ealdormen in their efforts against the besieged Danes. He also knew that it would be folly to take his own fyrd away from the south and leave that part of Wessex undefended.

'This is killing me!' Alfred raged to Wulfric as they stared at yet another fleet of longships and the sea-wolves those vessels had deposited on the shores of Wessex. 'Our people are dying – Diuma has died! – while we march from one side of the kingdom to the other, and back again. And all the while Haesten and his bastard Northmen ravage the countryside, steal our crops and even our people, and undo all the good work we've done in Wessex over recent years. I'm too old for this nonsense.' He shook his head, knowing Wulfric would not appreciate his self-pitying rant but unable to hold the words back.

Diuma's death had severely shaken the king, and not being able to attend his friend's funeral was yet another kick in the teeth to add to all the others since Haesten had been shat out in Wessex by the heathen gods. He had never properly told Diuma that he forgave him for that distant night when the ealdorman had turned Alfred and his retinue away from the walls of Brycgstow. Well, he had told him, but he'd always suspected Diuma did not believe him. They'd become friends again – good friends – but now that Diuma was dead, Alfred wished he could speak with him one more time, just to tell him that he truly did forgive him and understood his actions on that far-off night. That, and to tell him he would miss him terribly.

'So many of our friends and loved ones are gone now.'

Alfred blinked. Had he heard Wulfric right? He looked up at his towering captain and saw the firm, hard set of Wulfric's jaw.

'Exactly,' said the king, suddenly struck by the notion that Wulfric had also been a close companion of Diuma and, although he would not show it as openly, he'd be hurting too.

'It's not easy, growing old,' muttered Wulfric, turning to meet Alfred's gaze. 'Make sure your family know how much you care for them, my lord. One day Diuma's fate will also be ours.'

Alfred absorbed that, wondering if his captain was rebuking him for availing himself of the services of the camp whores lately. Surely not – all the men did so. Even Wulfric on occasion! Wulfric's wife was dead, of course, but still… Bedding prostitutes was a sin whether a man was married or not. No, the ealdorman was not scolding Alfred, simply reminding him how lucky he was to have Ealhswith and such fine children. And friends too.

'I hope Diuma's exact fate will not be ours,' replied the king, forcing himself to smile. 'But I take your point, and you're right. So, as awkward as it will make us both feel, Wulfric – I want you to know I love you like I loved my own departed brother, Aethelred. You've been the best friend a man, a king, could ever wish for.' As he spoke his voice began to waver and he turned away, overcome by a sudden crushing wave of emotion.

'Thank you, Alfred. It's been an honour to serve you. Hopefully we have plenty of years left to put Wessex to rights together.'

They watched the army of Danes moving about on the land before them, little specks bustling about as they unloaded provisions, horses, and weapons from the beached longships.

'I think we've let them get settled in enough,' Alfred growled, stooping to lift the spear and shield that were lying at his feet. 'Come on. Time to chase yet another load of heathen rats back into the sea.'

Their fyrd was hidden from the Danes' sight behind a low hill and Alfred led the way back to them. The warriors were ready to move, indeed had been preparing to do so for some time now, since Alfred's outriders informed him of the enemy fleet's presence. Soon after Alfred and Wulfric rejoined them the army was streaming over the crest of the hill, framed in the early afternoon sunshine before charging down towards the landed longships.

'*Godemite!*' Alfred roared, face twisted in fury as the distance between himself and the closest of the Danes narrowed. 'For God Almighty!'

'And for Alfred, and Wessex!' Wulfric shouted at his side.

The first of the Danes that Alfred came up against did not last long. All the pent-up grief and rage within the king was unleashed, his spear making a great crimson hole in the screaming Northman, and then the king set about making as many of his enemies as possible pay for Diuma's death.

It was a savage, but relatively short, battle. The Danes were greatly outnumbered but fought with great courage and skill until, at last, there were too few of them left to stand against the Saxons.

'They're breaking,' Wulfric called, halting to catch his breath as their foes suddenly turned and ran for their longships. He sucked in a deep lungful of air, let it out slowly, and then lifted his arm and launched his great spear through the air.

Alfred watched, astonished by his captain's prodigious strength after such a hard fight, as the great missile tore through the air and thundered into the back of a routed Dane. The man did not even cry out as he was catapulted forward to lie face down on the beach, dead before he'd even hit the ground.

Wulfric was not a young man any more, however, and he did not run to reclaim his spear, instead leaning forward, hands on his thighs, breathing hard but with a grimly satisfied smile on his face.

Alfred's eyes searched along the Saxon line, trying to guess their casualties. Was it worth losing more men to hunt down the fleeing Danes, many of whom had at last reached their ships and were shoving them into the water?

'Let them go!' the king bellowed, deciding he did not want to lose any more good men that day. 'Let the bastards flee along their beloved whale road. We've killed enough of them for one afternoon.'

As always, it took some time for his command to spread throughout the ranks. It was a vast army after all. Eventually, though, the Saxons ceased the hunt and let the beaten Danes run to their ships. Some of the vessels were abandoned, their crews hacked to pieces by Alfred's cheering troops, but many made it into the water and quickly disappeared, eastwards, into the mist.

Alfred removed his helmet, shaking free his long, sweat-damp hair. He had no idea how many Danes he'd personally cut down that day, but every one was vengeance for Diuma, and all the other comrades the king had lost during this damn war.

'Think they'll be back?' a nearby soldier asked.

Alfred looked at him, seeing a young, beardless lad who held his spear with the confidence of a seasoned veteran. This was what so many years of conflict had done to his people, he thought sadly. Instead of learning to read and write, the children were handed weapons and ordered to stand against the savagery of the sea-wolves.

God help us all, he thought. Let us end this war soon.

'Aye, they'll be back.' Wulfric's deep, confident voice provided the answer to the boy's question. 'And we'll kick their ugly arses again, just like we did today.'

That was the cue for the army to begin cheering once more, a great roaring that filled the air with the sounds of victory and joy, and, Alfred thought sadly, loss.

Those particular Danes did not return though; at least not to the coast of Defenascir. When Alfred's army chased them back to their longships, leaving behind most of the booty and slaves they'd plundered from Wessex, they'd licked their wounds on the open sea, making their way to the east. Presumably the idea of returning to their families and homelands with nothing to show for their time raiding the Saxon lands had been anathema to them, so they'd decided to stop for one final round of plundering.

Alfred had been struck deeply by his conversation with Wulfric, and by Diuma's savage murder, so, believing his southern lands to be safe, he'd allowed most of his army to return to their homes and headed to Wintanceaster himself. He'd been away from Ealhswith for long enough and desperately wanted to see her, to lean on her in his grief.

It had been a bittersweet meeting. Ealhswith was overjoyed to see her husband safe and well, as she always was when he returned after a campaign bearing new scars both physical and mental, but she'd heard about Diuma and shared in Alfred's sorrow.

And his guilt.

She'd been furious with Diuma over his 'betrayal' when they'd rode for their lives from Cippanhamme some fifteen years before, and it had taken a long time for her to fully forgive him and accept him back into their inner circle of friends. Like Alfred, she feared her coldness towards him had hurt him so deeply that he never truly got over it. And now he'd given his life in service to Wessex. To Alfred.

Still, they'd lost many friends and kinfolk over the years, to war and illness and other things. God would take them all into his arms one day and there was nothing to be done about it, other than honouring the memory of those they'd loved.

To that end, Alfred held three days of feasting, to celebrate the lives of Diuma and all the others those in the royal court had said farewell to in recent years. Even those celebrations made Alfred feel guilty, thinking of Edward, Aethelred, and the rest besieging Haesten in the north. They would not starve, his system of burhs would see to that, but spending the winter months in tents was a far cry from Wintanceaster's great mead hall and the festivities Ealhswith was hosting.

Alfred spent many long hours with Asser at that time, seeking spiritual guidance as well as forgiveness for all his weaknesses and sins.

Life in the royal capital was not all doom and gloom, however. When the nights drew in and the wind whistled through the little gaps in his hall, Alfred gloried in the sight of his blazing firepit, his heavily laden table, his *hearthweru*, and his wife's loyal companionship. The ale went some way to cheering him too.

It was snowing heavily one night when word came of the Danes' latest raid. A rider arrived and was allowed into the hall, entering with a gust of wind, snow whirling around him. The guard announced the newcomer in a bellowing voice, naming him as Bryn, a messenger from Cisseceastre.

'News, lord!' the man shouted, and, although he was soaked through and clearly exhausted, his eyes were sparkling from more than simply reflected firelight.

'News,' murmured Asser, sharing a worried frown with Ealhswith who set down the leg of chicken she was eating and wiped her hands with a rag to listen to the messenger.

Wulfric had read the man's excitement as well as Alfred though, and he smiled at the king.

'Come forward then, Bryn, lad,' Alfred called, although there was no need for him to raise his voice as the place had fallen silent at the newcomer's unexpected arrival. 'Warm yourself by the fire,' the king went on in a normal tone. 'You there,' he gestured to a servant. 'Pour him some ale, that's right. Now, heat it for him with the poker, good man.'

The messenger, wide-eyed to be the centre of attention, gazed around at the noblemen and women, stamped the snow from his boots, and then, at Alfred's renewed urging, hurried over to stand before the firepit. He practically glowed as the heat steamed the damp from his sodden clothes and was soon smiling happily as the servant respectfully handed him his warmed drink.

'Your news,' Ealhswith asked, smiling herself now as she realised the messenger must bear pleasant tidings or he'd not look so happy with himself. 'Is it urgent? Must my husband prepare for battle yet again?'

There were worried mutterings and unhappy sighs at her question. It would not be the first time the Northmen had mounted an attack in the depths of winter. Even a blizzard would not be enough to halt the likes of Haesten when the notion for blood and fire filled him.

'No, my lady,' the messenger replied, removing his wet cap to reveal a thick head of damp, red hair. 'Well, that is, the news is urgent, that's why I rode so hard to reach you here. But the king needs not prepare for war just yet.'

Cheers and relieved chuckles filled the hall, and the folk raised their cups and mugs in salute, praising God for another peaceful night of feasting.

'Go on then, Bryn,' said Alfred. 'What brings you here in such haste, in the midst of such horrible weather? Are things well in Cisseceastre?'

'They are, lord,' Bryn replied, and visibly puffed up as he went on. 'Thanks to the courage and skill of my kinsmen! The Danes landed on our shores, my lord.'

Alfred scowled and Asser made the sign of the cross.

'Fear not, though,' the messenger went on, looking apologetically around at the concerned faces of Alfred's guests. 'They're gone now.'

'Must be the same lot we chased,' Wulfric said to the king. 'We thought they'd head home to East Anglia, or Northumbria, or wherever they hailed from.'

'And instead they've chosen to make one final attempt at plunder in Cisseceastre,' Alfred agreed sourly. 'They probably heard about Haesten's successful attack on Eorpeburnan at the start of this war and hoped to find similar easy pickings.'

Wulfric nodded grimly. 'Only Cisseceastre isn't half finished, like Eorpeburnan was. It's heavily fortified, and fully garrisoned.'

Bryn saw them conversing and waited until the king waved for him to continue before he spoke up again.

'Our lookouts saw their longships landing on the beach,' he said, 'and brought word to the town. We were able to muster the fyrd and march out to wait for them coming.'

The hall was quiet, with everyone waiting eagerly to hear how things had turned out at the burh. Even Ealhswith's knuckles were white, Alfred noticed, as she clenched her fists, willing the warriors of Wessex to victory.

'We had the advantage,' Bryn crowed, 'of knowing the local terrain. We set up our forces in strong positions so, when the Danes came trudging across the countryside, gloating and boasting of what they would do to the unsuspecting Saxons, well, they got quite a shock, my lord.'

'Excellent.' Alfred grinned, rubbing his hands together like a gleeful child who'd been handed a shiny coin.

Bryn's eyes were dancing merrily as the warmed ale flowed through him and he grinned in return at the king. 'Our missiles took a terrible toll on the sea-wolves,' he said, shaking his head at the powerful memory. 'We must have killed or maimed dozens of them with our thrown spears in those first attacks.

Hundreds, maybe! It was carnage, my lords and ladies, I don't mind telling you.'

Alfred looked around, seeing normally gentle folk glorying in this tale of slaughter but he felt no pang of guilt or Christian charity for the dead Northmen. If they'd not been stopped by Bryn and the townsfolk Cisseceastre would have run red with Saxon blood. God be praised that things had turned out as they had. Even Asser was laughing and nodding with Wulfric as the messenger spoke on.

'The Danes tried to rally, and even threw their own missiles back at us, but we'd positioned ourselves too high for them to reach us. When our own arrows and throwing spears were used up, we charged.' Again he shook his head, eyes glazing over as he became thoughtful, picturing the scene he was describing in his mind's eye. There was an awed expression on his face as he recalled the casualties his people had inflicted on the enemy raiders and the pitiful cries of those too wounded to run back to their longships.

'How many escaped?' Wulfric asked, breaking the man's reverie.

Some of the revellers had started to eat their food once more, and supped their drinks with cheery, red faces, enjoying the entertainment. None expected a tale as exciting as this when they'd come to the hall that evening!

Bryn pursed his lips thoughtfully and slowly shook his head. 'Not very many. A few hundred maybe. We must have killed at least half of them, and captured many of their longships.'

'A good day for the people of Cisseceastre,' Ealhswith noted with a graceful bow of her head towards the messenger. 'A very bad day for the Danes.'

'Indeed, my lady!' Bryn laughed, bowing low from the waist in return. 'Needless to say, I don't think those bastards will be returning to our shores any time soon.'

Alfred felt elated by the messenger's tale. It proved once again that his system of burhs – and the astronomical cost of them which his thanes had been so against – had been a worthwhile undertaking. Similarly, providing Wessex with a standing army meant would-be raiders should find it much harder than it had once been to ravage Alfred's kingdom.

No, the war was not over as long as Haesten, Ulfhild, and their army remained besieged at Botingtvne, but at least the rest of Wessex was free of threats. Winter was covering the land with its icy blanket at the moment, but spring would arrive soon enough and, with the green shoots and bleating lambs, so too would come a reckoning for the grizzled king of the Danes.

'More ale for Bryn of Cisseceastre,' shouted the king, standing and raising his cup in salute to the proud messenger. 'More ale for all, by God! Tonight we celebrate Ealdorman Diuma and all our fallen friends, and the victorious heroes of Cisseceastre!'

The hall erupted in a deafening cacophony of cheers and whoops and laughter at his words, and so began one of the greatest nights of feasting Wessex had ever seen.

CHAPTER TWENTY-SEVEN

The winter was not particularly hard that year, at least compared to some that Edward had experienced – and Aethelred agreed. The ealdorman said he always felt that Wessex was a little more temperate than his own Mercian lands, and so it proved throughout December and January. It was cold, of course, but there was little snow or ice, and the ground did not harden quite as much as it had in recent winters. Instead, it rained. Edward believed it had rained every day throughout January although he had to admit the days were blurring into one for it was exceedingly boring maintaining the siege at Botingtvne. At first, Edward and his fellow commanders had sparred with one another and their hearth-warriors; they'd gone amongst their fyrds encouraging the men, sharing stories and ale with them; they'd scouted the nearby land on foot and on horseback; they'd even tried to hunt, although there wasn't much sport to be had at that time of year.

Eventually, everyone in the Saxon army had grown fed up with the continual rain and endless days of inactivity. There were only so many times a warrior could sharpen his seax or buff his mail coat before the task grew irritating.

'At least we still have plenty of this,' Ealdorman Aethelnoth said, lifting the chunk of buttered bread he was eating and holding it aloft like a priest would do with a communion wafer. 'The bastard Danes won't have much left by now.' He chuckled nastily, and Dunstan joined in, raising his overflowing ale cup again, as if part of some holy Mass.

'This too,' the thane agreed. 'Any supplies of ale, mead, or wine the whoresons would have had will be depleted after all these weeks.'

'They'll be getting drunk on one another's piss,' Aethelnoth laughed. 'Good enough for the heathen scum.'

Edward gazed at the earthen ramparts that Haesten's host remained imprisoned within and felt a pang of sorrow. Not for their enemies – after what they'd done to Diuma and his companions they could rot in hell – no, Edward felt for the horses many of the Northmen had ridden to Botingtvne. With no food for man or beast, and no way to forage for any, the horses would be first to die. Haesten's men would have butchered all the animals by now, desperate for meat of any kind to fill their swollen, empty bellies. Edward liked horses, and the thought of so many proud, useful beasts being slaughtered like mere cattle was a deeply unpleasant one. The aetheling knew his guess was right too, for the sounds of horses squealing and screaming had become a common one for a few days until the Danes must have killed them all.

That had been weeks ago now. The butchered carcasses would have offered decent meals to the Northmen for a while, but it would all be gone by now. Edward could only imagine what state their enemies must be in at this stage. Haesten and his family, along with the other higher-status sea-wolves, might still be eating at least one meal a day, but the rank-and-file *vikingar* would be wasting away surely. If Edward thought the siege was tough, he could only imagine what kind of hell the Danes must be experiencing every day. Bored, and starving to death! He reached out and helped himself to some salted pork, chewing it slowly, savouring every tasty morsel.

How long would it be before Haesten surrendered to the Saxon commanders? Edward felt sure it wouldn't be much longer now. Maybe another week or two at most. And then, Haesten and his wife would suffer the same gory fate as Diuma.

'You must find us food, Haesten. You call yourself king? Well, provide for your people!'

The old warlord scowled at Rune Eriksson, and he could practically hear Ulfhild beside him growling like an angry guard dog. He could not afford to anger the jarl who'd questioned him though. Morale was already low, and Haesten knew very well that his men were losing faith in him, as evidenced by this confrontation with his own second-in-command.

'Where would you have me find food, Rune?' he demanded, sweeping out his arm. 'You know as well as I do that the horses were the last thing we had to eat. Would you have us turn to cannibalism? Eat one another?'

Rune glared at him, eyes smouldering like hot coals. 'My own son has starved to death,' he grated, fingers clenching and unclenching around the handle of his sword. 'You promised to lead us to wealth and glory, Haesten. You and your wife. Big words, big promises, but you have failed to deliver and now we are penned like cattle in the arse-end of Wessex while the Saxons fill their bellies out there and laugh at us!'

Haesten felt rage building within him. How dare this fool speak to him so, and in front of a dozen other jarls and hersirs?

'Are you a child yourself?' the king asked caustically. 'You knew there would be risks when we sailed here. There is always a risk — that is what war is all about!'

'Look outside,' Rune shouted, his weak chin trembling with fury. 'Look out at the skinny, dying people you are supposed to provide for.' His eyes moved to Ulfhild, and then to Haesten's own two sons who were standing behind their mother, eyes wide. None of them looked much thinner than they had when the siege began. Certainly, they did not appear on the verge of death.

Haesten saw his look and guessed his thoughts, knew he had to divert the conversation in another direction. 'What would you have us do?' he asked Rune in a calmer voice, almost pleading, as if only Rune Eriksson had the wit and wisdom to guide the Danes out of their predicament.

The jarl's eyes snapped back to Haesten's and he shrugged. 'You are the king. It is your job to guide us, not mine.'

'I am asking for your advice, old friend,' Haesten replied, hoping he did not come across as condescending or patronising. Rune was only in his mid-thirties after all, and not really an 'old friend' of the king. Not by the standards of Haesten's own long decades on Midgard, at least.

'Send out foragers,' Rune suggested harshly. 'At night, when the Saxon guards won't see them.'

'We've tried that,' Haesten objected. 'They are always caught and killed.'

'Besides,' Ulfhild put in, 'there is nothing to forage anywhere near here, not at this time of year. Your suggestion is ludicrous.'

Her eyes bored into Rune's with an intensity most men would have found unsettling but now, with his son's death a fresh, open wound, he plainly cared little for her opinion.

'Then what are we to do?' Rune asked, returning the warrior-woman's venomous look. 'Just sit here and wait to die?'

'The Saxons will tire of the siege eventually,' Haesten replied soothingly. 'They always do, don't they?'

'They always did,' Rune retorted. 'But they are different now to what the old tales say about them, Haesten. We expected to find easy pickings when we sailed here from Francia, and our first, early success at that half-built town in the south gave us confidence. But that was a one-off. Alfred and his ealdormen are no fools. We made a mistake coming here with you.'

'Perhaps,' Haesten admitted dourly. 'But it was your own choice, freely made. All of you.' He balefully eyed the rest of the unhappy jarls behind Rune Eriksson. 'No one forced you to follow me.'

'Maybe not,' Rune granted. 'But you are our king, and unless you act like one and find us food, we will not follow you any longer.'

Ulfhild actually laughed at that, a harsh bark that filled the tent and drew every eye to her. 'You will not follow him?' she asked, wiping a tear from her eye before her face turned sour once again. 'Follow him where? We're not going anywhere, in case you hadn't noticed.'

'You know what I'm saying,' Rune replied coldly, visibly holding his temper in check.

'Peace, Ulfhild,' Haesten murmured, fearing his wife would push the jarls into open mutiny.

'Come outside, my lord,' Rune said, and his tone now was less confrontational. He tilted his head and held his arm out to the tent's opening. 'Please.'

For a moment, Haesten felt panic, his throat tightening and an icy chill rushing up his forearms. He stared at Rune, wondering if he should draw his sword, fearing his time – and that of his wife and children – had come. His warriors were going to slaughter them and surrender to the Saxons!

But Rune Eriksson's face was not murderous. If anything, he looked a little confused as he tried to make sense of Haesten's expression.

The king pushed himself to his feet, using the arms of his chair to help his aching knees and doing his best not to groan or curse. 'What would you have me see?' he asked.

'Come,' Rune said, gesturing again, then adding 'lord' in a respectful tone, as if he'd sensed Haesten's trepidation.

'Remain here,' the king said, turning to Ulfhild and nodding towards their sons. She opened her mouth to protest but changed her mind at the dark look he threw her. It would not do to undermine him at this crucial moment, said his expression, not when his men were already losing respect for his leadership. If he could not even control his wife, why should any proud *vikingar* do his bidding?

Meeting the gazes of the dozen or so jarls and hersirs that had crammed into his tent, Haesten walked proudly past them, shading his eyes from the pale sunlight that assailed him as soon as he stepped outside. He shivered, unable to help himself, for his tent was kept warm at all hours of the day by his servants and it was bitterly, shockingly cold despite the sunshine.

He pulled his heavy fur-trimmed cloak around his neck and cursed under his breath at this annoying intrusion. Damn Rune Eriksson to Hel, no man should be out on a day like this unless he had a job that needed done!

'Have you walked around the camp recently?' Rune asked, following him out of the tent, the other noble Danes at his back.

Haesten hesitated. In truth, he had barely left his tent lately. It was not just his knees that troubled him – most of his ageing body ached nowadays, and the cold and rain made it much worse than it had been in summer. Since there was nothing else to do, the king had taken to lying abed most of the day, listening to his skald telling tales or playing hnefatafl with Ulfhild and his sons. The servants kept them all fed, and there had not been much of a shortage of mead and ale – at least, not within Haesten's tent.

Of course, Ulfhild and the boys went abroad during the days, taking what exercise they could, but his wife had not said much about how things stood in the camp.

He realised now that she'd been hiding things from him, and what he saw shocked him.

Rune had not waited for him to answer the question, instead walking across to point down at a middle-aged, grey-haired *vikingr* who was lying listlessly just a short way from the king's own tent. Haesten looked at the man, not recognising him, but astonished at just how skinny he was. There seemed to be absolutely no fat or muscle on him. He was little more than a collection of bones held together by skin. The man did not even look up at them although his heavy, rasping breaths told Haesten that he was still alive. After a fashion at least.

When the initial shock at the man's appearance faded, Haesten mentally shrugged. Let him die. It was one less mouth to feed.

Then, as he followed Rune past the rest of the tents – large ones, small ones, and others only big enough to cover a single person – Haesten realised that everyone they saw was little more than skin and bone. He gaped at these people, feeling totally out of place standing there, practically as well-fed as ever.

He saw fear in his people's eyes. Fear, and hatred which bordered on murderous as they took in his fleshy body. Well, fleshy compared to them which was telling, as old age had robbed Haesten of most of his own muscle tone yet he seemed like Þórr in comparison to the emaciated wraiths that now populated his camp.

Rune was watching him for his reaction, but he was not sure what to say or do. To admit he was oblivious to this suffering would make him look like a doddering old fool, not the mighty warlord he'd played for decades. And besides, by Óðinn's hairy arse crack, what did Rune expect him to do? Share his own food with everyone in the camp? If Haesten did that he would starve too, and he could scarce afford to lose any more weight.

'What would you have me do?' he demanded, looking from Rune to the rest of the lordly Danes, hollow-cheeked and gaunt. 'I can't magic food out of my arse, and to surrender to the Saxons would mean my death. Yours too, probably. I doubt our enemies will be merciful to any of my commanders.'

'We must do what we should have done weeks ago,' Rune growled. 'Before we became walking skeletons.'

Haesten felt a sudden pang of fear as he saw the grim determination in his captain's stare. Rune Eriksson was not suggesting they surrender.

'We must leave the safety of our earthen walls,' said the jarl to murmurs of agreement from the others encircling Haesten. 'We must break out of here and attack the Saxons. I would rather die like a warrior, with axe in hand, than waste away like a coward.'

Haesten had never felt so old. When he was younger he'd have felt only excitement and perhaps a little trepidation over the prospect of another battle – now, he felt like his legs might give way and shame him in front of everyone. What could he do though, other than agree to his men's demand?

Taking a long moment to steady himself he nodded at last. 'Let it be so,' he said, and his voice came out as little more than a croak. 'Prepare your warriors. We will leave at first light on the morrow—'

'Our men are already packed and ready to move,' Rune replied coolly. 'There is no need to wait any longer, allowing more of our people to succumb to starvation during the night.'

Haesten's anger flared as he understood now what was happening; what had been happening behind his back. Rune Eriksson and these others had made preparations to leave the camp, regardless of Haesten's opinion. He knew that if he tried to stand against them it would be the end of him, and not just as king.

He forced a grin, praying to Óðinn that it would not appear as a terrified grimace. 'Yes,' he agreed, nodding. 'It is time to leave. Let us see how confident these Saxon sheep-humpers feel when they see our army bearing down on them.'

With satisfied grunts, the jarls and hersirs turned and hurried away to join their men. Rune Eriksson remained there for a short time longer, simply gazing at Haesten. He appeared disappointed in the old king but said nothing and eventually walked off, leaving Haesten standing by himself.

When Haesten spun to head back to his tent he looked down at the emaciated middle-aged *vikingr* lying on the ground and fearfully made a sign to ward off evil. Sometimes an omen was difficult to read, requiring a völva to interpret. This one was unmistakeable, and heavy with portent, however, for the man was dead.

CHAPTER TWENTY-EIGHT

'What's going on?' There was a distinct note of alarm in Ethelhelm's voice as he ran to Edward's command tent, pulling on his helmet and buckling it securely in place as he came. 'What's all the commotion?'

'Something's happening in the Danes' camp,' Edward replied. He was already dressed for battle, just as he was every day, although he had not yet lifted his spear or shield. 'Whatever it is, we'll find out soon enough.'

Ethelhelm smiled. 'The bastards must be about to surrender,' he crowed. 'At bloody last!'

Ealdorman Aethelred joined them, also appearing pleased. 'We can go home then,' he said. 'And finally spend a night in a real bed, in a real hall! Praise be to Christ and all the saints.'

Edward stood in silence, not sharing his comrades' optimism. If Haesten wanted to surrender why hadn't he just come to the wall and shouted his terms across to the waiting Saxons? Or come out through the gap in those walls that had remained stubbornly filled with logs and rubble for weeks? Instead, the guards posted to keep an eye on, and patrol the perimeter of the enemy encampment had come to report the sounds of movement within. A lot of movement.

Edward thought about it. Perhaps Haesten's people were simply making ready to move, knowing the Saxons wouldn't allow them to remain camped there once the Northmen's commanders were taken prisoner. That made sense. And besides, considering the squalid conditions that must prevail inside the walls, it would be no surprise if the inhabitants were desperate to get out as quickly as possible if they knew they'd be granted safe passage.

'We just need to wait on Haesten coming to parley with us then,' said Ethelhelm.

'Parley?' Aethelnoth asked, joining them with a raised eyebrow and a sardonic smile. 'If by "parley" you mean "be blood-eagled" then yes, let's do the deal!'

They laughed darkly and Edward couldn't help joining in. He'd been waiting for this day – for the chance to avenge Diuma. It seemed he was about to get his chance, and without anyone else's blood being spilled. A good result, all things considered.

Still, Edward had dealt with the sea-wolves enough, and heard so much about their nature, that he would take nothing for granted.

'Ready the men for battle,' he said to Dunstan who'd just come into the tent. 'Full armour.'

'Battle?' Ethelhelm demanded, still chuckling away to himself as Dunstan disappeared again. 'What kind of battle could they possibly hope to fight? They'll be starving, without energy or confidence in their leaders.'

'Exactly,' growled Edward. 'They'll be desperate. There's not much more dangerous than a cornered beast, my lord Ethelhelm. I suggest we prepare for anything.'

'He's probably right,' Aethelred agreed with a sigh, straining up on his tiptoes to try and see if anything was happening atop the enemy's walls. 'Only a fool tries to predict how a sea-wolf will think. A wise man would surrender to us in Haesten's situation, and save the skin of his family and followers, but Haesten is not wise, I think.'

Edward nodded. 'There's a chance they'll come spilling out of that camp in all directions, fleeing for their lives. It's possible they won't trust us to spare them even if Haesten was to surrender. Maybe if my father was here, but none of us have his charitable reputation.'

Aethelnoth spat on the grass. 'Even Alfred has grown wise to the likes of Haesten. Perhaps he would not let the Danes off freely either.'

'Better get ready then,' Edward suggested, and the other ealdormen nodded, grasping wrists with him and wishing him luck before they went off to prepare for whatever the day might bring.

It was late afternoon by the time the first Dane appeared on top of the wall, his head turning from one side of Edward's shieldwall to the other.

'Ready, lads!' called the aetheling to his fyrd. The gap in the enemy walls which was supposed to be an entrance had still not been unblocked. It was as filled with rubbish as before, offering no way in or out. If the Danes truly were planning to make a run for it, they would not be going in that direction.

Edward had taken this side of the camp, while Aethelred, Aethelnoth, and Ethelhelm had taken their detachments to the other three walls, effectively sealing in the Northmen. It would be dark soon, and Edward wondered if that was Haesten's plan – to wait for nightfall, and then come streaming over the walls, running for safety while the Saxons blundered about in the blackness looking for them.

It was hardly a sophisticated plan, and many Danes would be hunted down in the process despite the dark, but it was probably the best option available to the enemy warlord. It was what Edward would do, he thought. Command his troops to run as fast and hard as they could, evading conflict if possible, and meet up again at some prearranged spot far from the Saxon army.

'Keep your eyes open, lads!' Dunstan shouted and his voice carried effortlessly for an expectant silence, heavy and oppressive, had fallen across the land. 'They'll make a run for it, but don't let 'em! Kill as many of the bastards as you can, or they'll just come back to haunt us another day!'

One of the men pointed, calling on him to turn and look at the earthen ramparts. The thane spun, seeing more Danes appearing there, and grinned savagely. 'The siege is coming to an end now,' he said to Edward. 'And we'll be home soon enough.'

Edward smiled at that but his thoughts quickly returned to the present for Haesten's men continued to fill their walls until a great mass of Northmen stood looking out upon the Saxons.

'Shit,' Edward muttered, trying to count them but giving up. He'd had a good idea of how many were in the camp, but seeing them like that, all gathered together, was quite a daunting sight. 'Remember, they've barely eaten for days,' he shouted, bolstering his own courage as much as his troops'. 'They're starving, terrified, and desperate to escape from us. Easy pickings, lads!'

'Here they come!' Dunstan bellowed and Edward raised his shield, feeling it touch the one to his left, and then the one on his right locked into position too. He took a deep breath, trying to calm himself, but the blood was thundering in his veins and he was muttering a prayer, begging God to protect him and those in the line with him.

He could see the Danes were carrying their weapons and knew now that he'd misjudged them. If they were hoping to simply run for safety, they would have waited until it was darker, but they would also not be carrying spears and shields. Such heavy armaments could only slow a runner down.

They were not going to make a break for it. They were going to fight.

'Loose!' The call went out, all along the line as the Danes slithered down the earthen walls, on their backsides, or doing their best to stay upright although many of them fell or rolled, landing hard on the ground just in time to receive the volley of spears that Edward's fyrd had thrown.

Screams and cries of rage went up as the missiles thundered down, tearing into flesh and shattering bones. There would be no let-up though, and Edward repeated the command, 'Loose!'

The Danes who'd survived the initial onslaught were running towards the Saxon shieldwall, but the next round of spears came down like a black rain, hammering into the ground and into bodies, a maelstrom of horror and death.

Still, the desperate *vikingar* charged forward, closing the distance to Edward's men with surprising speed. The third round of spears was thrown, and then the Danes slammed into the Saxon line and Edward was pushed backwards, off balance. A thrill of terror coursed through him, the face of a battle-crazed Northman filling his vision, but then the men behind the aetheling pushed back, holding him up. He regained his footing and thrust his spear out, into the belly of the cursing Dane.

The enemy soldier fell away, disappearing beneath the feet of his own comrades and an axe smashed one of the boards of Edward's shield, forcing him to adjust his arm. Momentarily defenceless, he breathed another desperate prayer to God Almighty and it was answered, one of the men flanking him thrusting his spear into the axeman's neck. Blood gouted, covering Edward's helmet and face.

Everything became a blur after that, as the young commander tried to survive. At last the front line moved back, allowing those behind, fresh and eager, to move into their position and Edward stumbled away to rest for a moment on the ground. His arms and legs ached and a great flap of skin had been ripped open on his forearm. It was bleeding heavily and he used his seax to tear a piece of cloth from his breeches, binding it tightly around the wound.

When he'd caught his breath he climbed back to his feet and tried his best to make sense of what was happening on the battlefield. He was amazed to see Danes still – still! – trickling down from their rough walls. How many of them had there been in that damn camp he wondered? Thousands!

How many had the Saxons killed? Not enough, he thought, and, grinning encouragingly at others who'd fallen back at the same time as him, he went to rejoin the rear ranks of the shieldwall.

The Danes were not beaten yet. Until they were, the butchery must go on.

CHAPTER TWENTY-NINE

AD 895, Wintanceaster

Wulfric stroked his stubbled chin as he watched Alfred pace backwards and forwards, leaving a track in the soft grass. The ealdorman knew his king better than any man alive, had seen Alfred anxious and upset before, but there was a new, strange gleam in his eye now, one Wulfric could not remember seeing before. It was an indication of the stress they were all under, having faced so many enemies, on so many fronts. So much was at stake, and, although the news from the north was good, Alfred clearly wasn't sure he'd done enough for his kingdom to withstand this sustained invasion by the Northmen.

Word had come from Edward that Haesten's starving army had attempted to defeat the combined Saxon army in battle, much to everyone's surprise. The missive sent by the Mercian had described a brutal fight in Botingtvne, with the Danes charging out from their walls – which they'd climbed down from apparently! – and throwing themselves with insane abandon into the fray. Despite the fact Edward, Aethelred, Ethelhelm, and Aethelnoth's fyrds outnumbered them with fresh, well-fed troops, the Northmen had shown tremendous courage as they'd traded blows with the Saxons.

Their bravery had availed them little though, as the besieging warriors of Wessex, along with their Mercian and Wealas allies, easily repulsed the Danes' charge. Edward reported few casualties for the allies, God be praised, while their heathen enemies were slaughtered by the hundreds.

It was, it had to be admitted, a stunning, crushing defeat for the Danes.

With all that said, however, Edward's message admitted that many of their foes did escape into the surrounding woods to fight another day.

Infuriatingly, Haesten had been one of those to escape.

'What of that crazy Valkyrie wife of his?' Wulfric asked as Alfred read Edward's report.

'They didn't find her body amongst the dead,' Alfred said, eyes scanning the parchment distractedly. 'But they did find Haesten's two sons.' He broke off and looked at his captain, a heavy, sorrowful sigh escaping his lips as he took in those dark tidings. 'Damn it,' he muttered, shaking his head and making the sign of the cross. 'They were good children. I'd hoped they might grow up differently to their warlike parents. Now we'll never know what they might have been.'

Along with Wulfric, Ealhswith, Asser, and John the Old Saxon were gathered around the king, with a handful of other noblemen. All shared worried glances, wondering what Alfred was thinking. Wessex had survived thus far, but with Haesten still alive, and so many Danes still populating East Anglia, eastern Mercia, Northumbria, and even parts of Wessex, would the kingdom remain safe for much longer? It was a question Wulfric had heard his peers discussing often during the winter, although they were always sure to do it when Alfred wasn't in earshot. The king did not take kindly to such defeatist talk, forever exhorting his men to place their faith in God and look to Him for support when their fears threatened to overwhelm them.

Of course, Wulfric could hardly blame the thanes for questioning how the war was progressing. It was only natural. Even someone like Wulfric, who'd seen many raids by the Northmen over the years, could tell this latest invasion was different. Wessex had a system of burhs mostly in place, and a standing army where no such thing existed during the raids by the likes of Halfdan and Guthrum, yet, even so, the sheer number of enemies was proving difficult to deal with this time. Even when the end seemed in sight as it had done during the winter, Haesten somehow escaped Botingtvne with a large number of his warriors, and the war rumbled on.

And, despite the fact Haesten was an elderly man, he'd turned out to be every bit as vicious as his predecessors. Even more so, for even Guthrum and Halfdan had never blood-eagled an ealdorman!

'I should have killed him when I had the chance,' Alfred was muttering, drawing murmurs of surprised agreement from his noblemen. 'But I couldn't.' He went on, talking to himself rather than the audience he seemed not to have even noticed. 'He was safely camped inside Middletun and we didn't have time for a long siege.' He shook his head, continuing to pace back and forwards, sometimes running a hand through his shoulder-length hair, other times convulsively grasping the handle of his sword as if he wished to draw it from its scabbard and use it to cut down his distant enemy counterpart.

'You dealt with Haesten the only way you could, lord,' said Asser, but his support for the king brought more than a few black looks for the monk was not universally popular. He was seen as rather sycophantic towards the king, and somewhat symbolic of Alfred's hated educational reforms amongst the thanes, who still resented being forced to read and write.

'Exactly,' Wulfric growled, meeting the eyes of those who had glared at Asser. None dared give him such a disrespectful look. 'Halting Haesten allowed us to deal with the other sea-wolf armies. We could still be besieging Middletun today if we hadn't parleyed with him. How you dealt with Haesten cannot be questioned,' he stated firmly, leaving no room for any argument. 'The only question is what the hell we do now.'

'He is the key,' Alfred said, finally giving up his pacing and turning to look at Wulfric. 'Haesten is their king, and the key to the gate that would shut the Northmen out of Wessex for good.'

Wulfric nodded, noticing others amongst the group doing the same. Any who'd met Haesten had been struck by his charisma and the loyalty he inspired in his followers.

'We must kill him,' said Asser, pursing his lips and shrugging.

'By God's hairy arse, that's what we've been trying to do for months!' a young thane noted gloomily. 'It's easier said than done, brother.'

'He's right, though,' said John the Old Saxon. 'If we could somehow get close enough to Haesten, and send him on his way to Valhöll, there's a good chance many of the *vikingar* would sail abroad, to look for easier plunder.'

'The old bastard is surrounded by his household guard at all times,' Wulfric said. 'And that warrior-woman he's married to. It would take a miracle for one of our men to get close enough to kill him, never mind carry out the attack successfully.'

'By Christ, he's an old man!' Alfred grated, kicking a pine cone that was lying on the grass beside him and sending it flying. 'Why hasn't he settled down?'

'Maybe he's never found anywhere he wanted to so do,' Ealhswith suggested.

'You could be right, my lady,' an old ealdorman said. 'Perhaps, if some nice lands were offered to him, he'd decide it might be time to settle down after all.'

'Where?' Asser wondered. 'Not in Wessex, surely?'

'Mercia?' the ealdorman suggested. 'We offer Haesten lands in Mercia. Tell him of our previous alliance with Guthrum and how that benefited both parties over the years.'

Wulfric thought about that. Much of Mercia was already in the hands of the Danes, as was the rest of the eastern side of the country. If it meant an end to the current war, it would be acceptable to give away some more land to Haesten, would it not?

The other advisors agreed that this was a good plan, but Alfred didn't like it.

'I can't ask anyone else to visit Haesten,' he said, shaking his head firmly. 'Not after what he did to Diuma. Absolutely not, it's too risky.'

'You must,' argued the ealdorman whose idea it had been, and it was clear he had a great deal of support. 'We've tried everything else, lord. Haesten will return soon enough, and every Dane in Wessex will flock to his banner! We know there's at least one other army in or near Wessex, led by Sigeferth of Northumbria. If they join Haesten...' He shook his head in despair. 'We can't let that happen, my king. This is our last resort.'

His gloomy words struck Alfred deeply, Wulfric could see, for they were true. Despite beating Haesten at Botingtvne, Wessex remained in dire peril.

'Haesten's army has scattered for now,' Ealhswith noted. 'But he'll likely end up in East Anglia, since it's always proved a safe haven for the sea-wolves. Who would take our offer to him there? Especially after what he did to Diuma and those other poor men.'

'I'll go.'

There were murmurs of surprise that anyone should volunteer for such a dangerous mission, and at who it was that had spoken out.

'Are you up to it?' Wulfric asked, not at all shocked that John the Old Saxon would offer to perform this important task. The abbot might be elderly, but he'd been a warrior in his youth and retained the hard core that was drilled into him throughout those formative years. Still, he'd almost been killed just a few years before in Athelney Abbey, and such a vicious attack would inevitably leave scars, both mental and physical.

'God will sustain me,' John said and, although his words were of the pious type someone like Asser would use, there was a twinkle in his eye that told Wulfric he'd be ready for any trouble. Just as he'd been that night when the would-be murderers had accosted him in his abbey.

'I don't like this plan, John, but thank you,' Alfred said resignedly. 'Although I'll miss you saying Mass for us. You can't go alone, however. It's much too dangerous. I'll send half a dozen guards with you. Who will lead them though?'

'I'll do it.'

Alfred blinked as if amazed, but it was Ealhswith who spoke up.

'You, Wulfric? You'd leave your king's side after all these years?' Her tone was light and it was clear she was speaking partly in jest, but it was a fair question. It seemed astonishing that the ealdorman, Alfred's closest advisor and hearth-warrior, would go off in the middle of a war to perform some other mission.

'The king has you to take care of him,' Wulfric said. 'You might not be as big, or as ugly as I am, but you're as formidable as any man in the kingdom. You'll do as his bodyguard until I return from Haesten.'

Ealhswith laughed. 'Fair enough, I'll do my best.'

Wulfric turned then to Alfred, knowing he should explain himself to the king as well. 'It's a long time since I last went on a mission like this,' he said. 'I miss the excitement, and I'm not getting any younger. I'd like to do this before the war ends and we all settle down to a blissful life of peace.'

It seemed to him that Alfred might refuse his request − a younger soldier might be better placed to carry out the job of protecting the abbot − but after a moment the king shrugged and said, 'All right, it's settled then. Choose a handful of men to take with you, Wulfric, and get some supplies packed for the road.'

'We'll leave on the morrow, lord,' John said to Alfred, and he was smiling as if looking forward to the journey. Like it was to be a pleasure trip, rather than a visit to the proverbial lion's den.

The meeting broke up then, with the thanes and ealdormen returning to the hall to discuss what had been agreed over mugs of ale. It seemed they were all happy enough to continue holding their burhs against the threat of the Danes as they had been while Wulfric and John went to broker peace with the enemy king. What else could be done? At least this plan offered a small chance of ending the war without too much more bloodshed.

'Are you sure about this?' Alfred asked once he and Wulfric were the only two left. His voice was stern, and he did not look happy.

'I like John,' Wulfric said almost defensively. 'I wouldn't want to see him get hurt by that degenerate old dog Haesten.'

'If Haesten decides to kill him, you won't be able to do a thing about it,' Alfred argued. 'He'll just kill you too.'

'I've had a good, long life,' the ealdorman said. 'Longer than most warriors.'

Alfred's brow furrowed. 'So you'd just throw it away now?'

'I'm not throwing it away,' Wulfric protested. 'Someone has to escort John, and I'm as good as any man for the job. Better, since Haesten knows me. We did meet at Middletun, remember. The fact you've sent me, your own captain, as part of the negotiating party will only prove to him how important you think this is. My presence will make it more likely he'll bargain with us.'

Alfred still seemed unconvinced.

'There's just as much chance of me being killed at your side as there is going to speak with Haesten,' Wulfric said. 'Standing next to you in a shieldwall is probably the most dangerous place in Wessex, Alfred! The Danes don't like you very much, in case you hadn't noticed.'

They laughed but there was a distinct feeling of melancholy as they stood and looked at the peaceful town around them.

'It's been my job to stand beside you in war and in peacetime for, well, more years than I like to remember,' Wulfric said, with a rueful smile. 'Maybe it's time for a younger man to take on that mantle.'

Alfred gazed at him. 'What's brought this on, old friend?' he asked with genuine concern. 'This isn't like you.'

'I'm not sure myself,' Wulfric admitted softly. 'I just felt like going with John would be the right thing to do. We're all getting older, and I have a good ten years on you. Maybe I'm tired of fighting, and see this as a chance to bring peace to Wessex at last.' He shook his head, unable to untangle his own emotions at that point and hoping understanding would come as they rode to find Haesten. 'I think I'm feeling like Guthrum did when he decided to stop raiding and settle down. Like we're hoping Haesten will feel when your proposal of alliance is put to him.'

Alfred nodded, staring out, unseeing, into the middle distance. 'Fighting always seemed like a waste of energy and resources to me,' he murmured, before chuckling. 'I mean, of course, I enjoyed it when we routed the likes of Halfdan. I still do! God, there's not much gets the blood pumping like spearing a Dane in the middle of a battle.' His enthusiasm faded and he patted Wulfric on the arm. 'You're right though, as usual. It seems more futile as the years go by, and we bury more and more of our young men while the Danes continue to return year after year. You go to Haesten, Wulfric. Go with John, and persuade our enemies that making peace will be more beneficial to them than having their people slaughtered here in a foreign land.'

Wulfric grinned. The thought of him being a peace envoy was quite amusing. It would be the abbot, John the Old Saxon, doing the negotiating however, not Wulfric, who would simply be there as protection against bandits on the road and, as he'd said, to show Haesten how important Alfred saw this mission.

'Just promise me one thing though,' the king said, deadly serious again.

'Of course, lord. Name it.'

'No matter what happens, Wulfric, you make it back here safely. Even if Haesten agrees to peace, there'll be another Dane along soon enough to make trouble and I want you by my side for it, as always. All right?'

Wulfric smiled, nodding, truly happy to know that the king – his friend – still valued him so highly despite the fact he was pushing sixty winters by this point.

'All right,' he promised. 'I'll return, Alfred, count on it. Just make sure you do your part though, and don't let anyone kill you while I'm away.'

'Kill me? Not a chance. I'll have Ealhswith here to look after me.'

'Aye, I suppose so,' Wulfric said, looking to the west, where the queen consort was standing with Asser, chatting quietly. The sight did give him some comfort, for Ealhswith was strong, tough, and courageous. Looking at her, however, Wulfric could not help but remember her as the young girl who'd married Alfred. The earlier melancholy returned as he thought of all the years that had passed them by, and all the things that the people of Wessex had endured in that time.

It was a rare thing for Wulfric to grow maudlin. He hoped it would not last long, for it was an unpleasant feeling.

'Come on,' said Alfred, reading his thoughts. 'Let's get a drink. It'll be the last one we share together for some time.'

CHAPTER THIRTY

Wulfric had been quite happy to leave Wintanceaster with John the Old Saxon. Although both men enjoyed a good feast, it seemed they'd done nothing but drink and eat in recent weeks. First there was the usual Christmas revelry, and then honouring Diuma's memory and sacrifice, and then, just before they left the royal town, word had come that Alfred and Ealhswith had become grandparents again. Edward's wife, Ecgwynn, had given birth to a healthy son named Aethelstan and, of course, that meant more days of feasting.

Wulfric looked down at his belly and smiled bleakly.

'What are you smirking about?' John asked. They were riding northeast and it was a dry, overcast day. Good weather for travelling, as long as the clouds that had been gathering all morning did not decide to open.

'I was just thinking,' Wulfric replied. 'If we'd remained in Wintanceaster any longer my horse wouldn't have been able to carry me.' He patted his stomach ruefully. 'I had to add another notch to my sword-belt!'

John nodded grimly. 'Fear not,' he said. 'A few days on the road will see the fat dropping off you. We can spar every day if you're willing. I could do with the practice.' He trailed off and Wulfric guessed he was having second thoughts about meeting Haesten.

They had no idea what the ancient warlord would be like when they met him, having been chased the width of the country more than once since he'd landed there with expectations of a season's easy plundering. The people of Wessex had lost many of their most beloved sons and daughters during the conflict, but so had the Danes. Haesten's own children had died, by God. There was every chance he'd simply murder Wulfric, John, and the dozen guards that accompanied them on this trip, especially with Ulfhild still alive. Even if Haesten had not been a particularly caring father, not seeming bothered in the slightest when the Saxons captured his boys, Ulfhild undoubtedly thought the world of them. She would be beside herself with grief to lose them, and that could mean bad news for Alfred's emissaries when they finally located the wandering enemy king.

'Yes,' said Wulfric. 'We should spar.' He wanted to be in the best shape possible to meet Haesten. If the Northman tried to do to him what he'd done to Diuma, Wulfric would make things as hard as possible for the old prick.

The journey proved to be extremely pleasant for both Wulfric and John. With their dozen guards – good, strong men, hand-picked by the ealdorman himself – they had no fears of being accosted by bandits. The weather remained mild for February too, and the horses made good time on the hard roads. By the fifth day they were within East Anglia, passing settlements populated with as many Danes as Anglo-Saxons, the two peoples seemingly living harmoniously enough.

Wulfric had not been in those lands for a few years, and he was struck by the change. It showed that people could co-exist, even when they'd been hated enemies not so long before. Still, the hierarchy was clearly in favour of the Danes – they were the ruling class and had been since before the days of Guthrum. Wulfric would not like to see Wessex going the same way, although it did reassure him somewhat that the common folk at least would be left alone even if Haesten eventually won the war against Alfred's forces.

'Where should we begin looking for the enemy warlord?' the commander of their guards asked as they journeyed deeper into East Anglian territory. 'He could be anywhere.'

Wulfric nodded. 'Aye, he could. He might not even be anywhere near here. The only intelligence we'd received by the time we left Wintanceaster suggested the remnants of Haesten's army had retreated east. For all we know, they could have sought solace in Northumbria, or even found ships and buggered off back to Francia.' He laughed humourlessly. 'If only.'

'We'll head for Hædleage,' John said to the guard.

'Guthrum's old capital,' Wulfric put in.

'Seems as likely a place as any for Haesten to seek sanctuary.'

'Or at least to find out where he is,' agreed Wulfric. 'Guthrum's son, Eohric, rules there now and his alliance with Wessex still holds firmly enough. Ostensibly, at least, even if the bastard has surely been supplying Haesten with men and materiel during this war!'

'Once a *vikingr*, always a *vikingr*,' John agreed dourly. 'But we should be safe enough in Hædleage. Eohric will not want to openly break the alliance with Alfred.'

'He's not a bad sort anyway,' Wulfric noted with a rueful smile. 'As sea-wolves go.'

The guard's mind set somewhat at ease, he returned to his position just behind the two noblemen, allowing them to take point as they passed the pleasant little towns and villages that, before the great heathen army had arrived almost thirty years before, had once been ruled by Christian kings.

They were watched suspiciously by the locals, but not challenged – their arms, helms, and quality armour, not to mention the horses they rode, marked them as men of power and influence, not folk to be troubled without good reason. Bothering the likes of Wulfric could mean a premature death; that was something everyone learned at an early age whether they hailed from East Anglia, Wessex, or even in the Danes' homelands. On top of that, Wulfric's party carried good silver, so the merchants and alehouse keepers along the road were more than happy to furnish them with food, drink, and even beds for the night in the larger settlements.

Considering he'd told Alfred he was bored with living the easy life at court, hence his volunteering for this mission, Wulfric did not think the journey had been a hardship at all so far. Still, he was not feasting any longer, and his nightly sparring sessions with John the Old Saxon and their guards had served to harden his muscles and firm his belly again. He was not quite the lean fighting machine he'd been when he first swore to serve Alfred decades before, but, for his age, Wulfric still cut an imposing figure and could defeat even their guard commander who was a renowned swordsman in his own right.

Hædleage was not too far from the border with Wessex and, on the afternoon of the sixth day, they reached the town.

Wulfric led them to the large mead hall that had been built by Guthrum and now served as King Eohric's home.

John the Old Saxon looked up at the building, admiring its size and quality of craftsmanship. 'Impressive,' he murmured, nodding approvingly. 'They always were master woodworkers. Their homes and halls are as finely put together as their longships.'

Wulfric could only agree. He'd seen the mead hall before, but it had been extended and upgraded since his previous visits, and it seemed Eohric's carpenters were as skilled as his father's had been. The hall was sturdily built in the Norse style: rectangular, with a crest running the length of the roof, while the main entrance was framed by a beautifully carved portal.

Word of their arrival in town had preceded them, and stablehands were there to take their horses before the men guarding the hall door ushered them inside. Eohric was waiting for them along with two dozen of his hearth-warriors.

'My lords, come in, join us!' The King of East Anglia stood up to welcome them respectfully enough although Wulfric detected something in his tone that suggested his greeting was not as freely given as it might have been. 'I am always happy to receive Alfred's captain into my hall. Eat and drink, my friends. You will be tired from your journey.' He waved a hand at the servants who were already bringing refreshments for the newcomers. 'Sit and rest,' the king said to Wulfric and his companions. 'You can tell me the purpose of your visit once your bellies are full.'

Wulfric thanked him, pleased to discover Eohric's cooks were just as skilled as his carpenters, for the beef broth set down before them was bursting with flavour and had almost as much meat in it as vegetables.

John the Old Saxon and the warriors who'd accompanied them there set about the food with relish, murmuring in pleasure as they tasted the broth, dipping fresh bread into it and tearing off great hunks with their teeth.

Wulfric shook his head, smiling to himself, knowing this simple but tasty repast would forever endear Eohric to his travelling companions. He wiped butter from his beard with the back of his hand and took a sip of the ale, finding it rich, dark and flavoursome, with no hint of the spices that were often added to mask a stale batch.

Looking around at the interior of the hall he could see the alliance with Wessex had proved good to the lords of East Anglia. The planks that formed the walls were in excellent repair, and Wulfric guessed no draughts wheezed through even in the wildest of winter storms. Hanging on those walls were weapons and shields of various design, some quite new, others clearly vintage, and all undoubtedly with some story or legend attached to them. There were tapestries too, depicting scenes from war or from the hunt. Wulfric judged some were imported from far-off, exotic lands, for their style was different to that of the Northmen.

The ealdorman's eyes moved from the building and its furnishings to the people who occupied it. Eohric's hearth-warriors were typical Danes – tall, well built, almost all sporting impressive beards of various hues, and every one with the appearance of battle-hardened veterans. They returned Wulfric's interested glances with good humour, eyes sparkling with mead, ale, and merriment, and the men of Wessex relaxed, feeling quite at ease within Hædleage's great hall.

Wulfric finished his broth, wiping the remnants from the bowl with another piece of buttered bread, sighing in contentment as another sip of the dark ale washed it all down. And then he froze, staring in astonishment at a pair of Danes who were seated at the bench next to Eohric's own.

'I see them,' John the Old Saxon muttered, as Wulfric surreptitiously tapped him on the forearm. 'Looks like your guess was a good one. Our journey's over already.'

Wulfric nodded, meeting the malevolent gaze of one of the Danes he'd marked and feeling a chill run down his spine at the sheer hatred he felt emanating from them.

'Isn't that—'

'Aye, it is,' John replied, cutting off their guard commander's surprised question. 'It seems Haesten and Ulfhild are guests of Eohric too. What a stroke of luck!'

'Lucky. Aye.' Wulfric nodded and supped his ale, feeling anything but lucky.

CHAPTER THIRTY-ONE

Although Haesten's army had been soundly beaten and no longer posed a great threat, another large force of Danes remained in Wessex, formed from the remnants of the various other warbands that had been raiding in the kingdom. Alfred's tactic of stealing or destroying their longships had left them with no way to escape. So they'd come together at Meresig, on the east coast, their army growing in size as stragglers from all over flocked to the banner of their leader, Sigeferth of Northumbria.

Alfred, pleased to have dealt with Haesten for now, knew that if the old warlord was to join with this swelling horde at Meresig the war would erupt once more and all the good work by the warriors of Wessex might be undone. So, although desperately feeling the loss of both Diuma and Wulfric at his side, the king commanded his son Edward, who was now responsible for the security of eastern Wessex, to march on Meresig.

Gathering more fyrds from the burhs and towns on his way there, Edward's army grew, and word soon reached the Danes.

Sending their families and baggage into East Anglia where they would be safe, Sigeferth and his soldiers, desperate to restore their reputations as proud *vikingar* after so many recent defeats in Wessex, chose not to escape with their women and children. Instead, using the few ships still in their possession, they sailed up the River Tamyse, towards Lundenburh, then turned north, following the River Lea, and set up camp at Herutford, neatly avoiding Edward's burgeoning force.

As usual, the sea-wolves fortified their position which was right in the very heart of Wessex and a direct threat to Alfred and Aethelred's newly expanded Lundenburh, an important trading centre.

Sigeferth and his men were not giving up the war just yet, not while their king, Haesten, still lived.

'What do the fools hope to achieve by overwintering at Herutford?' Ealhswith asked as Alfred explained the situation to her. 'We've defeated every army they've thrown at us so far. They must know by now that their numbers are too few to take control of Wessex, especially with the system of burhs in place.'

Although he'd always sought his wife's advice, recently he'd grown even more reliant on her counsel with Wulfric away travelling with John the Old Saxon.

'You're right,' he said, nodding at her insightful grasp of the situation. 'I'm sure Sigeferth knows he can be little more to us than an annoyance at this stage.'

'What does he want then?' Ealhswith muttered irritably, fed up, as everyone was, with the ongoing war that was now into its third year. 'Money?'

Alfred grunted agreement. 'Exactly. At least, that must be his ultimate goal. Camp at Herutford and cause as much trouble as possible. Their fortress is near the river, so it'll be much harder to besiege than their position was at Botingtvne.'

'And we'll be forced to pay them a wagon load of silver to leave,' Ealhswith said.

They sat in thoughtful silence, their dark thoughts contrasting with the beauty of the scene they were looking out over. Although Alfred would have liked to spend some time at his estate in Ceodre – where he and Ealhswith had enjoyed so many wonderful times, especially in the early years of their marriage – Wintanceaster continued to be their home. Its location near the centre of Wessex meant it was easier to travel should the Danes strike again. Alfred had instructed his gardeners to plant flowers like the ones which grew near the royal hall in Ceodre though, making a small part of that beloved place there in Wintanceaster. The sight and scent of the blooms lifted Alfred's heart and he stood up, looking into the pond that was near their favourite bench.

'Look,' he said, smiling and nodding downwards at the white, daisy-like flowers that were growing in the pond. 'The water-crowfoot are flowering already.'

'They're early this year,' said Ealhswith coming to take a look and grasping his hand. They enjoyed the sight, and the sounds of insects buzzing softly around the grounds, and the gardeners going about their business. 'So what are you going to do about Sigeferth and his army?'

She asked the question almost reluctantly, as if she hated ruining the peaceful moment, and Alfred turned to her, drawing her into a hug and kissing the top of her head. He wished that moment would extend out forever, so content was he, but the loud clatter of a gardener dropping his shovel on the other side of a hedge, and then cursing loudly, rather spoiled the happy moment.

'Sigeferth thinks we'll be tired of war, perhaps even afraid of another battle. His army are seasoned veterans after all, even if most of their fights have been at the likes of Exanceaster, Cisseceastre, and Botingtvne, where they lost.' He gave his wife a grim smile and they walked back to sit on the bench again, basking in the sunshine. 'I am tired of war,' he admitted. 'Heartily sick of it, by God. But, until it's over and Wessex is free of heathen raiders, I will not give in.'

Ealhswith gripped his hand, signalling her full agreement as he continued.

'I'll send word to the garrison at Lundenburh to march north and surround Sigeferth's position as best they can. Then I'll muster my fyrd and march to join them.' His voice grew hard. 'If Sigeferth thinks he'll simply be handed a fortune in silver without even needing to face us in battle, he's in for a nasty shock. I mean to destroy his army, and send out a message to every other sea-wolf with thoughts of attacking Wessex!'

There was another thump, and an even more blasphemous oath came through the hedge to them, coinciding with a heavy grey cloud slowly covering the sun and drastically lowering the temperature.

'Come, my love,' said the king, laughing and helping Ealhswith up.

'Where are we going?' she asked, sharing his humour at the hidden gardener's outburst.

'To see Asser,' Alfred replied. 'It's about to rain and the bishop has a new book to share with us.'

'Oh, how nice,' Ealhswith said. 'And while we're there, we can ask him to pray for the soul of that blaspheming gardener!'

—

Alfred's plan did not quite go as he'd intended. He mustered his fyrd and began the march to Herutford, a journey of almost one hundred miles. He was in no great hurry, having sent word ahead to the garrison in Lundenburh to contain Sigeferth's troops within their winter fortress. Ealdorman Aethelred had spent some time back in Mercia with Aethelflaed but, with the continuing troubles with the Danes, he'd returned to take command of Lundenburh. Alfred knew the garrison was in good hands, since his son-in-law had by now beaten the Danes in more than one battle over the years and was fresh from his victory beside Edward at Botingtvne.

With Edward returning to look after his lands in the east, Diuma dead, and Wulfric somewhere in East Anglia, Alfred trusted Aethelred as much as any of his other commanders and was looking forward to joining him at Herutford to finally put an end to the sea-wolves' years of bloody raiding.

The thunderhead that had spoiled his afternoon in the garden with Ealhswith had merely been the precursor to days of persistent spring rains, and the king's mood was grim as they covered the miles.

In Wulfric's absence Alfred had called on one of his most trusted warriors to act as captain – Aedan, the thane of Hrofescester. He was a familiar, comforting presence, still sporting a short, red beard and wearing his hair shaved in at the sides. He'd been a loyal hearth-warrior to Alfred, supporting him during his time on Athelney before becoming thane of Hrofescester. Having lost two fingers on his left hand fighting the Danes at Readingum, Aedan knew better than most what it meant to face their savagery in battle.

'You think we'll be able to starve the bastards?' asked the thane as their horses trotted along the sodden road towards Herutford. 'Like Aethelred and Edward did at Botingtvne?'

Alfred shrugged. 'Probably not. Sigeferth has chosen a better place for his fortress. We should be able to contain them there, however, until they get fed up and come out to face our shield-wall.'

Aedan chuckled menacingly, absent-mindedly massaging the knuckles of his missing fingers. 'I'm looking forward to that day,' he said. 'It's always good to slaughter Northmen. Bastards, the lot of them.'

'Indeed,' Alfred smiled, glad he'd brought this man back into his inner circle. Aedan came from Irish stock and had the wit those people were famous for, making him a fine travelling companion. He also had fine eyesight, and he lifted a hand to his forehead now, shading his eyes from the rain as best he could.

'A rider approaches,' he noted. 'No... four or five of them.'

Alfred spotted them too, wondering who they were. As the distance between them narrowed it became clear these riders were warriors, men clad in furs and wearing shields on their backs, helmets on their heads. Danes? Why so few?

'My lord!' The lead horseman called out to them, his shout needing repeating more than once as his words were lost in the rain.

'Not Danes then,' said Aedan, saying what Alfred was thinking. 'Messengers, most likely. From Aethelred?'

Alfred groaned inwardly. This scene seemed oddly familiar, as if he'd experienced it before. He had, of course, more than once, damn it! The demeanour of the riders was not triumphant. They'd not ridden out to meet Alfred with good tidings, that much was clear. He braced himself, wondering what the hell could have gone wrong now.

'The Danes must have attacked Aethelred's fyrd,' Aedan guessed. 'We've got here just in time if that's the case, or Sigeferth would have the freedom to sack Lundenburh!'

As it turned out, Aedan was wrong.

The riders galloped up to them and came to a halt. The horses were sweating, while the riders were wide-eyed but obviously relieved to have met the king.

'Well?' Alfred demanded, uncharacteristically rude but in no mood for niceties. 'What's wrong?'

'Danes...' the lead rider said then halted to take a breath, as if he'd run there on foot rather than on horseback.

'We already guessed that much,' Alfred prompted. 'Spit it out, man! Did they attack Aethelred's men?'

The rider turned and shared a look with the nearest of his companions before hesitantly replying. 'Er, not exactly, my lord.'

Alfred stared at him and then, as the realisation hit him, he rolled his eyes and stared up at the sky, screaming in his mind, Why do you test me so, lord?

'Ealdorman Aethelred attacked them,' the rider reported, confirming what Alfred had already surmised. The man went on hurriedly, defending Aethelred's tactics, describing why the king's son-in-law had thought it a wise course of action, but Alfred broke in.

'How bad is it?' he demanded.

Another rider spoke up, a heavyset, bald man, as the first turned away sheepishly beneath the withering gaze of Aedan.

'We lost a lot of men, my lord,' said the bald rider. 'And sadly sent very few of the sea-wolves to their graves.'

'Oh for fuck sake!' Alfred exploded, patience now entirely worn through. 'I told Aethelred simply to contain the enemy within their damned fortress!' He drew in a long breath, forcing himself to calm down. He had a sharp pain around his right temple, and he took off his helmet, bending in the saddle to massage the sore spot, telling himself all would be well and that his army would reinforce Aethelred's. The Danes would soon be vanquished, God willing. Then a sudden fear struck him. 'Is Aethelred alive?' he asked, looking up at the riders, knowing Aethelflaed would be devastated if her husband was killed.

'He is, lord,' said the first rider, eager to redeem himself in the king's eyes.

'But we lost four thanes during the battle, along with a great deal of spearmen and supplies.'

Alfred took that in. This was a disaster, and such a great victory would only embolden the Danes, perhaps even bringing more to join Sigeferth from other lands. And when Haesten heard word of his kinsmen's strong position at Herutford he would undoubtedly come to join them. If that was allowed to happen there was every chance Alfred would lose Wessex forever.

'Come,' he commanded, waving at the riders to fall into place beside him. 'We'll talk on the road, and you can fill me in properly. Let's get to Lundenburh and set about repairing the damage done to our plans.'

CHAPTER THIRTY-TWO

Aethelred was alive but ill by the time Alfred reached Lundenburh. The ealdorman had come down with some malady that confined him to his bed and made him throw up almost anything he swallowed. Barely a crust had passed his lips in two days when Alfred was ushered in to speak with him, and the sight of his pale, red-eyed son-in-law softened the king's heart. Aethelred had been guilty of overconfidence, that much was clear, but could anyone blame him? He'd successfully beaten Haesten after all – twice – and must have felt invincible by the time he came to face Sigeferth's army.

'What the hell are you doing lying around in bed?' Alfred asked as he saw the sickly ealdorman's eyes open and blearily focus on him. 'Lazy turd, come on! I need my best men by my side if we're to slaughter these Danes north of the city.'

Aethelred must have been relieved to hear such a jovial tone, but he seemed too weak even to muster a smile.

Alfred spent a few more moments in the room, reassuring the ealdorman that – although he'd made a monumental arse of things – he was forgiven, and would be welcomed back to the army as soon as he was over his illness. It was stifling in the chamber, however, and Alfred could not force himself to remain there for long; sickrooms always reminded him of his own recurring stomach ailment, which still pained him to that day. It stank too, even with the shutters flung wide open, and the king was glad to leave the room with as cheery a farewell as he could muster for his poorly son-in-law.

He met Aedan standing there waiting for him, and the thane informed him that another ealdorman, Ethelhelm, had arrived in the city. As the aetheling, Edward, was bringing his fyrd as well, it did not seem like Lundenburh would be in great, immediate danger.

'The crops will need harvested soon though,' Aedan noted, having spent the morning speaking with the local thanes who hadn't been killed in the recent battle. 'And the folk here are worried the Danes will do it first, burning everything that's left and leaving Lundenburh with nothing for the winter.'

Alfred swallowed, imagining the famine that scenario would bring. The numbers of people who would die. It did not bear thinking about and could not be allowed to happen.

'We can't simply attack Sigeferth,' he mused, standing back to allow a healer carrying a jug of clean, warm water and some cloths into Aethelred's bedchamber.

'No,' Aedan agreed. 'We've seen how that turns out. The whoreson has got his army dug in pretty deep and the fortress they've thrown up is formidable. If we had more men we could probably attack them.' He looked uncomfortable, then said almost apologetically, 'What about Aethelwold's fyrd? We could bring them here to join us.'

The king shook his head. He still feared the aetheling's machinations and wanted him kept out of the way, where he could not cause any mischief. Besides, Aethelwold's warriors might be needed if more Danes landed on the southeastern coast, which they would do if they knew it lay undefended.

Alfred concluded that the tactics Edward and Aethelred had used at Botingtvne would be the safest way to deal with Sigeferth's hordes. The terrain was different, especially with the proximity of the river, but not so much that the Danes could not be mostly confined to the area near their fortress.

The crops though, they would be the key. And Sigeferth would likely be coming to the same conclusion, if he had not already…

'Forget Aethelwold,' Alfred said to Aedan. 'Come on. We need to protect the harvest with as many men as we can spare.' He strode out of the hall, not even noticing the guards' salutes as they passed. 'I want guards set all day and night, with the promise of severe punishment for any found sleeping or pissing about.'

Alfred fell silent as they walked. There was something in the air, he could feel it. A sense of something momentous about to happen that summer. If Wulfric's mission with John the Old Saxon was successful, and they persuaded Haesten to put down his axe in favour of a life of ease in Mercia, then all Alfred had to do was send Sigeferth's heathen host to Valhöll and then... Wessex would be free. The burhs would continue to grow in strength and number, the fleet would expand, and, with the war won, surely no other Northmen would even attempt to raid there, never mind mount a full-on invasion.

He breathed deeply, taking in the wonderful scents and sounds of Lundenburh – cooking food, wood smoke, children laughing, dogs barking... It was a city worth fighting for, just as all the settlements in Wessex were. Alfred felt a great surge of pride that he'd been given the task of shepherding these people. So far, he'd mostly kept the Danes at bay, unlike the rulers of the neighbouring Anglo-Saxon kingdoms. Now, at last, Alfred would go one step further, defeating the enemy armies and finally – *finally!* – achieve his dream of uniting all the Anglo-Saxon people.

One banner, one kingdom, one country.

Ængleland.

—

Over the next few weeks Alfred's army, combined with the garrison at Lundenburh, camped around the fields of wheat, rye, oats, and barley that grew close to the Danes' fortifications at Herutford, making sure the enemy army did not try to damage the crops or steal them.

'It's a boring job, my lord,' one of the men said to Alfred when he asked how things were going. 'But much better than getting killed by one of those big bastards.'

The soldier grinned, black teeth glinting in the sunshine that had helped the crops grow throughout the summer. Alfred shared the man's laughter and clapped him on the back, thanking him for his service as he moved on to continue his rounds.

Aedan and his ealdormen did, of course, continuously patrol the army, making sure no enemies threatened and also that the Saxon troops remained alert at all times.

'The future of the whole kingdom rests on your shoulders,' Alfred had told his warriors after hearing them complain about standing guard 'over a bloody field all day'. He'd ordered the thanes and ealdormen to drill that mantra into the men for he truly believed it and wanted the army to believe it too. It would be all too easy for a man to rest his eyes one night and fall asleep, allowing Danes to sneak through to slaughter the rest of the sentries and set alight to the fields. Far-fetched perhaps, but the very least Alfred expected from his troops was to stay awake and alert.

Sigeferth's army had made a nuisance of themselves by sailing up and down the River Lea during the summer months attacking villages, although Alfred's men harried them constantly so there was no great damage ever done. The Danes did steal food supplies during those raids, but Alfred and his commanders all agreed that the enemy fortress was not large enough to store a full winter's supply for so many hungry warriors.

The Danes would need to find food during the winter months if they did not leave Herutford before the weather turned. It seemed Sigeferth had little inclination to sail away though, as he remained within his fortress, sometimes appearing to taunt the Saxons who patrolled near enough to hear him.

'He's still hoping we'll grow tired of him and pay him silver to leave,' Aedan growled as the sea-wolf appeared on his fortress wall to shout obscenities at Alfred's guards again.

'Either that,' the king agreed, 'or he's waiting for Haesten to reform his scattered army and sail here to join him.'

Aedan sucked his teeth, shaking his head at the very thought of that.

'John the Old Saxon is a wily fellow, though,' Alfred said, lip curling at the sight of Sigeferth debasing himself in the middle distance. Even Ubba Ragnarsson would not have behaved with such little class.

'You really think the old priest will persuade Haesten to form an alliance with us?' Aedan asked doubtfully.

Alfred nodded. 'Perhaps not an alliance like the one we enjoyed with Guthrum,' he admitted. 'But I'm hopeful peace will be agreed. Haesten must know he's done. He can't defeat our armies, as we've shown him, and he's an old, old man now. Giving him lands in Mercia must be preferable to us hunting him continually across the country. He has very few ships left, remember.'

The thane listened but his uncertain frown softened hardly at all. He stared at Sigeferth, as if fearing Haesten would choose to join the capering Dane on the nearby earthen wall rather than settling down to a life of peaceful obscurity in Mercia.

'Come, my friend,' Alfred said softly, smiling at his temporary captain. 'Today is Lammas.'

Aedan's face brightened instantly. 'The feast!'

'Indeed,' Alfred agreed, eyes shining with expectant pleasure. The first day of August marked the beginning of harvest. The first sheaves of wheat had already been taken to be ground up and baked into loaves which would be blessed in the church. Lammas was an ancient celebration that continued from pagan times into the present day and Alfred's people looked forward to it immensely. It was, essentially, another excuse for a feast, and few did feasts better than the queen consort.

'The Lady Ealhswith always puts on a good Lammas celebration,' Aedan noted, rubbing his belly in anticipation of the delights they'd enjoy later that day.

Alfred agreed happily. Not only did he have the feast to look forward to, but he would enjoy it with his wife by his side for the king had sent word for her to join him there in Lundenburh. The roads were as safe between there and Wintanceaster as they'd been in a long time and a large armed escort made sure Ealhswith arrived in good time and in one piece.

Even the sight of Sigeferth was not enough to dampen Alfred's spirits as he and Aedan headed back towards Lundenburh. Barrels of fresh ale, warm buttered bread that had been blessed by Asser himself, for he too had come from Wintanceaster to join the king and Ealhswith, would all make for a very pleasant Lammas feast. He suspected the Danes would not enjoy such a happy night, and their troubles would only grow worse as August's scorching heat faded into winter's icy embrace. That day seemed a long way off as the swishing of scythes and groaning of wagons filled the country air, but Alfred was forever noting how fast the time moved as he neared his fiftieth birthday.

Alfred thought then of Wulfric, wondering where the bluff ealdorman was, and how his mission was going. With any luck Wulfric would also be enjoying the harvest celebrations somewhere with John the Old Saxon, and the pair would safely return to Alfred's side long before the roads grew treacherous with frost and snow.

CHAPTER THIRTY-THREE

Wulfric and John had spent an uneasy night at Eohric's hall after noticing Haesten and Ulfhild were also there. Of course, it had been great luck to find them so easily – in the very first place they looked, too! – but the knowledge that the enemy king would not only be there with his wife made the West Saxon delegation somewhat nervous. Haesten's warriors would surely be somewhere nearby as well.

The West Saxons did not believe Eohric would forget the laws of hospitality, especially since Wulfric was well known to be Alfred's closest friend and advisor, but still... Eohric was a Dane, and one could never tell how the heathen lords would behave in a situation like that.

As it happened, Eohric was not feeling any more relaxed than Wulfric, judging by the constant dark looks he threw Haesten.

John the Old Saxon had also noted those glances and nudged Wulfric as he spotted Eohric casting yet another glare in Haesten's direction. 'Something tells me King Eohric is not too pleased about his other "royal" visitors.'

Wulfric gave a low grunt of agreement, hiding his face behind his upended mug as he surreptitiously watched their host. 'Can you blame him? He's a decent king but he's no Guthrum. What great battles has Eohric ever won? What fantastic raids has he led?' The ealdorman sipped his ale and set the mug down again, turning to look at John so they could converse in low tones without anyone overhearing. 'He's no mighty *vikingr* like his father. No skalds sing songs about his exploits.'

'As they do about Haesten,' John noted.

'Indeed.' Wulfric looked at Haesten, wondering how the Dane's recent defeats had affected him. The man appeared much more aged than he had when Wulfric first met him — more wrinkled, more stooped even when seated, and rather scrawnier. Yet Haesten must have some power, some strange charisma even in his advanced years, to be able to command the loyalty of so many men — not to mention a strong woman like Ulfhild who appeared as imposing and physically attractive as ever to Wulfric's searching eye.

He remembered what the pair had done to his friend, Diuma, and the complimentary thoughts were dashed from his mind, leaving only a wish for vengeance. It would give him great pleasure to call both of them out there and then, demand single combat, and dispatch them to the twisted, murderous afterlife their kind called Valhöll. Eohric might well agree to the request if Wulfric was to make it, for, as long as he was in East Anglia, Haesten might prove a threat to Eohric's rule. Usurping the throne of a fellow Dane would not be at all out of character for the grizzled old whoreson.

Unfortunately though, killing was not what Wulfric was there to do, and he forced himself to forget thoughts of battle and simply enjoy their host's hospitality.

And enjoy it they did, for the ale was potent and Wulfric found himself thoroughly enjoying the evening's entertainment. He even accepted a cup of mead from King Eohric's own hand and the pair, along with John the Old Saxon, ended up singing tunelessly along with some skald's battle song.

It was quite uncharacteristic of Wulfric and he berated himself for letting down his guard when he awoke the next day, John and their guards snoring loudly on the benches nearby. Of Haesten and his wife, and of Eohric too, there was no sign. Presumably they'd slept off the drink in more comfortable quarters, or perhaps Haesten had stumbled back to be with his own army whom Wulfric discovered were camped not far from the hall.

None of the Wessex group had spoken to Haesten. Eohric had purposely kept the two factions apart, admitting to Wulfric that he feared a fight would start. Haesten had been most upset at his defeat at Botingtvne after all, and Wulfric was known to be the kind of man who did not ignore insults or challenges.

The ealdorman groaned and rubbed sleep from his eyes. His mouth was unbelievably dry, and he felt somehow unclean. One of Eohric's slaves was working nearby, tidying the place and replacing any straw that had been... soiled. Wulfric tried not to think too much about that, fearing he might soil the floor himself if he did.

'Where can I wash?' he croaked at the slave. The woman eyed him dully then pointed at the door.

'There's water on the western side of the hall,' she replied, returning to her work without another word.

Wulfric muttered a word of thanks then made his way outside. To his surprise, it was raining hard, and he allowed the cool water to run down his face, imagining it cleansing him of the hangover that made it seem like the town blacksmith was forging a new sword within his skull. He found the barrel the slave had told him about and used it to properly rinse his face, scrubbing it as best he could with his hands before he hurried back to the sanctuary of the hall. The rain, so refreshing at first, was now making him shiver and he strode to the firepit which was burning low but enough to warm him. He looked at the slave who pointedly ignored him so he found a mug and some ale himself, forcing the lot down his throat, gagging as he did so but knowing it would do him a power of good.

John the Old Saxon sat up on his bench, swung his legs onto the floor, and smiled across at Wulfric. It looked like the old man had enjoyed the best night's sleep imaginable. His eyes were clear and his expression that of someone well refreshed and not at all hungover.

Lucky bastard, thought Wulfric, wondering what the abbot's secret was.

Eohric appeared then and, rather to the ealdorman's chagrin, the Dane also seemed quite happy and not at all nauseous. Maybe they were just more used to nights of heavy drinking than he was.

'You're awake,' Eohric smiled. 'Good. Walk with me.' His gesture encompassed both Wulfric and John. Their guards were roused now but remained where they were at a signal from Wulfric, and the three noblemen went outside, taking their cloaks at Wulfric's suggestion.

The rain was not so heavy now, but they put their hoods up and wandered away from the hall so no one could hear their conversation.

'You're set on this course of yours?' the East Anglian king asked them when they were a good distance away, next to a pen with a house that must surely be home to a large pig. 'You mean to parley with Haesten?'

'We do,' John confirmed. 'That was the mission Alfred set us, and we'll carry it through.'

Eohric nodded, casting surreptitious glances about as if he feared spies were watching them. Clearly Haesten's presence nearby was a great source of anxiety for him. 'All right, if you insist. But I will not be able to offer you protection once you enter his camp.'

Wulfric and John glanced at one another. It was not the most reassuring of statements, but both had known from the outset that this could be a dangerous mission. They nodded.

'Where is he camped?' John asked. 'We might as well get it over with as soon as possible. I'd like to sample some more of that strong ale of yours before we make the ride back to Wessex.'

Eohric smiled and pointed. 'There,' he said, his finger picking out smoke rising into the sky about a quarter mile distant. 'That's their fires.'

'Haesten is there now?' Wulfric asked, wanting it confirmed before they walked into the lion's den.

'As far as I know,' Eohric said. 'Are you going alone? What about your travelling companions? The guards?'

Wulfric shook his head. 'Either we'll be safe with Haesten, or we won't. A few more soldiers won't save us if the old bastard decides to do away with us. You'll protect them if that happens, my lord? They are still under your roof.'

Eohric nodded gloomily. 'Ja. I'll do what I can.'

Wulfric frowned but held his tongue. Eohric truly was not the equal of his father, but, then again, perhaps that was just as well. If he'd been half the *vikingr* Guthrum had been in his youth the alliance with Wessex might not still hold...

'Well,' said John, clasping his hands and smiling beatifically at both Wulfric and Eohric. 'Let's get this over with.'

The rain drummed on the roof of Haesten's tent as Wulfric and John stood waiting to meet him. They'd been brought in by one of his guards, a massive bear of a man who towered over even Wulfric. The missing ear that had badly healed over was not concealed beneath long hair, either. It was openly displayed, a badge of honour for the Dane who'd obviously seen his fair share of battles.

'Wait,' the huge man growled, casting them malevolent glances. 'Haesten will see you when it pleases him.'

Wulfric stared coldly back at the man, almost daring him to start a fight. John simply smiled and nodded. The Dane appeared more put out by John's reaction than Wulfric's as he stepped back outside the tent to take up his post once more.

The only sound was the pattering rain on the roof and walls, and the occasional creak of leather armour as the guards shifted position at the entrance. Wulfric listened for some sign of Haesten's approach. It was a large tent, split into two sections, and he assumed the Dane was in the other 'room' with his wife. There was no sound, however, and the ealdorman wondered what the hell they were doing. Making love? From the rumours he'd heard, Wulfric doubted that. There was no conversation either though, so he assumed Haesten was simply making them wait. A transparent attempt to gain the upper hand in their meeting before it even began. Well, Wulfric was a soldier and used to waiting in silence for long periods.

John the Old Saxon had his eyes closed and he was silently mouthing a prayer, apparently completely at ease as he communed with God.

Time stretched out and Wulfric could smell lavender, which he guessed must be from the water Ulfhild used to wash herself, Haesten too probably. The Danes were notoriously fussy about personal hygiene after all, a trait Wulfric thought strange in such a warlike people. He tried to guess how many warriors were camped there with Haesten. They'd been forced to walk through the army to get to this tent, drawing black gazes and even insults from the enemy soldiers. Wulfric thought there could be as many as four hundred men in that camp, and more would be filtering in every day, making their way back to their king after scattering in all directions at Botingtvne. Not a huge force, but one that could be devastating if allowed to join with Sigeferth's army at Herutford.

The ealdorman's thoughts drifted this way and that as he waited until, at last, Haesten stepped through the partition separating the second room from the main one.

Standing so close to him, Wulfric could see each line, each furrow in the older man's brow. His skin seemed like leather, so tanned and weather beaten it was. He had not bothered to dress in his armour or heavy fur for it was a humid day, so his scrawny shoulders were easily visible.

Wulfric thought Haesten cut a pathetic figure at that moment. An old, old man, stooped, and moving with all the grace and speed of his many years. Then the ealdorman reminded himself of this geriatric warlord's cruel reputation and the many men he still commanded. Men that despised Wulfric and John, and were only separated from them by the walls of a tent.

Then Ulfhild stepped in from the other room and the West Saxons bowed to the enemy king and his wife.

'What do you want?' Haesten demanded without preamble. The charm that he'd displayed before at Middletun was gone, replaced by irritation, grief, and hatred. Wulfric winced inwardly. This was not a good start.

'They want to offer us some pitiful deal,' Ulfhild spat, before John the Old Saxon could even open his mouth. 'To sail away and leave them in peace.'

'Yes,' John agreed coolly, addressing Haesten. 'We are here from King Alfred of Wessex to make you an offer, my lord. Not a pitiful one at all, though. A very good one, given your weakened position.'

Wulfric held his breath, expecting one of the Danes to react angrily to that, but they merely smiled bleakly at John.

'Go on,' said Haesten, lowering himself into the seat that had been placed near the centre of the tent.

'King Alfred asks that you cease all hostilities against the Anglo-Saxon people,' John intoned, getting directly to the point. 'In return he will grant you land in Mercia, which you may rule, as King Guthrum did before you, here, in East Anglia.' He avoided giving Guthrum his Christian name, Athelstan, knowing it would annoy Haesten.

'That's it?' Ulfhild asked scornfully. 'You would offer my husband, the greatest *vikingr* in all Midgard, some land in the shithole that is Mercia?' She seemed furious, barely holding her temper in check, and Wulfric surmised it was not from the offer, but from the loss of her children.

For his part, Haesten had seemed extremely interested in Alfred's offer of land. It was not every day one was granted a kingdom after all. He stared at his wife, seemingly unable to speak out against her harsh words and Wulfric wondered if they'd have been better trying to parley with Ulfhild from the start. She appeared to be the one in charge in the tent at that moment.

Before Wulfric could react, Ulfhild took one step forward, and her right fist shot out, hammering into John's chest. The abbot cried out, hands grasping, blood spilling through his fingers.

Wulfric was unarmed for they had not worn any weapons to come here, knowing the Danes would simply confiscate them and maybe even steal them. He had no chance to defend himself or his companion anyway, as something struck the back of his knees and he collapsed onto the ground. He tried to stand but his legs wouldn't support him, and he saw the massive guard's boot just before it hammered into his face and everything went black.

CHAPTER THIRTY-FOUR

Alfred shaded his eyes with his hand and looked upriver, nodding in satisfaction. 'What about here?' he asked the riders who'd accompanied him.

Aedan nodded, while Aethelred rode closer to the River Lea, examining its flowing waters and squinting across at the far bank.

'It seems all right,' the ealdorman said thoughtfully, wiping perspiration from his forehead and lifting his water-skin to take a quick sip. Thankfully God had seen fit to heal him of his previous malady and today was the first time he'd felt strong enough to ride out with the king. It was a hot day though, and he'd been advised by the surgeons to drink plenty of fluids if he wanted to remain fit and healthy as he accompanied Alfred.

The reason for their ride was simple: Alfred guessed Sigeferth's Danes would try to escape soon, and he wanted to make that impossible for them. The fields around Herutford had been completely emptied of crops, with oxen growing fat on the stubble left behind by the reaping sickles of the workers. Lundenburh's storehouses were filled to bursting with the harvest and the people should enjoy a winter of plenty.

In contrast, the Danes within Sigeferth's fortress would soon run out of food, and the frosts of winter would make it impossible for them to find more. Botingtvne was a fresh, recent memory for Sigeferth, and many of the men with him had actually been there, escaping from their doom only to join Sigeferth at Herutford and face the prospect of the same thing happening again. Swollen bellies and horses butchered in desperation would not be an appealing prospect to the heathen army encamped by the Lea.

Surely they would use their longships to escape, Alfred guessed. They would sail along the river, rejoin the Tamyse, and then, no doubt, find some other town with well-stocked grain stores to attack and spend winter in.

The king was not going to let that happen.

'We could build a small fortress here,' Aedan said, nudging his horse into a trot that carried him along the riverbank. 'The ground is flat and should allow us to make a decent foundation.'

Aethelred nodded agreement, gazing across the river at the far shore as if seeing the future in his mind's-eye. 'And another fortress there,' he said.

'With a bridge joining them,' Alfred agreed, imagining the finished construction. 'Allowing men and horses to move across the river, and, crucially, to block the sea-wolves' longships.'

Aedan looked upstream, thinking this over. 'It will block our own ships too, lord,' he pointed out. 'Unless we're able to build a bridge that can be moved out of the way when needed.'

'Anything like that would take a lot more time and resources,' Aethelred noted. 'And make the whole bridge less sturdy, which would somewhat defeat the purpose.'

Alfred dismounted and arched his back, stretching out muscles that had tightened up already, despite the fact they hadn't ridden very far that morning. Groaning as he rolled his neck, feeling the tendons stretch, he pushed aside his aches and stamped a foot on the ground. 'Aye, this spot will be ideal for a fortress,' he said. 'And don't worry about the river being blocked off for good. I only want a bridge here for as long as Sigeferth's army remains at Herutford. The two fortresses will be small affairs, quickly thrown up but sturdy enough to withstand all but the most concerted attacks. The bridge itself will be the same – heavy enough to take the weight of a few horses crossing, or to withstand a longship ramming directly into it, but quickly constructed with simple materials.'

Aethelred nodded, pleased by the king's plan. 'Sounds good,' he agreed. 'No point in constructing some magnificent structure, only to tear it down a few weeks later.'

'You think the Danes will be gone so soon?' Aedan asked sceptically. 'The whoresons hung around at Botingtvne for a lot longer.'

'And look where it got them,' Alfred replied with a grim smile. 'No, they'll have learned their lesson. They'll surely look to move on soon.'

'We'd better get the builders to work immediately then,' Aethelred replied.

'Indeed,' said the king. 'I'll leave it up to you, my lord. You're in charge of Lundenburh after all, so it'll be your workers and craftsmen making the bridge.' He looked around, finding a long branch beneath a nearby bush. This he brought to the exact position he'd picked out as the site for the first fortress and rammed it into the soft grass, grunting as his elbows protested against the rough movement. 'There,' he said, trying to ignore the pain and pointing at the branch. 'A marker so your builders don't get the location wrong.'

The three men stood side by side, looking at the land and the river in quiet contemplation. Summer was fading, but there were still birds singing in the nearby trees, and bright blooms added vibrant colours to the mostly green and brown terrain that surrounded them.

'How quickly d'you want it built?' Aethelred wondered aloud, lifting a rock and skimming it downstream, the smooth, flat stone bouncing a handful of times before disappearing with a little 'plop'.

'As soon as possible,' said Alfred. 'When the Danes discover what we're doing they won't hang around to let us finish so... the sooner the bridge is in place the better.'

'You're assuming, my lord, that Haesten isn't on his way to join Sigeferth,' Aedan said.

'No,' the king replied, shaking his head, lips pursed. 'If John the Old Saxon can't make peace with Haesten, and he brings what's left of his army to join Sigeferth, he may well come along this river in longships borrowed or traded from other Northmen.' He held out both his hands towards the water which was moving fast that day despite the fine weather, its water rippling in the sunshine. 'A bridge here will allow us to cut the bastards off before their two separate armies join to become one.'

'Well,' Aethelred demanded, walking back to his waiting horse. 'What are we waiting for, my lords? Let's get back to town and I'll have my men start construction this very afternoon!'

Wulfric opened his eyes and stared at what he saw in front of him, trying to make sense of the confusing images. What was he looking at? It took a while for the fog to lift from his mind and the memories returned, shocking and painful, and he understood then what he was seeing: the bars of a cage.

He did not move, although the temptation to reach out and try to break free was almost overwhelming. He stared, keeping his eyes hooded in case anyone was watching him, examining the prison that he'd been placed in. The bars were not incredibly thick, but they were made from iron, and, without some kind of lever, Wulfric knew he would not be able to pry them apart or snap them.

Tilting his head slightly, he realised he was lying in a foetal position and, even if he wanted to, he could not stretch out. The cage he was in was small and narrow. Fear clawed at his throat, gorge rising as the sense of confinement threatened to unman him – what was happening? And, more importantly, how the hell was he going to get out of this prison?

He took a deep breath, forcing himself to remember who he was, and how he'd been trained. He was Wulfric, ealdorman, warrior, and he'd been in worse situations than this.

It was daytime at least, for it was light, and he seemed to be outside, judging by the warm breeze that tousled his hair. Would he remain there, outdoors, in the cage, when night fell? Had he already spent nights unconscious there? The thought was not pleasant, and he feared freezing to death before he could even attempt to break out of his prison, for he was not dressed warmly at all.

The sudden memory of Ulfhild attacking John the Old Saxon hit him and all other thoughts paled into insignificance. At first Wulfric had thought the woman had punched John, but, as he went through it in his mind now he recalled the abbot's hands grabbing desperately at his chest, and the blood that appeared through his gnarled fingers.

A punch would not do that. A terrible black rage filled Wulfric then, as he knew Ulfhild had murdered his friend. There was no way the old clergyman could survive a knife to the heart, even if the Danes had given him immediate treatment, which would not have happened.

The only question was: Why had they not killed Wulfric? Fear rose within him again, but he shoved it aside, knowing it would do him no good. The only real reason they could have spared him was to kill him at a later date – would he suffer the same fate as Diuma? He gritted his teeth and vowed to do whatever he could to avoid that horror, but the very idea was terrifying.

He rolled onto his side, needing to do something to take his mind off his imagined fate. On the cage floor beside him was a wet pile of vomit. He had no recollection of throwing up, but he was the only one there so it had to have been him and, judging by the fact it hadn't dried out yet, it must have happened only a short time ago.

He'd only been there for a few hours at most, he guessed. That was good, he told himself, for his strength would not have faded as it would have done if he'd been unconscious for days. He would be able to fight the bastards when they came for him. Assuming they didn't just leave him there to starve to death.

'You're awake.'

Wulfric saw no sense in pretending to be out cold, so he grunted and pushed himself up to his feet. He had to use the bars of the cage and, even at that, the roof was too low for him to stretch out to his full height. As he was well over six feet tall, being forced to crouch or sit in such a cramped area for long would not be pleasant. He prayed to God that he would be let out soon.

'Why am I locked up?' he demanded, turning to see Haesten sitting on a stool beside the cage. The old warlord was holding a cup and seemed to have been enjoying the sunshine as he waited for Wulfric to awaken. Thankfully, Ulfhild was not there.

'Well, you can blame my wife for that,' Haesten replied, laughing apologetically and looking over his shoulder as if he was afraid she'd hear him. It was supposed to be a joke, but Wulfric could tell the Dane genuinely feared Ulfhild. 'I would have let you go, but she said it would be better to keep you here.' He smiled again, this time apologetically. 'I'm afraid you're not going to have a very pleasant death.' He sucked his teeth, enjoying himself. 'She has some plans for you, ealdorman.'

Wulfric's lip curled but he held his discipline, refusing to give this twisted old king the satisfaction of an angry retort.

'Alfred will not allow this to pass without reply,' he growled.

'What will he do?' Haesten demanded, and he was angry too now. 'My sons are dead! My second-in-command, Rune, dead! My army cut in half, or more! My ships burned or stolen! What exactly will your Alfred do to me that could possibly be worse?'

Wulfric leaned back against the bars, staring at the enemy king, imagining placing his hands around the old bastard's scrawny neck and squeezing until...

'Alfred thinks he's won, doesn't he?' Haesten asked, taking a sip from his cup. The moistness on his thin lips disgusted Wulfric but the warlord continued, oblivious. 'He thinks I'm beaten, but I'm not. Many of my warriors have travelled south to join my comrade, Sigeferth. And every day more come here to serve me once more.' He laughed nastily, rheumy eyes boring into Wulfric. 'Preparations have already begun, Saxon. Preparations for me to also make the journey south. I will take control of Sigeferth's army, making one great force that will be big enough to smash Alfred into his weak God's waiting arms.'

Wulfric felt his heart sink. He had failed in his mission and there was absolutely nothing he could do about it. Wessex was doomed.

'You're a fool, Haesten,' the ealdorman said scornfully. 'A bitter old fool being manipulated by your woman.' He spat, smiling without humour. 'What kind of *vikingr* are you, old man? I've met great heathen leaders like Halfdan, Guthrum, Ivar the Detestable... You are nothing compared to them. Nothing!' He could see his words were enraging Haesten and he took great satisfaction from it, even though he knew it would merely make his own demise more painful when it came. 'Even Ubba was more of a leader than you, Haesten. Even Ubba, drunken oaf that he was, never attacked the wrong city, thinking it was Rome!'

Haesten glared at him, chewing his cheek wrathfully, but then he smiled. 'Whatever, Saxon,' he muttered. 'None of those great leaders were able to defeat Alfred, but I will. Wessex will fall to me within weeks but, long before then, you will have died screaming in terrible agony.' He got up from his stool and threw his empty cup at Wulfric. It clattered against the bars, missing the ealdorman but making him flinch instinctively. 'You will be pinned to the ground, face down,' Haesten said, staring through the cage at his captive. 'And then I will watch as your ribs are sawn from your spine. Imagine it, ealdorman. Imagine the pain you will feel! Look. Look there!'

Wulfric's eyes moved down to the spot Haesten had indicated. There, about ten feet away from his cage, lying on another stool, was a hand axe of the kind used to chop wood, and a short saw with wickedly sharp teeth. A wave of ice washed over

Wulfric as he looked at the tools that were to be used to end his days on God's earth.

The enemy king continued, describing in horrific detail what awaited Wulfric and, as much as the West Saxon warrior tried to ignore him, the thought of Diuma's agonising end filled him with terror and it was all Wulfric could do to remain standing, fingers grasping the bars in a white-knuckle embrace.

He would die in torment, Haesten promised, and then the sea-wolves would march upon Lundenburh. The war would be over soon, and Alfred's long reign would be too.

God help us all, Wulfric thought, as Haesten departed, cackling with vicious glee and promising to return soon to watch Ulfhild bring the ealdorman a lingering, savage death.

CHAPTER THIRTY-FIVE

Haesten did not return as soon as Wulfric had feared. For hours, the West Saxon warrior sat in his cage, muscles tensed, ready to fight whoever appeared to take him to his doom. He would not go quietly, he vowed, but he imagined all the various scenarios in his head, picturing how things might happen. Or would happen, if he was in Haesten's place. The Danes would expect him to fight back, so they would incapacitate him quickly. He shuddered as he thought of that. Would they simply crack him across the head with a bludgeon of some sort? Enough to render him pliable, but not dead. Or would they smash his leg bones so he'd be in no state to resist what was being done to him?

Wulfric knew from long experience how brutal the sea-wolves could be to their prisoners. He remembered back to that time, around twenty-five years before, when he'd watched from a distance as the sons of Ragnar Lodbrok murdered King Edmund of East Anglia. And that had been a relatively quick, easy death the Christian monarch had been given! Compared to what Haesten had planned for him, Wulfric knew he would soon be screaming for mercy, no matter how stoic he hoped to be.

Even the hardest of men would cry for their mothers once the torturers set about their bloody work.

Wulfric had moved position within that infernal cage numerous times, sitting down, standing to crouch beneath the solid wooden roof, kneeling as if in prayer, all the time keeping himself alert and his muscles warmed up. Occasionally one of the Northmen would pass and call out in mocking laughter at him. Some spat through the bars on him, and one even pulled down his breeches to send a steaming, stinking stream of piss towards him. There was nothing Wulfric could do to avoid it; all he could do was mark the man and pray that God would one day – either in this life or the afterlife – allow him to meet the whoreson on equal terms.

By the time night fell neither Haesten nor Ulfhild had reappeared and he sank to the sodden grass, utterly exhausted after his long ordeal. The sounds of feasting and laughter came to him and he guessed his death would not come until the morrow. Haesten would let him stew in his own juices – and that of his laughing warriors – for one more night. They'd not even bothered to set a guard on him but he soon discovered there was no way to break out of the cage. The damn thing had been as skilfully put together as one of the Danes' longships, and attempting to escape would merely tire Wulfric further.

He could not help it when tears came to his eyes, and he lay his head on the cold grass to rest for one final time. Thoughts of his wife, Sunngifu, came to him and he cried to remember her, how beautiful she'd been and how happy their life had been together. If only they'd been granted more years together, before she was cruelly taken by the illness. Then he thought of his daughter, Deorwynn, living contentedly as a nun in Ilminster. Wulfric would have given anything to see her then, to tell her how proud he was of her, how much he loved her, and how she'd helped him deal with the loss of Sunngifu.

He thought too of Alfred, his friend, and the times they'd shared over the decades. Bad times, aye, many of those, but Wulfric's memories were mostly of happy events they'd enjoyed by one another's side. Now they would not see any more of those times together…

—

He awoke with a start, eyes wide, nostrils flaring, instantly remembering where he was and struggling to sit upright, fists clenched. His tears had dried and he mentally berated himself for allowing himself to become maudlin before the gloomy mood had passed and he felt more like his usual self. He was about to die, but he would not go to meet God meekly, sobbing.

A sound came from behind him and he turned, staring into the darkness. It must have been the middle of the night by now, for the sounds of revelry that had emanated from the tents all around had been replaced with snores. He heard the noise again and tried to make out what was causing it. A fox? An owl?

It was as black as Haesten's heart in the sea-wolves' camp so Wulfric shrank back in surprise when a massive, dark shape suddenly filled his vision.

This was no fox – it was a man.

Wulfric gritted his teeth and balled his fists, ready to deal with this nocturnal shade who'd been sent, undoubtedly, by Haesten to disturb his slumber and torment him even further.

'Stand back,' the shadowy figure hissed. 'I'm here to help you, you big fool.'

Wulfric tried to make out the man but there was barely a sliver of light to distinguish his features. There was a grunt as the newcomer tried to work loose the bolt that held the cage door shut at the bottom. It came slowly free with a metallic shriek that Wulfric felt sure must bring every Dane in the place running.

Who was his would-be saviour? The man spoke with as thick an accent as any of the other sea-wolves, which made sense, since no Saxon would have been able to sneak into such a heavily armed camp.

The second bolt, the one holding the door closed in the centre, came free, the shadowy figure dropping the padlock into the grass beside the first, and then the door was open and Wulfric didn't hesitate to step out.

He was free, but for how long?

Something glinted in the meagre light cast by some distant, smouldering campfire, and Wulfric froze, knowing it was a blade. His rescuer did not plunge the steel into Wulfric's belly though. The handle of the sword was pressed into the ealdorman's grip, and he felt a surge of elation – he knew this grip, had killed countless Danes with his hand grasping it. This was his own sword!

'Come, hurry.' The shadowman moved away, bearing to the west of the encampment where there were fewer campfires and less tents. Hopefully, thought Wulfric as he stepped stiffly, quietly, across the ground, there were less guards as well. As much as he would like to shove his newly recovered sword deep into sea-wolf guts, he wanted even more to escape from the blood eagle that had haunted his dreams that night.

A sudden shout came to the side of them and Wulfric stopped, straining to see in the gloom. Should he run for it, or stand and fight? The sounds of a man coming towards them were unmistakeable and Wulfric's blood was thundering in his veins as the footsteps came closer. He felt his companion grasp his wrist and lower the sword just as another figure reeled out of the darkness, stumbling into Wulfric.

'Who's that?' the man demanded, and the stench of stale mead filled the air. 'Can't a man go for a shit without folk disturbing him? Go on, fuck off you big bastard, or I'll stab you to death.'

Wulfric gagged at the vile smell emanating from the drunk but remained silent for fear of incriminating himself with his Saxon accent. He felt his wrist pulled onwards and trotted into the night again, away from the muttering sot who was still threatening to kill the empty space they had just occupied.

'Who are you?' Wulfric asked when it seemed they'd moved away from the tents. The sun was just beginning to brighten the eastern sky with its orange-red glow and the ealdorman was able to make out more of his rescuer. The man was small, much smaller than Wulfric but, as he turned to speak, Wulfric did not recognise him at all.

'King Eohric sent me,' the Dane replied in a low tone. 'Keep moving, Saxon. They'll notice you're gone soon.'

They walked on in silence and Wulfric's mind raced as he tried to make sense of what was happening. Had he not been so exhausted by his experiences of the past day or so he would have understood immediately, but, as it was, it took him a while to grasp things.

King Eohric had known Alfred would blame him personally for the deaths of John the Old Saxon and Wulfric. Two noblemen of Wessex, and personal friends of Alfred. Such a crime would cast a heavy shadow over the alliance between Eohric's East Anglia and Wessex. True, it would be Haesten who was truly to blame for the murders, but these were Eohric's lands, and the Saxon emissaries were under Eohric's protection.

Wulfric looked up at the brightening sky and murmured a soft prayer of thanks. It was not in his nature to look for God's hand in every event, good or bad. That was more Alfred's thing – but sometimes in a man's life a miracle occurred. This was surely such an occasion, and it would be churlish not to recognise it, and give thanks.

'Here.' The Dane did not stop moving but he turned and handed Wulfric his scabbard. When the ealdorman had buckled it in place his rescuer handed him his seax and a small bag of food. 'We're out of Haesten's camp now, but you're not safe as long as you remain here. Your men are waiting for you at the town gates, go there and join them, then get the hell away from here. Ride back to Wessex and, if you wish to thank my lord Eohric, keep this a secret. He fears Haesten almost as much as you do.'

Wulfric nodded, taking in the man's commands as any good soldier would do. When it was all clear in his mind he held out his hand, grasping the Dane's wrist and thanking him profusely for saving his life.

'If ever I'm able, I will return the favour, my friend,' he said.

The Dane grinned then wrinkled his nose. 'The only thanks I want from you right now, Saxon, is for you to keep well away from me. You stink of piss, ealdorman. I suggest you ride hard for Wessex, but stop at the first river you find and have a good bath!'

Wulfric laughed and nodded, joy filling his heart at his good fortune. Smelling of urine was far better than being sawn apart rib by rib while Haesten and his men looked on in glee.

They were some distance from the enemy king's camp but, even so, the sudden shout of fury reached them quite easily, carried in the dawn quiet by a cool breeze.

'Go!' Wulfric's rescuer commanded harshly. 'And my Óðinn be with you, Saxon.'

They parted, Wulfric hurrying towards the town gates which were not far off. The guards there pointedly ignored him as he passed, turning their backs as if they couldn't see him. When he was about a quarter of a mile along the road the sounds of shouting and arguing behind him were starting to worry him. Haesten knew by now that he'd escaped, and the enraged king would send riders after him, scouting the lands all around Eohric's capital for the fugitive.

Where the hell were the guards that had travelled there with Wulfric and John?

He saw them then, sitting atop their horses beneath a pair of trees. Wulfric ran to them and tried to jump onto his own mount. His ordeal had left him tired and drained though and it took three attempts before he made it onto the beast's back.

'Come,' said one of the guards, staring back at the town fearfully. 'King Eohric ordered us to be gone as soon as you reached us.'

'Then what are you waiting for?' Wulfric demanded with a weak laugh, kicking his heels into his mount and grasping the reins tightly for fear of sliding off onto the road, such was the depth of his exhaustion.

They followed his lead, a small cloud of dust forming in their wake as the horses gathered speed, cantering along the road, sending early-morning travellers scattering for safety lest they be trampled beneath thundering hooves.

Wulfric held on for dear life as his horse sped up, the effects of his captivity truly beginning to tell on him. He glanced backwards repeatedly, fearful of Haesten's pursuit. Each time he looked he expected to see Ulfhild galloping after them, hair flying behind her like a halo in the rising sun, sword held aloft in challenge. The Saxons had left behind any pursuit though for there was no one riding after them and, at last, Wulfric allowed his horse to slow, not wanting to sap its energy too much.

'What the hell happened back there, my lord?' one of his guards asked when they were a good mile or two distant from the town. 'Where's the abbot?'

Wulfric felt a lump in his throat as he thought of John the Old Saxon and his fate. He had not even seen the abbot's body. What had the sea-wolves done with it? He was afraid to imagine.

His companions cried out in impotent fury as the ealdorman recounted the events of the previous day. Had they known what was happening, they said, they would have come to rescue him themselves, rather than Eohric sending someone.

'I appreciate that lads,' Wulfric said with a grateful smile, believing them. 'But Eohric's man was a Dane, he was able to pass through Haesten's camp without being detected, and he knew where to find me. You lot would have stood out, even in the dark.'

The soldiers absorbed his description of the events and one whistled softly. 'And it was Haesten's wife who killed the abbot?' He shook his head. 'The woman's a bloody demon.'

No one replied to that, simply nodding gravely. Wulfric thought back to Ulfhild's attack, jaw clenched in righteous anger. She'd moved with astonishing speed, he remembered, taking both Wulfric and John by complete surprise. Her thrust had been delivered with grace and precision, marking her as a skilled fighter. No wonder Haesten kept her close – she was an ideal bodyguard, especially given his own weakening body.

They continued along the road and then, coming to some woods, Wulfric led them beneath the trees, casting another glance back the way they'd come to make sure no one was following them. Soon they were completely hidden from the road by the dense undergrowth, and they began to relax, knowing they were safe at last. They rode on for a while longer and then, knowing he would fall off his mount if they didn't rest, Wulfric called a halt.

Eohric had furnished the guards with food and refilled their ale skins. The king had even had the foresight to fill a pack for Wulfric and he accepted it gratefully from one of his companions, finding some cheese and bread to still the rumbling in his empty belly. When he'd washed it all down with a little ale and felt more like his usual, strong self, he stretched up and looked at the other soldiers.

'There's a stream there,' he said, pointing. 'I stink, so I'm going to bathe as best I can.'

None of the men said anything out loud but their relieved looks were enough to tell him bathing would be a fine idea.

'Don't be too long, my lord,' one said, earnestly but respectfully. 'We want to get moving again as soon as possible. I don't fancy being caught by Haesten and blood-eagled.'

Wulfric was already walking towards the stream, stripping off his clothes as he went. 'You can ride on lads,' he called over his shoulder. 'I won't be coming with you.'

Predictably, his words sparked consternation amongst the riders and they demanded to know what the hell he was talking about. Where was he going?

'Haesten has gathered the remnants of his army to him,' Wulfric replied, stepping gingerly into the stream and shuddering at its chill. He steeled himself to go deeper although it only came up to his ankles and he was forced to crouch down and use his hands to splash the icy water over himself. 'He's going to lead that army – probably bolstered by some of Eohric's warriors desperate for glory – to Lundenburh, where he expects to defeat Alfred.'

'So come back with us and tell the king what you know,' the guard commander said.

Wulfric scrubbed his piss-stained clothes as best he could in the stream, more used to its cold now, and then he stepped out, dripping, to place his wet things on a large rock, hoping the sun would dry them quickly.

'What's the point in me coming back with you?' he asked, more to himself than his comrades, thinking things over and praying he was making the right decision. 'My mission was to neutralise the threat Haesten posed. With the murder of John the Old Saxon that mission has failed.'

'So?' the guard sergeant asked. 'Not every mission is a success, you know that, lord.'

'No,' Wulfric admitted. 'But Haesten remains the key to Wessex's survival. He can't be allowed to join his army with Sigeferth's.'

'What are you planning to do then? Attack Haesten all by yourself?' It was asked in jest but no one laughed, especially when Wulfric gave his answer.

'Aye,' he said grimly, drawing his sword from its sheath and examining the blade. 'That's exactly what I'm going to do.'

CHAPTER THIRTY-SIX

Wulfric was stunned by what he saw when he circled back around to Hædleage. He'd journeyed on foot, with only a pack of supplies and his weapons for company, keeping off the road and using the foliage and contours of the land to remain hidden from travellers or any who might be hunting him. He'd spotted bands of riders galloping along the road and guessed they'd been sent by Haesten to find him, but they did not look very hard and soon returned to the town. Wulfric hoped Eohric would not suffer for helping him.

In truth, Wulfric had not thought there was any danger of that, but now, as he sat hidden within the branches of a yew tree just outside Hædleage he realised his reading of the situation was off. When he'd enjoyed the hospitality of Eohric's hall, and then spent an unpleasant night in Haesten's camp, the true scale of the old warlord's army had not been known to Wulfric.

Now, as the *vikingar* marched past him, heading south-west to attack Alfred, the ealdorman felt his guts tighten with fear. Haesten had suffered a crushing defeat at Botingtvne, yet somehow he'd managed to rebuild much of his army. How he'd done it, Wulfric could only guess. Promises of a great victory with enough plunder to make them all rich must have brought more Danes who'd settled in East Anglia and the other neighbouring lands to Haesten's banner.

Wulfric could see that banner now, a black eagle on a red background, fluttering in the air over the column of enemy warriors that snaked out along the road.

On its own, this army would not be enough to defeat Alfred, but combined with Sigeferth's…? And there was always the possibility that yet more Danes were sailing to attack other parts of Wessex, as they'd done earlier in the war.

Damn the old bastard, Wulfric thought gloomily. Why couldn't he have been killed at Botingtvne, and his witch of a wife too? How the hell had the man survived for so long, given his penchant for violence? Sometimes Wulfric wondered if Þórr and Óðinn really were protecting the likes of Haesten. Maybe he should start following those old, heathen gods too.

The thought made him smile as he imagined Alfred's reaction if he was to even suggest such a thing. How amusing it would be to meet the king while wearing one of the hammer amulets the Northmen wore to honour Þórr!

His smile faded as he remembered where he was, what was happening, and what had already happened to John the Old Saxon. Thoughts of pagan gods disappeared from his mind and, despite not being much of a Christian, he mouthed a silent prayer for the murdered abbot's soul. With that out of the way, Wulfric's mind turned to a job more suited to his particular set of skills: vengeance.

He knew Haesten and Ulfhild would be near to the eagle banner flying at the head of the Danes' column, but he also knew they would be well guarded, and not just by the hundreds of sea-wolves in the marching army. Wulfric remembered the massive boot of the warrior who'd attacked him from behind in Haesten's tent, and of the man who'd pissed on him when he was caged like a beast. They were not important, but Wulfric hoped he would meet them again soon.

The column moved on at a steady pace, some on horseback, some on foot, with the supplies packed into wagons that came along at the rear, hauled by teams of oxen. Those wagons would slow the army's progress but, even so, they would meet up with Sigeferth within six or seven days.

Wulfric had told the guards who'd accompanied him to Hædleage to ride hard for Lundenburh, warning Alfred and the people there to prepare for a great battle. He could only hope that those messengers completed their mission and Wessex was able to muster as many fyrds as possible. The alternative did not bear thinking about.

Truly, it seemed like this would be the final, great battle to decide the fate of all the Anglo-Saxon kingdoms forever. Could Alfred's Wessex stand against these numbers, after losing so many warriors during the recent years of constant fighting?

Wulfric walked along, remaining hidden from the road, pondering how things had turned out. It was a depressing day, seeing the might of the enemy war machine up close like that. Yes, the Danes were not disciplined, their army being formed of disparate units loyal ultimately only to themselves rather than their king, but, for as long as they sensed victory they would march – and fight – as hard as any warrior of Wessex.

At times Wulfric was forced to hang back, allowing the wagons to roll on ahead because there was no way for him to remain concealed. Although he felt horribly exposed to take the road at those times, he was never seen and it was easy enough to jog along until he'd caught up with Haesten's horde.

So the day passed until, eventually, Wulfric realised he would be safer wearing the same clothes as the Danes he was trailing. With that in mind, he waited until the road passed through a stretch of woodland, and he waited for his chance.

It came mid-afternoon, when he heard a man pushing his way through the undergrowth. Wulfric moved as fast as possible, dodging between the trees while doing his best to avoid stepping on any branches or otherwise giving himself away.

Before him one of the sea-wolves was squatting, bare arse visible as he emptied his bowels noisily onto the moss. Wulfric, eyeing the enemy soldier with disgust, edged closer, his footfalls masked by the splattering and grunting of the Dane.

When he was almost upon him, the soldier turned and the pair locked eyes for just a moment.

Wulfric was amazed that the enemy moved so quickly from his squatting position, standing upright and pulling the axe from his belt. It did the Dane no good though, as Wulfric's sword pommel smashed into his temple. The man collapsed backwards, cracking his skull on a log. He did not suffer long, falling silent and unmoving as Wulfric hammered his pommel down repeatedly on the Dane's forehead. Sure he was dead, Wulfric hastily grabbed the man around the armpits and dragged him further back into the woods, away from the road.

The Dane was heavy, and Wulfric felt like he'd committed a great sin as he bumped him across rocks and old, fallen leaves still with his trousers around his ankles, cock flailing this way and that like a worm chopped in half by a curious child's spade.

'Dying while taking a shit,' the ealdorman muttered breathlessly to himself. 'What a way to go.' He decided he was far enough from the road now that, even if the dead sea-wolf's kinfolk came looking for him, they would not find him. They would, with any luck, see the shit splattered across the rocks and think the dead man had simply got lost within the marching column.

Hastily, Wulfric stripped the man and put on his clothing. First there was a simple, red cloth cap, then a blue tunic fastened by a button at the neck and held in at the waist by Wulfric's sword-belt. Over it all he threw the dead man's red cloak, pinning it in place with a nice golden brooch. It was no thrall that Wulfric had killed – this fellow had been a warrior of some standing. That just made his manner of death all the more grim to Wulfric who'd not enjoyed the brutal work.

It had been necessary though, if he was to blend in with the Danes.

One last thing caught his eye and he bent to lift it from the corpse, examining it closely, a small smile tugging at his mouth. It was an amulet, shaped like a great hammer – Mjölnir Wulfric had heard it called – on a leather thong. He dipped his head and slipped the thong over, wishing he had some way of seeing himself with it, and the rest of the Dane's gear. He had no doubt he would pass for one of the enemy army unless he came under close scrutiny.

Piling small rocks and brush over the pale body, Wulfric murmured an apology for giving the man such an ignominious death, and then he moved on, hurrying to make up the time he'd spent getting his disguise.

Alfred had felt very old as he washed his face and shrugged on his byrnie that morning. His stomach pains were never far away although, mercifully, they were merely a dull ache as the sun rose in the pale blue sky. His joints felt stiff though, particularly his elbows, which was no great surprise given the harsh treatment they'd received over the years wielding spear and shield. Every day seemed to bring a new ache and recently it had begun to affect his mood.

'When I was young physical pain didn't bother me,' he told Asser as they mounted horses and rode out with a dozen hearth-warriors, patrolling the land around Herutford. 'Well, other than my stomach of course. But apart from that, I almost felt invincible. Wounds taken in battle always healed, and any aches and pains would fade away over time.' He sighed and looked downriver at the bridges that were being constructed across the glittering waters. 'Now I know my elbows will always hurt, my knees will feel stiff, and a hangover will take forever to shake off.'

Asser smiled sympathetically. 'That's all part of getting old, I think, lord,' he said. 'If only we could remain forever young, eh?'

Alfred nodded and turned his horse, moving away from the river and riding north, towards Sigeferth's camp. He was glad Asser was with him although he felt a little guilty as there had been times he'd felt irritated with the bishop, comparing him unfavourably to his old friend, Oswald. Asser was more of a 'yes man' than his predecessor had been and, for a time, that had grated on Alfred. If he'd ever looked to Oswald for advice, the priest would give it without hesitation and without worrying what the king would think – he had been an excellent advisor as a result, offering a slightly different perspective to Wulfric and Ealhswith, and Alfred had missed his old friend terribly ever since his death.

It had annoyed Alfred when he'd looked to Asser for input on matters of great import within Wessex and had only platitudes in return. For a time Alfred even thought of leaving Asser behind with Ealhswith whenever the king had to go on campaign, but, eventually, it had dawned on Alfred that he was being extremely unfair to Asser. He was, for some reason, expecting the bishop to act as a complete replacement for Oswald, which was ludicrous. He did not expect any of the other scholars he'd brought to his court to act exactly like his dead friend, did he? Plegmund or John the Old Saxon wasn't expected to be like Oswald, so why expect Asser to be so?

They were very different people, and Oswald had been in Alfred's service for many years, so of course he would feel more comfortable being critical towards the king's policies and plans.

Asser had come to Alfred's court to act as a teacher and a spiritual mentor and, on reflection, the bishop was superb at both those roles. He was, despite not being Oswald, a great friend and Alfred realised he should be thankful to have him beside him.

With that in mind, the king had stopped expecting political or even military advice from Asser and instead focused on learning from him, even when they were chasing Danes around Wessex. Teaching was one thing Oswald had never enjoyed, but Asser was patient and had helped Alfred learn so much during their time together.

'*Nu wæs ðeah-hwæðere þæt halige mæden Maria, Cristes moder, Godes beboda gemyndig, and eode on ðysum dæge to Godes huse mid láce, and gebrohte þæt cild þe heo acende, Hælend Crist, gelácod to þam Godes temple, swa swa hit on Godes æ geset wæs.*'

Alfred looked at Asser and they shared a smile. The bishop often recited prayers or passages from the bible, and his Latin was excellent, spoken clearly and slowly enough for the king to try and make sense of. Indeed, Alfred recognised the words as coming from 'On the Purification of St Mary', one of the homilies the pair had been studying lately.

'Now was, nevertheless, the holy maiden Mary,' Alfred said slowly, doing his best to translate the passage in his mind, growing in confidence as Asser nodded encouragingly at his efforts. 'Christ's mother, mindful of God's commands, and she went on this day to God's house with a gift, and brought the child that she had given birth to, Jesus Christ, to be presented to God's temple.'

'Excellent!' the bishop cried, beaming at his royal student. 'Your Latin is quite good, now, my lord. I'm proud of you.'

Alfred grinned at him, feeling like a child being praised by his mother for learning to do up the laces on his breeches. 'I wouldn't say it's good,' he said self-deprecatingly. 'But it's passable now, thanks to you, my friend.'

'No, it's good,' Asser argued. 'Let's try some more of that homily, shall we?'

He recited some more and Alfred did his best to translate it, then they discussed the deeper meaning and significance of that and other homilies and, as they skirted the edge of Sigeferth's camp, Alfred realised he was enjoying himself. All thoughts of his aching elbows, or the simmering pain in his guts, or even the fate of Wulfric, had been pushed aside by his conversation with Asser.

No, the bishop was not Oswald, and Alfred would never quite get over the loss of his old priest, but Asser was as good a friend in his own way and that, he thought, was truly a gift from God.

CHAPTER THIRTY-SEVEN

By the time Haesten's army stopped moving and started to set up camp, Wulfric was more tired than he'd expected to be. The constant threat of being spotted, and taking care not to be, had taken a toll on him both physically and mentally, and he was glad to finally get a proper rest. With the setting of the sun there was little chance anyone would stumble upon him by accident. Still, he'd found a good place to catch some sleep at the top of a steep but small hillock surrounded by saplings and bushes. No one would sneak up on him there.

He was glad he'd taken the extra clothes from the dead Dane as it grew cold and he was able to use his own tunic and cloak as blankets. Suitably wrapped up, he allowed himself to fall asleep just as the last orange rays of sunshine were filtering through the leaves of the trees around him.

He came to with a start, grabbing for his sword which he'd left unsheathed next to him. Whatever animal had woken him – a fox, Wulfric guessed – did not come any closer though, for he heard it slinking away down the slope, leaving only silence in its wake.

The ealdorman looked up, seeing that the moon had risen although there were quite a few clouds in the sky that might cover its glowing white crescent at any moment. It could even rain he thought, feeling just a hint of chilly dampness in the air. Well and good if it did, for it would add a layer of confusion to the Danes' encampment and surely help Wulfric in what he was planning to do.

It was madness, he knew that, but Haesten and his men would think he had escaped with his guards and be halfway back to Alfred by now. The last thing anyone in the nearby enemy camp would expect was the West Saxon ealdorman to be lurking nearby.

He ate some salted pork and an apple, took a long swallow of water from his skin, and steeled himself for what lay ahead. If he failed, the agony of the blood eagle would be the reward for his what? Bravery? Hubris? Arrogance? Stupidity? All of those and more he thought with a humourless chuckle, making his way carefully down the benighted hillock that had allowed him a few hours of rest.

He walked slowly, listening intently with every step, knowing the Danes would have guards around their perimeter. If he was spotted, things would go badly, but he was confident he could slip through them without being noticed. The guards would be on the lookout for a Saxon warband large enough to be a threat, not a single man dressed like one of their own kind.

Besides, they were still within East Anglia – territory that belonged to Danes – so Haesten's army would be filled with confidence at this stage in their journey. Only when they drew closer to Wessex would they begin to fear attacks.

No, Wulfric had to strike tonight.

He told himself all this as he walked, hands touching his weapons as he went. Sword, seax, smaller knife held to his calf by a thong, axe he'd taken from the soldier he'd killed... All were in place. The only thing missing was a shield, but the weight would slow him down too much. Besides, if he was discovered, a shield would not offer much protection against the spears of hundreds of irate Northmen.

The enemy soldiers were not making any attempt to be quiet – why would they? They were legion, after all, and any threat to them was miles distant in Wessex. The camp was lit by fires, and the mouth-watering scents of roasting meat and warming stew filled Wulfric's nostrils as he approached. So too did the sounds of hundreds of men, confident and safe in their numbers, chattering, laughing, arguing over tafl and games of dice, and the exaggerated squeals of the women who followed any army, providing their services in return for silver if they were lucky, or as slaves.

Wulfric took it all in, utterly familiar with the sights, smells, and sounds, feeling strangely at home as he crouched beside a juniper bush, eyes scanning the darkness for the guards who must be nearby.

His guess that anyone on watch would not be paying too much attention proved correct. As he observed from his hiding place he saw two dark shapes, large in size and in sound, conferring together near a small fire. The fools were on the far side of the flickering flames, allowing Wulfric to see them quite clearly, and blinding themselves to anything outside their camp's perimeter. Either they were too stupid to know what they were doing, or, more likely, they believed the threat of danger to be so minuscule that their turn on guard duty was merely a chance to warm themselves and down some mead.

Haesten would likely have them flogged if he caught them, but the king was surely resting in his command tent, enjoying the company of his wife.

The thought of them living — literally — like royalty, while John the Old Saxon had been so cruelly sent to God, made Wulfric's jaw clench in anger and he tested his sword in its sheath, making sure it would draw out easily.

He knew there would be more guards evenly spaced along the camp perimeter, and it was possible the others would be more diligent, more alert, than the pair allowing the bright firelight to destroy their night vision. With that in mind, the ealdorman crept a short distance to the left, keeping to the cover of the bushes where possible, and then he moved forward, passing the invisible barrier that marked the enemy camp's boundary.

He was inside, and it had been as easy as he'd hoped. Now came the hard part, though.

Crouching would merely draw attention to himself so, drawing in a deep, steadying breath, he rose up to his full height beside a tent, using its shadow to compose himself. He was wearing the same clothes, for the most part, as the Danes he reminded himself. He could easily pass for one of them in the gloom.

'Fuck it,' he murmured, throwing any further sense of caution to the wind and walking boldly out from the shelter of the tent.

A group of Northmen were seated on the ground around a fire just a few paces away from Wulfric. They were chatting quietly amongst themselves, grumbling about the toll the day's march had taken on their feet, or the chafing their armour had caused. One was staring dazedly, fixedly into the flames, drunk or merely exhausted – he was the only one to look up as Wulfric passed, eyeing him dully, not responding when the ealdorman nodded a greeting.

Then Wulfric was past, letting out a sigh of relief as there was no shout of alarm or challenge, and he walked on. He did his best to portray the confident swagger of a jarl or hersir who had every right to be striding through the Danes' camp, praying silently all the while that God would allow him to blend in.

The thought struck him then that someone might recognise the cloak he'd stolen from the dead Dane and a moment of panic brought bile into his throat, but he realised there was little chance of that happening in the dark and he forged on, passing more lounging Danes, none of whom gave him a second glance. Some hardly even granted him that – his bearing clearly marked him as a nobleman, and the rank-and-file troopers had no desire to draw the attention of such a one. An easy life was all they prayed to their gods for, and attracting the attention of an arrogant jarl was not how one attained such a thing.

A couple of the men he passed did nod greetings to him and Wulfric returned them with the hint of a smile and a grunt, but no one challenged him or sought to strike up a conversation and, as the eagle banner that marked Haesten's tent drew closer, the ealdorman felt the blood begin to pound in his veins.

What was he going to do when he reached his destination? He had no real idea for there were too many variables in this entire venture. All he'd planned – hoped – to do was somehow make it to the command tent and then... kill the bastards within!

He knew it was a ridiculous idea and momentarily thought about turning back and heading for the safety of his little hillock. He even slowed, as if his feet wished to carry him no further, sensing the magnitude of Wulfric's mission. A suicide mission, he knew.

So be it – he was prepared to die. As long as he could take Haesten with him, it would be worth the sacrifice.

Beside him, a drunk sea-wolf stumbled and kicked the iron tripod that supported a pot of bubbling stew. The scalding liquid spilled and landed on the Dane's leg, drawing a howl of pain and a furious berating from the nearby cook who'd been looking forward to his supper.

Wulfric felt a laugh brewing within him, almost a hysterical reaction to the incredibly dangerous position he'd put himself in, and then, in another few steps, he saw the familiar tent that belonged to his quarry. Outside stood the same massive guard who'd battered Wulfric unconscious not so long before and the ealdorman smoothly turned to his left, walking between two more large tents as if he knew exactly where he was going and had every right to be there. He felt the eyes of the guard boring into his back as the shadows swallowed him – there was one Northman who was neither drunk, exhausted, or incompetent.

If Wulfric wanted to kill Haesten he would need to find a way past that big, hard bastard. He hoped he would not have to fight the man, at least not before he reached the enemy king, for it would likely be a very messy encounter, and a noisy one. He would do whatever he could to avoid it.

The sound of footsteps made him turn and his eyes widened as he realised the big guard was standing right behind him, spear in hand and a look of malevolent suspicion on his battle-scarred face.

'You,' the Dane growled. 'Who are you? Wait. I know you!'

CHAPTER THIRTY-EIGHT

Wulfric stared back at the guard but he had no idea what the hell the man was saying. His speech was guttural and harsh and, although the Danes shared many common or similar words with the Saxons, whatever this one was saying was unfathomable to Wulfric.

It was, however, very clear that the guard was not in a friendly mood. He repeated his hostile question again but, before he could finish speaking, Wulfric's sword came free of its sheath with a soft sound and plunged deep into the Dane's belly.

The man's question was choked off as Wulfric dragged the blade upwards, doing as much damage as possible, feeling the steel grinding through flesh and bone. There was a horrific stench as the enemy warrior soiled himself, falling heavily to his knees as Wulfric withdrew his sword and stared breathlessly down at the dying man.

'That,' said the ealdorman quietly, 'is for what you did to me back at Hædleage, you bastard.'

The light went out of the Dane's eyes and Wulfric grabbed him, letting his body fall softly to the ground.

What now? The ealdorman knew there would be at least one other guard posted on Haesten's tent, and they would wonder where their comrade had disappeared to if he didn't return soon. They were probably already coming to find the big guard—

'By Óðinn, what's this?'

Wulfric jumped, thrusting his sword at the surprised sea-wolf who'd peered around the edge of the tent. This guard moved faster than his dead companion had done though, and used the shaft of his spear to knock aside the Saxon's blade. The shock of the situation worked in Wulfric's favour, for the spearman seemed too amazed to process his thoughts quickly. Rather than calling out for aid, the man simply gaped down at his friend's prone body.

'He's a Saxon,' Wulfric hissed, pointing at the dead man.

The sentence was so incongruous, so unexpected, that it caused the spearman even more confusion. As he stood pondering what to do next, Wulfric pointed over his shoulder and the guard turned instinctively.

Amazed that his childish ploy had worked, the ealdorman thrust his sword up through the Dane's chin, pushing it so hard that the tip broke through the man's skull.

Well, thought Wulfric as he pulled this second corpse into the shadows between the tents, *that's the guards out of the way*.

It hadn't been what he'd expected, or even hoped for, but he felt sure the way into Haesten's tent was now open and unguarded.

Praise be to God, he couldn't have asked for a better opportunity.

—

Haesten was sitting within his tent, wrapped in a great wolfskin for, although it was a mild night, he felt cold. Slaves had brought heated stones in for him and he believed he must have downed a barrel of mead that evening as his bloated guts seemed to grumble each time he shifted position.

He was alone for now, Ulfhild having left to take a walk around the camp. She often patrolled the area nearest to their command tent when they were on the march, perhaps finding her husband's company rather boring although she never said as much. He smiled ruefully, knowing she would not have found him a boring companion forty years ago. He belched and reached for his cup, set it back down again without raising it to his lips. He'd had enough for one night – the pleasant haze the drink had imparted was wearing off and leaving him with a sick feeling that only sleep would cure.

He closed his eyes, knowing there was no danger of him dying in a fire as his slaves or Ulfhild would douse the candles, and he tried to drift off thinking pleasant thoughts. He imagined what they would see when they reached Herutford, picturing Sigeferth's army ready and willing to join with Haesten's. Sigeferth was a good man, a good *vikingr*, and he would allow the older man to take overall command without argument. He'd sent messengers saying as much, which was why Haesten was travelling to join the Danes besieged at Herutford. In the old warlord's mind he could see the green fields and lush foliage of Wessex stretching out before him, the glistening River Lea with triumphant longships massed upon it, and hundreds of tall, proud warriors eyeing Haesten with awe and devotion. Travelling overhead, as if he'd taken the form of a great raven, the king looked down, seeing the terrified faces of the Saxons he'd come to slaughter. He heard their wailing and cries of anguish as they understood their doom was upon them.

There was a tearing sound and he sleepily wondered what it was. He couldn't be bothered turning to look for he was lovely and cosy within his wolfskin and his blankets and the dream he was creating seemed all too inviting.

He smelled something then and, at first, thought it was part of the scene he was imagining: leather and sweat. And blood. He opened his eyes and wondered if he had actually fallen asleep, or if the mead he'd taken was rancid for what he saw seemed impossible.

'Saxon?' the old king muttered, squinting up at the apparition before him. He saw a very tall, lean man with a bloody sword in hand, and dressed like one of his own sea-wolves, but Haesten recognised his face and knew this was the ealdorman he'd planned to inflict the blood eagle upon. 'How did you get in here?' he asked, feeling no fear yet, just curiosity.

Wulfric nodded and the warlord turned stiffly, seeing a great slash in the wall of the tent.

'You're here to kill me, eh?' Haesten asked, mind sluggishly beginning to put everything together. Where were his guards? He was not terribly afraid, for he knew Ulfhild would return soon and, if this hulking brute of a Saxon had planned on killing him, he'd already have done so.

He smiled and gestured at the cup beside him. 'Have a drink, my lord,' he said. 'Tell me the tale of how you managed to find your way past all my warriors and here, into my own tent.' As he spoke he looked into the eyes of the big ealdorman and felt a shiver run through him.

This man was not here to talk after all.

The sound of quick, light footsteps came to him then and a moment later Ulfhild ducked into the tent.

'Where in Hel are your guards?' she demanded, looking from Haesten to Wulfric, eyes widening in shock as she realised it was no loyal Northman sharing the tent with her husband.

The king watched in satisfaction as she drew out her seax with astonishing speed, the blade shining like fire in the meagre light from the candles dotted about the tent.

The Saxon moved just as fast as Ulfhild though, his left arm coming up and hammering into the warrior-woman's wrist. She gave a small cry of pain at the savagery of the parry, and Haesten watched in horrified fascination as time seemed to slow down. The Saxon kicked out, catching Ulfhild on the knee and, as she fell, the big man hacked down with an axe drawn from his belt. It was not a powerful blow for the ealdorman was forced to make it shallow so the iron head didn't catch in the tent's roof, but it caught Ulfhild on the skull. The hollow thump made Haesten wince, but the attacker was not done, and he repeated the hammering movement two more times and then, when Ulfhild was no longer moving, the Saxon's sword was thrust into the back of her neck, severing her spine.

Haesten stared, mouth hanging open at the savagery of the Saxon's assault. Never before had Ulfhild been beaten in single combat, as far as the king knew, and certainly not so comprehensively. The sight of his woman on the ground with her skull caved in was too much for Haesten to process.

'You've killed her,' he gasped, tears blurring his vision. He'd not been too bothered when Ulfhild and his sons were captured by the Saxons at Beamfleote, but now that they were all dead and he faced a life alone the weight of his years came crashing down upon him. He wondered how he would go on, but those fears disappeared as the thought of vengeance filled him. He threw off his wolfskin, or at least he tried to, finding the weight of the thing made it impossible for him to stand quickly.

'Bastard,' he sobbed, struggling to free himself, embarrassed by how ludicrous he must look when such a moment demanded a heroic response. 'You bastard, I'll see you blood-eagled for this, you'll never make it out of my camp alive.' Adding weight to his words, there came a shout of alarm from outside as the king's dead guards were discovered.

He opened his mouth to parley with the Saxon and saw the ealdorman's axe just before it hammered into the side of his head. Stars filled his vision and he knew he was lying down again, the crushing weight of his wolfskin across his chest, making it impossible for him to catch his breath.

'Wait,' he croaked, hearing the cries and footsteps running towards his tent and desperately sought to buy time for his guards to save him. 'I have silver...'

The huge Saxon did not say a word; had not, Haesten now realised, said a single word since he'd come into the tent. He did now.

'Your guards are coming to kill me, sea-wolf,' he grated, 'but I've done what I came here to do. Your wife is dead, and now you'll follow her to burn in hell. God curse you both!'

With that, the ealdorman bared his teeth and brought his axe down in another vicious swing.

CHAPTER THIRTY-NINE

Ealhswith laid her hand on Alfred's arm and squeezed reassuringly. He looked down at her and forced himself to smile although his guts were tight with anxiety, and he knew he would be forced to take to his bed soon.

The terrible stomach pains of his youth had abated, somewhat, during his middle years but they'd returned with a vengeance recently. He suspected it was not a punishment from God, but rather a punishment from himself, a rebuke for failing in his duty as King of Wessex.

They stood looking at the massed ranks of Sigeferth's army, which had been forming all throughout the morning. Having built the towers and the bridge that joined them across the River Lea, Sigeferth's army had no way to escape downriver, and no easy way to gather more food. Alfred had thought that the best way to force the Danes into submission but then the guards who'd travelled with Wulfric and John the Old Saxon had returned from Hædleage bearing their terrible tidings.

Not only was the beloved old abbot dead, but Wulfric most likely was too by now and, even more pertinently for the people of Wessex, Haesten's army was on their way to join Sigeferth.

No wonder Alfred's guts were roiling – everything he'd built over the past two decades was about to be torn asunder. Smashed by the spears and shields of the Northmen whom the West Saxons just could not defeat once and for all! How could Alfred defeat such an implacable, resilient enemy? For every warlord or king he killed or battered into submission there were a dozen others ready to take their place, coming in their despised longships with their tall, bearded warriors who wanted nothing but silver, slaves, and glory. Even dying in the hunt for those riches was no deterrent to the sea-wolves, who believed they would spend the afterlife feasting with their heathen gods.

It was hopeless. Wulfric was dead and Wessex was doomed and there wasn't a damn thing Alfred could do about it. God, he felt so tired of it all.

'What the hell are they actually doing?'

Alfred turned to see Aedan squinting at the scene before them. He was frowning and shaking his head as if confused.

'You've seen more than your fair share of battles, Aedan,' Ealhswith said, smiling in an attempt to lift the mood. Alfred's ill humour had spread throughout the ranks of the thanes and hearth-warriors around him. 'You must know what they're doing,' she went on. 'Preparing for war.'

Aedan did not look at her, a mark of his bafflement. He continued to crane his neck and to raise himself up on his horse to try and get a better view of the land around Herutford. 'That's the thing, my lady,' he replied. 'If they're making ready to fight us, they're going about it in a strange way.'

Alfred wanted to groan with the mounting pain in his guts. He wished his son, Edward, was there with him, to share the load of leadership, and the thought made him feel old. What kind of father would want to put this stress on his own boy? No, Edward was better – safer – on his estates to the east, far away from Sigeferth and Haesten and the death that was about to descend upon everyone near Lundenburh. Even those who avoided the fighting would face hardships no matter how this battle turned out.

No, Edward would have his own troubles to face when he was older and Alfred was no longer around to take command. This recent pain he'd been suffering though… It was like nothing he'd experienced before, and he knew that, if it struck him within the next hour or so, he'd not be able to lead the army. How would the people see that? At best, it would be seen by his troops as a bad omen, at worst everyone in Wessex would think him a coward, despite the fact he'd proved his mettle countless times over the years.

He realised he was letting his fears get to him and looked to the cloudy sky, begging God to give him the strength to get through the battle at least.

'Maybe they're just preparing,' Ealhswith suggested, not noticing her husband's discomfort. 'They may have had word that Haesten's army are approaching and making ready to join his ranks.'

Aedan still did not look at her, so focused was he on the enemy gathered in the middle distance. 'Perhaps,' he admitted. 'Although our scouts have not reported any Danes on the road from East Anglia.'

'Maybe Haesten is coming by longship,' Alfred muttered, doing his best to keep his voice level. 'We destroyed or took most of their vessels, but their allies may have brought more. Damn heathens seem to have limitless numbers of men and longships.'

Aedan continued to stare ahead, forehead lined with worry.

Alfred understood the thane's trepidation. The Danes were usually quite predictable when it came to battle. They would rarely fight unless they had superior numbers, preferring to remain within their earthworks until the Saxons paid them off or returned to their homes for harvest or planting.

What was Sigeferth planning, and how could Alfred protect his army against it?

'Send out riders,' he said to Aedan. 'Have them scout all the rivers that Haesten might use to transport his sea-wolves here. There's a chance we've missed them and they're much nearer than we thought. It wouldn't be the first time the whoresons had marched overland at great speed and taken us completely by surprise.'

'Yes, lord,' Aedan returned with a bow, and turned his horse to find men to carry out the orders.

'What will we do now?' Ealhswith asked. She did not appear worried or frightened, a mark of the faith she had in Alfred, and it raised his spirits to know she believed he would lead them right, no matter what the enemy leaders were up to.

'Now,' the king said, with a tight smile, 'I'll hear Mass. Will you join me?'

Ealhswith smiled. 'Of course.'

'Come, then,' he said, dismounting and helping his wife down from her white palfrey. 'Asser?'

The bishop nodded and came to join them, leading the way to the little tent that contained everything he would need to celebrate Mass. Some of the thanes and ealdormen followed, while others went to rejoin their fyrds, making sure their men were all alert and ready for whatever Sigeferth would do.

Asser's beatific smile alighted on Alfred, and the king felt suddenly reassured. Asser had seen his discomfort and God's power seemed to thrum in the air as the Mass started. It was not unheard of for Alfred to enjoy the rite outdoors, but it was uncommon enough to be something of a novelty. Rather than the silence of a church, with thick timber or stone walls dampening the sounds from outside and imparting a reverential, almost otherworldly ambience to proceedings, hearing Mass in a field like they were in now was different. The buzzing of insects, low murmuring of men chatting nearby, birdsong in the trees with their gently creaking branches, the breeze ruffling the king's long hair... Alfred's pain eased a little and he felt blessed as Asser led them in the opening hymn.

As was usual, the king found himself becoming lost within the ritual, allowing the bishop's words to penetrate deeply to his very soul. Tears formed in his eyes as Asser recited '*De Dominica Oratione*' – one of Alfred's favourite homilies – and the thought of driving the heathen invaders from their shores forever filled his heart. The pain in his stomach was forgotten and righteous power seemed to flow through him. He would fight Sigeferth that day, and his sword would be the implement of Christ's justice. Justice for all those of his flock who'd fallen to the hunters from across the whale road.

'We beg you, lord,' Asser intoned near the end of the Mass, head bowed, eyes on the soft grass before him. 'We beg you grant our brave warriors the strength to defeat our enemies this day. To bring us victory against those who follow the false gods. To protect our King Alfred, and all who reside within these blessed, green lands.'

'Amen,' Alfred murmured and then he looked up, scowling. Someone was shouting nearby, and there was nothing the king hated more than being disturbed while he was praying.

The shout was louder now, and it seemed to be spreading quickly amongst the West Saxon ranks although it was still too far away to make out the words the men were crying out.

'What's going on?' Alfred growled, turning to see what the commotion was. He saw a man on horseback thundering towards them from the direction of Sigeferth's camp and, as the rider grew closer Alfred recognised him as Aedan. Warriors parted from his galloping mount as the waters of the Red Sea had parted for Moses and, as he passed them, his cry was taken up by the men.

'What are they saying?' Ealhswith asked, hand gripping Alfred's arm although whether it was in excitement or fear he could not say for he could not tear his eyes away from Aedan who seemed to be framed in rays of golden sunlight.

At last the words of the rider and of the men he was hurtling past grew loud enough and close enough that Alfred could make them out.

'It's a miracle!' Aedan was shouting.

'A miracle,' the men agreed in joyful tones.

'What does he mean?' a thane standing close to Alfred asked, hand grasping his sword, ready for trouble.

'Look!' another nobleman shouted. 'Look at the Danes!'

Alfred could see movement at Sigeferth's camp and he ran then, vaulting on top of a wagon filled with sacks of vegetables that had been drawn up nearby. From his higher vantage point he was able to finally make sense of Aedan's claim of 'a miracle'.

Sigeferth and his Danes were moving, but they were not forming into a shieldwall and coming towards the army of Wessex. Instead, the *vikingar* were taking to their longships or marching away.

'They're going northwards,' Ealhswith said, jumping up onto the wagon beside her husband and looking from the Northmen to Alfred with glittering eyes and the biggest smile he'd seen on her face for a long time. 'They're leaving!' she shouted, grabbing him around the neck and hugging him fiercely.

'It's a miracle, lord,' Aedan shouted, reining in his horse beside the wagon and he too had a broad grin on his face. 'They've given up. They're leaving!'

Alfred could see that what Aedan reported was true and he joined in with the ripple of laughter that was spreading all throughout the West Saxon army.

'But where are they going?' the king demanded, not yet willing to believe things were turning out as nicely as they seemed. 'It might be a trick. Maybe they're just going north a short distance, to join Haesten and then come back here.'

'Haesten is not on the road to the north,' Aedan returned, shaking his head vigorously. 'We'd have had reports of them by now. No one's seen them since our men returned from Hædleage with word from Wulfric. Something else must have happened.'

Alfred stood with his arms around Ealhswith, joyful but unwilling yet to believe Asser's Mass had truly had such an immediate and miraculous effect. Could it really be true? Was Sigeferth simply giving up and leaving Herutford?

Even if they were, they could not be allowed to attack the settlements they passed on their way out of Wessex. He smiled at Ealhswith, kissed her happily on the lips, and then bellowed to his commanders, 'Make ready to march, lads! We'll follow the heathen scum all the way out of our lands, and kick their arses if they try to steal as much as a loaf of bread!'

It was a happy army that began the chase after their retreating enemy. Some, led by Ealdorman Aethelred, followed the course of the River Lea which flowed to the west and would, ultimately, end up in Mercia. Aethelred was happy to take this course, looking forward to being reunited with Lady Aethelflaed.

Alfred himself took the larger force and went on foot, or horseback, after the majority of the Danes who had no longships to depart in.

Lundenburh's garrison remained at Herutford, ready to deal with any threats from Haesten or any other Dane who might suddenly turn up although that now seemed highly unlikely. Sigeferth's one and only chance of beating the West Saxons had been to combine his numbers with Haesten's. Without those extra troops the Dane had no chance of winning any battle.

Ealhswith rode beside the king, as did Asser, and Alfred's heart was light as they travelled. The sea-wolves showed no inclination to halt and fight or even to turn back and hurl insults at their pursuers. They marched steadily, practically in silence, and it looked a dejected, ragtag column that headed out of Wessex.

'I don't understand,' Ealhswith said as it became ever clearer that Sigeferth was truly giving up his war with Wessex, for now at least. 'What made them leave?'

'God answered our prayers,' Asser said seriously.

Alfred nodded in hearty agreement with the bishop. 'Indeed. But also the fact that we'd blocked off the river to the south, and taken in all the harvest leaving them with no food for winter and no way to get any.'

'But Haesten's army,' the queen consort mused. 'They were on the road to join Sigeferth. We know that from those warriors who journeyed with Wulfric. Did Haesten just change his mind?'

Alfred had been asking himself that very question and the answer seemed obvious, if too incredible to believe.

'Maybe Wulfric succeeded in the mission he gave himself,' he murmured gravely.

Asser and Ealhswith both looked at him in disbelief.

'No. Surely not,' said the bishop, laughing. 'I mean, God is great, but that would be asking too much of Him, would it not?'

'How could Wulfric have made it into Haesten's camp,' Ealhswith asked. 'Never mind found his way to the king's tent, got past the guards, and then killed him?'

'Not to mention that wife of his,' Aedan added. He was riding just behind them, still grinning at the 'miracle' they'd witnessed that day. 'I know Wulfric is a great warrior, but Ulfhild would give any man a hard fight.'

'Exactly.' Asser nodded emphatically, swaying slightly as his horse moved around a boulder. 'It's too incredible. Something else must have happened to divert Haesten from his course. Perhaps he simply decided he'd suffered enough beatings at your hands, lord, and those of your commanders.'

'Maybe,' Alfred shrugged. 'But Wulfric has never let Wessex down. It would not surprise me to find out he's killed Haesten.' The thought made him swell with pride, but it also frightened him for if Wulfric did make it into the old warlord's camp and put an end to him, there would be no way back out for Wulfric. The alarm would be raised, and hundreds of Northmen would fall upon Alfred's friend like a pack of ravening wolves.

The king's joy dimmed as he contemplated that bleak scenario. It hardly mattered that Wulfric was already old, as warriors went, and had led a storied, honourable life. Had done things that truly mattered for his king and his people.

Alfred had already lost friends like Diuma. To lose Wulfric to the blades of the Danes as well... How could he bear it? He was not sure he could.

CHAPTER FORTY

Alfred sat eating some food and, although his ale was warm for it was a muggy day, the liquid was doing more than enough to slake his thirst and leave him feeling somewhat content.

They'd been trailing Sigeferth's Danes for two days now, Alfred's outriders occasionally going on ahead of the main army to pepper the rear ranks of enemy soldiers with arrows and throwing spears. They did not do much damage for the Saxons simply wanted to show the Danes what would happen if they stopped moving, and it was doing the job so far, as Sigeferth's men had moved at a quick pace and only stopped when necessary. They had not marched northwest as some expected. Rather than heading for East Anglia they seemed to be aiming for Mercia. Perhaps Sigeferth had no firm destination in mind and simply hoped to escape Alfred's pursuit. Whatever the case, there had been no real fighting, and the Danes had clearly lost any will they once had to fight the army of Wessex.

'Maybe we should turn back,' Aedan had suggested that morning. 'They pose no threat to our lands now, lord.'

Alfred shook his head firmly although he would have gladly returned to Wintanceaster to enjoy the autumn. 'Mercia is our ally,' he reminded his captain. 'My daughter is married to Ealdorman Aethelred! We'll see Sigeferth dead, or gone completely, before we turn back.'

Ealhswith agreed with him. 'We might even get to see Aethelflaed,' she'd said to Alfred as they rode in the early-morning sun, and the thought had made him smile. He would like nothing more than to spend a quiet afternoon with his wife and children, watching the world go by without the need to fight, or for anyone to die...

There had still been no word of Haesten or Wulfric, and the king naturally feared the worst for his old friend. Their scouts had returned having scoured the lands near Herutford and finding no evidence of any invasion force or any Danes whatsoever so it really did seem like Haesten had chosen to give up Wessex forever and take his raiders elsewhere for plunder. Somewhere the locals wouldn't put up as much of a fight as the West Saxons had done.

Still, it did not quite feel like a victory for Alfred. Perhaps it would when Sigeferth's army was defeated or scattered, or perhaps that glorious feeling of triumph that usually followed the winning of a battle would never be Alfred's. That might well be the case if Wulfric was never heard from again.

Sighing, feeling his joints aching again, and annoyed with his inability to simply feel pleasure on such a glorious day, he tossed the remainder of his bread to a jackdaw that was staring at him expectantly from its white eyes. He looked away, knowing the bird would not come closer if it thought he was watching it, and then all thoughts of jackdaws were shattered by what he saw coming towards him.

'Wulfric!'

Alfred was on his feet and running like a child, laughing and shouting, oblivious to the looks of amazement from his thanes and hearth-warriors. Those looks of amazement were nothing to the shock on their faces when they saw the big, bluff ealdorman coming, also at a run and also laughing almost maniacally.

'You're alive, you big bastard! How the hell are you not dead?'

They embraced and Alfred stared in wonder at Wulfric. He'd convinced himself, deep down, that he would never see his friend again. That he'd been killed while trying to sneak into Haesten's camp. The plan of a lunatic if ever there was one!

'Wait,' he suddenly exclaimed with a frown. 'God's blood, Wulfric, have you become a heathen?'

The ealdorman looked down and grinned, pulling a Mjölnir amulet from his neck. 'I took it from Haesten's body, thinking it would disguise me if the Saxons spotted me in their camp,' he said. 'And so it did! But I suppose I can stop wearing it now.'

Alfred felt something thumping into his back and then he was laughing again as Ealhswith had her arms around both him and Wulfric, and even Aedan ran up to add his weight to the embrace.

'Really, Wulfric,' the king demanded, freeing himself from the tangle of arms and stepping back to eye the ealdorman happily. 'Haesten is dead then? But how did you come to be here?'

'It's a long story, lord,' Wulfric replied. 'And I look forward to telling you all about it. For now though, it's enough to say Haesten and his wife are dead, and his army have turned back from Wessex. I was almost captured after I killed the king, but the alarm was raised and there was so much confusion I was able to slip away. I managed to find a horse in a nearby village then I met one of your scouts on the road to Herutford and he told me you'd come this way, chasing Sigeferth along the River Lea. So, here I came!'

'Did you hear that?' Alfred shouted, turning to face the crowd that was gathering around them. 'Haesten is dead!'

'Haesten's dead!' The word went out, spreading like fire in a field of dry grass, passing from fyrd to fyrd until the air was filled with the cry. 'Haesten's dead!'

'God be praised,' said Alfred, tears of joy filling his eyes. 'The war is over, Wulfric, finally, after all these years. We've won!'

CHAPTER FORTY-ONE

AD 896, October 26th, Wintanceaster

Sigeferth's longships and his army continued west along the River Severn until, at last, they came to Cwatbridge where they finally stopped retreating and dug themselves in once more.

Cwatbridge was far from Wessex and the Mercian ealdorman, Aethelred, brought his own fyrd, along with Aethelflaed, to meet Alfred there.

'Father!' Aethelflaed looked even more confident than when Alfred had seen her last and he embraced her happily after she'd ran to him. She looked older too, of course, and that made him wonder just how ancient he must appear to her.

Ealhswith joined them and Aethelflaed hugged her mother, laughing and complimenting the queen consort's hair. Alfred smiled, knowing Aethelflaed cared more for weapons and armour than for hair or fine clothes, but he appreciated his daughter's attempt to please Ealhswith.

'How have you been?' the king asked. 'How is our granddaughter, Aelfwynn?'

Aethelflaed's laughter rang out, her love for the little girl evident in her joyful expression. 'Oh, she's wonderful. We've left her in Gloucester with her maids and Ealdorman Morcar.'

Alfred nodded, disappointed but understanding the decision. 'I would have liked to see her but it's not safe for a child here.'

'Especially one like Aelfwynn,' Aethelflaed agreed. 'She's a law unto herself. Likes to wander.'

'That reminds me of someone else,' Ealhswith noted, eyebrow raised. 'You were the same as a child.'

'Never did me any harm.' Aethelflaed grinned. 'But let's get some refreshments. I'm hungry, and it looks like the mess tent has been setup.'

The next few days were happy ones for Alfred as he was able to spend time with his beloved daughter. They feasted and talked of the war with the Danes, of God, of little Aelfwynn, and of their hopes for the future of Wessex and Mercia. They also went out riding together as they used to do when Aethelflaed was a child and that in particular brought back memories of happy times for Alfred.

Sigeferth remained within his fortress and, as time went on, Alfred knew he must take his fyrd back to Wessex. He would have liked to spend a few more days with Aethelflaed, as would Ealhswith, but duty called and there was no need for the armies of both Mercia and Wessex to maintain the siege. With smiles and tears of farewell, the king embraced Aethelflaed and then reluctantly led his people back to Wintanceaster, leaving his daughter and Ealdorman Aethelred to deal with Sigeferth.

Throughout the rest of the year, messengers continually travelled the roads between Mercia, and also Hædleage. King Eohric happily informed Alfred that, when Haesten was killed in East Anglia, his army disintegrated, following individual jarls and hersirs to find glory and fortune elsewhere, vowing never to return to Wessex for it had proved too dangerous a place to raid.

Similarly, in the west, Aethelflaed reported that Sigeferth's army gradually sailed or marched away, with most of the Danes choosing to follow the warlord across the sea to Ireland.

It was an anticlimactic end to the war that had consumed Alfred and his people's lives for the past four years but the lack of a great, final battle was clearly a blessing for all except the scops, who would have preferred an exciting end to their tales. Still, there had been more than enough acts of bravery, and heroes, during the fighting for the storytellers to celebrate over the next few months and years.

Diuma, Aethelred, Edward, Aethelflaed, Alfred himself, and, of course, Wulfric – all of them, and more, were immortalised in songs and stories that entertained and warmed the hearts of the people of Wessex during even the coldest winter nights.

The king oversaw the rebuilding of the towns and villages damaged or destroyed by the Northmen, and his burhs were strengthened once more. Never again would marauding *vikingar* find the shores of Wessex an easy target.

Peace came to the kingdom then, and the people found themselves growing in wealth and in learning too, for Alfred continued to insist that as many of his people as possible should learn to read, rather than wasting their leisure time in frivolous or carnal pursuits.

The king also made the most of his days, overjoyed to spend them in prayer and contemplation instead of war. He translated more Latin books, completing work on Boethius's *Consolation of Philosophy*, and St Augustine's *Soliloquies* during this period. He also spread his riches amongst the monasteries, his school, and the poor, but it was not just in material wealth that he praised God, vowing also to serve the Almighty with his own body and mind, day and night.

This notion made him realise that he had no way to accurately judge the time thanks to darkness, or rain and cloud obscuring the sun and stars. Ruminating on the problem, he eventually came up with an ingenious solution, making candles of uniform size and marking the wax so they would burn down to each mark at twenty-minute intervals. Six of these candles would last for twenty-four hours, allowing Alfred to know exactly what the time was. To stop the flame being extinguished he designed a lantern constructed from wood and transparent white-ox horn, ensuring the candles would always burn at the same rate no matter the draughts that blew through the doors of the church they were located within.

Three years of peace Wessex enjoyed, as Alfred and Ealhswith's other children grew into adults and went out into the world to make names for themselves. The aetheling Edward's wife Ecgwynn died after an illness and he took Aelfflaed, daughter of Ealdorman Ethelhelm of Wiltshire, as his new bride.

Alfred, now in his fiftieth year, spent much less time indulging the carnal pleasures that he'd been renowned for in his early days. He ate healthier, drank much less ale, and took no women other than Ealhswith to bed, truly doing his best to live a Godly life.

Those earlier indulgences had taken their toll on his body, however, and the aches in his joints and, particularly, the stomach pains that had beset him through his whole reign grew worse until he was forced to spend much of his time in bed.

One morning the king summoned Asser, Wulfric and Edward to his chamber. When Wulfric walked in he smiled to Ealhswith who was already there, but the sight of his friend in bed reminded him painfully of the priest, Oswald, who'd died of a similar stomach malady to the one Alfred suffered from. Oswald had withstood much pain and should have died sooner than he did, his latter days and weeks being spent inebriated in an attempt to dull the agony he was going through. Wulfric prayed that Alfred would recover from this recent bout of illness but, if he could not, that God would not force him to linger in his sickbed for as long as Oswald had done.

Surely God would not be so cruel to his faithful servant...

'I am weak,' Alfred said to the three men as they crowded around his bedside with worried frowns. 'Each day saps me further.' His face was damp with sweat and his hand rested continually on his stomach. Every now and then he would grimace and grit his teeth as if in terrible pain.

'We pray for you, lord,' said Asser, who'd also seen his fiftieth birthday come and go. He looked rather younger than the king though, whose years of hard living had visibly taken a toll upon.

'I pray for myself.' Alfred chuckled gloomily. 'Perhaps God will heed our prayers and I can get back to translating those books of ours, eh?'

Asser nodded and, to Wulfric, it seemed like the bishop had faith the king would recover. Wulfric was not so sure.

'Edward,' Alfred said, turning his eyes on his oldest son. 'You've become a fine man. A fine leader. It will be time for you to take the throne soon.'

Edward looked at his father in anguish but did not argue. Instead he merely nodded. 'I'm ready, my lord,' he vowed.

'Good,' the king nodded. He groaned and Ealhswith, who was at his side as she usually was those days, squeezed his hand and wiped a damp rag across his forehead before holding a cup of cool wine to his lips.

He only took one long sip and then turned his head away, almost like a child when their mother tries to feed them another unwanted spoonful of gruel. Alfred thanked his wife though, even managing to smile at her before turning back to their son.

'When you become king there may be some who will challenge your right to the throne,' Alfred murmured.

'Aethelwold,' said Wulfric to the king. 'Your nephew.'

'Yes,' said Ealhswith as another stab of pain made Alfred wince. 'Your father has done all he can, Edward, to make sure you take the throne legally. His will should leave no room for argument.'

'Aethelwold is a little shit though,' Wulfric noted dourly.

'He is,' Alfred said, recovered somewhat now. 'Which is why I want you to become Edward's captain, Wulfric. He'll need your experience and your wisdom to deal with whatever Aethelwold decides to throw his way.'

Wulfric frowned. He was sixty-one now: a relatively old man. 'Wouldn't it be better to find someone... younger than me?' he asked. 'Someone that can support Edward in years to come?'

'You mean as you did for me?' Alfred asked with a small smile. 'Yes, and Edward has good men his own age to advise him throughout his reign. For now, though, while the kingdom is going through the transition of power, I would like you by his side. You have so much experience, my friend. You would be a valuable addition to Edward's court.'

No one spoke for a time and Wulfric wondered why Alfred was talking this way. Did he expect to drop down dead any moment? Surely not. The priest, Oswald, had lingered for a long time, deteriorating markedly, before he finally passed. The ealdorman examined Alfred surreptitiously and was somewhat surprised to realise the king's beard hid a hollowness that had not been in his cheeks before. Still, Wulfric could well remember the vile stench that had emanated from Oswald's sickroom, and the agonised cries as the pains wracked his failing body.

Alfred had not suffered so, had he?

'Will you do it?' the king asked and Wulfric was jolted back to the present, thoughts of Oswald fleeing from his mind.

'Of course, lord. I am your family's servant.' He looked at Edward, wondering if the aetheling would even want his help, but the young man nodded gratefully.

'Good, that's settled then,' Alfred said. 'Thank you, Wulfric. You have been the best friend I could ever have wished for.'

Wulfric nodded, a little taken aback by the king's praise in front of the others. 'As have you, my lord,' he replied gruffly. 'I've been lucky to serve you for so long, as Wessex has been lucky to have you as king during so many hard years.'

Alfred smiled and gazed at the wall as if lost in thought. 'Do you remember that first, great victory we had at Ascesdune?' he said to Wulfric.

'How could I forget?' the ealdorman replied. 'Your brother wouldn't join the fight until he was done with his prayers. We almost lost.' He shook his head, thinking back to that day nearly thirty years before. 'You fought like the devil himself that day, Alfred.'

'We all did,' the king nodded happily, eyes glazing over as the wine took effect. 'I was terrified. Then, not long after that, my brother died, and I took the throne.' His good humour faded and the atmosphere became oppressive, but his smile returned.

'Aethelflaed was just little then, and a while later, you were born, Edward.'

The aetheling reached out and grasped Alfred's hand, squeezing it gently but saying nothing.

'You were always a good boy,' the king murmured, and it seemed to Wulfric as if he was only partially in the room with them. As though some part of him was in the past, reliving those earlier, happy days.

'We made some fine children, didn't we, my love?' Alfred said to Ealhswith, and it was her turn to take his hand and kiss his forehead, eyes brimming with tears as she did so.

'We did,' she agreed. 'Praise God, we did, Alfred.'

'What about those days on Athelney? We were cold, frightened, hunted… but they were some of the best times of my life.' Alfred's voice became hard as he reminisced. 'I was glad to leave there though, and reclaim our lands from the sea-wolves. Diuma came back to us then, remember? Ah, Diuma, how I wish you could be here with us now…' He trailed off and then his eyes flicked up to Wulfric. 'Remember that whoreson – what was his name, now? – Hjalmarr! That was it, Jarl Hjalmarr.'

'I remember you foolishly taking him on in single combat,' Wulfric scolded him.

'Won, didn't I?' Alfred retorted with a wry grin.

'Aye, you did,' the ealdorman laughed. 'Then stuck his head on the end of a spear to warn other Danes not to come to Lundenburh.'

'They never did stop coming though, did they?' the king said dreamily. 'Haesten, Halfdan, Ubba, Ivar, Guthrum.' He chuckled at the latter's name. 'Who would have thought Guthrum would become a friend, eh? After all the things he did.'

'We defeated them all, lord,' Wulfric said proudly. 'You led us to victory against every one of the bastards.'

'I had some help,' Alfred said. 'From all of you, and Oswald, and Diuma, and the others who have gone ahead of me to be with God. I've been blessed to know you all.'

'I think you should rest now,' Ealhswith said with a worried frown as the king's voice faded weakly again. 'You're getting tired.'

Alfred weakly raised his hand in farewell as both Wulfric and Edward were ushered from the room by Ealhswith. Asser remained and the queen consort went back in, gently closing the door behind her.

'Well,' said Edward. 'That explains why my father asked me to visit him here in Wintanceaster. You'll be my new captain, eh?'

'Is that all right with you?' Wulfric asked. He had been the aetheling's tutor years ago and they knew one another quite well, but kings often liked to choose their own staff, particularly those who would be working the closest beside them.

'Of course,' said Edward emphatically. 'You've been a rock for my father, and for the kingdom. I'd be honoured to have you by my side, my lord.'

Wulfric smiled broadly, pleased to still be so much in demand at his advanced age.

'Hopefully I won't have any need of you for a while yet though, eh?' Edward said jovially, beginning to walk towards the bench beside the firepit in the hall. 'My father's suffered these gut pains for as long as I can remember, and he always gets over them.'

'True,' Wulfric agreed. 'The first time was at his wedding to your mother. It's been a constant source of anguish for him, yet, as you say, he's managed to survive and turn Wessex into the great kingdom it is today in spite of those pains.' He nodded thoughtfully, a warm wave of affection for his old friend filling him as they came to the bench and a servant hurried across to bring them refreshments.

'Edward. Wulfric.'

They turned and saw Ealhswith standing at the open chamber door, hands clasped by her abdomen as she looked at them with a strange, unreadable expression.

Edward was already moving, hurrying back to his mother as Wulfric followed, a sick feeling in the pit of his stomach. He could feel tears forming even before he reached Ealhswith and she bent her head, gesturing for them to go back in.

Alfred lay on the bed with his eyes closed, looking as if he was simply enjoying a peaceful nap. Asser was reciting a soft prayer and Wulfric looked at Ealhswith although he already knew what had happened.

'He's dead,' the lady whispered, her voice breaking as Edward took her in his arms and held her tightly against him.

Wulfric gaped, amazed, a lump in his throat and tears now spilling unashamedly down his cheeks. 'But how?' he asked in confusion. 'We were literally just talking to him. He looked, sounded, fine! Oswald…'

Ealhswith was sobbing quietly, face buried in Edward's tunic, but her words were clear enough. 'Oswald was a priest,' she replied. 'And a fine one too, may God rest his soul. But he was a man of peace – Alfred is, was, a warrior. He's been suffering terribly these past few days, Wulfric. The pain has been unbearable at times, yet, unlike Oswald he was able to hide it from everyone except me, and Asser.'

Wulfric felt a sudden pang of jealousy at the tonsured man who was still praying over the king's unmoving body. He angrily pushed the feeling aside, knowing Alfred would of course have sought Asser, for the bishop would be needed to pray for him in his final days. Wulfric did not have that connection with God.

Ealhswith continued to cry as Edward lightly detached himself and went over to look down at the face of his father. The young man was masking his emotions well, doing his best to play the part of the proud king, for that was what he was now. Wulfric could see the tightness of the young man's jaw though, knew Edward was just as upset as anyone in that room. Had he been younger himself, Wulfric would also have hidden his feelings. But, as he'd grown older such things seemed less important. Especially when one had just lost someone who'd been their dear friend for decades and been through so much beside them.

'Halfdan, Guthrum, Haesten...' the ealdorman murmured, sucking in a shuddering breath through his nose. 'No Dane could best him. Only God would decide when his work here was done.'

Ealhswith looked up at him in amazement. 'Yes, you're right, Wulfric.' She even laughed a little through her tears as she came over and grasped him by the arm, sharing his grief. 'I never would have expected such words from you, but you are exactly right.'

They stood like that for a long time, Asser continuing to say prayers for the king's soul until, at last, Wulfric looked down at Ealhswith and wiped his face with the back of his hand. 'We must tell the people, my lady,' he said, and she nodded.

'Yes, we must, Wulfric.' She sighed and looked down at the floor. 'Remember the last time this happened?'

Wulfric nodded. 'I brought you and Alfred the news of his brother's passing.'

'You did,' she agreed. 'You told us Aethelred had died, but you also reminded us what that meant.'

The ealdorman looked at her and then he understood her meaning and they turned together to look at Edward. 'You're right, my lady,' he said. 'The people must be told – they have a new king.'

Ealhswith slumped against Wulfric then, finally overcome by her loss and by the memories of that long distant day when Alfred had become king. The big ealdorman grasped her, supporting himself as much as he was supporting Ealhswith.

'The king is dead.' She sobbed, drawing back and taking a long, deep breath as she gathered her composure and stared proudly at her son. 'Long live the king.'

CHAPTER FORTY-TWO

King Alfred was buried in Wintanceaster and he was given a magnificent send-off, with Asser proclaiming him 'the magnanimous king of the Saxons, unshakeable pillar of the western people, a man replete with justice, vigorous in warfare, learned in speech, above all instructed in divine learning'.

All the important clergymen, thanes and ealdormen were at the funeral to celebrate the life of the man who was already being called the greatest king in Wessex's history. Alfred's children were there to support Ealhswith: Aethelflaed with her husband, Ealdorman Aethelred of Mercia; Edward; Aethelgifu, Abbess of Sceaftesburi Abbey; Aelfthryth who was now married to Baldwin, the count of Flanders; and the beloved youngest son, Aethelweard, who was not yet twenty.

One member of Alfred's family was notably absent, though, and it came as no great surprise when word came from Wimborne while the funeral feast was still underway.

'That little bastard,' Wulfric growled as the messenger explained what Aethelwold, Alfred's nephew, had done as soon as the king's death was announced. 'We should have killed him that night he made a scene over Alfred's will.'

Ealhswith had never wanted to make an enemy of Aethelwold, having loved the boy when he was an infant and his father, Aethelred, had still been alive. But now... She nodded her head in grim agreement with Wulfric's sentiments.

'So he's seized the royal estates at Wimborne and Twineham,' Edward stated matter-of-factly, mulling over what the messenger had told them. 'And locked himself within Wimborne.'

'Why there?' a young thane wondered. 'Is there some significance to the place?'

'His father is buried at Wimborne,' Ealhswith said. 'Aethelwold wishes to remind us that he is also the son of a king, and, by his logic, has as much right to the throne of Wessex as Edward.'

'This is ludicrous,' a red-faced bishop erupted. 'No one would support Aethelwold, surely. Edward has every legal right to be king, I mean, the Witan agreed. And, on top of that, Edward has proven himself a capable and courageous commander, defeating the Danes on more than one occasion!'

'You're right.' Wulfric nodded gravely. 'But Aethelwold is the son of a former king of Wessex, and there was once an argument that he, or his brother, should have been next in line when their father died. Instead, Alfred was crowned and Aethelwold has been bitter about it ever since he came of age.'

'Let's not discuss all that again,' Ealhswith said. They were in Wintanceaster's hall surrounded by Alfred's hearth-warriors as well as Edward's, and the thanes and ealdormen who were still in the city. Everyone there knew the history between Aethelwold and his now deceased uncle. 'The question is: what do we do about this pretender to the throne?'

All eyes turned to Edward and he swallowed. This was his first test – a major one – and he hadn't even been crowned king yet. He thought of Aethelwold and how well he had performed during the battle at Scobrih two years before.

His cousin was an angry young man who seemed to think the world was against him – that was a weakness but also gave Aethelwold the drive to have now captured Wimborne and made his play for the throne. Edward did not know him well, but he knew enough to respect him as a dangerous opponent.

'Do any of you here support Aethelwold?' he demanded, standing and running his gaze across the noblemen and warriors within the hall. 'Do you believe he has a greater claim to be king than I?'

He knew that some of the men there did believe Aethelwold had a decent claim to the throne, indeed had probably been in contact with his cousin, hence Aethelwold's bold attacks on Twineham and Wimborne. Some, perhaps all, may not even think Aethelwold should be king before Edward, but they saw Alfred's death as an opportunity to gain more power for themselves. If Aethelwold was to defeat Edward, any who supported him would be very well rewarded.

It was a dangerous time in Wessex.

No one there spoke up to support Aethelwold – it would have been a very rash move, marking any who did as an enemy of Edward. Not the wisest move when surrounded by Wulfric, Aethelnoth, and all the other warriors who were firmly on Edward's side.

'I have not been formally crowned yet, but I *am* king of the Anglo-Saxons now,' he said. 'By right of birth, by my father's will, and by force of arms.' There were nods and loud rumbles of assent at this and he forged on, filling with confidence. 'Aethelwold is a rebel, and I'll deal with him as one must deal with any who threatens the safety of his lands and his people: we ride to war, gentlemen.'

Edward felt it was a good speech, unplanned and delivered off the cuff, but it did not quite rouse his men as he'd hoped. Still, no one wanted to fight this battle, Saxon against Saxon, so it wasn't really surprising that the nobles gathered in Wintanceaster did not meet his pronouncement with cheers of joy. They would do as he said though, he hoped, and follow him to meet his cousin, which was all he could ask of them at that moment.

'We will ride to Wimborne, and deal with Aethelwold,' he said firmly.

Wulfric stood up beside him then, bowing towards him. 'And then, when the upstart aetheling is no longer a threat, we'll crown our new king, and Wessex will move forward in a position of strength and wealth that none before us have ever known!'

That thought did rouse the noblemen – the idea of getting richer was a sure way to win the support of a warrior, and Edward smiled gratefully at his experienced captain. Still, many of the noblemen remained reticent to fight their own kinfolk at Wimborne. Many of them were old enough to remember King Aethelred and respect him. Killing his son did not seem at all right.

'There is one other thing, my lord,' called Asser, coming into the hall at that moment, all eyes turning to look at him. 'We've just had more dire news from Wimborne. Aethelwold has abducted a nun from the nearby Sceaftesburi Abbey.'

That caused uproar, with everyone demanding to know why the aetheling would do such a thing. How could this possibly strengthen his cause? Edward understood immediately though and, by the shocked expression on his mother's face, she did too.

'The nun he's abducted,' cried Asser in outrage, 'is Lady Aethelgifu, abbess, and daughter of Alfred himself!'

Aethelwold's motive became clear then – he intended to force Aethelgifu to marry him, further cementing his claim to the throne. If he truly thought this a cunning move, he could not have been more wrong.

'Let us ride then, lads,' Edward cried, praying that, this time, his words would garner an enthusiastic response.

They did, thank God, and soon a great army was marching behind him to deal with the rebel who'd kidnapped the Abbess of Sceaftesburi and sought to steal the throne of Wessex.

—

When they came within four miles of Wimborne, Edward chose to camp there, at an iron age hillfort known as Badbury Rings. This allowed his army to dig in and fortify the area, but, crucially, it also allowed Aethelwold a chance to escape should he wish. Edward had no great desire for battle if things might be settled peacefully, somehow, with his rival.

Emissaries were sent from both camps and a meeting arranged at a location midway between both armies. Scouts had reported that Aethelwold's force numbered much less than his, so, as they came to meet, Edward felt confident.

Taking with him Wulfric, Aedan, Aethelnoth, and Aethelred of Mercia, Edward stood on a low hill with a view of the surrounding area and waited for his cousin's arrival. He could see there was no gathered army nearby, no treachery afoot of that nature, and it wasn't long before the rebel appeared with four of his own *hearthweru*.

'Wait here,' Edward commanded, dismounting and walking to meet his rival. He was armed with his sword and his seax, and he had no doubt Aethelwold would come similarly outfitted, but Edward had learned from the best swordsmen in Wessex and did not fear his rival, physically.

'What have you to say, cousin?' Aethelwold demanded when they were within touching distance. No preamble, no commiserations for Edward's loss, or respectful greeting. It seemed a mark of Aethelwold's lack of not only manners, but moral fibre.

'You have abducted my sister,' Edward returned with a similar frosty tone. 'I should have known you'd do something like this when you spoke of coveting her before. Return her to me, Aethelwold, or I'll tear down the walls of Wimborne and see you hanged.'

'Is that all?' the rebel aetheling asked with a mocking smile.

'No, I also command you to give up any spurious claim to the throne of Wessex and, if you do so, and leave these lands in peace, you will not be harmed.'

Aethelwold's lip curled and his face flushed. Edward was reminded of the stories he'd heard about this young cousin of his – stories of a youth with a terrible temper who'd even gone so far as to attack Alfred himself. It seemed the aetheling's dark disposition had not improved over the years.

'I will not leave Wimborne,' Aethelwold spat. 'There I will live, or I will die. Alfred is gone at last. I pray the devil takes him, and I demand my throne!'

Edward was stunned by the venom in his rival's blasphemous words.

'This is a waste of time, you bitter fool,' he retorted, hands balling into fists instinctively at the insult to his beloved father. 'You'll return Aethelgifu safely to me, or you will die in agony. Do you understand me, cousin? You have no support, you have no power, and you are a weak oaf, twisted by hatred.'

Aethelwold moved fast, but Edward had been told the story of him punching Alfred and he'd been expecting the attack. He brought up his forearm and knocked his cousin's fist aside, rocking Aethelwold back on his heels with an uppercut.

He saw his cousin's hearth-warriors running forward and knew his own supporters would be doing the same, but he did not want this to descend into a full-on brawl. Before Aethelwold could regain his senses, Edward punched him again, this time in the guts, knocking the wind from him. When he doubled over, Edward shoved him hard onto the grass and then drew his sword, pressing the tip against Aethelwold's throat.

'Halt!' he commanded the four warriors running towards him with murderous intent in their eyes. 'Or I kill him, and then you die too.'

Wulfric and the others were lined up beside him now, all with swords drawn.

'Disarm him,' Edward growled. 'And if you move, Aethelwold, I will tear your windpipe open, do you understand?'

Aedan stepped across and took seax and sword from the fallen aetheling who glared at them in sheer hatred.

'Now,' Edward ordered him, stepping back, his men doing the same. 'Return to Wimborne in disgrace, swordless, and beaten like a washerwoman's sheets. When you get to the town, command your men to disperse, and leave Aethelgifu unharmed in the minster. Will you do so? Remember, Aethelwold, she's your cousin – harming one of your own blood will not be looked on kindly by God.'

Aethelwold said nothing and Edward pressed his sword down, drawing a line of blood along his pale neck. 'Swear it you squirrel's turd, or I'll kill you right here and save us all a lot of trouble!'

'I swear it, as God is my witness,' the aetheling shouted, furious, but also now quite frightened for his victorious enemy was obviously in earnest.

'Get out of my sight,' Edward commanded him.

Scrambling to his feet, Aethelwold cut a pitiful figure as he stumbled across the grass to his men, embarrassed and humiliated. They did not wait, following him away, towards Wimborne.

'You should have killed him,' said Aethelnoth.

'Probably,' Edward replied. 'But he's my cousin, and my parents loved his parents. Besides, who knows what his army would do to Aethelgifu if I killed him here.'

They waited in silence until the five figures receded into the distance and finally were lost from sight.

'Come, let's get back to the army,' Edward said, turning and walking towards Badbury, sheathing his sword as he went.

'That must have felt good,' Wulfric guessed. 'Putting the horrible bastard on his arse like that.'

Edward grinned and there was great relief as well as pleasure in it. 'Oh, it felt good, my friend!' he agreed. 'So damn good.'

Aethelwold held to the oath he swore to Edward, leaving Wimborne peacefully, and marching northwards. Aethelgifu was unharmed and safely returned to her home in Sceaftesburi Abbey.

Yet, although Aethelwold did march out of Wessex, the rebellious aetheling was not quite ready to give up his claim to the throne, travelling to Northumbria where he forged an alliance with the Danes there, vowing to return and take the kingdom by force with their support.

On the Whitsunday after Alfred's passing, on June 9th AD 900, Edward was crowned King of the Anglo-Saxons at

Kingston. The location was symbolic, being located on the border with Mercia, marking the new king's desire to continue the close relationship with those people who had been so ably led by his own sister, Aethelflaed, and her husband.

'Your father would be proud of you,' Ealhswith told him as they celebrated his coronation in a hall filled with happy supporters. Music filled the air and men and women danced merrily, overjoyed that their kingdom was once again intact and free, for now, of threats.

'What are your plans?' Wulfric asked. 'We've not really had a chance to discuss it since your father passed.'

'My plan for tonight is to get roaring drunk and thoroughly enjoy myself.' The king chuckled, upending his third mug of ale and gesturing for another to be brought.

'Just like Alfred,' Ealhswith chided but she was smiling, happy for her son to enjoy himself on this auspicious day. 'He never knew when to put down his cup either.'

Edward laughed and hugged her, then stood up and held out his hand to his wife, Aelfflaed. 'Right now, I plan on dancing,' he cried over the sound of the musicians' tune. 'And then, in the coming weeks and months? My father always said he would like to see all the kingdoms united under one banner – a new united kingdom named Ængleland.' He pulled Aelfflaed in and kissed her as they wheeled onto the floor, scattering other dancers as they went, all laughing together. 'I think that is a good plan, don't you, Wulfric? Will you be at my side for the journey?'

The ealdorman smiled and nodded. 'Aye,' he said, softly, for Edward had disappeared with his partner amongst the raucous throng of revellers before them. 'Ængleland. A kingdom for all the Anglo-Saxons, with no Danes to threaten us. I like that plan.'

'What about Aethelwold,' Ealhswith asked, tempering his happy mood slightly.

'We'll cross that bridge when we come to it,' Wulfric said. 'But I wouldn't worry too much about your nephew. Edward, like his father, has been marked by God for great things. You'll see.' He lifted his own mug and smiled at Ealhswith. 'Long live Edward,' he said.

She raised her cup, eyes sparkling as she watched her son dance and make merry in the Wessex that her beloved Alfred had built for them all. 'Long live Edward,' she repeated with a hopeful smile. 'King of the Anglo-Saxons.'

Author's Note

It might have seemed strange for me to begin this book in 887 on Athelney and, in fact, the abbey there was probably not built until 888. It *may* have been in use as early as 886 though and, honestly, when I read the story about the abbot being attacked in Asser's *Life of King Alfred* I felt like it had to be included in this novel. It was just so exciting and must have further influenced Alfred's opinion on the terrible state of his country at the time. He desperately needed men like Asser to help him reverse the moral decline in Wessex, and the attempted murder of John the Old Saxon would have really hammered that home so, to me, it was the ideal way to kick off *King of Wessex*.

Similarly, the story about Haesten and Bjorn Ironside sacking what they thought was Rome but was, in fact, the much smaller town of Luna, needed to be told. It's possibly a myth, made up to make the Danes look bad, but I thought it was a great tale and wanted to share it with my readers.

There were two significant characters named Aethelhelm in the book which I feared might be confusing, so I've changed the spelling of one – Edward's eventual father-in-law – to Ethelhelm for clarity.

Speaking of Edward, I wish the old chroniclers had wanted to share more about him but for some reason he fades out of the histories during the war with Haesten – he was clearly doing something, somewhere, though. He was a commander now after all. So, I decided to keep him paired with Aethelred for the raid on Benfleet and the siege at Buttington. The *Anglo-Saxon Chronicle* doesn't even name the commanders of the army Alfred left behind to deal with the Vikings from Appledore/Thorney, so historians have concluded it must have been Edward and Aethelred. Why was Edward ignored by chroniclers, when other Saxon commanders were given their due? We'll probably never know, but I thought I'd give him some credit in this book.

Another piece of artistic license was my killing off of John the Old Saxon in 896. In reality he probably died after 904 and not at the hands of a Viking warrior-woman, but I liked the dynamic of him and Wulfric in the prologue so thought I'd pair them up again for the visit to Haesten's camp.

You might have thought Wulfric's part in that little adventure was unrealistic – wandering into the enemy camp and making it all the way into Haesten's tent. However, I was a gas/electric meter reader for eighteen years and, trust me, people simply ignore you if you look and carry yourself as if you have every right to be in a place. I used to walk right through restricted areas of supermarkets and industrial units without anyone ever challenging me. The uniform I wore, and the fact I carried myself as if I belonged there, meant I was simply accepted. At the time, we wore the same uniforms as a security company, and I remember going into my local grocery store to buy bread – the cashier asked if I was there to collect their takings and was ready to hand over the strongboxes to me until I put her right! So, as incredible as Wulfric's entrance into the Danes' camp might have seemed, I think it could well have happened.

One thing that did not happen, I must admit, was Sigeferth being in command of the Danes at Herutford in 896. History suggests he'd given up attacking Wessex two years earlier, in 894, and sailed off to attack the remaining son of Ivar the Detestable, Sitriuc, who was king of Viking Dublin. Asser and the *Anglo-Saxon Chronicle* do not name any other leaders of the army that invaded Wessex during this time though, so rather than inventing someone, I decided to use Sigeferth as the warlord for Alfred's final confrontation with the heathen hordes.

The claim that Alfred invented candle-clocks is not strictly true either, for they were used by the Chinese as far back as the sixth century. He was, seemingly, the first to use them in Britain, however, and it's thought that he did invent the horn lantern that protected his candles from the wind so credit where it's due, he was a great forward thinker as well as a warrior.

What *is* true, is the whole thing with Aethelwold kidnapping Alfred's daughter, Aethelgifu. Well, he kidnapped a nun, and it must have been with the idea that it would strengthen his claim to the throne, so some historians believe the nun must have been Aethelgifu. Marrying Alfred's daughter, a powerful abbess in her own right, would certainly not do his claim any harm. I thought it an interesting addition to what had already been a pretty wild story, so it had to be included.

I've thoroughly enjoyed researching and writing this trilogy, but it's been hard at times including all the events and characters from known history, while making the story exciting. It would have been nice to go into more detail about Alfred's children, especially Edward and Aethelflaed, but there simply wasn't enough space – maybe one day I'll write more about those two and how their lives turned out after their father's passing. For now, I really hope you enjoyed the story of Alfred, King of Wessex, and agree with me that he truly deserved to be known as 'the Great'.

Steven A. McKay,
Old Kilpatrick,
May 28th, 2024

Acknowledgements

I'd like to thank my beta-reader, Bernadette McDade, for her invaluable help with these three novels. Thanks also to my editor, Kit Nevile, for his excellent suggestions and guidance in making the trilogy as strong as it could possibly be. Cheers to my readers for buying and reviewing the books, and sharing them on social media. Finally, I have to thank my wife, Yvonne, and my children, Freya and Riley, for supporting me always.